PAUL M. SCHOFIELD

TROPHY

ERIC & BARBARA...
ENJOY THE READ!
BEST REGARDS,
Paul M. Schofield

GALACTIC
PUBLISHERS
WWW.GALACTICPUBLISHERS.COM

MARBLE · MURPHY · ANDREWS

PUBLISHER'S NOTE

* * * * * * * * * *

* * * * * * * * * *

Published by: Galactic Publishers
North Carolina, USA

ISBN-978-0-9844780-0-2

ACKNOWLEDGMENTS

A novel is a long and strenuous effort … but ultimately rewarding and satisfying when one's labors finally come to fruition. The final result was not accomplished solely by myself and I wish to mention all those who helped me along the way. My sincere thanks go to:

Monica Harris, MHM Editorial Services, LLC, in New York City, mhm68@me.com, for her professional editing, insight, direction, and encouragement. She was a joy to work with.

Ronda Birtha, the catalyst who inspired me to continue in this endeavor. I am grateful for her technological expertize in photography, graphics, editing, proofreading, prodding, and cheer leading. She is a gifted artist, writer, and good friend. www. rondabirtha.com.

Laura Fitch, for getting the ball rolling by typing the first chapters into the computer.

Larry Breazeale, for his timely and important contribution.

My loving family for all their encouragement, technical help, and emotional support. These include:

Ellen, my wife, for her constant support, ideas, proofreading, and business and marketing efforts.

Rachel, my daughter, for her creative ideas and proofreading.

Jared, my son, for his thoughtful insight and proofreading.

Kris, my sister, for her support, creative ideas, and timely proofreading.

And finally:

Norman Stark, for his initial instruction in our adult education creative writing class, Plantation, Florida, 1991.

DEDICATION

This book is dedicated to the countless animals that are mistreated or die each day at the hands of man. Although their existence is viewed by many as simple and mundane, these precious lives, both large and small, are worth our esteem, protection and preservation.

TROPHY

Chapter I

Earth Date: 475 N.V.A.
Location: Kuiper Belt: trans-Neptunian region

Janet Rogerton carefully studied the NAV screens. Her large blue-green eyes, tinged purple from years in space with artificial gravity, intently searched for the subtle clues that would locate a cloaked ship. "Kolanna, have you picked up any anomalies or shimmers on the screens yet?" the young Lieutenant-Warden asked her pilot.

"Nothing, Ma'am," Kolanna stated, looking over her instruments. "The particle-stream sensors are also showing nothing. He has to be here – the coordinate models all indicate this is the correct position."

"I do not like it," Rogerton said nervously. "The squadron is bunched too tightly ... we are like sitting ducks. I know what our orders say, but I hate being the bait in the trap. The bait always gets bitten," she said, looking over, her eyebrows raised.

Kolanna turned to her: "I know what you mean, Lieutenant. Who will take the first hit? Our shields are set at minimum to appear unsuspecting, but the first blow could be lethal. At least our cruiser is close – ready for action."

"I hope they are close enough," Rogerton said. "They are cloaked, too, and their exact location is unknown. Let us hope we are not caught in a cross-fire."

"Ma'am, the NAV screen is showing a shimmer on the starboard flank," said Warden Elizabeth Archer.

"Yes, Warden Archer, I see it now."

"It seems to come and go," Archer stated. "Now it is stronger ... no, it is weakening. Wait ... it is growing stronger again. If it is a ship, it is quite large. Could this be the Victorian Cruiser? Why would it be in this position? Now it is growing stronger ... stronger ... Ma'am! A large ship is decloaking! ... Its weapons are powering up! ... It's firing! ... It's firing! Pulse-cannon and hyper-lasers!"

"Raise all shields to maximum!" Rogerton ordered her squadron. "Take evasive maneuvers, pattern Epsilon Two! Target his engines! Full power to all forward hyper-lasers!" she yelled, her attention fixed on the NAV screens. "It is Galen Bestmarke! We have him now if we can take out his shields!"

"Bestmarke has targeted Ship Three!" Kolanna shouted. "He is breaking down their shields ... their shields are almost gone!"

"Cruiser decloaking behind Bestmarke!" Archer confirmed. "Now we will see some fire-power!"

"Ship Three's shields are gone!" cried Kolanna. "Bestmarke is cutting them up with his hyper-lasers! We have to stop him!"

Suddenly the powerful weapons of the Victorian Cruiser *Laurel* blazed into action in a terrifying display of power. Brilliant crimson colored hyper-lasers chiseled away at the shields of Bestmarke's ship while the continuous blue pulses of the ion-cannons slammed his rear shields, weakening them, blow by blow.

In response, Bestmarke's ship focused its formidable arsenal on the cruiser in a barrage of devastating energy. His ship's mighty fusion engines surged and it began to pull away from the Victorian Cruiser. The deadly volleys of both ships continued to crackle and dance along the edges of their mutually weakening shields.

Meanwhile, Rogerton directed her remaining nine ships into an attack pattern. "Alpha Squadron, circle tight to his stern and target both engines! If the *Laurel* can break his shields, we may have a chance to stop him. Go in straight and fast ... pull up at the last second! Use attack pattern Gamma Four!" she shouted as her own ship led the charge directly at Bestmarke's screaming engines.

TROPHY

"The shields of the *Laurel* and Bestmarke's ship are collapsing!" yelled Kolanna, her purple tinged eyes wide with adrenaline.

"Concentrate your hyper-lasers on the port engine!" bellowed Rogerton. "When it stops, target the starboard engine. He will pay dearly for his attack!"

"Pull up in five seconds!" Kolanna quickly said.

All nine ships continued firing. Breaking off at the last second, they angled out in a precision move, sweeping around in tight circles for another run at Bestmarke's ship.

"Port engine weakened," stated Rogerton. "Continue the same pattern. His engines are powering up ... watch his wake!"

"The *Laurel's* shields are totally collapsed!" shouted Archer. "They are continuing to attack – but now they are vulnerable."

"They are taking the heat and giving us one more chance! Hit Bestmarke with everything you have!" Rogerton ordered as all nine ships targeted Bestmarke's fleeing ship.

"The *Laurel* is hit!" cried Kolanna. "They are backing off ... they are losing power and falling behind!"

"Bestmarke's shields are gone!" shouted Archer. "His port engine is losing power!"

"Brace for his attack! Now he will concentrate on us!" cried Rogerton. "Continue to target his engines! If you are hit once, break off your attack. Do not sacrifice yourself!" she said. "Ship Four ... break off your attack!"

"His engines are shutting down! Now we have him!" yelled Kolanna. After a few seconds her sudden hope was dashed. "He is engaging his cloak ... and running wave silent ... he has disappeared."

"Calculate his trajectory and target your probe-bombs," ordered Rogerton. "He will make steering changes with his thrusters so pay attention to the particle-stream sensors and your NAV screens.

TROPHY

We have hurt him – we will not give up now. Remember our Sisters on Ship Three and the *Laurel*."

* * * * * * * * * *

After forty-eight hours of continuous pursuit Janet Rogerton was tired, longing for sleep that duty consistently denied, and her frustration was growing as she struggled to smother her anger. Anger was her last resort, her admission that she could not think her way through a situation, and find a suitable conclusion that remained within her definition of self-control. Anger, if allowed at all, must be harnessed and channeled, not through the heart, but through the mind. For anyone this was a difficult chore, but it was required and expected from a trained officer of the New Victorian Empire.

Her uniform was dark forest green with brass buttons and a distinctive badge by the left shoulder, signaling her rank. Fine black and purple striping finished the appearance, enhancing the unique color of her eyes … and it fit her tall, athletic frame well. She sighed as she ran her fingers through shoulder length auburn hair.

The Planetary Control Corps, the military arm of the Empire, was stretched thin in this vast empty region of the outer Solar System. Rogerton's small squadron struggled to keep up with its normal duties of maintaining civil order, regulating trade, and search and rescue. But the situation grew more complicated when criminal activity became the focus of attention. Here at the fringes of the Solar System, far from the central government on Earth, the darker elements of human society held more sway in a subtle and often hidden system of operations not easily discerned at first inspection. Far from the sun all life literally existed in darkness, and deep within that literal darkness the figurative gloom was pervasive and easy to hide in.

Her squadron had been viciously attacked by Galen Bestmarke, and even though Bestmarke had escaped in the ensuing fight, Rogerton was still after him. He was wanted for crimes against the Empire, but more importantly for harboring in his employ a brilliant, eccentric, and extremely gifted engineer now desperately wanted alive by the Empire.

"Kolanna, what is our estimated time to the Keyhole?" Rogerton said, looking at her ship's pilot. "Bestmarke is headed in that direction and will probably make a run for it."

"At full speed ... roughly twenty minutes, Ma'am, without knowing the exact location," Kolanna said, her eyes fixed on the NAV screens.

"We have to somehow position the squadron between Bestmarke and the Keyhole. It may be our last chance to stop him. The Star-Commander ordered that Franelli be taken alive. I would rather destroy Bestmarke's ship and be done with it. I am tired of this cat and mouse game."

"Yes, Ma'am. Full thrust in ten seconds, on my mark. All crew members strap in," Kolanna said mechanically, her exhaustion evident.

The small ship trembled as their engine surged to full thrust and the g-forces settled the crew deeper into their gravity seats. Rogerton was on the COM system relaying orders to the remaining ships in the squadron. "Ships two and six, continue your advance with the probe bombs. All other ships fan out and continue the same general heading at full speed. The target is probably headed for the Keyhole. Remember, Franelli must be taken alive. Remain on full alert until further notice. That is all," she said in her rich, feminine voice.

Her tired eyes made a final sweep of her instruments and NAV screens. With a deep sigh she leaned back in her gravity seat and closed her eyes, content to savor even ten minutes of precious sleep.

* * * * * * * * *

TROPHY

Galen Bestmarke nervously stared at the NAV screens. "Fifteen lousy minutes," he muttered, pulling at the collar of his charcoal colored jacket. His ship shuddered as probe bombs detonated nearby. After a two day chase they were finally closing in. His ship was cloaked, essentially invisible, but the searching pattern of explosions was growing closer. "Louis, are you done repairing those circuits? We have to fire up the engines now!" he demanded, raising his voice, his face beginning to flush.

Chief engineer Louis Franelli answered slowly without looking at him. "I'm almost finished, boss. I have to get it right the first time. You know those PCC ships won't give us a second chance." Exhausted and annoyed, he scowled at Galen. "It wasn't me that got us in this ridiculous situation in the first place!"

"Just fix it, Louis!" Galen said, his face and neck reddening.

Space exploded directly behind them and the ship shuddered violently as Louis rushed to finish his repairs.

"Hurry up, Louis!" Galen yelled. "Somehow they have narrowed us down."

"Calm down, Brother, and give Louis some room to think," said Terran, trying to defuse the tense situation. Full partner, ship's pilot, and Galen's identical twin, Terran was emotionally his opposite. "Louis is right, you know. You got us into this mess. You just had to take a shot at those PCC ships, didn't you?" Terran said, looking him straight in the eyes. "We could have coasted right on by, fully cloaked and undetected."

"How did I know a cloaked Victorian cruiser was with them?" Galen shouted in defense. "They got a lucky shot at us, that's all! But we nailed their cruiser, didn't we?"

"It was more than luck, Brother. They skillfully broke down our shields and knew just where to hit us. Their technology has improved and we have grown lax. Only our speed and our cloak saved us. And only Louis can get us out of trouble now."

"It was still a lucky shot!" Galen yelled. "Hurry up, Louis!"

TROPHY

Terran rolled his eyes and sighed. "I will be glad when this expedition of yours is finished and we can start making money again. Ever since Louis made it possible for us to use the Keyhole, you have been obsessed with your collection."

"This will be the final trip for my collection," Galen said, starting to calm down. "After this we can concentrate on business again. Do not forget, this trip is our concluding test before we fully implement our human relocation program. Once that is underway we will have more power and money than you ever dreamed possible! I promise!"

"You promise ... right. How many times have I heard that?" scoffed Terran.

"No! I promise! This will be ....."

"Cloak down! Shields up!" yelled Louis as the great ship trembled from the fierce explosion of a probe bomb hitting the rear shields, now intact and fully operational.

"Louis! What are you doing?" yelled Galen, veins bulging in his neck. "Why did you drop the cloak? Now every PCC ship in the region will see us!"

Louis turned from his screens and stared at him with a measured silence, finally answering in his deep voice. "That probe bomb would have hit us if I hadn't dropped the cloak and raised the shields. I had just finished repairing the circuits with a few seconds to spare. That gave us a comfortable margin."

"A few seconds? ... A comfortable margin?" Galen exclaimed. "You are sure of yourself, aren't you?"

Louis maintained his piercing stare. "Boss, the circuits held, the shields are intact, the probe bomb exploded harmlessly. There is no problem."

"Right," he said, looking down at his NAV screens for a moment. "You're good, Louis. You're good. But don't scare me like that." Galen glanced at him again, his wide mouth and thick lips turning up at the edges to reveal white teeth, trimmed at the edges with gold. The ship shuddered again as another probe bomb hit the rear shields.

"We need to lose these patrol ships now!" he said impatiently. "Begin the engine start-up sequence, Louis."

"Start-up sequence commencing," Louis said as he turned away, a faint smile forming on his haggard face.

Galen scanned the NAV screens. His ship was twelve minutes from the Keyhole and the PCC ships were desperate to stop him before he could gain the entrance. Cursing the Empire for its controls, regulations, and constant harassment, he contemplated the gauntlet before him and hoped his ship was up to the challenge.

TROPHY

Chapter II

Galen flipped the COM switch and barked out: "Stelle! Are you and the Pouncer connected and ready for action?"

A mechanical affirmative emanated from the defense control cube located in the very front of the ship. Estelle Fairfield, a guider, was strapped and wired into her control seat next to her partner, Tommie. Tommie was a five kilogram orange striped tabby cat, also known as a pouncer.

They were a mentally-linked defensive team designed to protect the ship from incoming projectiles. The ship's energy shields were effective against the probe bombs, lasers, and other beam weapons, but the projectile weapons were increasingly more effective and difficult to counter. The combined consciousness of the feline-human mind-link was superior to control strictly by computer, but a strong bond was essential for a guider and pouncer to work smoothly together. If a guider did not love cats, the pouncer sensed it immediately, dooming the chemistry of the partnership. There was no faking it.

Estelle wore a wireless head-gear set that was tightly strapped over her short, blond hair. A tiny chip had been implanted surgically near her brain-stem creating a direct, wireless interface between her central nervous system and the head-gear she wore. This arrangement connected her to the ship's central computer. Tommie was connected in a similar manner and then strapped into a special seat to prevent any movement. When the interface between Estelle and Tommie was activated, they were essentially of the same mind and interconnected to the ship's main computer. This enabled them to make instant decisions to defend the ship.

The concept of a human-animal mind link was first discovered by a Guardian nearly a century ago who had owned an

exceptionally intelligent and responsive pet cat. Her studies and those
of scientists after her had led to the development of one of the
Empire's most useful tools. Of all the domestic animals researched
and tested at CENTRAL, cats were the overwhelming choice for
this kind of training. They easily accepted space travel and most
ships allowed and encouraged them because they helped control the
vermin that always found a way aboard. But the Thought Modified
and Controlled training, known as TMC, was limited to just the few
meeting the rigorous requirements. One of the key requirements
was their ability to think of doing things without the actual physical
movement. With special training that modified their thought
processes, some cats could accomplish this superbly, remaining
completely motionless while in their minds they were running,
pouncing, and killing their prey. Most cats could not separate these
actions and remained normal cats with all their associated movement.

TMC cats could be trained to achieve various skill levels and
were given a rating from one to seven, seven being the most qualified.
Tommie was a seven, one of the best trained ever. But even properly
TMC-trained cats needed guiding and control; they could sometimes
panic or behave erratically. A competent guider could do wonders
with a properly controlled pouncer. Guiders were carefully selected
women who were mentally matched with the cats, always for the
life of the cat. Estelle had been matched with Tommie for three
standard years and it was necessary to maintain daily training sessions.
During these sessions their thought processes were harmonized in
an interactive program much like a game. Estelle would guide and
encourage Tommie through the game, giving him commands and
exercises to keep him mentally sharp, and their relationship one of
love and trust. During a real situation Tommie would continue seeing
the program as a game. Only Estelle would know the true danger
at hand. She was trained to control and suppress any feelings of
fear or panic and to mentally project calmness and well-being. This
promoted stability and defused any panic situations as far as the cat

was concerned. Training sessions were at random times to prevent any regularity or anticipation of their time together. As a defense team they had to be ready at all times, so they trained that way.

The rank of guider was a secretive position in the Planetary Control Corps. Society in general and even some in the Corps were uncomfortable with the mental linking of humans and animals, but CENTRAL deemed it logical and necessary for the defense of the Fleet. Only graduate women from the Academy with the brightest, most adaptive minds were chosen, and the training was intense. A high level of honor and dark prestige was associated with the skill. But if an officer became a renegade, it paid handsomely on the black market.

She checked her instruments, confirming the status of the shielding. "All shielding restored to full levels, boss," she said mechanically.

Galen was happy to have a guider/pouncer team, a real defensive luxury not many ships had, and he was pleased with their performance. Although Estelle had been with him for two and a half standard years, he still harbored doubts about her loyalty. Only a former Victorian officer could have her guider training and possess a fully trained cat. No other organization had the resources for the extensive and complicated training necessary. By her own admission she was a renegade of the New Victorian Empire and willingly submitted to full internal and external scans before he hired her. She hadn't given him reason to doubt her, Galen just had a gut feeling. He didn't trust women and he hated cats.

He had asked her why she went renegade. A woman with her abilities could go far in the New Victorian Empire. What would cause her to give up the benefits and luxuries afforded to her? Was it hatred for the Empire? What was it that made her not only walk away, but become an enemy of an Empire that would have cultivated her talents and awarded her handsomely for them? She said it was something on a personal level. Questions like these gnawed at Galen at less intense times, occupying his mind more than he wanted to admit. Did she hate the Empire as much as he did? For as long as he could remember, he and his twin brother Terran had despised the controlling, authoritarian government that had been in power for nearly five centuries. He hated the absolute rule by women alone; total female rule was completely unnatural. Did not the male animals assume dominance and lead the others? Did not ancient history also prove the rightful place of men as rulers? He would never accept or submit to total rule by women. He would always resist in any manner he could.

Louis's voice sounded over the COM system indicating one minute until the engines fired up. "I have the PCC ships on the NAV screen, boss," he said. "They know where we are headed and they are all on an intercept course. We may outrun some of them, but now we have to show our hand. Now we go back into the fire."

Galen's ship was huge by any standards, nearly five hundred meters in length, and with the armament of a Victorian cruiser. Everything was the best to be had. Louis had also added his own touches to try and keep one step ahead of the Planetary Control Corps technology. Galen strapped himself in at the controls. He wanted his fingers on the trigger in the fight he knew was coming. He entrusted the piloting of the ship to Terran. He trusted him implicitly and the two had used the link for five years. As a guider and pouncer were mentally-linked together, a pilot and gunner could also be mentally-linked. A Level I interface was all that two humans needed or could endure. A deeper level interface would invariably lead to dominance by the stronger mind. A Level I interface had restraints and buffers to prevent total mental interaction, thus preventing dominance. Two linked individuals needed to trust each other implicitly and be well matched in thought processes. Having an identical twin made this much easier to do.

Galen put on the headgear and hooked in the link. Terran was already connected and Galen immediately felt the dream-like confusion of mixed emotions trying to focus as the interface gently pulled their independent thoughts together into the same flowing stream. Each maintained his individual side thoughts, like currents or eddies along the edges of a clear but frighteningly deep river. There were shapes in that deepness that took no form, but could be felt. Some were fearful, some vague, but all were seemingly at the edge of a dream and just out of reach. He wondered if a Level II interface lead to those depths but his thinking was interrupted as he felt his thoughts come into focus with Terran's.

"Welcome to dreamland again," Terran thought.

"Right. I'll feel better when we enter the Keyhole," Galen thought. "Is it on time and in the same position? I have planned and waited a long time for this trip. With my collection nearly complete the Empire is not going to stop me now, not when I am so close."

"It is always on time, Brother, but the location continually shifts. It always occurs in the same general location. The PCC ships won't know the exact location either."

The thirty second warning light flashed on. "Maximum starting thrust in twenty-five seconds," Louis calmly said.

Remembering to use his voice, Galen barked out commands. "Everyone strap in. Rough ride coming up!"

Check lights clicked on one by one as the rest of the crew members strapped in … six, seven, eight … nine … one more to go. "Johnny, are you in?" he yelled at his First Officer. The last light clicked on as the last seconds ticked off.

"Here we go!" said Louis, an uncommon note of excitement in his voice. "Maximum starting power!"

The fusion thrusters shook the ship as they fired up to fifty percent. Any more would push the thrusters right through the ship, which was not designed for the substantially more powerful engines replacing the originals. The G-forces increased tremendously, pushing them all deeper into their specially designed gravity seats. The skin of their faces pulled back and their eyeballs sank in. The inertia dampers controlling the G-forces were at full, lowering the forces to a tolerable level, safely lower than the life crushing pressure of maximum starting thrust. Louis could now bring them up steadily to full thrust in fifty seconds, twice as fast as any PCC ships nearby. His fine tuning was paying off.

Galen and Terran were glued to the NAV screens, their thoughts racing together far faster than any verbal communication would allow.

"Where is that blasted Keyhole?" Galen immediately thought.

"It's somewhere in the designated area, probably on the far side. Scanners will pick it up soon. Wait ... it's there ... near the edge ... ten minutes away," thought Terran. "Look! Nine PCC ships! We're ahead of five already and with luck we can beat three more coming in from the sides. That leaves one directly ahead and any more that might be cloaked."

"Cloaked? I thought they didn't have that technology on these small patrol ships."

"They don't ... yet. But if they have another cruiser in the area, it might be cloaked. All we can do is wait and see."

"Full thrust in ten seconds," croaked Louis, straining against the G-forces. "Dampers at one hundred ten percent. All circuits holding."

Galen watched the seconds count down to zero and felt the increased rumble and vibration as the two Zenkati fusion engines roared like a matched binary star, somehow harnessed and barely controlled. He loved the raw power of his star ship. The vibration and G-forces shot up oppressively but started leveling off as the dampers struggled to compensate, slowly gaining. The heavy gravity began to subside and Galen smiled, and then laughed to himself. Action like this is what he lived for, and his eyes gleamed with the rush of adrenalin.

"You're ready for the fight, aren't you," Terran laughed in his mind. Not a mocking laugh, but of understanding and camaraderie, as two knights side by side eagerly joining the battle, laughing as they ride forth to a nameless enemy.

"Shields up and guns out!" roared Galen. "We have a fight ahead!" He twitched in his seat, straining against the subsiding G-forces. The smile on his face was one of pure anticipation and pleasure.

TROPHY

Chapter III

"Their ship is firing up the engines, Ma'am. Look! … Look at that! … The acceleration is incredible! How can they possibly survive?" said Warden Elizabeth Archer, her eyes wide as she stared at the screens.

"It is impressive," agreed Lieutenant-Warden Janet Rogerton. "Do not forget, they have Franelli. Bestmarke was no fool when he acquired him years ago. Those two are a dangerous combination, genius and ambition. It is rumored that Bestmarke interfaces with another human like a guider/pouncer team. Franelli, no doubt, worked that one out." With a ring of disgust in her voice, she looked up from the screens. "Franelli would have been on our side, but for the compu-courts. Efficiency at all costs … and the cost this time has been dear."

A junior officer broke in, "Two minutes to intercept, Ma'am. Shall we raise our shields and ready our weapons?"

"Do it!" barked Rogerton as she turned to her NAV screens again. "Status on our sister ships, Warden Archer," she said, running her fingers through her thick hair.

"Five behind him and three at the sides, but they cannot intercept. Bestmarke has outrun them all. Only we are in his path now and we have seen his armament … we are greatly out-gunned, Ma'am. Remember what he did to the *Laurel* and Ship Three," she said, her voice softly trailing off. Rogerton could sense her fear, a legitimate fear.

"We alone cannot go against him. He is heading directly for the Keyhole with only our small ship in his way. He could go any other direction and outrun us, yet he continues toward the Keyhole. It is all very odd."

TROPHY

She studied the weapons inventory only to be interrupted by the ninety second intercept warning. "Deploy all the projectile mines we have and target them in the enemy ship's path. On my mark!" she ordered. "Pilot Kolanna, get us out of here quickly, full thrust, full rear shielding! Move, now!"

The Planetary Control Corps ship lurched as the single fusion engine roared to full power. Speeding away from the oncoming ship, five projectile mines were deployed with a burst resembling sparks exploding from an ancient campfire. The PCC ship continued its arc and began to pull away on a course perpendicular to Bestmarke's oncoming ship.

"Sixty-seconds to mine intercept," announced the soft voice of the computer over the COM.

"Go to one quarter thrust and hold. We will soon see if there are any pieces to pick up. Take us out of weapons range, Kolanna, and change to a parallel course. Keep the shields at full strength, focused towards his ship."

"Full strength, Ma'am?" questioned Warden Archer.

"Yes, keep them at full strength. Never trust Bestmarke," she muttered. "He is a despicable man lacking any honor. He hates the Empire and has resisted all of our efforts to deal with him in an honorable way. Franelli has only emboldened him in his arrogance. It will be a momentous day in the Empire when both of them are in custody ... or dead."

* * * * * * * * *

"Projectile mines," thought Terran. "We don't need these right now."

"Getting worried?" thought Galen, grinning as he glanced at Terran. "We'll just pick them off with the hyper-lasers."

"It won't work on these, they're fully shielded."

TROPHY

"Then we'll use the pulse-cannon to break down the shielding!" countered Galen. "Then the hyper-lasers!"

"We won't have time. Recharge time on the cannon is one and a half seconds. We may destroy a couple of mines before the rest unload on us. Two projectiles per mine, if they're standard issue. At best, we'll get two mines. That leaves three mines, six projectiles. Can Estelle and the cat handle what is left?"

"Leave them out of it! We can handle this!" Galen thought, his temper flaring and his raging anger clouding the river of their combined consciousness. Frightening waves and deep whirlpools seemed to grow as if a vast dark storm were approaching. Terran's calming thoughts, like clear skies peeking under the edges of that darkness, seemed remote and insignificant. But minutely, steadily over what seemed long moments, which in fact were only a few seconds, Terran's peaceful steadiness soothed the rage from Galen's mind. The waters calmed as the murkiness gave way to clearing, even to the greenish depths of their mysteriously joined consciousness.

"That's better, my brother," said Terran. "We need control now and clear thinking. There is always a way out. Space has many directions."

Galen steeled his self-control and opened the defense channel. "Stelle, can you and the Pouncer handle ..."

"Maybe nine, eight for sure. If you clear one mine, we'll get the others," Estelle urged. "You have fifteen seconds. Awaiting your command."

The command was obvious as Galen fired the pulse-cannon. He fired again after it recharged and continued to fire three more times. First one pulse and then another flashed out from the ship like hot blue stars, streaking to their targets. The first one hit the mine, causing it to glow a dull burgundy, turning to flame red, brightening to electric orange, and flashing to purest white as its temperature soared, finally exploding in a brilliant burst of light. The second pulse intercepted the second mine and destroyed it. The third, fourth

26

and fifth mines were destroyed, too, but not before all three had unloaded their shield piercing projectiles.

"Nine projectiles!" yelled Estelle. "You have to give me control! There are too many for partial control! I must have total control of the ship! Ten seconds!"

Galen looked in dismay at the NAV screens. Cursing, he muttered something about standard issue and tapped in the code that gave total ship control to the defense cube.

"I know you don't trust her," thought Terran. "But at the moment she's the best we've got, she and Tommie."

"Don't remind me" answered Galen sourly. "We'll all be feline fricassee if they don't pull us out. And it will happen quickly, if that's any consolation."

The ship trembled slightly as Estelle mentally coaxed the engines to one hundred-ten percent. For brief periods they could handle that and more without overheating. The projectiles bore down on them in a great pincer-like pattern. The three closest were ten seconds away on the lower port. Estelle banked hard to upper starboard and pushed the engines to one hundred-twenty percent. The projectiles banked hard in pursuit, straining to catch the ship. The hard turn spread them out just far enough that she and Tommie gained a few more milliseconds between each projectile, enough additional time for them to catch the deadly incoming intruders.

Flipping the separator switch off and engaging the mind-link, Estelle felt her thoughts racing across what seemed like a vast, closely trimmed, bright green lawn, stretching off into infinity. It was filled with small, smooth, round bumps or hills, and shallow valleys between. Everywhere was the same smooth, bright green grass, bathed in golden yellow sunlight. Every time she saw it she was amazed and briefly awed, like a baby seeing its first brilliant spring flower or butterfly. "Ah, the playing field," she thought and felt intensely happy. An orange striped tabby cat, glistening in the sunlight, sat on the nearest small hill, looking at her with anticipation, his ears straight ahead, and his eyes a soft golden glow.

"Play?" thought Tommie with almost a musical quality. "Play?" he questioned again with more insistence.

"Yes, play!" thought Estelle with anticipation. She projected love and well-being to ensure calmness and total concentration on the task at hand. "Let's start now," she thought. Tommie immediately went to a heightened alert, scanning the area all around. From a distance away he saw the first three projectiles approaching, although to him the program made them appear as small white rats scurrying straight for them … small distinct white shapes over the green bumps of lawn.

The speed of the cat always amazed Estelle. Like a shot he bounded forward to the back side of a hill, tail twitching, and awaited the first rat. It didn't swerve, but came straight over the top. He pounced and quickly grabbed it in his outstretched claws. Instantly, Estelle mentally hit the trigger and in a dynamic burst the hyper-laser swept out, vaporizing the first projectile. Tommie only saw the rat disappear and shifted his attention to the next. He caught it without any difficulty and Estelle triggered the laser again. Each one, though, became progressively more difficult. The ship jerked and banked hard again and again following Tommie's pattern as he hunted down the projectile rats and Estelle triggered the hyper-laser.

The last two came together and Estelle could see the danger if Tommie could not reach them in time. "Quick, Tommie! Quick!" Estelle thought, trying to suppress her anxiety. Tommie's ability was unusually keen, which was why he had a TMC-7 rating. Although he was near exhaustion he did not give up as a lesser ranked cat might have done by now. He leaped toward them and with great maneuvering caught number eight. Estelle fired and number eight disappeared.

Number nine, the last one, was running quickly toward Estelle. It was apparent it would reach her before Tommie could get it. She had to slow it down. Banking the ship hard to starboard, she mentally rammed the engine controls to one hundred-fifty percent. The ship shuddered violently and the inertia dampers struggled as the increasing G-forces pushed them back in their harnesses. The warning light and horn jolted on screaming thirty seconds to fusion overload.

"Come on, Tommie," she coaxed. "Just one more ... you can do it!"

Tommie turned and looked back at the white rat half way to his partner. The rat was moving more slowly as the ship's speed increased, but steadily it drew nearer to Estelle. Tommie wearily lunged forward, straining, his thinking distracted by the heavy gravity. The rat was six meters from Estelle and gnawing as if trying to chew through something. Suddenly, it resumed moving steadily closer. Another horn and flashing light snapped on. "Shield breach! Shield breach!"

Tommie leaped faster. Four more bounds and he would have it. The rat was two meters from Estelle. With a last powerful jump, Tommie was on it, claws and teeth gripping tight. This one wouldn't get away.

Estelle mentally hit the trigger. The ship rocked and shuddered as the last projectile vaporized in a blinding flash, engulfing the ship for a split second. The ship burst through unscathed. Backing the engines down, she breathed a sigh of relief.

"Tired," thought Tommie, as he stretched out full-length on the nearest small green hill. His musical tone was subdued and Estelle could sense his fatigue.

"Rest, then eat," thought Estelle, warmly directing her emotions to Tommie.

"Yes, eat," Tommie continued, his attention recaptured. "Rest, eat."

"Good boy," she commended and flipped the separator switch on, ending the mind-link. She felt her thoughts racing backwards and the golden sun reddening as it set over the infinite green lawn. The lawn glowed silver in the white moonlight that gradually darkened and glimmered out. A last star twinkled out as the program gently put her down, back to the stark gray reality of the defense cube interior. Her hand gently stroked Tommie as he lay sleeping beside her. He stretched and purred softly, quickly falling back to sleep.

Mentally exhausted, Estelle sank deeply into her padded gravity seat. As she tapped in the return control code giving Galen back his ship, she absently loosened her harness and stared tiredly at the NAV screens. The PCC ships were all out of range, trailing further and further behind as Galen's ship raced onward to the Keyhole.

The Keyhole was there on the screen, growing larger. She would have been more excited to finally see it but for the deep exhaustion that gripped her, leaving her clammy with nervous sweat. She longed for a shower and change of clothes. Tommie was totally asleep, not even dreaming. The nearness and timing of the attacking projectiles had been close this time, too close, exhausting them both more than ever before. She was thankful of the results, but even more for the rest and relief from combat.

"Good work, Stelle!" boomed Galen's deep voice over the COM system. "I knew you could do it, not a doubt in my mind! You'll get bonus credits for this one. And give the cat some extra tuna." The COM system snapped off.

"I wonder what he really thinks," said Estelle. Muttering something about being too tired to care, she reclined her gravity seat, shut her eyes, and immediately fell asleep.

"She did all right, and the cat, too," thought Terran. "Maybe you should trust her."

"I have never trusted any woman. If I could find a guider that was a man, I would hire him. But the Empire only trains women because they are the best match for the cats. Estelle is the only choice we have, so I put up with her to get the additional protection for the ship," countered Galen. "You know I do not even trust our own mother. She tried to brain-wash us with all of this Empire propaganda and her authoritarian control. You are the only one I can really trust. There are no secrets between us."

"No secrets, Brother ... only differences," thought Terran, his thoughts flowing smoothly. The placid river of their joined consciousness was clear now, yet deep and mysterious, although somewhat threatening, in a remote, detached way.

"Yes, differences," reflected Galen, his thoughts more subdued and cautious.

TROPHY

Chapter IV

Lieutenant-Warden Janet Rogerton watched the NAV screen in total fascination. She expected the first two mines to be taken out before they could unload their projectiles, but she could barely believe the speed and agility of Bestmarke's ship as it dodged, countered, and one by one destroyed the remaining projectiles.

"Kolanna!" she commanded. "Take us to full pursuit."

"Ten seconds to full thrust," Kolanna said. The computer counted down to full thrust and the engine roared, straining and mildly shaking the ship.

As their small ship accelerated, Rogerton contemplated the superb defense handling of Bestmarke's ship. He must have a guider/pouncer team and it has to be Victorian trained. It was too good to be anything else. But is it a plant or a renegade?

She switched her computer console to 'Privacy: Commanding Officer'. The micro-shield immediately enveloped her and the console, allowing her to speak freely with the system in total privacy. "Computer, scan for any Victorian officers that have gone renegade. Narrow the choice to ones trained as guiders within the last standard year."

"Two renegade, but no guider training."

"Check back two standard years," she said.

"Three renegade, but no guider training."

"Check back three standard years," she asked again.

"Five renegade, one with guider training."

"Give me all the information on the one. "Code name: 'Star Point'. Renegade 2.75 standard years."

"That is all?" Rogerton said. "What is the priority rating?"

"Priority 50-C1. No more information is available."

TROPHY

She knew she was locked out tight on this one. 50-C1 was highly classified. She scanned back five additional years. There were a number of renegade officers but no guiders. Just the one.

"One in eight years," she thought. "And she appears on Bestmarke's ship?"

The COM light interrupted her train of thought. She dropped the privacy shield and answered: "Go ahead, Kolanna."

"Ma'am, we are seven minutes from the Keyhole and maintaining pursuit. Do we continue our heading?"

"Yes, and prepare for braking thrust. Keep us a thousand kilometers distant. Are all circuits stable?"

"Yes, Ma'am. Holding steady."

"And, Kolanna, keep a close eye on the NAV screens. There may be unusual activity soon. One of our cruisers could be near the Keyhole, cloaked and waiting. That is all."

The Lieutenant-Warden studied the NAV screens herself as she absently caressed the badge by her left shoulder. Her purple tinged eyes were even more pronounced with fatigue and she could not recall how many hours it had been since she last slept. Sleep, what a glorious thought. The last time she felt thoroughly rested was two months ago back on Planet Earth. She and her crew were on shore leave, before they were hurriedly called back to duty. Her squadron had been a year in space and all were anticipating a full month on solid ground with real gravity, sweet unrecycled air, warm sunlight, beautiful scenery, growing plants, and fresh wholesome food straight from the productive soil. With the entire planet under weather and climate control systems, deserts and unproductive, inhospitable lands had been transformed into a beautiful paradise of global proportions.

She loved to visit the New Sahara region with its vast green savannas, dotted with flourishing stands of date palms and exotic tropical plants. A profusion of African wildlife lived and roamed there, many brought back from the edge of extinction to numbers reminiscent of a thousand years ago. Every day brought exciting and entertaining vistas, and each night cool breezes and intoxicating fragrances of night-blooming flowers under a brilliant canopy of stars.

Rogerton was proud of what the New Victorian Empire had accomplished in five centuries of rule and was content to serve in any capacity that opened up to her, just as her mother and grandmothers had done. Nearly five hundred years of relative peace was the result of the ruling power of CENTRAL, the massive computer governing the Solar System under the watchful care of the Guardians.

Most of the citizens of this authoritarian government were happy and content, but not all. The Planetary Control Corps was born of necessity to care for those who were not happy, who were discontent, and who fought against the rule of CENTRAL. Men like Galen and Terran Bestmarke would not submit to a government overseen only by women, so a life of crime was their only natural conclusion.

Now Bestmarke was headed for the Keyhole. Every other ship or probe entering it had disappeared, never to be heard from again. What did he and Louis Franelli know about this unusual anomaly in space? Was it a worm-hole to another part of the galaxy? Was time affected when you entered it? Where did you go and how did you return? What does CENTRAL know about this? What did my mother know about this before her ship disappeared? There were so many questions, hard questions, for which she had no answers.

"If anyone could figure out what the Keyhole was, and how to use it, it would be Franelli," she said out loud. She cursed the judicial league again for their unbreakable rules, and their refusal to recognize his unique genius. "He could have been on our side," she muttered and leaned back in her gravity seat, her head resting on the soft upper cushion. A light sleep stole upon her, relaxing her face, softening the hard edges, and revealing a tender expression usually

TROPHY

masked by concern and duty. The long desired sleep, repeatedly denied, was sweet ... but it was not to last.

TROPHY

Chapter V

"Louis, are your calculations done yet?" Terran asked. "We are at three minutes and I'd rather not go to braking thrust."

"Thirty more seconds," Louis said, narrowing his eyes with annoyance. The stress of the whole ordeal was showing, intensified by the lack of sleep. Finally Louis's voice crackled on again. "My calculations are done. The guidance system is locked on. Go to fully automatic in ten seconds, on my mark."

He counted down the seconds and Terran locked in the ship's guidance controls to the computer. The Keyhole loomed larger and larger through the front viewing portal, always closed during battle, but now momentarily opened to reveal the incredible sight in its grandeur. The pale blue outer cloud was tiny by galactic standards – a thousand kilometers in diameter. The color intensified toward the middle to an electric cobalt blue and concentrated to jet black in the center with a shape similar to an old-fashioned keyhole ready to receive a skeleton key. The intense blackness of the ten kilometer wide opening was enhanced by brilliant flashes, like lightning bolts in stunning ever changing neon-rainbow colors, penetrating into its abysmal depths. The flashes were mesmerizing, like the flames of a campfire that flickered and danced. Shimmering background stars could faintly be detected, twinkling and changing shape, as if seen through a fast moving stream of clear water.

It took a few seconds to realize the defense alarm had sounded, like a nagging voice faintly calling to a dreamer lost in blissful thought, only to be awakened by cold, loud, sudden reality.

"Where did THEY come from?" Galen said, his eyes riveted to the NAV screens. He lunged for the shielding controls and yelled: "All shield power to the stern! Charge up all the weapons! Get connected, Stelle, this is no drill!"

TROPHY

Galen's face flushed with adrenalin and anger. He spit out curses in an unending stream, finally muttering in disgust to Terran: "They had to come now, now that we're locked on fully automatic. I thought we had outrun all their miserable little ships. Where did this Cruiser come from? Is there anything you can do with the controls?"

"Not unless we abort the Keyhole and override Louis's calculations."

"No way!" Galen hissed. "I've waited too long and invested too much time and money to stop now! We're not giving up yet, not without a fight! No Victorian cruiser is stopping me!"

Unlocking the activator controls, he jabbed at the pulse-cannon trigger sending the hot, blue pulses behind them followed by the tight, continuous beams of the hyper-lasers.

Estelle awoke with a start at Galen's shouting. Adrenalin-laced blood pounded through her head and chest as she began focusing her thoughts and actions. Gently waking up Tommie, she studied her NAV screens and felt a chill of apprehension run down her spine. "Victorian Class Cruiser ... and close, right behind us. They must have come in fast and cloaked. Their shields are holding against the pulse-cannon. That's odd, they're not firing back," she quietly said and then gasped. "They want us alive."

* * * * * * * * *

Strapped in her battle chair on the bridge of the Victorian Cruiser *Daniela*, Star-Commander Abigail VanDevere smiled as she watched Bestmarke's frenzied but futile attack. She was thankful their new shielding was holding at full power. A few months ago a barrage like this would have severely damaged them.

"Lieutenant-Commander Gornect, report on shielding circuits, please."

"Holding steady, Ma'am," she replied in her thick Martian accent.

37

TROPHY

"Good, good." VanDevere was pleased. She had been alerted by Rogerton's squadron and now Bestmarke had suddenly appeared on the NAV screens of their cloaked Cruiser as they coasted along toward the Keyhole. Having Bestmarke in this position was something she had desired for a long time.

"Disable his ship – shut down the reactor and engines. I want him and Franelli alive."

Gornect quickly pressed the controls and the blue-green beam of the Phase Interrupter Laser softly swept out toward Bestmarke's ship. After five seconds, his engines were still glowing and his ship moving faster toward the Keyhole.

"Status, Lieutenant-Commander!" snapped VanDevere. "Why are we not effective against him?"

"I don't know, Ma'am. Their shield frequency is unreadable and we can't lock down on it. It's impossible to focus the Interrupter through his shielding."

"Franelli!" The Star-Commander spit out his name like a curse. "How in all of the New Victorian Empire can we deal with him!" she snapped, fighting for self-control. CENTRAL was desperate to apprehend Franelli and had recently updated her orders. Now they wanted Franelli alive. To follow them into the Keyhole meant risking ship and crew. "Keep the shields up and back off pursuit, Lieutenant-Commander," she said in a voice heavy with frustration. "We will have to wait."

* * * * * * * * *

"Louis! Why aren't their shields breaking down?" demanded Galen.

"I don't know, boss. I'm trying to get readings to analyze it," he said calmly.

Galen was speechless at Louis's nonchalance, staring at him in disbelief. As if to read his mind, Louis fixed his eyes on Galen.

"Don't worry, boss. I'll figure it out," he said in his deep voice. He fastened his gaze on Galen until Galen uncomfortably withdrew his eyes. Louis then turned back to his controls. Galen sighed to himself and turned back to the NAV screens. He watched the cruiser steadily gain on them, contemplating his next action. Suddenly he yelled. "They're powering up! They're going to fire at us!"

They all watched the screens as the blue-green beam of the phase interrupter laser swiftly came toward them.

"What is it?" said Galen speaking softly, almost hypnotically.

"It's an interrupter type weapon," Louis said. "It shuts down fusion reactors. It would seem they want to capture us. Don't worry, I anticipated them this time. They won't get through the shields."

Louis had already punched in commands to the shielding controls. The interrupter beam crackled and arced along the shield edge but came no further. After a few seconds the cruiser began to retreat and Galen yelled in delight, spewing more curses at them.

"They are backing off now," he gloated. "We will be safely through the Keyhole soon ... we have beaten them again!"

In contrast, Terran's calm voice came over the COM system. "Thirty seconds to the Keyhole. Everyone strap in. Set all remaining controls to full auto in fifteen seconds."

Apprehension of another kind grew in the minds of all the crew, that is, except Tommie. He just purred as Estelle gently stroked his thick fur. She wished it were that easy to calm her inner turmoil and fears that the unknown generated. So many ships and probes had disappeared into this anomaly called the Keyhole.

Her decision to take this employment two and a half years ago had not been easy. As a renegade and a guider her options were limited. The pay was excellent, but there were many unknowns when you worked for a man like Bestmarke. She sighed and tightened her restraint belts. She looked down at her cat, checking his restraints. "You're not worried, are you, Tommie?" He looked up at her with eyes half-open, blinked, stretched, and continued to purr. He waited

TROPHY

for Estelle's hand to gently scratch his furry head. His wish was soon granted.

Even Terran was apprehensive as their ship approached the Keyhole. Having been through it before he knew the procedure, and he also knew the risks. He told himself that risks came with a pilot's job, but he wasn't convinced. He watched the screens, expecting them to soon become erratic, as the ship plunged deeper into the Keyhole. Every move and reaction the ship did now had been programmed by Louis.

The audible alarms began sounding as the screens showed erratic fluctuations throughout the ship's circuitry. This time he knew better – adjusting the controls produced nothing. Just ride it out, don't touch anything, there is nothing you can do. As he watched, the screens gave the illusion of the ship spiraling and tumbling into a great void or tunnel as the G-forces seemed to slowly grow and grow. He imagined the crushing pressure of deep waters that steadily increase as one sinks uncontrollably in a never ending abyss. The shrieking alarms were like the groaning of the ship's titanium alloy and hardened plastic structure that molecule by molecule was crushed and compressed into nothingness and empty waste, even beyond time.

Terran fought the urge to grab the controls. He told himself to relax and let the Keyhole swallow them down. Even his thoughts began to be submerged as he and the others drowned in unconsciousness, falling into deep and untroubled sleep.

The ship seemed asleep, too, its mighty engines now silent, as it tumbled on deeper and deeper into the abysmal void, into the gigantic and frightening maw of this unexplainable phenomenon.

* * * * * * * * * *

Lieutenant-Warden Janet Rogerton, awakened by her crew, watched in fascination as the Victorian cruiser, shedding its cloak, suddenly appeared on the screen directly behind Bestmarke's ship. Both ships were far in front of hers and the fire-power coming from Bestmarke's was impressive. Her ship could never take that abuse, how was the cruiser doing it? The whole scene played out with the cruiser finally backing down while Bestmarke's ship sped directly into the Keyhole and quietly disappeared.

"I wish I could quietly disappear," she said. "The Star-Commander will be furious this time. This is one debriefing I really wish I could avoid."

"Continue present course" she reminded the crew. "Take side-dock number three, port-side at the *Daniela*. That is all." She sighed and sank back into her seat thinking of uninterrupted sleep that would still have to wait.

TROPHY

Chapter VI

Earth Date: 475 N.V.A.
Location: CENTRAL, Earth

"I just cannot accept what the future is unfolding. Can all our hard work and that of the generations before us really come to nothing? My heart cannot deal with that," sighed Guardian III as she walked along the rushing, boulder strewn creek that foamed and splashed down the tumbling mountainside, weaving its way through the dense hardwood forest toward the sun filled valley below.

"My thoughts and fears are similar ... but we must never give up hope," said Guardian I as they walked together by the thick ferns and tiny wildflowers crowding the edge of the winding trail. "Our ancestors were at this point more than once. They struggled to give us everything we now have. It seemed impossible for them, too, but they succeeded ... as we will," she reassured her.

"I am sorry to be so gloomy ... it's not like me to be this way. But when I realize we have only two generations left, perhaps three if we are fortunate, I am overwhelmed. Plus the fact that only ten of us know what the truth really is. If even a hint of this leaked to the general populace the very existence of the Empire would be jeopardized. What do we do now?" Guardian III said, turning and looking into the aged face of the tall woman beside her.

"I see a glimmer of hope, though at present I have no substantial facts to back up my thinking. My feelings tell me that somehow Franelli is the key to our great puzzle. I have considered so many other possibilities, but my thoughts and hopes keep circling back to him. It is imperative that he be captured alive and brought back to CENTRAL. If he truly has an understanding of the Keyhole, if it is a conduit through time as he once said so many years ago, he must be persuaded at all costs to help us. If we cannot convince him, then we must force him to cooperate, though I would be loath to do so. The Star-Commander is aware of our request for his capture and is committing as many resources as possible to accomplish the task," Guardian I continued.

"You encourage me, but I admit that I have serious doubts about Franelli. Guardian V will likely agree with you concerning him. The others will probably agree with me. I remember him as being unpredictable and difficult to read. Will he ever want to help us? I am willing, of course, to see what help he can provide, but I cannot place any hope in that solution just yet."

They were silent as they descended a group of steep switchbacks that led to the edge of a shimmering emerald pool, twenty meters below the top of the cascading waters surging down the uneven layers of sedimentary rock. Rainbows glinted briefly in the mist as the late afternoon sunlight filtered through the trees. The fragrance of wildflowers intermingled with the earthen smell of rock and moss and clamorous falling water.

"It is so beautiful here, this is one of my favorite locations," Guardian I softly said, gazing with renewed wonder at the familiar scene. "And now there is similar beauty throughout the whole earth. We have accomplished much, haven't we, my friend?"

"Indeed we have ... indeed we have," mused Guardian III. She paused in thought, and then with a troubled face, turned to Guardian I. "But will there be anyone at all to enjoy our beautiful planet after our grandchildren have lived out their lives?"

* * * * * * * * *

TROPHY

Earth Date: November 1, 1975 Ancient Calendar
Location: En route to Earth from the Kuiper Belt

Tommie was the first to awaken. His long dreamless nap was over and he was hungry. He wanted attention. Still strapped in, the only thing he could do was meow. He did again and again until Estelle started to move, gently roused from deep sleep.

The sound of Tommie's meowing triggered a bizarre waking dream involving Tommie and countless ships and cats, all floating above a vast green plain that stretched off into infinity. Tommie was meowing as if pleading with Estelle to play, but she couldn't answer or move, only watch and listen. The other cats and ships slowly faded until it was only Tommie, still meowing.

Slowly, Estelle's waking consciousness took control, and she realized Tommie indeed wanted her attention. She felt happy that he was there. And then pity, realizing he had probably been strapped in a long time and was, no doubt, hungry. She reached out and affectionately stroked and scratched his furry head while loosening his restraints. She told him to be patient, there were other things she had to do before he could be fed. Tommie purred and blinked his eyes as if to say he understood.

Estelle looked at her controls. All readings looked normal, not erratic as they had been. She continued scanning computer functions looking for any abnormalities. She found none. She was switching to the COM System when her eyes caught one sub program display blinking on and off with the words "System Error". A sub-program wouldn't be vital to the ship's immediate safety, but she was curious. She punched into Terran's console and gently woke him up. "All systems fully functioning," she told him. "But one sub-program is erratic, and you might want to check it out."

"Which one?" he asked sleepily.

"The program base date," she replied cautiously. "The one that tells us the date."

"What does it say?"

"November 1, 1975, in the Ancient Calendar. That is ninety years before the New Beginning, which was four hundred and seventy five years ago. How can this be correct? What does it mean?"

"Don't worry," he said as he awakened more. "That's exactly what I expected. That subprogram always shifts when we travel through the Keyhole. I will correct it immediately. It is nothing to worry about."

"Thanks, Terran, I'm glad it is nothing serious."

Terran didn't say anything more and Estelle didn't ask. She contemplated his explanation; it seemed reasonable, but she still had questions. If we traveled through the Keyhole, then where are we and can we travel safely back? Why did we come here? Does the rest of the crew understand our situation? Why would only the date subprogram be affected? She had many questions but she knew there would be few answers. When you work for Galen Bestmarke, you do what you are told and do not ask questions. She knew this when she took the job. "I will just have to be patient and see if I can figure out any of these questions myself," she said out loud. She checked the subprogram again and it was reading today's date. It had already been corrected.

Putting it out of her mind she turned to more immediate matters. "Okay, Tommie," she said, smiling pleasantly. "Let's get you out of that harness and feed you something." Tommie just looked at her and slowly blinked, continuing to meow.

TROPHY

Chapter VII

"I'll be glad when these g-forces subside," Galen said, confined to his gravity seat while the engines were accelerating. "Are the inertia dampers working as they should? I don't remember it being so oppressive the last time we came back," he growled, tugging at the tight collar of his jacket. "Have you checked with Louis?" he said, looking over at Terran comfortably relaxing in his gravity seat, his eyes closed.

Terran turned his head and slightly opened his eyes. "It is the same, it hasn't changed. Louis says all the systems are working perfectly. Last time was our first trip back. You were excited and didn't notice the discomfort," he said annoyed. "Soon the engines will shut down and we will have standard gravity during the coasting mode." Turning his head back and shutting his eyes again, he continued to speak. "With the power of these Zenkati engines it is a wonder that Louis has come up with a design to keep us alive and not be crushed. If you want speed, there has to be some discomfort. The fact that we can make the trip in about thirty days is a testament to the man's genius. No ship in the Empire can even come close to that speed," he said with finality, trying to stifle his brother's constant complaining.

Galen recalled his first impression of Louis Franelli: tall and thin with droning speech and intense, merciless eyes. Louis's ordinary looks mocked his brilliance – a perfect disguise. Louis's intelligence was legendary to those who cared about cutting-edge research. Galen cared. He schemed to somehow attract Louis away from CENTRAL, and his chance finally came. In a tip he learned that Louis had been banned from research work at CENTRAL and sentenced to a prison term. He didn't know the details but the compu-court was firm in its decision. His informant had detailed that a Victorian Cruiser would transport Louis and other prisoners to the Rehabilitation Institute at Luna One. Cloaked, his ship followed the unsuspecting Cruiser. Halfway to Luna One, he suddenly decloaked his ship and attacked the Cruiser, targeting its reactor and engines. The Cruiser lost all its main power and weapons systems. With lightning speed he took his crew, boarded the Cruiser, and successfully abducted Louis after an intense laser-rifle battle that left many PCC personnel dead or wounded while his forces suffered only minor injuries. He offered Louis the choice of working for him or being abandoned to his fate. Louis was bitter against the Empire and grudgingly accepted his offer, a position Louis had kept for nearly ten years.

"I admit, Brother, Louis is a genius. I am reminded every time I remember how much I am paying for his genius!" Galen said. "But when I win the wager with the Izax, I will get all of it back and then some!" With satisfaction he slapped his palms on the armrests of his seat. "He really doesn't think I can complete my collection. I will show that impudent swine a thing or two. Too many times he has beaten me ... but not this time!"

"We owe him a few, don't we," Terran said, opening his eyes. "Remember the time he cheated us out of the shipment of premium Martian burgundy, direct from the slopes of Olympus Mons?"

"How can I forget, that is my favorite," said Galen bitterly. "And the time he underpaid us for the Laconian Lager from Titan Station?"

"Yeah, that stuff is good!" said Terran, putting his hands behind his head, reminiscing.

"Somehow he always cheats us," Galen said. "This time he will pay dearly and we will have the last laugh."

"Revenge will be sweet," said Terran. He paused for a moment. "And yet, we do not want to anger him too much. He is a powerful man with many friends, some even within the Empire itself. That could be useful some day."

TROPHY

"You always have to be so practical, don't you," Galen countered in jest. "You are absolutely correct, though, so we will anger him just enough to annoy him. We do not want to burn any bridges behind us, that is, unless the Izax is standing on one of them," he said. "I will try to control my gloating when it becomes time."

The COM snapped on with Louis announcing engine shut-off in ten seconds. "Standard gravity will soon be restored."

Terran stretched, happy to be free of the oppressive heavy gravity. He stood up to walk around. "Estelle was the first to awaken. She noticed the date change before I could mask it. I told her the date subprogram always shifts when we travel through the Keyhole. She accepted my explanation without anymore questions."

"Good. She has always kept to herself and her cat, not socializing with the rest of the crew," replied Galen, also standing and moving about, stretching his muscles. " As long as you corrected the date, we won't worry about her unless she starts asking more questions."

* * * * * * * * *

Earth Date: December 5, 1975 Ancient Calendar
Location: Earth, geosynchronous orbit

"You will essentially be invisible to their primitive radar detection system," said Louis, standing at the controls in the space-plane port. "The space-plane will still be visible to the eyes, however, so go in and leave during darkness. The ground cloak will hide you during daylight. It doesn't use much power."

"Thank you, Louis," Terran answered, standing beside him, arms folded across his chest. "Galen has given you control of the ship until we return. Hopefully that will be in two days, three at the most. The expedition gear is stowed and ready. The preservation chambers are in stand-by mode, ready for use. If you have any problems or questions, contact me. I will do the same. At all times I will be staying in the space-plane. Only my brother will be hunting."

Galen could be heard slapping the walls of the corridor as he walked noisily to the space-plane port. He was obviously in high spirits and anxious to depart. He grinned at Louis and slapped him on the back. "It is about time things were ready. You probably wish you could come along, too, don't you, Louis? Though I doubt you could stand to have so much fun!"

"Don't worry about me, boss," Louis said. "Just remember the instructions I gave you for the chambers."

Louis watched patiently while the two brothers finished loading the tiny space-plane. Standing behind the thick window in the control room, he depleted the atmosphere and artificial gravity in the port and opened the main doors to space. The extension arm moved the space-plane out the doors and released it into the deft hands of Terran, sitting in the pilot's seat. They slowly moved away from the massive cloaked ship and powered up their chemical engine. Picking up speed and arcing away they aimed for Earth's upper atmosphere. Their scorching descent to the lower atmosphere led them to their final destination; the rugged, snow covered mountains of Southwestern Montana, North American Continent.

TROPHY

Chapter VIII

Earth Date: December 5, 1975 Ancient Calendar
Location: Gallatin Range, Southwest Montana, U.S.A.

Terran Bestmarke brought the space-plane in and hovered over the snow clad meadow on the east face of the mountains close to Windy Pass. With a muffled roaring of the exhaust he lowered it straight down to a landing at the meadow's edge near a stand of tall fir trees. Shutting the engine down he engaged the ground cloak and the ship took on the appearance of a large snowdrift, completely concealed. For a moment he and Galen sat quietly listening to the wind breathing through the fir trees and scattering the dry, finely grained snow that stung against the hull of their small ship.

"It is cold out there," whispered Terran. "It is minus twenty degrees Celsius. I will be happy to stay in the ship and let you do the walking."

"That is your choice, my brother. For me, I cannot wait … this is what life is all about. The thrill of the hunt is matching wits against a wise and subtle animal in its own environment. It makes my blood course and surge through my veins. This is the way a man is meant to live, not controlled and emasculated," he said, his purple tinged eyes flashing and his gold rimmed teeth glowing softly as he turned his thick lips upward into a greedy smile. "This is what I live for."

"Well, what I live for is a good night's sleep," Terran said. "I suggest we get some. The morning will soon be here and it will still be dark and cold."

*   *   *   *   *   *   *   *   *

TROPHY

Earth Date: December 6, 1975 Ancient Calendar
Location: Gallatin Range, Portal Creek Drainage

The stars were still shining as Martin Bucklann locked the cabin door and carried his thermos of coffee and lunch to the old truck, rumbling at low idle in the crisp mountain air. The exhaust hung around the truck in layers, sweetly acrid, reminiscent of other early morning starts. Five degrees Fahrenheit and no wind. Perfect. The Constellation, Orion the Hunter, was slipping behind the western mountains as the stars Arcturus and Spica were rising in the east. "Time for another hunter," thought Martin as he slid onto the cold seat. The deep-lugged tires squeaked in the powdery snow as he turned the steering wheel and shifted the old 4x4 pickup into gear, heading down the snow-packed road west of the cabin to the main road by the river. It was only a ten minute ride along the Gallatin before he reached the Portal Creek turn-off that loomed up abruptly in the darkness. Turning up the untracked road, his headlights seemed feeble among the towering firs that guarded the entrance to the narrow canyon. The firs gave way to large open rock slides bordered by Engelmann spruce and quaking aspens, leafless and spindly, invisible in the dark. The narrow road became steeper and more snow bound, forcing him to chain-up the struggling truck. Finally reaching the upper meadow he climbed out, breathed in the faint refreshing scent of the conifers, and looked around, allowing his eyes to adapt to the darkness. The starlight-illuminated snow gradually became brighter, but the trees remained an impenetrable black wall, their dark tops silhouetted against the night sky like jagged picket fences, back-lit by diamond dust. It was quiet and still except for the squeak of the dry snow under his boots, and the faint ticking of the hot engine as it cooled.

Windy Pass was to the northeast of him, faintly discernible as a treeless dip between the mountainous ridges on either side. As he looked in that direction he noticed a small, bright point of light like a

51

star, but much brighter, as if coming from the pass. It faded in a few seconds and was gone. Martin passed it off as a hunter's flashlight or a meteor just above the pass.

He remembered mornings like this when he was a teenager, hunting with his father. He was happy then. But now, standing in the snow under the bright starlight, a wave of sadness suddenly swept through him, ripping open the empty place in his heart he usually kept tightly closed. He missed his father so much. Memories washed over him like a gentle snowfall; memories still clear and not yet dimmed with age. Pleasant memories of good times long past, but always followed by a perpetual and unshakable sadness.

Seventeen long years ago his father had disappeared on opening day of hunting season. Martin was sick and did not go with him – something Martin had always regretted. Searchers found his father's truck intact and parked where he had left it. But no trace of his father was found. Even human remains discovered the next summer were unidentifiable, and just intensified the lingering doubt.

The only common thread in all the months since his disappearance were three empty cartridge casings, two of which were found only days later and a third one the next summer, close to the human remains. He still had them, and questioned their bright metal construction. Casings were usually made of brass, but these were foreign to him, with different, odd-shaped primers. The metal was like stainless steel, but with rainbow colors shimmering faintly on the surface, ever changing like sunlight reflecting from an oil film on still water.

The searching had continued for Martin. He feared what he would find in the end, and yet he knew he had to discover the truth to fully realize his pain, and find closure in his mind and heart. Now, standing in the snow, his spirit weary again, he forced himself to climb back into the truck for one more cup of coffee before he began his hunt.

TROPHY

"Do you want any of this coffee, Terran?" Galen said as he finished his breakfast in the tiny galley of the space-plane. The aroma of sausage and toast lingered in the stuffy cabin air.

"No," Terran groaned. "It is too early for anything except sleep. You are crazy to go out now. It is still cold and dark. Hurry up and leave so I can have some peace!" he said, hiding his head under the blanket.

"You are jealous," Galen teased. "You will not have any fun sitting in this plane all day. Come with me."

"You are crazy!" was the muffled reply.

"At least have the preservation chambers ready. I feel lucky today."

"I will," Terran said. He uncovered his face and looked up at Galen. "Take a laser-rifle and an infra-red scanner with you. You could easily find what you are looking for and quickly be done with it. Then we could leave this frigid place."

"It is not nearly as cold as space," Galen said, rolling his eyes. "Besides, you know I am a sportsman. My equipment is a projectile weapon, a rifle, the same as the hunters of this time era. That makes the hunt more challenging. All that other stuff would definitely attract attention if someone saw me. Some of those things have not even been invented yet."

"Right, I forgot about that. But you are still wearing a shielding-suit."

"That is different, Brother. That is my insurance. I have to draw the line somewhere."

"I hope you are successful, Mr. Sportsman," said Terran. "But not too soon – I still want to get more sleep."

"Sleep. That is all you ever think about," said Galen as he pulled on his hat and gloves, cradled his rifle, and stepped through the open hatch to the snow covered ground below.

TROPHY

"Close the hatch! You are letting all the heat out!" said Terran, pulling the blanket back over his head.

Drawing a deep breath of cold, dry air, Galen smiled and walked up the short distance to Windy Pass. The pine scented breeze was steadily increasing. He allowed only enough illumination from his hand-light to faintly see his way through the scattered boulders. His footsteps, squeaking gently in the powdery snow, came to a stop at the top of the pass. He risked a brighter light to examine the descending mountainside stretching off into the west.

*   *   *   *   *   *   *   *   *   *

Finishing his coffee and stuffing a sandwich into another pocket, Martin climbed out of the truck and put on his down parka. He loaded five cartridges into the magazine of his 8mm Mauser, slung the rifle onto his shoulder, turned to the northeast, and walked into the darkness of the trees. The road became a wide trail lit by the fading stars and the glimmers of dawn on the dry, powdery white snow. The delicate crunch of snow under his lugged boots was the only sound a deer or awakening bird might hear.

The air began to move. The vaguely brightening dawn was starting the great wind engine that drove these peaks and passes. A few snowflakes from the Lodge Pole pines drifted down, caressing his warm face. Soon all the trees would be dumping their snowy loads on any unfortunate soul beneath them.

*   *   *   *   *   *   *   *   *   *

Turning his back on the westerly wind, Galen slowly worked his way back down the eastern side of the pass and turned south at the edge of a small meadow flanked by fir and spruce thickets, still black in the fading starlight. Studying a topography map he located a trail and continued his southerly direction, finally turning west again around a shoulder of the mountain. With the wind once more in

54

his face, Galen moved stealthily along the trail with a minimum of illumination from his light. Suddenly a fresh set of large deer tracks entered the trail, moving in the same westerly direction. He smiled to himself and continued on even more quietly.

* * * * * * * * *

Martin was suddenly surprised by the shock wave of a nearby rifle firing in the dark. The rolling roar of the large caliber continued to echo down the canyons and roll back, finally dying out, leaving only the faint rustle of the breeze tipping the snow out of the top branches of the tall pines. The chickadees were silent, not even moving. Everything was silent. Standing still, Martin strained for a sound but only silence floated back.

Then he heard it. A branch snapped, and then another, mixed with the muted thuds of hooves in the dry snow coming down the hill ahead. Another branch snapped followed by a heavy thud, and then stillness. Listening carefully he began to recognize the sound of a winded and severely injured animal. He guessed it was a deer. But why had it been shot now? Daylight was still to come and a true sportsman wouldn't be hunting deer at night. He stood silently, listening to the faint rhythmic breathing. But another faint sound, also rhythmic, intruded gently on the first. The steady squeak of deliberate footsteps in the snow descended the hill. Slowly and steadily the steps drew closer. The animal's breathing quickened, and it gasped and coughed as it struggled to get up. To Martin's amazement, an intense white light illuminated the animal, a five point muley buck, one of the largest he'd ever seen. The buck, bloodstained on its lower chest, panicked and struggled to leap away. It crashed into a Hawthorne bush, sending up a sparkling cloud of snow. Desperate and blinded by the light, the deer could only guess where to jump. The rifle roared again, echoing through the mountain sides. The hapless buck leaped again down the mountain side as the intense light faded to darkness. Quick and heavy muted steps followed. The crashing of the wounded deer continued, growing fainter as it descended toward the creek bottom.

Martin remained motionless and silent. He couldn't hear the buck or the hunter anymore. He waited for more light to continue walking up the trail where the deer had crossed. Tufts of brownish gray and tan hair hung from the thorns of the Hawthorne Bush, and dark drops of blood drilled the snow below it.

"Why didn't he kill the deer?" he said, noticing the footprints in the snow. "He was plenty close enough. Using a light is illegal." Anger began to grow in his heart. "I'll turn him in to the Fish and Game if I find out who it is."

Minutes later as Martin rounded the heavily timbered mountainside below the southeast ridge, the boom of a distant rifle again caught his attention. His anger rekindled as he remembered the agony of the wounded animal as it tried to escape, and the hunter using a bright light. Martin's face flushed hot with indignation.

Martin had long ago lost the thrill and heart racing feeling of the kill. As the years went by, he found himself more reluctant to squeeze the trigger to end an animal's life. The protection and preservation of them had grown in his mind and heart, and he wondered how long he'd continue to hunt. He reasoned that hunting was necessary for the health of the animal population, and he truly did like the meat, depending on a supply of it to carry him through the long winters. And the ritual ... could he ever really stop? He loved the mountains and the hunt; the battling of wits with a creature his own size or larger that survived not only by instinct, but by caution, cleverness, and speed.

Following the ridge north for half a mile, he turned eastward again at the head-wall along the upper end of the valley, crossed a frozen stream, and approached the eastern base of Windy Pass. The rising wind was at his left as the dawn approached. Martin slowly shifted into position in the deep woods at the eastern edge of the

TROPHY

pass. It was only a matter of time until hunters worked their way up the western side of the pass and drove the big bucks to him. He'd done this before and he could wait.

Martin watched and waited for a long time, but nothing came his way. With no activity but the rising wind, he retraced his steps on the trail that had brought him. He turned onto a different trail that dropped down lower on the mountain. The wind lessened and the jays and chickadees reappeared, lightening his heart and reconfirming his love for the forest's inhabitants. The usual satisfaction of the first day's hunt was unfulfilled; his heart wasn't in it after seeing the hunter with the bright light. The ritual seemed empty. Was it something his father would have done, or something that memory and loss drove him to do? Thoughts and memories like these brought back the ache of his father's disappearance. Only the soothing balm of the forest lifted his spirits.

The weak winter sun at mid-morning signaled a stop along a south facing hillside. Several hundred feet below him ran a small stream, virtually unseen for all the snow and ice except for a few dark holes in the snow. After a sandwich, he worked his way down the steep hillside to the stream and scooped up the cold, refreshing water with his hand. Scooping up another palm full, he glanced upstream and froze, water dripping through his fingers. Partially hidden by a bush was the body of a large mule deer laying in the creek. But to Martin's surprise and disgust he discovered the deer had no head.

"Trophy hunter," he muttered, deep anger stirring in him again. He vividly recalled the consuming rage of his father many years ago when the two of them discovered the headless carcasses of three magnificent bull elk. He still mirrored his father's sentiments.

"Nothing is more wasteful or arrogant!" his father had said. "To kill these stately animals just to hang their heads on the wall is criminal. The hunter should use the meat or at least give it to somebody that needs it. It's too bad this hunter's head isn't hung up on a wall for us all to jeer at!"

TROPHY

He pulled the deer up the bank some distance for the coyotes to finish. Dropping the legs and turning to go uphill a brilliant gleam caught his eye. He bent down and reached for a small metallic object caught in the crotch of a double tree. It was a rifle cartridge ... the metal was iridescent like an oil film on water. Stunned, he looked at it carefully. It appeared the same as the three unusual casings that had been found when his father disappeared so many years ago. Long years of unanswered questions and agonizing memories once thought conquered suddenly sprang alive in a hideous rebirth.

For hours he scoured the area for anything that would provide a clue. The wind had erased any tracks but could not blow away the lingering doubts and nagging questions. Was this the same hunter that left the previous casings years ago? Was this the same hunter that used the bright light? Did this hunter have anything to do with his father? Does it all fit together or is it just coincidence? Finally, he returned to the trail and made for his truck.

The chickadees were still flitting about and chattering in the upper branches when Martin reached the old truck sitting forlornly by the big firs. Small drifts of snow had banked against the wheels. The truck door opened with a groan and he tiredly climbed in, started the engine, and let it run while pouring himself a cup from his thermos. The coffee smelled so good. It was a relief to be out of the wind enjoying the warmth of the heater and his favorite brew.

Still full of questions, Martin started back down the rough road, easing the old four-wheel drive down the steep hills that didn't seem nearly so steep going up.

"I should have left an hour ago," Martin said out loud. "The sun would still be shining." The southwest mountains now hid the lowering sun and silently signaled the approaching twilight.

A half mile down the road, his retreat was halted by a fallen Lodge Pole pine. "Wind must have knocked it down" he muttered and climbed out to assess the situation.

TROPHY

The twelve inch diameter tree was wedged between standing ones. With no ax or saw, and no winch on the truck, he wasn't going anywhere except on foot. He walked slowly to the butt end of the tree where it was still attached to the stump. Looking closely, he realized it had been cut and made to appear as if it had blown down naturally. Both sides of the road were too steep and tree bound to drive around the fallen tree.

"Who would do this? This doesn't make any sense," he said, shaking his head. "Now I have a long walk back to the main road, most of that in the dark. Oh well, at least it's all downhill," he said, trying to cheer himself. "I might as well finish my coffee and sandwich in the heated truck," he said, climbing back in. ""I'll have to get back out in the cold soon enough."

TROPHY

Chapter IX

"I told you I was feeling lucky," beamed Galen. "Look at the size of this buck....five points on each side. Have you ever seen such antlers on a deer? He is almost the size of an elk!"

"He is impressive, Brother. But you know more about this sort of thing than I," Terran said. "Did you take him with the first shot?"

"You had to ask. No, I did not," Galen said in a disgruntled tone. "It took three shots to finish him off and he led me on a wild chase. But it was worth it."

"How is the preservation chamber working? I don't notice the gamey smell anymore."

"Perfectly!" Galen smiled. "I am anxious to fill the other one and I think I can do it soon."

"How is that?"

"I back-tracked on my trail and discovered another set of tracks. They match what I am looking for, as best as I can tell. I will rest awhile and then resume my hunt."

"Will you return in time to leave tonight?"

"I will try. I am prepared to stay out all night if I have to. If this is the opportunity I have been waiting for I do not want to pass it up."

"Well, if you must stay out all night, I hope you do not freeze."

"I will be prepared," said Galen smugly.

* * * * * * * * *

Martin finished his coffee and shut down the old truck. He started the long walk down the road in the early darkness, his rifle cradled in his arms. The tree purposely blocking the road, the hunter with the light, the headless deer, and the empty cartridge casing made him suspicious. Bears were hibernating now, but mountain lions were still a threat. He also might need to signal with his rifle in an emergency.

The wind had abated for the night and the quietness was broken only by the soft crunching of his boots in the crusted snow. The young moon slowly encountering the mountains softly lit the road ahead. It was accompanied by a host of brilliant winter stars. But the thick trees, close and dense, formed impenetrable black walls on either side. The road was a faint, sparkling, narrow ribbon of white between them.

He had gone only a half mile when something tugged a corner of his consciousness forcing him to look behind where he had been. Back where his truck was parked the tops of the trees were lit up as if illuminated by a brilliant light at ground level. He stood listening quietly but no sounds came. After a few seconds the light subsided back to darkness. He remembered the wounded deer and the hunter's light from earlier that morning – thoughts that were troubling. It aroused his curiosity but heightened his feeling for caution. Quietly, Martin climbed up the steep bank to his left until he was a hundred feet from the road. He then doubled back in the direction of his truck. Without a trail it was difficult and slow going among the dark trees. He moved skillfully, making little noise, and stopped from time to time listening carefully for any approaching sounds. After going some distance he turned back toward the road, quietly making his way down fifty feet before turning left again in his original direction. He slowly paralleled the road. He stopped often. He waited patiently. Finally, faint crunching footsteps floated to his keen ears. Martin remained motionless. He strained to pick up every nuance. The footsteps continued on by him at a steady pace. Martin slowly followed through the trees, gradually working his way down toward the road.

TROPHY

He could now see a darkened figure ahead of him steadily moving down the road in the soft moonlight. Suddenly it stopped and Martin quickly checked his own movement. A brilliant white light illuminated the road ahead and swept continuously around just as Martin ducked behind a densely needled spruce tree. White slivers of light on each side of him finally moved off as the light continued sweeping around. The figure focused the light on Martin's footsteps going up the hill. The figure hesitated and looked around once more with the light. Looking up the bank again, the figure quickly climbed up as the light faded out.

At that moment Martin's suspicion was confirmed. He was being hunted. He quickly made his way back to the road and carefully walked in his own tracks a short distance before dropping off the right side at a rocky spot with little snow. With more regard for speed than stealth, he worked his way down toward the creek bottom that lay below him. He had only gone a short way when the trees around him were stabbed with a sharp white light, followed seconds later by the deafening roar of a large caliber rifle. A tree only a foot from Martin's shoulder splintered as the bullet tore through it. Martin plunged a zigzag path down the mountain while questions raced wildly through his mind. "Who is it? Why is he after me?" he kept repeating in his head.

More than once the dead fall tripped him in his headlong plunge toward the creek bottom. He clumsily fell numerous times, gouging himself on the snag ends of broken branches, all the while struggling to control his panic. Gasping for breath, he huddled behind a tree and flicked off the caps of the scope. Loading a cartridge into the chamber of the 8mm and clicking the safety off, he waited behind the tree. With his breathing settled, he strained for any sounds. A branch snapped in the distance above him and then another one. Martin continued to wait. Suddenly the snow beside him was illuminated in brilliant light, and the patterns of bark on the tree trunks jumped out in rugged detail. He squinted to avoid losing all his night vision and continued to wait. "Not yet ... not yet ...," he said to himself. Suddenly, it was dark again. The breaking branches continued and drew slowly and steadily closer. Martin readied the rifle at his shoulder and waited. The throbbing pulse in his head quickened in anticipation. Time crawled slowly. The waiting seemed like it would endure forever.

Suddenly, brilliant light illuminated his surroundings. Martin was ready. With his right eye to the scope, he swung the rifle around the base of the tree and aimed directly at the top edge of the light. The light's brilliance through the scope was painful, like staring at the noontime sun, but in a disciplined split-second he found his target and squeezed off the shot. The 8mm roared as the bullet found its mark and the light fragmented into a thousand sparks. Finally there was blackness again.

"Maybe that will even things out a bit" he said, quickly turning downhill again. No shots followed him this time as he zigzagged down through the dead fall. With a haunting suddenness the sound of laughter floated down from the hillside above. Martin stopped abruptly behind a tree.

"Well met!" boomed a deep and richly melodic voice followed by more laughter, this time harder and longer.

Martin continued his plunge down the ravine to the creek bottom. The laughter had sent an uncommon shock of terror through him. This person was playing with him, hunting him like an animal.

He lunged forward, straining his stiff and aching muscles, trying to follow the creek in the dense darkness. He continued along the creek for a long distance, slipping and falling many times in his haste. He reached a point where the ground fell more steeply and he struggled down the backside of an ancient rock slide. Anxiety and fatigue caused him to be careless. He proceeded too quickly and slipped again, instinctively grabbing for a tree, but only grasping a rotten branch that slowly pulled out of its socket, causing him to

TROPHY

slide slowly backwards in the dark toward what felt like the edge of a cliff. Clutching his rifle in his left arm, he frantically pawed at the ground with his right hand, hoping to find anything to stop him. With a sickening dread, he slid over the edge feeling the rocks scrape along his belly and chest. In terror, he plummeted down in the darkness. The cliff sloped out at the bottom, causing Martin to slide and tumble into the snow-covered boulders below. He stopped abruptly and lay still.

The loud snap of a branch and the tumbling of small rocks jarred Martin to painful consciousness. He reached out for his rifle which was surprisingly right beside him. The chatter of rocks again brought back the danger that pursued him. As he slowly stood up he wondered how long he had been lying there. Testing each footstep he painfully made his way down to the trees a few yards away. In a short distance he discovered a large spruce tree with dense, low growing branches so thick the snow and wind barely penetrated. There was a thick blanket of dried needles on the ground hidden beneath it. Martin realized how cold and near exhaustion he was and decided against going on. As quickly and comfortably as he could, he buried himself in the thick bed of needles. He kept his rifle, with the safety off, beside him. He would trust the tree and the forest that he loved to watch over him for a while.

Laying there in the dark, Martin remembered the night his father had disappeared. The following seventeen years he had grown very close to his mother. She worried about him during hunting season since this was the time of year she lost her husband. He wished he were with her tonight, talking and laughing about old memories, instead of cold and hungry, waiting for dawn, and hiding under a tree from an unseen predator. Thinking of his mother cheered him, and fostered his inner strength, compelling him to be positive and never give up. Under the spruce needle blanket with its faint refreshing smell, his warmth began to return. In minutes he fell into a deep, dreamless sleep under the guard of the giant spruce tree.

64

TROPHY

Chapter X

The first sounds Martin heard were familiar. The faint morning light stole through holes in the roof of his den as he opened his eyes. The huge tree trunk rose above him as a dark shadow, like the mast of a great sailing ship. Chickadees were fluttering close by and the raucous cry of a jay high above shattered the silence. He painfully sat up and rubbed his battered legs and arms. He ached everywhere including his stomach. He was hungry. Searching his pockets, he found only a squashed candy bar and a strip of forgotten jerky … not his idea of breakfast. He wolfed them down but the ache in his stomach remained.

The upper branches of the trees creaked and swayed as the morning wind began. The blue sky of the day before was replaced with gray, and he could smell the heavier, humid air marking the change in the weather. Now and then a tiny snowflake drifted by, a prelude to something greater. It was a mixed blessing. A storm would make the going difficult but also provide the cover and secrecy he needed if the hunter was still after him. He shuddered again at the thought and wondered why anyone would go to such lengths to pursue him. He couldn't resolve it in his mind, but he had to escape the mountains soon or succumb to exposure and hunger. He was thirsty and needed to find the creek he had been following.

The cold wind slapped Martin's bearded face as he crawled out from under the great spruce tree. He paused for a moment, listening carefully, before slowly working his way down toward the creek. He found an open patch of water hidden behind a massive boulder and satisfied his thirst. With his rifle in his hands, he followed the creek downstream as the sky continued to darken with thickening snow clouds, driven by the increasing wind. He reached a narrow point in the canyon and climbed up the northern slope to a deer trail a hundred yards above the creek bottom. He spotted footprints recently made that were just beginning to fill with windblown snow. The footprints followed the trail as it descended the mountain, paralleling the creek. To continue along the trail would mean an ambush, no matter how stealthy he was.

Martin glanced at his watch. 8:45 A.M. Looking again at the sky he decided to go south, up the left side of the canyon. As soon as he begun climbing up the snowflakes started down, lightly at first, swirling in the wind, but quickly thickening until it was difficult to see ahead. He found another deer trail about the same distance above the creek. This one was untracked and led through denser growing pines and firs. With his rifle pointed forward and the safety off he trudged along the trail, barely able to see, snowflakes stinging his eyes.

Suddenly he heard a muffled snap, like a hidden branch trodden down beneath the snow. He stopped moving, even breathing, as he strained to pick up any more sounds. He flicked the caps off his scope and scanned the trees on the opposite side of the narrow canyon. It was difficult to see anything but white snow. Martin moved the scope slowly and soon his concentration was rewarded. Through the falling snow he could barely make out movement – a figure in dark clothing hugged the trail as it wound around the bottom of an overhanging cliff.

He remembered that cliff from a summer hike he had taken last year. A rock had nearly fallen on him at the time so he had investigated to see why. Another cliff jutted above the lower one creating a talus rock slide at its base which precariously hung just above the lower cliff. Wind, thunder, or too much rain would bring down the slippery rocks. Now the rocks were loosely frozen together and the snow was piling up, arching out in a cornice – anything would bring them down.

In a split-second decision, Martin aimed the 8mm at the cornice and fired off three rounds as fast as he could. A handful of rocks and snow tipped off the edge and chattered down toward the creek below. Time stood still with only the sound of the rising wind streaming through the swaying branches. Suddenly the mountain groaned as the snow cornice and a slurry of talus rock thundered down the lower cliff upon the darkened form cowering below. A hoarse, muffled scream was briefly heard and then only the continuing slide and chatter of the falling rock.

"What have I done!" Martin said in shock. "Have I just killed a man? Was I thinking too fast? Should I try to help him?" he said to himself, his mind racing from the adrenaline surging through his trembling body. "Why should I help him? He tried to kill me!" he argued with himself. "He got what he deserved. The mountain killed him," he said, though his reasoning felt hollow. "But what if that wasn't him?" he suddenly said. "What if that was just another hunter, an innocent man?" With doubts beating his conscience, Martin decided to at least find the dead man's broken body for identification. He crept along the descending deer trail to a small open meadow where he struggled across the creek and began climbing back up toward the rock slide, two hundred yards above him through the thick timber.

The steep climb was treacherous and he slipped many times. He finally slung his rifle over his shoulder so he could pull himself up through the trees with both hands. He pulled on a rotten branch that snapped, sending him back down the last ten feet he had just scaled. At the same instant, a tree exploded just above him and the powerful roar of a rifle shocked his senses. Somehow his hunter had survived! He not only survived, but was seemingly unhurt and still bent on his malevolence.

In desperation Martin slid down the mountainside nearly to the creek and positioned himself behind some rocks and thick brush. Peaking through the leafless branches, he searched through his rifle scope for his assailant. The swirling snow was blinding and coated the lenses, but he wiped them off and persevered in his search until he saw the dark movement of a man. This time he ignored his conscience and firmly squeezed the trigger. Nothing happened. He had forgotten to load another cartridge into the chamber of his rifle. He quickly cocked another one in place and looked through the scope. The figure was gone. Martin kept searching.

Suddenly the rock beside him sparked and sang as a bullet ricocheted close to his head, followed by a deafening report and the pungent odor of pulverized stone. Martin noticed movement and instantly aimed and fired at the barely visible form above him. With the roaring of his 8mm he watched the figure of a man tip and slide down the mountainside to a point above the creek where he could no longer be seen. That was enough for Martin! No pangs of conscience were going to hold him this time. He turned and labored through the deep snow back to the creek where he quickly followed it downstream without resting. He found the deer trail again and slogged along for a mile before turning south, heading up the mountainside towards the ridge.

He was sweating and gasping for breath as he made the ridge top. Like a bare shin on the mountainside, the ridge was clear of trees for some distance down its long face. He welcomed the easier walking across the open ridge although the wind-whipped snow stung his face. He was close to the tree line on the opposite side when he suddenly felt uneasy with a need to hurry. With quickening steps he lunged for the cover of the trees. At the same instant a bullet splintered the tree beside him at chest level, only inches away, and the powerful roar flooded his mind with fear. Panic drove him stumbling down through the trees on the south-facing slope. Falling and sliding, he scrambled to pull himself behind a large fir tree but was thrown behind it with a hard slap on his leg and intense pain burning in his left thigh. The thundering report in his ears sickened him. He had been hit! "No! No!" he moaned in despair. But his despair turned to rage at this loathsome beast hunting him like an animal. Enduring the pain, he shifted his position, took the rifle's safety off, and carefully peered around the base of the tree. Through the scope he could barely make out the gray outline of a figure steadily moving closer. His leg was throbbing as he lightly touched the trigger. He started to squeeze it, but the figure disappeared behind some trees. He kept searching through the scope as the agony became more intense. If Martin didn't do something to stop his attacker, he would soon be dead. Suddenly he saw movement. Desperate, Martin squeezed the trigger of the 8mm.

The roar of the rifle filled his ears as he watched his target through the scope. The bullet should have found its mark; the figure was still, but standing upright. It seemed as if a faint luminescence flickered and then went out from the gray outline. Fear clutched at Martin's heart. What was he up against? Was there anything he could do to stop this monster? Seized by panic, he struggled to stand and hobbled down the mountainside, every step bringing waves of pain. The bullet had missed the bone and his bleeding was light but he felt weak and nauseous, wondering if the nightmare would ever end. He stumbled down the mountainside toward the creek at the bottom expecting to be shot again at any moment. It didn't happen and he collapsed behind a boulder at the edge of the stream, trying to calm his thoughts and collect his strength. This creek was bigger and not totally frozen over, but quick running and shallow for some distance – an opportunity to hide his obvious trail of footprints and blood. With no choice but to walk the creek he slung his rifle over his shoulder in case he fell. The snow was falling heavily as he stepped into the creek and the icy water seeped over the top of his boots. His leg was numb and now his feet as he struggled and slipped along the icy creek bottom, stumbling numerous times and nearly falling, but somehow catching his balance. He slipped on an ice-covered boulder, painfully falling with his hands, arms, and forehead upon the rocks protruding above the freezing water, leaving him dazed, swollen, and bleeding. Fighting for concentration as numbness spread throughout his body and mind he took his rifle in his hands and stiffly climbed up the south bank of the creek. In swirling clouds of snow, he struggled up the steep, thickly forested canyon wall, slipping many times, and falling against rocks and sharp branches. He didn't feel the pain anymore. He was numb everywhere. Only sheer concentration and strength of will compelled him to continue his climb until his breath came in great heaving gasps, his lungs aching from the cold that now penetrated to his core. He stiffly propped himself under a large fir tree to rest and catch his breath but the tree offered little protection from the wind driven snow that stung his eyes. Shutting them for a moment to ease the pain, he huddled down behind the tree and fell very still.

With a jolt, he shook himself awake. He had fallen asleep from exhaustion. He didn't know how long he'd been asleep, probably only minutes, but it frightened him and wiped away the numbness in his mind. The intense pain in his leg throbbed as he struggled to his feet and hobbled across the wind swept ridge, starting down the other side to what he hoped was the main Portal Creek Road far below. Clutching his rifle, he stumbled forward on unfeeling leaden feet, constantly slipping and falling as he descended the steep mountainside, the howling wind swirling around him, and each jolting step racking him with pain.

Without warning, he was thrown to the ground with a deafening roar from behind. Martin struggled to bring up his rifle but it was gone, fallen in the snow. He had no feeling in his right arm, only an intense burning pain and he screamed with fear and desperation, struggling to crawl away from the horror behind him. Staggering to his feet he tried to run but another blast slammed him to the ground, sending him skidding face first and sideways down the mountainside in the icy snow. A tree stopped his slide and Martin lay there motionless. The pain and pressure in his chest was intense, excruciating, with his breath coming in short, painful gasps.

"Why?" he groaned. "Mother... father... I haven't found you yet..." He tried to move, but it was too hard, too painful. It was so much easier to just lie there. He felt numb all over, even warm, but he was so tired … so tired. He wanted to rest and sleep.

The snow swirled thickly about him as he laid face down, a reddish cloud slowly spreading out in the snow under him on both sides, fading as the falling snow quickly covered it like multiple gauze blankets, layer upon layer, diluting red to pink, and pink to white, with a serene purity.

Slowly approaching footsteps in the snow, the steady squeaking of boots, grew closer. To Martin it seemed remote, as if in a dream. It frightened him and he wanted to run away, like a young boy escaping his nightmare, fleeing to the arms of his mother. He yearned for that peace and comfort.

With a swift kick an icy boot was in his ribs turning him over. Martin stared up glassy-eyed at the hunter. The kick was painful, like a lightning bolt surging through him, but the relieving numbness quickly returned. He tried to speak but his mouth and face were too cold to move and all he could do was gasp and stare with half-opened, glassy eyes.

As if from a great distance he heard a rich, deep voice with an unusual accent slowly speaking to him. "We meet again, young hunter. You were a worthy chase, you almost beat me. And now I am going to give you the honor that you so richly deserve!"

The words echoed in Martin's mind. Then he heard a merciless laughter that made him shudder with anguish and complete despair. He helplessly watched as the hunter pulled a long, strangely luminescent knife from a black sheath and move steadily closer to him. Memories of the headless deer floated through his mind as he felt an icy touch at his throat. He felt no pain, and Martin finally drifted off to sleep, to the rest he yearned for.

TROPHY

Chapter XI

Earth Date: December 10, 1975 Ancient Calendar
Location: En route to the Kuiper Belt

The light was soft and muted when Martin first opened his
eyes. All he could see was a light gray sheen that wrapped around
him. He tried to move his head, but his muscles didn't respond. He
could hear a faint whir or hum that seemed to pervade all other
sounds. He strained to hear something else … anything. But the
humming noise, or sensation, was all there was. All there was. That
thought disturbed him and increasingly so as he reflected on what
had happened in the last few days and hours. Everything was a blur,
surreal, leaving him confused and disjointed in his thinking. He
vividly remembered the ordeal he went through to its ghastly end, but
how could it have been real? It must have been a dream but where
was he now? He needed answers about what was real and he needed
time to think because now his only reality was his own consciousness,
the light gray sheen that encircled him, and the almost undetectable
but all pervasive hum.

A wave of panic and fear swept over him when he realized
he wasn't breathing, and yet he was still alive and conscious. He
could see parts of his face as he moved his eyes; the top corners of
his mouth and the edges of his cheeks covered with his auburn, gray
flecked beard. He could move these as well as his eyes in what felt
like a normal fashion. An indistinct smell lightly touched his nostrils,
vaguely reminding him of overheated electrical components. But
he was almost afraid to speak for fear that he could, even without
breathing. He tried and was surprised to hear his voice, although
it sounded flat and confined as if in a small space. He shouted,
marveling at the volume with seemingly little effort. Shouting again,

he began voicing his frustration. "Where am I? Why am I here? Is there anybody here?"

Almost imperceptibly, the light gray sheen began to darken. As it darkened the vague outline of a man's head began to emerge as if out of a thick fog, which the bright morning sun slowly burns away, until details are sharp and crisp. The softly lit face of a man, strangely familiar, looked squarely at Martin from about three feet away. All was dark around him and only his face could be seen. Martin stared at him. Martin was full of questions with an apprehension he couldn't explain. The man was a big man, as far as he could tell, completely bald with full thick lips, strong facial features, and dark brown eyes ... but the whites were a purplish color. His right cheek had a fresh, nasty looking gash. A slow broad grin was spreading over his face, revealing gold rimmed teeth that gleamed softly in the dim light. His smile was not benevolent. Martin recognized his unusual foreign accent immediately.

"We meet again, indeed, my young opponent. From your shouting, it was obvious that you finally awoke. It has been some time, almost three standard days, and I was starting to grow impatient.

"But in answer to your questions ... I'll answer them in random order. My name is Bestmarke, Galen Bestmarke. And where you are? You are on my ship, although it is probably much different than any ship you have seen before. Let me just say that it is a very powerful ship, a very fast ship.

"And now your best question, 'Why am I here?' That is, of course, why are YOU here? First, let me explain that I am a businessman, a very good businessman. And because I am rich, as you would say, I can well afford to do more than just work. I can do what I like to do. I like to collect things. Rare things. One-of-a-kind things. And I am much like you, Martin Bucklann, or shall I call you Marty? Yes, you and I have a lot in common. You see, we are both hunters. Yes, Marty ... hunters ... sportsmen! Are you beginning to see why you are here? Come now, my worthy opponent, it is so plainly obvious. You belong to me now. Yes, I know it is shocking to think about, but it is true. You belong to me. I have collected you, so to speak, and now you join my other collections in my grand display room. My trophy room, if you will. Yes, now ... you ... are ... my ... trophy," he slowly said, letting each word sink in. He gloated, savoring the shock on Martin's face.

Grinning broadly, Galen studied Martin's face for a few more moments and then asked him quietly, almost whispering, "Do you want to see my other conquests, my prize trophies, my now complete collection?"

Martin could only stare blankly, wondering what bizarre and horrible creations this madman had invented. But Galen wasn't waiting for an answer. Stepping back and turning around with both arms held out, he said arrogantly, "Behold, my grand trophy room!"

As the illumination spread and grew, Martin realized he was at the side of a circular room, richly finished in dark, polished woods on the walls with deep forest green carpet. The ceiling was not defined, but was like the blue sky of a sunny afternoon. Its height was difficult to judge as the walls seemed to diffuse into it with no corner or pronounced division. But these things were secondary to what caught Martin's widely opened eyes. All along the perimeter and at various points near the center were heavy carved wooden pedestals or platforms of different sizes and shapes. A shimmer like very clear glass, almost invisible, sparkled faintly above each. One by one, starting at Martin's immediate right and working around the room counter-clockwise, the sparkling sheen above each pedestal gave way to a shape, the head of an animal. Martin watched and listened with growing horror as he recognized different animal heads. He heard a cacophony of different noises: bellowing, roars, and bleating. Screams of terror and growls of anger filled his unbelieving ears while his eyes tried to comprehend the sheer ferocity, the lunacy, of this visual circus, with the sickening realization that all the heads were somehow alive. They were alive and he was like them. Living trophies captured and put out for display.

Watching silently with a greedy smile, Galen carefully observed Martin's terror struck face as each pedestal's hideous treasure was fully revealed. Finally having seen them all, Martin stared at Galen with outrage.

"Why?" he said almost inaudibly as Galen continued to grin with an irritating smugness. "Why!" screamed Martin with all the hatred and rage he could summon. So intense was his outburst that the room quickly fell silent. Even Galen stopped grinning and stepped back, but he quickly regained his mocking composure and moved close to Martin's face.

"Why?" he said in a more serious tone. "You are asking me why, you of all people? You know why!" he said with a sarcastic harshness. "I am a hunter, just like you. And you ask me why?" He looked incredulously at Martin. "I am just like you, only this time I won which proves I am the superior hunter. Barely, I will humbly admit. You almost beat me with that rock slide – that was brilliant! But I won just the same," he said arrogantly, grinning again. "And now you are mine!" he gloated triumphantly.

"I'm not like you," Martin said with a growl. "I'm not like you at all. I hunt only for the meat. I'm not a cold blooded killer!"

"Oh, no, I am sure you are not," Galen mocked. "And yet you love the hunt, do you not? You love the power of life and death in your hands, do you not? And do you not love the kill, that most visceral and intense feeling of all?" he said hungrily with surprising intensity. "Oh," he mournfully cried. "You just kill for the meat … I have so misunderstood you," he scornfully continued.

Martin just stared at him blankly, totally taken aback, feeling the acute impotence of his position. Before Martin could utter a sound, Galen screamed: "Liar! You love to kill! You are a hunter just like me!" Galen paused and then more quietly continued. "In one respect I am different, I admit, but in a superior way because I do not kill. You are the killer. I am the collector, a collector of living things," he coldly said with emphasis on the word 'living'. "YOU are the killer, my young and worthy opponent" he said again with an accusing superiority. His intense laughter showed his complete satisfaction with the outcome of their verbal sparring. He continued to laugh for a long time, and all the mixed orchestra of sounds seemed to join together in a great, hideous, overwhelming crescendo, bent on driving Martin to madness.

But Galen, composing himself, looked at Martin with a menacing twinkle in his eye and said: "I have one more surprise for you, Martin Bucklann." He turned Martin's pedestal ninety degrees to the left where another pedestal of equal height was sitting, its trophy hidden by the sparkling iridescence.

"Behold!" he shouted, bursting with wretched glee. Martin numbly watched, wondering what could possibly be worse than his present situation. The sparkling diminished as a man's head began to form in front of Martin's bulging and dismayed eyes. All he could do was gasp and blink his eyes. In total disbelief, he finally said in a breathless whisper: "Father ..."

Galen's triumph was supreme. He was beside himself in the glory of the moment. "Father and son!" he shouted. "A matched pair of hunters! And I took them both! Is it not both ironic and wonderful?" he said, laughing long and hard, totally pleased with himself.

"I will give you a few minutes to get reacquainted," mocked Bestmarke. "Perhaps you can tell each other hunting stories," he chided maliciously, and walked away continuing to laugh and gloat.

Martin just looked at his father in total disbelief, feeling completely wretched. How could they ever get out of this deplorable situation? Who could ever help them? It seemed totally hopeless.

"Son, we're finally together," said his father softly. "I've dreamed of seeing you and your mother again for a long time ... but not like this ... not like this. How long has it been? You look older.

Somehow he shuts me off and I sleep almost constantly without dreaming. I have lost all track of time."

"Seventeen years, Dad. Seventeen long years. Now, we're both gone. Mom's heart must be broken again. I feel so helpless and miserable. We missed you so much, Dad. We searched for years to try and understand what had happened. I wish this were just a nightmare and that we would both wake up."

"I'm afraid it is a nightmare, Son, but a nightmare we can't wake up from. This maniac told me every detail of his plan to capture you, and how he'd accomplish it. Oh, how I hoped he would fail! He's completely wicked, totally evil. How could he just rip us away from our families, from the ones we love so much?" he cried, his voice breaking. "He's worse than an animal!"

"Why did he pick us? Where did he come from and where are we going?"

"He picked me at random, Son. I was just like another animal out in the forest. But he specifically chose you. He forced me – he tortured me – to find out about you. He put all the details together so he could trap you. Now the pig gloats about having a matched pair of hunters."

"Oh, Dad, I've wanted to tell you how much I've missed you for so long. And now it seems so hollow. What are we going to do?" Martin continued. "How can we ever help mother? How can we ever let her know the truth about what's happened to us? We're like helpless animals in a zoo, totally controlled by this beast. It's totally hopeless!"

"It might seem hopeless, Son, but never give up. We don't know what the future holds. Somehow, something might change. We can never give up hope!"

"I wish I could feel that way, Dad. I don't know what we can do. He's such a cruel and wicked man. I wish I could ..."

TROPHY

"Could what, my young opponent?" challenged Bestmarke as he walked toward them. "You have had enough time together. It is time to shut you off!" he shouted as he walked to the pedestals.

"Son, I love ... "

Martin felt his energy drain away and quickly fell asleep.

*   *   *   *   *   *   *   *   *   *

Galen locked the vault door on the trophy room and walked forward through the central corridor that threaded the core of the long ship toward the forward compartments. The trophy room and cargo compartments comprised about a third of the ship in the center, with the fusion reactor and engines in the stern behind the massive blast/thrust plate. He continued forward past his quarters, past weapons and engineering, and finally through the crew's quarters to the bridge in the bow of the ship. The defense cube, buttressed in the heavy front shielding, was all that was forward of the bridge.

Terran was at his console looking thoughtfully at the screens, rubbing his chin, deep in contemplation. He barely noticed Galen standing beside him, also studying the screens. Terran spoke first, not looking up. "Did the reunion go as you expected, Brother?" After a few seconds of silence he looked up at Galen.

Galen caught his gaze and smiled a self satisfied grin. "It went very well," he beamed. "Very well, indeed! I was just now contemplating my good fortune on acquiring a matched pair of hunters. They are truly unique! I cannot wait to see the Izax again. I have beaten him this time! It is a resounding victory for me. He will be insanely jealous. What a pity," he mournfully mocked, chuckling softly with great satisfaction. "Are we ready to go back through the Keyhole?" he asked, on a more serious note.

"Louis is working on his preliminary computations. He needs an hour or two and wants to be left alone. He made a point of that," he said, shrugging his shoulders. "Then it should be smooth sailing until we reach the Keyhole."

Galen just grinned. "I feel so good I'll be generous with him … THREE hours of peace." He laughed again, heading to the mess hall for a bowl of pretzels and a few Laconian Lagers.

TROPHY

Chapter XII

Earth Date: 475 N.V.A.
Location: Kuiper Belt: trans-Neptunian region

Star-Commander Abigail Vandevere wasn't smiling this time. Her mood was tense and foreboding, like a volcano about to erupt. The lines on her face and set of her jaw revealed her locked-in rage. Her steely-gray eyes were brimming with anger.

She was not an imposing figure at first glance: medium height, slender build, and smartly styled short blond hair with natural highlights of gray, giving her a dignity befitting her high rank. Her lightly purple-tinged eyes accented her modest, impeccably presented uniform. A single ten pointed star of pure platinum was near her left shoulder. Only that star and the platinum buttons, instead of brass, signaled her rank, the pinnacle an off-worlder could attain. A higher rank would land a desk job on earth or on one of the big bases in the solar system. However, she had what she wanted, command of the flagship *Daniela*, the most impressive Victorian Cruiser of the fleet.

The Star-Commander's self control was exemplary. She obviously didn't achieve her position by flying off the handle when situations went awry, but her patience was nearly spent as she listened to the reports from the officers that had tried to disable Bestmarke's ship.

"What level did you have the probe-bombs set at, Lieutenant-Warden Kanopolis?" said the Star-Commander.

"They were at half strength, set at level five, Ma'am," she said nervously. "We had concern for Franelli … we thought a higher setting might rupture the hull of the ship. We did not want to take that risk."

"Let me worry about Franelli, Lieutenant," VanDevere said sharply. "We are not nursing mothers here. This is battle. As long as Franelli is not dead, that is all that matters. He deserves to be roughed up. Bestmarke deserves even more. Someday we will get both of them."

"Yes, Ma'am!" Kanopolis said.

"Lieutenant-Warden Rogerton," said the Star-Commander, shifting her gaze. "You have oversight of Alpha Squadron. How would you rate their performance?"

"They followed my orders explicitly and did all they reasonably could, Ma'am," Rogerton said with a strong voice. "I gave those orders to reduce the probe-bomb intensity."

"Your orders? I see," said VanDevere calmly. She began to pace slowly along the line of officers. "Is it not standard procedure to set them at seven, if not full strength, Lieutenant? Do you, perhaps, know more than the designers of these devices?" she said, raising her voice.

"I do not pretend to know more," Rogerton said. "But with all due respect, Ma'am, we are not in the lab now. We are on the battlefield. Bestmarke's engines and shields were damaged. We needed to compensate to keep Franelli safe," she said, her eyes straight ahead.

"Oh, yes, our dear Mr. Franelli," the Star-Commander said, continuing to pace. She stopped suddenly in front of Rogerton and turned to her, standing close. "Tell me, Lieutenant, what did you discern about the performance of Bestmarke's ship when he dropped his cloak and made a run toward the Keyhole?"

"He has a ... a very fast ship," Rogerton said quietly, momentarily looking down. "It is ... very maneuverable."

"And that is your description?" VanDevere said, staring at her. "Very fast ... very maneuverable? What do you think that would indicate, Lieutenant? As you said, we are not in the lab now."

TROPHY

"I am not sure if I know what you mean, Ma'am," she stammered, looking straight ahead."

VanDevere looked into her eyes for a long moment, a faint smile forming on her lips. "Never mind, Lieutenant."

The bridge was unnervingly quiet and tense. VanDevere again began to pace, and slowly moved her unflinching gaze from one officer to another as they stood rigidly at attention, eyes straight ahead. Finally she spoke, exasperation heavy in her voice.

"I really thought we had them this time. They were in our grasp but for Franelli!" she said, spitting out his name with obvious disgust. "We had them ... we had them," she repeated as if murmuring to herself, shifting her gaze downwards.

And then, raising her spirits and her eyes, she said: "You all are to be commended. Under the circumstances you could not have realistically done more. Thankfully, the *Laurel* suffered no loss of life and only moderate damage. She will be back in action soon. Ship Three of Alpha Squadron was nearly destroyed, however. Two crew members were critically injured but have been stabilized. The rest are in fair condition, receiving treatment for their burns. Now we must prepare for Bestmarke's return. We can only assume that he will soon bring his ship back through the Keyhole. It may be the next time the Keyhole appears, it may be farther in the future, we do not know. But we must be ready!" said the Star-Commander. She paused momentarily before giving her final order. "There is time before the Keyhole's next appearance, so get some rest and give your crews time off on the *Daniela*. Strategy briefing tomorrow at 14:00 hours. Dismissed."

The officers saluted with their left fists over their hearts and a crisp, "Yes, Ma'am!" They began filing off the bridge.

As almost an afterthought, the Star-Commander said: "Lieutenant-Warden Rogerton, would you accompany me to my office, please?"

TROPHY

"Yes, Ma'am," was the immediate, emotionless reply. Rogerton's heart rate increased and she wondered what other difficult questions awaited her. The slumping shoulders of her fellow officers revealed their relief as they quickened their pace to leave, gratified their names weren't mentioned.

A brief walk brought them to the austere but pleasantly comfortable private office of the Star-Commander. As was usual on a battle-ship, there was no loose furniture. Everything was built-in or firmly anchored and secured. The muted pastel colors were comforting and tastefully coordinated with VanDevere's personal preferences. A single ten pointed star was the only decoration on the wall behind the desk. At the side wall was a single picture of a fashionably dressed and younger Abigail VanDevere standing beside another young woman, obviously her sister, similar in age. On the opposite wall were two pictures: the same younger Abigail VanDevere in a simple cadet's uniform fresh out of the Planetary Control Corps Academy, and a similar looking young woman but with dark walnut-colored hair, also in a simple but more updated cadet's uniform. It was her daughter Elizabeth, still in her last year at the Academy, and VanDevere was very proud of her. School officials said she was well on her way to becoming a fine officer.

"At ease, Lieutenant, and make yourself comfortable. I want you to tell me everything you haven't told me yet. I felt during the debriefing that you were holding something back. I assume you felt it necessary and had good reason," she said as she sat at her desk. "Oh, I'm sorry," VanDevere continued. "I meant to offer you some refreshment. I would really like some coffee. Would you like some, too?" she said, touching the control of the intercom.

"Just water for me, please, Ma'am," replied Rogerton, sitting down on the edge of a wall couch.

VanDevere called for the beverages. They sat in an awkward silence as her Personal Specialist quickly brought them and quietly disappeared. The redolence of the coffee filled the room as

TROPHY

VanDevere poured a cup from the carafe and savored the first sip. Then with a gentle smile, she looked directly at Lieutenant-Warden Rogerton.

Rogerton felt the power of command keenly focused on her and it was intimidating, to say the least. She swallowed, put her drink down, and collected her thoughts. Looking straight into the eyes of the Star-Commander, she began: "I thought we had a chance against Bestmarke's ship with our mines, especially the new issue SPM-3's. We deployed the five we had. He took out the first two before they unloaded, but the last three had time to unload, nine projectiles in standard "C" formation. Nothing should have escaped ... but his ship seemed alive. I am thinking a guider/pouncer team and suspecting Victorian trained."

The Star-Commander's widening eyes signaled the Lieutenant had gained her interest.

Rogerton continued: "Using the micro-shield, I had the computer search for any renegade Victorian officers specifically trained as guiders. It found one back three standard years. I searched back five more years ... nothing. Only one in eight years."

Lost in thought, the Star-Commander wasn't looking at her anymore.

"I asked for everything in the data-bank on the officer and here is what it gave me: Code name – "Star Point", renegade 2.75 standard years."

It took several moments before the Star-Commander looked intently at the Lieutenant and sharply asked: "That is all? What is the Priority Rating?"

"Priority 50-C1. No more information was available."

With a deep sigh Star-Commander Abigail VanDevere seemed to age in the Lieutenant's eyes. She looked absently to the picture of her sister and quietly said: "Now I am beginning to understand ..."

TROPHY

Rogerton kept respectfully silent. She also had questions that demanded answers, but now was not the time to ask.

Heaving another deep sigh, the Star-Commander stood, signaling the end of their meeting. The Lieutenant-Warden quickly stood.

"Lieutenant, keep this confidential," VanDevere said in a low voice. "Speak to no one about this, no matter their rank. I cannot explain more at this time. You are one of my most discerning officers. You possess a keen and observant mind and will understand this situation more distinctly as time and circumstances unfold. Thank you for your discernment in not disclosing this information at the debriefing. Dismissed, get some well deserved rest."

"Thank you, Ma'am," expressed Rogerton with affectionate concern in her voice. She had never seen the Star-Commander in such a mood. She was always the model of self-control, logic, and finality in her command. Yet she had revealed to her, a junior officer, strong emotions about some hidden situation that was deeply troubling. Why now and why her? These thoughts raced through her mind as she smartly saluted with her left fist over her heart and quickly walked through the door.

Lieutenant-Warden Janet Rogerton was tired, exhausted from hours of continuous duty, but not ready to sleep just yet. Not now. She needed to walk and think. Usually confined to her small ship, walking for any distance was a luxury to her. But a Victorian Cruiser, especially the *Daniela*, was immense, six hundred meters long. Walking without repeating the scenery was possible, although all the decks and corridors were essentially the same. Still, to walk and think, oblivious to your surroundings, was something to savor in the depths of space.

As a commanding officer most of the ship was open to her and she walked for some distance. Finally she came to one of the canteens near her ship's docking port. The smell of food combined with the sounds of laughter and conversation drew her in. Walking through the door automatically set one "at ease" with no distinction of rank observed. Everyone was equal here, although discipline, order, graciousness, and the dignity of the service were always required.

Glancing around she noticed her pilot, Kolanna Montoombo, seated at one of the booths, obviously enjoying a plate full of food.

"Hi Kolanna, do you mind if I join you?"

She looked up with an inviting smile, revealing white, perfect teeth that seemed to stretch from ear to ear. She was tall and willowy with gracefully long arms and legs, smooth brown mahogany skin, and a regal elegance about her reminiscent of an ancient African princess. Her large, almond shaped, dark brown eyes had a light purple tinge. Closely cropped black hair gave her a professional and athletic appearance. Gold jewelry, not worn on duty, often completed her look.

"Welcome, Lieutenant! Please! Please! Sit down!" she said enthusiastically, obviously enjoying herself. "Look! Can you believe it? Biscuits and gravy! Real biscuits and gravy! I could just drink in the aroma itself! Do you know how long it's been since I've had them? I can't even remember. Probably back on Luna One. Here, try some! I have plenty!" she said, sliding over her plate.

It was impossible to refuse her generosity and the Lieutenant tried a small portion.

"It's very tasty, but heavy," she said, raising her eyebrows. "If I eat too much, I will never get to sleep."

"I always sleep better on a full stomach," said Kolanna, wielding her fork.

"How can you eat so much and stay so thin?" said Rogerton, protesting in mock exasperation. "There has to be something in the regulations about such gross unfairness."

Kolanna laughed, smiling infectiously, and continued to eat with complete delight.

The Lieutenant realized that all the walking had done its job ... she was exhausted. "Thanks, Kolanna, I need to get some sleep.

TROPHY

We will have a crew meeting tomorrow after we know our orders from the Star-Commander. Rest well."

"Rest well, Lieutenant."

TROPHY

Chapter XIII

Star-Commander Abigail VanDevere was again the model of self-control, logic, and finality of command. Her impeccable standards of punctuality and professional comportment were obvious as she strode briskly into the briefing room at precisely 14:00 hours. All the officers were wisely there early and now stood respectfully at attention, all smartly dressed in their best uniforms, presented as they were expected.

Standing at the right side of the front row Lieutenant-Warden Janet Rogerton couldn't help but notice the difference in the Star-Commander's attitude from her private meeting the day before. There was almost a smile on her face as if something in the past hours had brought her new hope.

"At ease. As you all are aware, Bestmarke and Franelli know something about the strange anomaly, the Keyhole, which has eluded us. So far we know nothing of what causes it or controls it. All we know is that it appears precisely on time and remains for precisely the same length of time at each appearance. This has remained absolutely the same for over two centuries since it was discovered. Also, as you know, it never appears in the same exact location but shifts randomly inside a large bubble of space. Since its discovery we have run countless calculations to determine a pattern to these appearances, but to no avail," she said, speaking clearly and pacing back and forth.

"We know Bestmarke's ship came back out one time before. We were too far away to do anything but watch him on the NAV screens. After a short time he disappeared from those, too," she said as she stopped pacing and faced them.

"But now we know something even Franelli does not know," she said reassuringly, gesturing widely with her arms. "We may have cracked the code on where the Keyhole will appear next."

TROPHY

She let the import of this statement sink in to her officers for a few moments. The subtle nodding of heads and widening of eyes underscored the importance of this announcement.

"No doubt you all will have many questions," she said, radiating confidence. "In the days and weeks to come we hope to use this new information from CENTRAL to accomplish the following: First we must capture Franelli alive and whole. Second, once Franelli is caught and persuaded to cooperate, we will press on with our investigation and study of the Keyhole. CENTRAL believes this anomaly plays a crucial role in our future, in the continuation of the Empire, and even in the survival of the human race."

VanDevere paused again to emphasize the importance of this latest revelation. She could sense in her officers different feelings; apprehension and uncertainty in some, confidence and boldness in others. All, though, showed rock-like courage and fearlessness, instilling deep pride and camaraderie in the heart of the Star-Commander.

"We have narrowed the choice to three possible locations where the Keyhole will next appear. This is based on the latest communications from CENTRAL. We have assigned squadrons to each location anticipating Bestmarke's return through the Keyhole at its next appearance in nine standard days. Lieutenant-Commander Gornect will pass out the briefings. You will have one hour to look them over and formulate any questions. Please be thorough! One hour, my Sisters," she emphasized, leaving the room as quickly as she had entered it.

TROPHY

Chapter XIV

Earth Date: January, 1976 Ancient Calendar
Location: Kuiper Belt, 'Keyhole'

"There it is," murmured Terran. "It's almost in the
same location. Thirty minutes and we will be there. Louis's final
calculations are already locked into the guidance system."

"Nothing to it this time," chided Galen. "We are making life
too easy for you, aren't we Louis?"

Louis's expressionless gaze revealed his contempt for small
talk.

"The calculations are different each time, boss, and very
difficult. Miscalculations could be fatal," he said, thoroughly annoyed.
"Speed, timing, and the energy harmonics of the ship have to be
perfectly synchronized with the Keyhole. We could miss our target
date by years, even centuries, with a slight miscalculation. Many
probes and ships have been lost since the Keyhole was discovered
and nobody knows where they are or even if they still exist. You
don't want to end up in that situation, do you?"

Galen just smiled and held his tongue. Louis certainly had
been testy lately and most likely needed some time off on solid
ground. He had to coddle him a bit more than usual but he didn't
mind. There was no one else with a mind and creative genius like his.
He was unique. Galen was keenly aware of this and handled him with
kid gloves, patience, and high pay ... a winning combination in his
estimation.

Galen methodically went through his gunner's checklist
and reassured himself on his weapons inventories. These might
be necessary after emerging from the Keyhole though all weapons
systems needed to be off during the transit. Louis had strongly

warned all of them about leaving any weapons systems on, or using the link between himself and Terran, as well as Estelle and Tommie, as they unconsciously passed through the Keyhole. Their vulnerability during the waking moments on the other side worried him. The unpredictability of the Keyhole's location gave him some assurance but nagging doubts and fears remained. He wanted every edge he could gain. Being prepared as much as possible was absolutely essential.

The minutes ticked by and the silent tension on the ship climbed.

Finally Terran's voice announced over the COM: "One minute to fully automatic, the guidance system is locked on. Everybody strap in."

Anticipating the possibility of battle, the viewing portal was closed this time so the beauty and frightening immensity of this strange galactic phenomena wasn't visible as they entered the abyss. Terran sighed in resignation as he gave up the controls, once again placing his life in Louis's hands and brilliant mind. His instruments became erratic and he felt the building g-forces and sluggishness of his thinking as they were swallowed down deeper and deeper. He didn't fight it, but welcomed the deep, dreamless sleep.

The ship flew on, ever deeper into the Keyhole, as if it were asleep again, too.

TROPHY

Chapter XV

Earth Date: 475 N.V.A.
Location: Kuiper Belt, approaching the 'Keyhole'

Lieutenant-Warden Janet Rogerton's PCC ship was coasting through space with her assigned squadron. Their single fusion engine was silent now, only steering thrusters were occasionally needed. Nine other Patrol Class ships like hers plus a Victorian Cruiser made up Squadron Alpha. They were approaching their tactical location, one of three possible areas for the Keyhole's reappearance. The fact that the cruiser they accompanied was the *Daniela* only emphasized that this location had the highest probability of intercepting Bestmarke's ship when it reemerged from the Keyhole. What they would do, or could do, when they finally encountered Bestmarke's ship was still uncertain.

At their final briefing, the Star-Commander had emphasized the importance of quickly taking his ship. VanDevere had recounted the one instance of seeing Bestmarke reemerge through the Keyhole. His ship had shown no control or activity for a few minutes. How many minutes were uncertain, but everything about the ship, including its engines, appeared to be shut down. Their window of opportunity was brief and the safe capture of Franelli was paramount. To guarantee Franelli's protection, they must avoid a fight with Bestmarke. Once Franelli was safely removed from Bestmarke's ship, the squadron would be free to attack Bestmarke with all their power.

The Star-Commander's voice came over the COM system: "Ten seconds to braking thrust ... on my mark."

Kolanna synched her controls with the flagship and went to standard braking power. "Braking thrust and steering, Ma'am," she reported to Rogerton. "Reappearance of the Keyhole in ten minutes."

The minutes slowly ticked by. All eyes were on the NAV screens to see how close they would be.

"Stand by alert," the Lieutenant-Warden calmly said, with two minutes remaining.

Tension on the ship began to grow as the seconds trickled down to zero. The Star-Commander's voice came over the COM again, and it was obvious the adrenaline was flowing. "The Keyhole is right on schedule!" she said, excitedly. "Pilots, steer us to our prearranged coordinates! Ships One and Two prepare for attachment and boarding procedures! Ships Three through Ten take flanking positions! Prepare to synch shielding! Coordinate harmonics, on my mark!"

"Shielding synched," confirmed Kolanna, steering ship One into position. Smiling, she looked up at Lieutenant-Warden Rogerton who returned her gaze with a nervous grin. With silent anticipation she continued monitoring the NAV screens.

Ten minutes showed on the screen as the Keyhole completed its formation. Its unstable forming time lasted nearly 12 minutes before it settled into its stable mode for just over an hour. It then began to collapse at the same rate it had formed, following the exact timing and sequence since its discovery in 261 N.V.A., 214 standard years ago.

"Two minutes to completion," monitored Kolanna. "No activity yet."

All the crew watched the NAV screens in silence as the tension mounted.

"Stabilization is complete, beginning countdown of 62.79 minutes. All circuits are steady. The Octopus Boarding Unit is at standby. All we need is Bestmarke," said Kolanna.

Two minutes went by, then three and four. Rogerton felt like a hunter, waiting for her prey.

TROPHY

"There is activity!" exclaimed Kolanna, nervously caressing her controls as she watched the screens.

Rogerton saw it at the same time on her NAV screen. "This could be Bestmarke's ship," she said cautiously, and then confirmed. "It is Bestmarke! His ship will clear the Keyhole in 30 seconds. Kolanna, set your final approach vectors and begin moving into position. Set the Octopus to full operation," she briskly ordered. "Specialists, take your boarding stations at the Octopus. Shielding suits on! Remember, we must be quick! Take Franelli first!" she said, clenching her fists.

PCC Ships One and Two positioned themselves to come in from behind as Bestmarke's ship cleared the Keyhole. Ship Two led the approach along the top of Bestmarke's ship. Octopus Boarding Units were attached to the bottoms of the two PCC ships and their arm-like tentacles were fully extended out, ready to grasp the ship when they lightly touched down.

Bestmarke's ship was huge. It was originally a high volume standard cargo vessel, but had been extensively modified and refitted with additional armor, formidable weaponry, and two Zenkati fusion engines, the best and most powerful available. The Star-Commander, however, was expecting no change to the location of the operations center of the ship. Franelli was an engineer and they were counting on him being in that section.

"Take us in, Kolanna," ordered Rogerton.

In unison, both ships gently touched down, the tentacles of the Octopus units clinging to the hull of Bestmarke's ship with barnacle-like strength. Ship Two was over the engineering area and Ship One over the general cargo area, closer to the stern.

"No response," whispered Rogerton. "It is like they are asleep. Quickly now, get the can-openers working."

The nuclear cutters of the Octopus units quickly and efficiently burned boarding holes through the thick skin of the hull, securing the lids quietly. Instantly, equalizer tubes extended in to eliminate sharp edges, seal any air leaks, and provide hand holds to scramble up or down. Four boarding Specialists on each ship descended down the tubes into the belly of Bestmarke's ship.

The Ship Two Specialists stealthily fanned out in the dim ambient lighting of the engineering section. They encountered no resistance, although they were armed with stun-phasers and wore shielding suits with blast helmets. They quickly found Franelli strapped in his control seat, completely asleep. As they touched him, he groaned and started to move but quickly slumped forward as they sedated him. Quietly, they unstrapped him and carried him to the boarding hole where they attached a harness and pulled him up into the PCC ship.

"We have Franelli secure and unconscious, although he was beginning to awaken when we encountered him," stated the Lieutenant-Warden on Ship Two. "The Specialists are returning to the ship. The cutter will begin sealing the plug."

Meanwhile, the four Specialists from Ship One had descended into the cargo area.

"Lieutenant-Warden Rogerton, we have the area secure, but we have never seen anything like this before," one of the Specialists responded.

"Please describe," Rogerton said.

"The room is circular, and it makes you feel like ... like being in a forest with blue sky above. It's hard to explain. There are many heavy wooden pedestals, and each has a shimmering, glassy-looking glow above them. Please advise."

Lieutenant-Warden Rogerton contemplated her options, finally responding. "Can you bring one or two of them up?"

"We will get a harness on them and bring two up."

"Very good, I am coming down to see for myself."

Also wearing a shielding suit and blast helmet, Rogerton quickly came down. The Specialists pointed to the pedestals as they deftly maneuvered two of them up the equalizer tube into the PCC ship.

"What is this place?" she wondered as she walked around. "And what are these pedestals for?"

She reached down and touched the small shiny plate on the side. Suddenly, the glassy sheen above began to darken and a shape appeared as if through a thick fog. Her fascination, though, turned to horror and intense fear as the snarling head of a huge, maned lion roared at her from only a meter away. She frantically jumped back with her stun-phaser raised, her eyes wide with fear. Visibly quite shaken, she realized it couldn't hurt her, but she had never been so frightened. As she turned to the Specialist beside her, alarms began shrieking. Bestmarke's huge ship rumbled and vibrated as the fusion engines began their start-up sequence.

"Back to the ship!" shouted Rogerton as she and the specialist ran to the equalizer tube. They both grabbed the harness and were steadily pulled up toward the ceiling.

* * * * * * * * *

Lieutenant-Commander Roxana Gornect was at the controls of the Victorian battle cruiser *Daniela*, the flagship of the Victorian fleet. All systems were battle ready, at full alert. Star-Commander VanDevere was pacing in front of the large multi-dimensional viewer used primarily for battle situations. She was carefully watching the ongoing operations.

"Good ... good ... right on schedule," she softly said. "All quiet and Ship Two is lifting off."

"Ma'am, they have Franelli," reported Gornect. "He is sedated. They captured him just as he was about to awaken."

"Good ... excellent!" she grinned, her first genuine smile in a long time. "Have him brought immediately to a maximum security cell. Double the guard. Have him fully scanned and keep him sedated. Do not underestimate him. Monitor him continuously."

"Yes, Ma'am, I am directing their ship to Security Port One."

Star-Commander VanDevere's gloating was cut short as Bestmarke's sleeping beast of a ship suddenly woke up.

"Bestmarke's ship is firing up, Ma'am, and Ship One is still attached. Our engines are at standby. Shield-synch power is at fifty percent. I am bringing it up to one hundred percent. We are ready for full pursuit as soon as Ship Two is safely docked."

"We cannot wait, Lieutenant-Commander. Squadron Alpha, all engines fully on! Match velocity to Bestmarke's ship as you can. Keep your shield-synch positions, but fan out to avoid his wake. Provide full power to forward hyper-lasers," ordered VanDevere, as she quickly strapped into her command seat. "Instruct Ship Two to fan out with the others. We must keep up with Bestmarke if we are going to get Ship One safely back!"

* * * * * * * * *

Galen Bestmarke fitfully awoke from a deep, dreamless sleep only to find himself in the middle of a nightmare. The defense alarm was braying loudly and crew members were trying to wake up. All of them were groggy, trying to awaken from deep, dreamless sleep.

"Terran!" he shouted at his brother. "Fire up the engines! They are here! They are here! How did they find us? Look at the NAV screens!"

The NAV screens showed a ring of eight PCC patrol ships and a Victorian cruiser around his ship as it exited the Keyhole. Hull sensors indicated two additional ships attached to his ship's skin. One was above engineering and another further back above the cargo area.

"Louis!" Galen yelled. His face was white with apprehension, and then turned red with anger after no response. "Louis, answer me!" he said, bellowing more loudly.

TROPHY

Loosening his straps, he ran stumbling down the corridor to engineering and threw open the bulkhead door. "No!" he shouted as his mind registered what had taken place.

"Boss, what's going on?" mumbled Johnny, his First Officer, just beginning to revive himself. He glanced around the engineering module at the debris on the floor. Looking up, he saw the fused plug in the ceiling still glowing at the edges. A slight scraping and jarring sound from the hull's exterior could faintly be heard. "Boarding ship with an Octopus," he muttered. "They must have captured Louis, and that's the sound of them leaving."

"But the sensors showed two ships! Grab an LR and follow me!" shouted Galen. The great ship trembled as the engines began their start-up procedure.

Holding laser rifles, the two ran back into the bowels of the ship past the cargo hold to the bulkhead of the trophy room. Galen unlocked the hatch and swung it open. Quickly sizing up the situation, they both jumped through the hatchway, firing their laser rifles at the intruders rapidly ascending up through the equalizer tube.

Fully realizing the extent of his loss, Galen screamed like a madman: "No! No! You can't take those!" he said continuing to fire at the equalizer tube, shreds of it falling to the floor.

*   *   *   *   *   *   *   *   *

Lt. Warden Rogerton and the Specialist felt the lasers hitting them like hammer blows. It was painful and they would be deeply bruised, but basically unhurt, due to the shielding-suits and helmets. The laser blasts were cutting through the equalizer tube as they reached the top and clambered through the Octopus opening into their PCC ship. The nuclear cutters fused the lid back into place as they quickly strapped themselves into their gravity seats.

"Kolanna, has Ship Two departed?" yelled Rogerton, quickly looking at the NAV screens.

TROPHY

"Yes Ma'am! Just lifted off and is rejoining the Squadron!" she shouted excitedly, her eyes open wide.

"Loosen the Octopus and take us out of here!" Rogerton quickly ordered.

But before they could detach their ship, they felt the terrific rumblings and vibration of the twin Zenkati fusion engines roaring to life at maximum starting thrust.

"Inertia dampers at full!" yelled Rogerton. "Kolanna, fire up our engine and try to match our velocity with theirs while the Octopus still has us secure! If we let go our grip now, we will be cooked in their wake! Our shielding is not strong enough to protect us!"

"We can't keep up!" shouted Kolanna. "In twenty seconds their velocity will exceed our engine's capacity and our synch-shielding with the Squadron will be out of range! It's at forty percent and dropping!"

The g-forces were oppressive. It was even hard to think, and Rogerton was losing her color vision. It was like looking down a gray tunnel to her instruments and crew around her. She knew she had to act quickly or they all would be unconscious with disastrous results.

"Kolanna," she strained. "Use the explosive bolts and give us your tightest one-eighty at full power! On my mark!"

As her consciousness diminished, she felt the small patrol ship veritably jump from the side of Bestmarke's enormous ship as the explosive bolts blasted free the Octopus's grip.

* * * * * * * * * *

"Thirty seconds to full ignition!" came Terran's voice over the COM. "Everyone strap in! Estelle, get plugged in!"

Cursing with anger, Galen ran back to the bridge and settled himself into his gunner's seat as the fusion engines roared to life.

"All ahead max!" he yelled, snapping on his weapons systems.

TROPHY

The sensors showed the one PCC ship still attached.

"So you think you can hang on, you miserable leech?" he said, as the ship's inertia dampers strained under the increasing g-forces. "We will shake you off and give you a little surprise, or crush you if you stay," he promised bitterly.

Suddenly the big ship shuddered as the PCC ship fired its explosive bolts, thrusting it forcefully away from the hull of Bestmarke's accelerating ship. As the small ship turned a tight arc in the opposite direction, Galen powered up the ion phase pulse-cannon, aiming it at the fusion engine of the fleeing ship. He pressed the trigger once and then twice more, sending three hot, blue pulses streaking to the shrinking target.

"That will finish them," he growled hatefully. "Get us out of here and go to full cloak. There are too many of them for us."

The ship rumbled and shook as Terran brought it up to full thrust.

"We WILL get Franelli back!" promised Galen.

* * * * * * * * * *

"They have blown the explosive bolts and are taking a tight one-eighty!" exclaimed Lieutenant-Commander Gornect. "Shall I focus the synch-shielding on Ship One?"

"Do it!" snapped VanDevere. "All of it! The other ships are far enough behind to be at minimal risk! Bestmarke will most certainly take a parting shot!"

"He is powering up and locking on to Ship One!" yelled the Lieutenant-Commander in dismay. "He is firing his pulse-cannon! One ... two ... three pulses!"

"Fire the forward battery! Burn through his shields and take out his weapons!" growled the Star-Commander.

"First pulse ... shields hit. Second pulse ... shields collapsed. Third pulse ... direct hit to Ship One!" reported Gornect. "The engine appears destroyed with critical damage to the rear crew quarters. All systems are off including emergency power and life support. The synch-shielding removed some of the sting but it does not look good, Ma'am."

They continued their barrage on Bestmarke's ship but his shielding held. His intense acceleration quickly distanced him and he finally blinked off the NAV screens, fully cloaked and wave silent.

"May he be damned," muttered the Star-Commander in disgust. "Get us to that ship now, Lieutenant-Commander! Let us hope we are not too late!"

The mission was successful, VanDevere thought, but at what cost? They finally had Franelli but Bestmarke still eluded them although he was more vulnerable without his chief engineer. Perhaps he wouldn't be so clever now and the Empire could finally put an end to him and all his illegal operations.

"Braking thrust and matching velocity to the drifting ship," noted the Lieutenant-Commander.

"Dispatch tugs and bring them to Repair Bay Two, starboard side. Coordinate trauma and radiation teams to RB2, on the double!" barked VanDevere. "Get Ship Two and Franelli here as fast as possible! Coordinate a rendezvous with Beta and Gamma Squadrons at full speed and inform CENTRAL that we have Franelli!" she ordered. "I am going to RB2, Lieutenant-Commander. You have the bridge!" VanDevere said quickly and briskly retired with her battle security Specialists closely behind her.

TROPHY

Chapter XVI

Earth Date: 475 N.V.A.
Location: CENTRAL, Earth

The river-rock fireplace was comforting in the Chambers of CENTRAL. The flames of the holographic fire crackled and hissed. The illusion was convincing. Everyone's eyes were hypnotically fixed on the dancing energy while each wandered through their own private thoughts, comfortable in their plush, dark-colored chairs. Bursting through the large doors at the end of the room, Guardian III walked quickly toward the fireplace across the polished stone floor, littered with appropriately placed woven carpets.

"They finally have Franelli!" she said, excitedly. "Star-Commander VanDevere has him sedated and under heavy guard in isolation! Three heavy cruisers and their squadrons are bringing him back!"

The energy in the room suddenly increased. This was an announcement they had waited long to hear.

"Good, good," said Guardian V, smiling broadly. She stood and walked over to Guardian III. "They should keep him sedated with no interrogations. We need to have him first hand. Perhaps there is hope for this errant one."

"Do you really think so?" said Guardian VIII, standing and turning to Guardian V. "You were the closest with him at one time. That he is brilliant is an understatement, but do not let sentiment cloud your logic and reason," she said, resting her hand gently on Guardian V's shoulder.

"You worry overmuch, my friend," said Guardian V, looking at her with assurance. "Sentiment does not enter into this, at least not too much, I hope. Truly, it is more hope than sentiment ... hope that we can exploit his incredible mind, and hope that we can finally find an answer. He is the first in many generations that has given us a glimmer of real hope." She turned and slowly walked to the front of the fireplace, staring at the flickering light.

"But hope at what cost?" interrupted Guardian III, walking quickly over to Guardian V. "He may have already started an avalanche that cannot be contained! No doubt Bestmarke has corrupted him, bought him off with trinkets and pleasures. Bestmarke's short-sighted selfishness may have destroyed our hopes with Franelli!" she said, her smile changing to concern.

Guardian V smiled at her and gently continued. "And that is what we hope against. We cannot afford to give up on him, too much is at stake. We do not have more generations to find another like him."

The room grew very quiet. Only the crackling fire could be heard. Finally Guardian II stood and walked to the front of the fireplace. She turned to face them all and spoke calmly. "Indeed, what you have said is cause for both hope and concern, but we are getting ahead of ourselves with speculation. We must stick to the facts. First, we have Franelli in custody. Second, he knows how to use the Keyhole and to a degree what it does. Third, he is possibly dangerous and corrupt, but perhaps not unreachable. More than that is pure speculation at this point, we need more facts."

Guardian X quickly stood. "This is true and here is another fact, Bestmarke will desperately want Franelli back. He was desperate to abduct him years ago after Franelli was sentenced and en route to the penal colony at Luna One. That was a bloody battle that Bestmarke won. He may again take unprecedented measures against us. Can our defenses handle it, realistically? He is extremely wealthy and can buy many allies, some even within the Empire," she continued. "And remember the 455 Rebellion ... Galen Bestmarke was a young firebrand and one of the main instigators. The Empire lost six ships at their initial assault before we could turn events our way. We finally captured or destroyed thirteen of their ships but we paid dearly for it. We lost one more Victorian cruiser and two cutters … nine ships in all. Bestmarke has nothing but hatred for the Empire. He is a master of greed and manipulation and is used to getting his own way. We must be prepared for his assault … it is just a matter of time."

They began talking quietly with one another for a few moments. With respectful silence they all gave their attention to Guardian I as she stood and concluded. "Our present course is clear for now. When we finally have Franelli back, we must do everything in our power to persuade him to share his knowledge and even contribute more to it. This will be no small task … we must be successful," she said and paused, gazing at them. "We must also fine-tune our defenses for the storm that is sure to come. Whether it is a whisper or a full blown battle remains to be seen, but it is coming. Knowing Bestmarke as we do there will, no doubt, be an evil twist to it, but we are forearmed with that knowledge," she said, turning momentarily to the fire. Slowly turning back around, she looked at them all. "Lastly, my Sisters, we must remember our overreaching goal. This is what we have sworn ourselves to accomplish, even with our lives if need be. We must not fail. The consequences of failure are unacceptable and unpardonable."

With these last remarks, they all stood and concluded, raising their clenched left fists over their hearts.

TROPHY

Chapter XVII

Earth Date: 475 N.V.A.
Location: leaving Keyhole, en route to Earth

The Star-Commander anxiously watched through the shielded windows as the tugs gently coaxed PCC Ship One into the repair bay and locked it into place. The bay doors closed and shielded access tubes moved into position, connecting to the hatchways of the damaged ship. When all the seals were tight and rechecked, the bay's artificial gravity was restored.

Radiation control crews in shielded suits entered and assessed the damage and radiation levels while trauma crews entered the ship through the shielded tubes. Thick radiation controlling foam was sprayed over the severely damaged engine and reactor and any other parts with high radiation levels. Upon a final inspection, the bay's atmosphere was restored.

The trauma teams found only moderate radiation levels inside the ship, nothing of immediate danger. They were relieved to find most of the crew in relatively good condition with only minor burns and injuries. However, they were visibly distraught and saddened when they opened the bulkhead door to the port-side Specialist's cabin. The cabin wall had taken a direct hit when the engine was destroyed and the hull had ruptured, opening the cabin to space. The pulse blast had incinerated the two Specialists inside including the one who had seen the lion's head with Rogerton. Their deaths were instantaneous. Even the battle hardened trauma crews were upset, many with tears running down their faces and bitter curses against Bestmarke. Lieutenant-Warden Rogerton was injured with deep contusions and bruises suffered from Bestmarke's laser rifle fire. Fast acting pain relievers were administered and all received radiation treatment for their burns. Rogerton was taken to sick bay where she was given a private space, a luxury on board ship. The Star-Commander had personally seen to that arrangement. Not only was she concerned about her injuries, she wanted to speak with her in private.

VanDevere consoled and thanked Ship One's crew before she entered Rogerton's room. The trauma team was just finishing and the Star-Commander waited patiently, allowing them to do their work.

After they left, she stood by the bed and smiled at Rogerton. "Good job, Lieutenant. That was a close one. How are you feeling? We were very concerned for your safety."

"Thank you, Ma'am," Rogerton said, tiredly. "The medication is working now and the pain is manageable."

"Manageable? Yes, I am sure," said the Star-Commander with admiration and pity.

"What about my crew, Ma'am, did they all survive? I must have blacked out, I cannot remember anything more."

"I am afraid the news is not good, Lieutenant," VanDevere said. "Two of the four Specialists that were added to this mission have not survived. Specialists Brandenburg and Chou were fatally burned when a pulse from Bestmarke's ship ruptured the wall of their quarters, opening it to space. They died immediately. They were good women, loyal and highly trained. They were well liked and will be greatly missed. It wrenches my heart to see this happen, and infuriating that we have not been able to stop this beast, Bestmarke. I rue the day that he and his brother were born into existence."

Rogerton sighed deeply and closed her eyes. Tears trickled down her cheeks onto the pillow. "Oh, Star-Commander, I feel so badly for them and their families," she softly said, her voice breaking up. "They were so good, so professional ... and now they are gone. I have never lost anyone under my command. I feel so helpless and so angry at the same time. I want to hunt down Bestmarke and destroy him ... he is nothing but vermin," she hissed, a pained expression in her face and eyes.

"I understand your feelings, Lieutenant. This is the difficult part of command. Unfortunately, it does not get easier. I think about the consequences with every major order I give. How many lives will my decision affect? What if I make a wrong decision? What do I have to do to be at peace with myself? I cannot tell you how to sort out your feelings about this, Lieutenant. You will have to do that yourself," she said. "I will always be available, though, if you need someone to talk to,"

"Thank you, Ma'am," Rogerton said, composing herself. "I am beginning to realize what you go through. It must be very difficult at times."

"I will not gloss it over, Lieutenant. The decisions and emotions can be overwhelming if we allow them to be. We must totally believe in and depend on one another. We have to look at the big picture with total commitment that what we are doing is right and good and true. If you are determined to command, Lieutenant, you cannot doubt." The Star-Commander paused a moment and then spoke determinedly. "Grieve and ponder the lives of our fallen Sisters, but never doubt them or your purpose."

"Thank you, Ma'am," Rogerton said, a milder expression returning to her tired face. "How is the rest of my crew?"

"I am relieved the rest suffered only minor injuries and burns," VanDevere said, offering a gentle smile. Pilot Kolanna did some excellent flying and you made good decisions. Well done! We now have Franelli in custody, Beta and Gamma Squadrons are joining us, and it is full speed to Earth CENTRAL to deliver him," she said. "Your ship is badly damaged. The blast shield saved most of you, but I am afraid the engine is quite destroyed. You and your crew will be guests on the *Daniela* until we get back to Earth. I am sure we will be able to find a suitable ship for you then," the Star-Commander said.

TROPHY

"Thank you, Ma'am. I am looking forward to being with my crew again, that is, once I have rested and healed up."

The Star-Commander gazed at her curiously, a faint smile on her lips. "Have you always been this driven to duty, Lieutenant? You have been in the Corps for only five years, though your distinguished record would suggest otherwise," she said, remembering her own meteoric rise up the ranks. "And you were at the top of your class at the Academy, too."

"I do not feel driven, Ma'am. It all feels normal to me – this is what I should be doing. The Empire has been mother and father to me – they have given me love, companionship, training, and a purpose in life. My loyalty and devotion is the least I can do in return."

"Your mother was in the Corps, was she not?"

"Yes, and her mother before her and so on, for six generations, nearly half the time the New Victorian Empire has been in power. I love the Empire, it is an honor to serve," she said with an unforced smile of pride.

"How old were you when you lost your mother?" VanDevere gently asked.

"Eight years old, Ma'am. She took the obligatory five year maternal leave and then resumed active duty. She was a Pilot on a research cutter ... and she loved it. Three months on duty and home for one. We had so much fun when she was home, but she did not spoil me. Her stories inspired a love of space duty and adventure in me. And her eyes... beautiful bluish-green with a touch of purple ... those are my strongest memories of her," Rogerton said.

The conversation lagged as both considered their own private thoughts. The Star-Commander was the first to speak. "What happened to her, Lieutenant?"

"Her ship, the *Rosella*, disappeared with all hands presumed lost. My mother and nineteen of our Sisters disappeared, simply vanished."

TROPHY

"The *Rosella*, you say?" questioned the Star-Commander. "I distinctly remember that the *Rosella* disappeared while studying the Keyhole. What really happened and why has always been a mystery. I am truly sorry for your loss ... for our loss. It must have been difficult for you."

"It was, although I was used to her being gone for extended periods of time. It did not really hit me for a few more months until the time she was supposed to be home on leave. I kept waiting and hoping, but I never saw her again. The unknown was the greatest fear and pain for me, but the Empire rushed to fill the void. The PCC arranged for a foster family to raise me. My foster mother truly loves me and I love her. I was never that close to my foster father but he was still very good to me. My fears and pain were gradually eased and my life again filled with purpose, a noble purpose to follow in the footsteps of my mother and the generations before her."

"I see, Lieutenant. And so you chose duty that could position you near the Keyhole?"

"Yes, Ma'am," she smiled. "It is encouraging for me to continue on in the dedicated service of my mother, who also loved the Empire."

"We are grateful for her dedication and for yours, Lieutenant-Warden. You bring honor to our profession and to the Empire."

"Thank you, Ma'am."

"Tell me now, what did you discover on Bestmarke's ship?" VanDevere said, tilting her head slightly. "The recordings the Specialist made were destroyed. We have no other records."

Even though she was exhausted, Rogerton explained in detail their every move, as well as the strange details of Bestmarke's ship, the unusual room, and its contents. The two retrieved pedestals were of great interest to both of them, and the Star-Commander agreed to wait until Rogerton had rested so they could examine them together. VanDevere had plenty to keep her busy: debriefing the other crews, checking on Franelli, and coordinating the return trip with the other squadrons.

A few moments after she left, Kolanna appeared in the doorway. She was unusually subdued, showing only a hint of her infectious smile.

"Kolanna, come in. How are you feeling?" Rogerton asked, trying to conceal her fatigue.

"I am fine, Lieutenant, just some radiation burns and nausea. The skin coating meds help me feel better, but it smells awful!" she complained, wrinkling her nose with a disgusted look. "I know you are tired and I am only here for a moment. How are you feeling? Did the Star-Commander tell you about our crew mates that were lost? We all feel so badly about them. Their poor families ... this is such a shock. It makes us all so angry."

"I am angry, too, Kolanna. My heart truly hurts. They were under my command and that makes the pain even deeper. The Star-Commander was comforting and gave me valuable advice."

"She is a great leader and I am proud to serve under her," Kolanna said. "Tell me, Lieutenant, are you in a lot of pain?"

"I feel no pain, I am just very tired. When the meds wear off, no doubt I will feel much worse," she said, laughing weakly. "That was a good bit of flying, Pilot. I was starting to tunnel vision and I blacked out. You pulled us through. Well done!"

Kolanna smiled a little wider. "The Star-Commander hinted that a new ship might be larger. I am thinking a Cutter, perhaps, in place of the Patrol Craft. And a Cutter is commanded by a Lieutenant, not a Lieutenant-Warden. Perhaps a promotion possibility?" she teased, giving her a sideways glance.

"You are too much," said Rogerton with a tired grin. "That is the last thing I want to think about. What I want most now is sleep and then a real vacation, even a short one, on real ground, breathing fresh air scented with living plants and flowers. That is all."

TROPHY

"I hope you get it all soon," whispered Kolanna softly as she quietly left the room. The nodding Lieutenant-Warden quickly fell asleep, fully realizing the first of her requests.

TROPHY

Chapter XVIII

Everything hurt; her skin was painful and her body ached when she moved. The meds helped substantially, but the Lieutenant-Warden limited their use in favor of a sharp mind. There were too many new questions to be answered, and she didn't want to keep the Star-Commander waiting.

With painful difficulty Rogerton walked to Repair Bay Two where she was to meet VanDevere at 09:00 hours. The Lieutenant was early, but the Star-Commander was already there assessing the damage to the decontaminated patrol ship.

"Reporting for duty, Ma'am," she said in her cheeriest voice although it barely concealed the pain.

VanDevere smiled. She liked this officer; smart, tough, punctual, and not afraid of personal discomfort. She also appreciated her sensitivity to situations … when to speak and when to keep quiet.

"It is good to see you up and moving about, Lieutenant-Warden, although somewhat labored. Are you in much pain?"

"It is manageable, Ma'am," she said without complaint, although the Star-Commander knew it barely so.

"Your ship is essentially gone from the blast shield back. The engine is destroyed … an ion phase pulse-cannon is a formidable weapon." They walked along the side of the ship, examining the blackened and twisted hull. "And here is where the hull was breached. You can see how it damaged the Specialists compartment. Without bulkheads on each compartment Bestmarke's attack would have destroyed the entire ship, killing everyone. The synch-shielding helped protect you … but it was thin at that distance. Another blow while your ship was tumbling would have been even more deadly."

"My crew and I are thankful you were there to help us, Ma'am."

TROPHY

VanDevere looked at her and smiled again. They continued to circle the damaged ship noting the levels of destruction. She was pleased to see the Octopus unit still attached with surprisingly little damage. Those units were expensive and difficult to replace.

After finishing their inspection of the ship they walked into the storage bay where the two heavy wooden pedestals had been taken. The pedestals had been placed immediately into a sealed blast proof chamber, and the Star-Commander herself had locked it with a retinal scan. The Specialists guarding the chamber stepped back as VanDevere and Rogerton approached. The Star-Commander opened the hatchway, and both officers went in, closing it behind them.

The chamber was cube-shaped measuring ten meters on each side. Every action was closely monitored and sensors for every possible condition were employed though none were visible. The chamber appeared essentially plain and unencumbered.

The two pedestals were sitting near the center about a meter apart. An almost invisible shimmer, like very clear glass, sparkled faintly above each one. The two officers just stood and stared. VanDevere was the first to speak.

"I can see why you were puzzled, Lieutenant. We have been scanning these since we brought them aboard. The sensors are showing life signs, but have failed to identify what they are. Most unusual ... they match nothing in the data-banks. Franelli's hand in this is obvious so we must be cautious," she said, her eyebrows raised.

"The pedestals have chambers and some sort of mechanism in them that appears to be nuclear, as best we can tell," said VanDevere perplexed. "Sensors show them to be stable with no radiation leakage ... essentially inert. They are doing something ... we just do not know what it is. And here is the small shiny plate on the side that you mentioned in your report. Upon close inspection it is really two plates very close together, perhaps switches of some sort. Would you like to try one?" she asked eagerly.

TROPHY

Rogerton distinctly remembered what happened the last time she touched the plate. Her heart began to beat faster with apprehension. She knelt down and closely examined the plate of the first pedestal confirming it was indeed two plates. With a deep sigh she touched the upper plate and quickly stood back by the Star-Commander. Nervously they watched as the nearly invisible shimmer turned to a sparkling sheen. It grew darker like a thick fog and gradually dissipated, giving way to a form that became more defined, distinct, and utterly recognizable.

There was no noise, no frightful surprise ... only awe and bewilderment. The two officers could only stare and then look at each other. With eyes wide open, they gazed at the large head and neck of a majestic black panther. Its eyes were shut as if asleep, and its mouth was partially open revealing enormous yellowish-white fangs and teeth.

With pity in her voice, the Star-Commander bemoaned: "What a magnificent animal! This is not the way for it to live, trapped as nothing more than an oddity, a toy for degenerate men. It should be in a forest, running, and hunting with room to breathe, to really live unhindered. What a great sadness this is."

With outrage in her voice, Rogerton continued: "This flies in the face of everything the New Victorian Empire stands for! Will this kind of behavior ever be eradicated from the human race? For nearly five centuries we thought we had this bloodthirsty dominance under control and even now it springs to life again in this beast of a man, this Bestmarke! The earth wide work to restore the nearly extinct species has been applauded for centuries. And now we have men like this who care nothing for the freedom and welfare of these beautiful animals, but only want to dominate and kill them. To make matters worse, there are others like him out there on the fringes which we know absolutely nothing about. Will we ever see an end to this brood?"

TROPHY

"Someday, perhaps," said VanDevere with a disgusted look. "For now our mission is clearly defined, and all the more so as we see abominations such as this. Shall we see if the lower switch awakens the creature?"

"I am tempted not to, especially after my frightening experience with the lion. This animal may not be as aggressive, though. If we are quiet and stand farther back, perhaps it will perceive us as less threatening," Rogerton said, nervously looking at the Star-Commander.

She reached down, gently touched the lower plate, and backed quickly to the wall of the chamber where the Star-Commander had already moved. With their backs to the wall, they stood completely still and silent, lowered the lighting level, and waited patiently. Thirty seconds passed and they noticed no change. A full minute passed and suddenly the golden feline eyes of the panther snapped open. Yawning widely it revealed all its fearsome teeth in their full glory. After licking its mouth with its large pink tongue, it began to look about. It had only gazed for a moment until the sight of the two officers brought it to rapt attention. It silently stared at them with intense concentration.

"What do we do now?" whispered Rogerton, staring at the panther.

"I am quite at a loss," the Star-Commander whispered, her gaze also fixed on the great cat. "They do not teach this situation at the Academy."

The panther continued to watch them intently.

"Unless there is a timer on that switch, we will have to get closer to turn it off," whispered Rogerton again, alarm beginning to show in her voice. "I will try it myself, one person will be less of a threat," she gulped, glancing briefly at VanDevere.

"Very well," said the Star-Commander, happy to remain at the wall.

TROPHY

As Rogerton moved slowly forward the panther started to growl with a low rumble. She stopped, and so did the panther. Rogerton again began to move forward, just inching her steps, and the panther began to growl again, a little more loudly this time. Rogerton stopped and slowly turned to the Star-Commander and whispered: "What now?"

VanDevere just shrugged, a grimace on her face. This was definitely unfamiliar territory.

Rogerton knew it couldn't hurt her, but she wanted to keep it as calm as possible. She continued to slowly move forward and began speaking softly in a monotone. "We do not want to hurt you. We want to help you. We know that you are trapped. We just want to help you," she repeated softly, avoiding eye contact, and not showing her teeth as she spoke.

The panther continued to growl, though not as strongly. She continued her slow advance and soft speech until she was close enough to reach down and touch the bottom plate. The panther was now softly growling and panting intermittently and as Rogerton slowly stood up, she risked a look into the big cat's face. She expected a fierce roar or scream, but instead sensed a depth of understanding in its big yellow eyes. A feeling of fear, loneliness, and even gratitude seemed to pierce her heart, as if she really understood its terrible plight. The sensation was fleeting and over quickly as the big cat fell asleep again, its eyes shut, and its mouth gently open as they had seen at first.

The Star-Commander approached and both continued to stare at the beautiful animal.

"Good work, Lieutenant," said the Star-Commander. "Well done."

"It seemed to touch my heart," replied Rogerton, struggling to control her emotions. "I feel so sorry for it. I did not know you could sense such feelings from animals."

TROPHY

"There is much we still do not know about them, and perhaps we never will," said VanDevere. "But not many have had an experience such as yours. Remember it … it will be useful to you in the future."

"Let us see what this other pedestal holds, now that we know a little more what to expect," said VanDevere.

Her words were not reassuring. Rogerton wasn't looking forward to another emotional roller-coaster ride, but professionalism to duty and obedience to her superior officer were paramount, so she reached over and touched the top plate. The nearly invisible shimmer above the second pedestal turned to a sparkling sheen and grew darker as the first one had done. The darkened fog-like sheen gradually dissipated, showing a somewhat different form, but left them no doubt as it cleared into horrifying reality.

They were quite taken aback. They stood speechless with their mouths open and their eyes wide with shock.

"Great heavens!" said the Star-Commander with a gasp. After a lengthy pause she said: "What is it? Who is it? What has Bestmarke done?"

They both continued to stare at the head and neck of a man, a man with a full head of hair and a neatly trimmed beard. His hair was auburn with flecks of gray and white and his skin was lightly tanned and freckled. Tiny crow's feet wrinkles at the corners of his eyes and the beginnings of forehead wrinkles indicated a man used to spending much time out-of-doors. The widow's peak and high cheek bones gave him a distinctive, pleasant, masculine look. He probably would have been close to two meters tall and thirty to forty years old. Probably, but at the moment his eyes were shut and his thin lips slightly separated. Like the panther, he appeared to be sleeping.

"How and where did he get this man?" VanDevere finally said, her face white with shock. "It would seem the appropriate question would be 'When did he get this man'? No man alive today has hair! Do you realize what this means, Lieutenant? Bestmarke

117

TROPHY

has somehow traveled through time! Franelli has figured it out! The laws of physics, as we know them, say it is impossible ... but Franelli has discovered the secret! This is why CENTRAL was so insistent to capture him. This is profound! How are these heads being kept alive?" questioned the Star-Commander, her color beginning to return. "Have you ever seen anything like this man before, Lieutenant?"

"I have never seen a man like this," confessed Rogerton, turning to the Star-Commander. "Only in the pictures of the ancient times, in the archives at CENTRAL University, do you see images that resemble this man. What has Bestmarke done? This is both profound and hideous. And what do we do with him? Do we awaken him? Can we speak with him and understand him? Can Bestmarke go back through time again without Franelli? Is the programming to do so built into his ship? This has enormous implications!"

"Enormous, indeed," agreed the Star-Commander, looking at Rogerton and then back at the man. "He must be taken to CENTRAL immediately. We dare not awaken him. Obviously he is a result of Franelli's twisted genius and Bestmarke's arrogant ambition. The experts at CENTRAL will certainly want to question Franelli before they awaken this man. I would hope to be there when they do awaken him."

"If Franelli has discovered how to use the Keyhole to go back in time, it could open up some dangerous complications. It could change the very fabric of our society, and completely undermine the Empire," admitted Rogerton, continuing to look at the man. She turned back to the Star-Commander with a fearful look. "If Bestmarke indiscriminately removed people living in the past, it could instantly change our reality and send us along a totally different time thread. Even the smallest change could be profound in its effects upon society, even the human race itself! We could each be standing here one moment and then the next be totally gone – never having existed at all. That is indeed frightening. And worse,

some killer like Bestmarke could be indiscriminately controlling it, manipulating countless lives, with no concern for the consequences."

The Star-Commander looked thoughtfully at her young officer. "For a long time, CENTRAL has suspected that Franelli was working on time travel through the Keyhole. Years ago he was a top researcher at CENTRAL, vigorously studying the Keyhole's secrets, and all forms of nuclear engineering. His brilliance was profound, and a bit frightening to some in authority."

"What happened to make him leave?" asked Rogerton. "I have heard it was a compu-court decision, but I know little else."

"Is that what you have heard?" quizzed the Star-Commander. "That is something most know nothing about. It is highly classified, but I can tell you this: Franelli was held responsible for a situation that cost many lives. He was sentenced and was being transferred to Luna One when Bestmarke attacked the cruiser carrying him. I was serving as Lieutenant-Commander on that very ship. We were soundly beaten in a bloody battle and Bestmarke escaped with Franelli. Our ship was not destroyed but we lost many lives and I nearly lost my leg in a laser fight. However, I did gain something ... a potent hatred for Galen Bestmarke."

Both paused and stood quietly, lost in memories of past battles. They looked at the sleeping heads of the man and panther, somehow kept alive by an ingenious mechanism located in the base of each pedestal.

"Ma'am," said Rogerton, breaking the silence. "You said there were compartments in the pedestal. May we see what is inside the one for the man? Hopefully, it will not awaken him."

"Let us try," said the Star-Commander. "I see little risk at this point. Perhaps we will find some additional clues."

Rogerton carefully searched the surface and finally found a small round plate, the size of a button, near the bottom at the rear of the heavy cabinet. She looked up at VanDevere who nodded in approval to touch it. A large panel opened smoothly and silently revealing a spacious interior with more compartments. The largest of them was obvious as to how it opened but the smaller ones seemed more inert, probably housing the power mechanism for the living head above. The large compartment gave up a number of interesting articles, the first being a heavy metal rifle with a wooden stock.

"This is an interesting weapon, and heavy," said Rogerton, holding it in both hands. "It is a projectile weapon of sorts." She put it back down and picked up a bright yellow plastic container, removing the cover. "And this must be the ammunition, these brass cartridges with the lead tipped copper ends. Bullets they used to call them. They look painful and deadly," she said, delicately touching one.

"What else is there, Lieutenant?" the Star-Commander asked.

"Here is a coat that is much stained, probably blood stains," said Rogerton with a grimace as she looked up at VanDevere. "Oh, look! There are holes in it! Made from bullets, I assume," she said, reluctant to continue touching it. Gingerly holding it up with one hand, she searched the inside with her other hand. "There is an inner pocket that is zippered shut. I can feel something inside of it. Here it is, Ma'am. It appears to be a leather clutch or wallet."

"Let us see what is in it," said the Star-Commander, opening it up. "Here is a plastic card with his picture on it, though not a good likeness at all!" she said, nearly laughing. "It is in old English, but readable. It says Driver's License, State of Montana. Are you familiar with the old geography?" She looked at Rogerton, her eyebrows raised.

"It also gives us a name: Martin Charles Bucklann, born in 1938. This document appears to be dated 1975 so that would make Martin 37 years old when Bestmarke captured him. The New Beginning was in what year?" said the Star-Commander, looking up again at Rogerton.

"It was 2065 of the Ancient Calendar, Ma'am."

TROPHY

"So this man is from 90 years previous to that pivotal year. That should be significant. I wonder how CENTRAL will use this information?" VanDevere said. She paused thoughtfully and then looked Rogerton directly in the eyes. "All that we have seen here is strictly confidential. All the records taken are classified 50-C1 and will be given to CENTRAL."

"Was there any other records from my ship that were usable?" asked Rogerton.

"A minimal amount – the Specialist would have had the most important information and she is tragically gone. The only other first-hand information is what is in your memory, Lieutenant. I am quite certain the experts at CENTRAL will want to talk to you personally," VanDevere bluntly said. "You will accompany me to CENTRAL when we get back to Earth."

"Yes, Ma'am," said Rogerton, feeling somewhat overwhelmed.

The two officers took a long, final look at Martin and the panther, both asleep and seemingly undisturbed, before shutting down the pedestals. The Star-Commander locked the chamber with a retinal scan and the guards resumed their positions. Both officers then walked silently alone, back to their separate quarters.

TROPHY

Chapter XIX

Earth Date: 475 N.V.A.
Location: CENTRAL, Earth

The fireplace provided its comforting glow, but at the moment, nobody was paying attention. The usually restful room in which all the Guardians were assembled was uncommonly alive with energy. Guardian II spoke first.

"We have all now seen Star-Commander VanDevere's latest report, sent from the Fleet on our most secure channel," she said, standing in front of the fire while the others remained seated. "It is, to say the least, absolutely mind boggling! What VanDevere and her young Lieutenant-Warden have done is given us time and an edge-up in our preparations for dealing with Franelli. We know for a certainty that he has successfully traveled back through time at least once, possibly twice, or even more."

The room buzzed as they all seemed to talk at once. Guardian II restored order and gestured towards Guardian I who stood up to speak. "We also realize that this beast, Bestmarke, has brought back these poor creatures, and Franelli has fashioned them into living abominations, living trophies, if you will," she lamented.

Guardian II continued. "Most importantly, though, we now have the ancient man's name, age, location, date of birth, and date of apparent death. Data specialists are researching this as we speak."

Guardian V raised her hand to speak. "Franelli's handiwork is certainly evident. The level of sophistication in these devices is astounding! If we could persuade him to share this knowledge, think of the huge technical advances we could quickly make!"

"Franelli is corrupt," interrupted Guardian III. "Do we dare put any measure of trust in him?" she said. "He may in pretense share knowledge with us that appears beneficial, but in reality is a dead end, even a trap. He has no love for us. He hates the Empire. We must use extreme caution with him. Would we ourselves attempt to use his knowledge of the Keyhole? That would be possible only if he himself went with us and that presents a host of security questions. It would, no doubt, invite an attack from Bestmarke. He will be desperate for Franelli's return."

Guardian V paused for a moment before she spoke again, carefully weighing her words. She thought back to the years she and Louis had worked side by side in Research. Their work had included small scale nuclear engineering and artificial intelligence. The most dangerous and controversial project involved the mysterious Keyhole. Louis's calculations on the Keyhole had indirectly led to the disappearance of a research vessel and crew of twenty. This landed him in the compu-courts. Guardian V had stood by his side, pleading for him, but to no avail. In her opinion his conviction was unjust, his prison sentence wrong, and his ban from CENTRAL a mistake. Those actions were now ugly memories.

"You are correct, my Sister," Guardian V calmly said. "We must be cautious. Franelli could very well be corrupt, but is he beyond help, beyond redemption? At one time he showed some good qualities, although he was always reclusive and difficult to read. That was over ten years ago, back before I became a Guardian. Time and circumstances could have changed him," she said tactfully. The possibility of a pardon came to mind, but she didn't mention it.

Guardian VIII sighed deeply. "We know what Franelli was working on ten years ago but nothing of what he has done since. If he has been with Bestmarke all these years we can only conclude that Bestmarke has treated him well. If that is the case, what can we offer him that Bestmarke has not already given him? We can never set him free and he knows that. Any cooperation from him will always be suspect. He will always have to be, at best, kept on a short chain."

TROPHY

"But do we really know Franelli? Do we know him enough to make that assessment?" Guardian V stood and asked. "In the past, he only cared about his work, his research. He was extremely passionate about it. Nothing could tempt him away from it. It could be that he has no love for Bestmarke, for the Empire, or for anything except his research. We may not know him as well as we think we do," she said candidly.

The room became silent with only the sounds of the holographic fire. Guardian II broke the quiet. "Whatever is in Mr. Franelli's mind will be ours to find out soon enough. More speculation now is pointless. What other areas need to be discussed?"

"What of the cat and the man?" asked Guardian VII. "We cannot restore them as they once were, but perhaps we can restore them enough to dignify their appearance, and provide a nearly full measure of motor control. We can even give them super abundant strength and speed if we can unlock the secrets of Franelli's power source," she said, becoming more animated. "Obviously the only truly living part of them will be their heads … most importantly their brains. Everything else will essentially be mechanical. But the possibilities are exciting. Think of what we could create. A super panther and a super man! An ancient one at that!"

"Do we want to take them off one pedestal and put them on another?" objected Guardian IV, a sour look on her face. "We must consider the moral issues here. If it is our place to restore them, then by how much? If it is our place to enhance them, then again, to what degree?" She paused, and continued in a more conciliatory tone. "The man at least needs to be heard. The cat also should be heard, though that will indeed be more difficult."

This last comment brought more simultaneous comments. Guardian II again had to restore order. "Please, Sisters, please," she said, imploring them. "Let us keep order. Do you have a point, Guardian VI?"

"Yes, thank you. What of the intricate genetics of this man, can we duplicate them? Can we duplicate him? Will it bring us any closer to solving our dilemma? If so, what are our guidelines?" she said, looking around to them all. "You now see the questions this new situation brings up. What do we make our priority?"

"This is an important question," said Guardian II, looking them all in the face. "Our first task will be establishing priorities, and then a procedure to accomplish them. We still have time before the Fleet arrives to establish at least a loose outline before we meet our subjects face to face." She turned and recognized Guardian IX.

"The question of time travel now takes on enormous importance," cautioned Guardian IX. "Should we attempt it ourselves now that we see it is definitely possible? Bestmarke has done it, apparently for selfish sport, with no regard for past and future generations. However, we could accomplish much good if used judiciously. We could solve our dilemma of perpetuating the human race and fill in all the gaps of our history as well as many other noble endeavors. But what if others discover how to use it for more ominous reasons?"

"What are you suggesting?" said Guardian II, intently looking at her.

"What if rebels or even organized crime establish a slave trade?" Guardian IX said with all seriousness. "What if they time-travel to a period before the Great Catastrophe and capture biologically sound people, bring them back to our time, and sell them to the highest bidders?" A collective gasp went up from the Guardians. "People could just disappear, not even exist, with the slightest tinkering of events in the past. This may have already happened, so we need to quickly investigate this possibility. Time travel, if at all attempted, should be meticulously researched and carried out only under the most stringent of guidelines. We could find ourselves in the position of playing God. The moral ramifications of that scenario are beyond us and unacceptable. We must be extremely cautious!"

All were in complete agreement with Guardian IX and the discussion came to an end as she sat down. The room buzzed with quick conversation as Guardian II sat down and Guardian I stood up to conclude.

"We plainly see the task in front of us," she said in her resonant voice. "Each of our areas of expertise will be fully put to the test. Our decisions in the near future will place us at the nexus of our foreseeable existence. This may be our only real opportunity to guarantee the continuation of our generations. Really, we are forced to seize this opportunity in spite of any misgivings or doubts. We must not fail!"

Once more they all stood and raised their clenched left fists over their hearts.

TROPHY

Chapter XX

Earth Date: 475 N.V.A.
Location: En route to Earth from the Kuiper Belt

The gnawing feelings and repetitive questions would not go away in spite of how busy she kept herself. Star-Commander Abigail VanDevere was finally caught up with her lengthy schedule of duties, and she had no more excuses. Ever since her first private meeting with Lieutenant-Warden Rogerton, where the code name 'Star Point' was mentioned, curiosity and dread had battled continuously in her heart. She had an idea of the identity of Star Point, but that knowledge and the risk of knowing the truth frightened her. She recognized that sometimes you can learn too much.

"I have to know," she resigned herself. "I will drive myself mad if I do not at least make an attempt to find out the truth."

She attempted to calm her emotions and finally sat down at her desk. "Computer, give me 'Privacy: Commanding Officer'," she said quickly before she could change her mind again. "Give me full clearance to Priority 50-C1 situations." The micro-shield enveloped her, providing total privacy.

"Please enter name, rank, password, and remain motionless for dual retinal scan."

"Abigail VanDevere ... Star-Commander of the New Victorian Empire Fleet ... 'Bestmarke must die'."

The scanner quickly verified both eyes and announced her clearance.

"Please give me all information on a Victorian officer, code-named Star Point, renegade 2.75 standard years."

"All information has been reclassified to 50-GX status. No further information is available."

TROPHY

"Is Star Point the code name for Michelle VanDevere, my sister, who became a renegade?" she said, trying again.

"All information has been reclassified to 50-GX status. No further information is available," said the computer.

VanDevere was at a loss of what to make of this development. 50-G indicated it was at a level that only a Guardian could access. And the "X" identified which Guardian had supervision.

"When was this reclassified?" the Star-Commander continued.

"That information is unavailable."

"How can I approach or talk to Guardian X?" she said.

"She will be waiting for you when you arrive at CENTRAL, Star-Commander VanDevere. You will receive further instructions when you arrive at Earth Space Dock. Please follow them implicitly."

The Star-Commander was stunned ... stunned in both thought and speech! It was frightening to be totally involved in a situation and yet know nothing about it. She felt like a puppet, a marionette, waiting for another string to be jerked. Yet, she could only do what she had been trained to do all of her life, follow orders. That was much harder when it didn't make sense or couldn't be understood. She shrugged, letting out a deep sigh. She would just have to wait and see how this drama played out. Did she have a starring role, or was she just part of the supporting cast? Did it really matter in the long run, or was her happiness dependent on the fulfillment of her ego?

"Happiness!" she snorted. "Why is it so elusive? What does it really take to find it? Computer, end privacy program and go to stand-by," she said tiredly. "Please awaken me at 06:30 hours."

She slowly walked into her small, austere apartment with one thing on her mind ... sleep.

TROPHY

Chapter XXI

Earth Date: 475 N.V A.
Location: Earth Space Dock, high earth orbit

Lieutenant-Warden Rogerton nervously rubbed her hands together as she sat in the window seat of the space-plane that was loading and preparing for the last leg of their trip to Earth CENTRAL. She preferred space travel to the bumpy atmospheric flights that ferried supplies and people back and forth to Earth's surface from the huge space dock facility that was orbiting the Earth. She had a lot of respect for the pilots that dealt with a multitude of problems unique to leaving and reentering the atmosphere. Of course, none of the Corps deep-space vehicles with their toxic fusion engines could be used in close proximity to the atmosphere. Anti-gravity propulsion systems for atmospheric and deep-space vehicles were still just a dream but were gradually coming closer to reality. Highly efficient chemical engines were still the tried and true workhorses for atmospheric flights.

Star-Commander VanDevere had the window seat across the aisle and was sitting quietly, deep in thought, her right hand absently caressing the ten-pointed platinum star near her left shoulder. With the Star-Commander's permission, Pilot Kolanna had been allowed to ride in the pilot's cabin up front. She was beside herself with excitement, her smile was even wider than usual, and her large dark eyes had a glow about them. Franelli was still sedated and under heavy guard in a special security capsule in the hold. The two pedestals and their precious cargo were also well anchored in a special cargo crate locked with a retinal scan from VanDevere. Two additional fortified space-planes along with two squadrons of ten

TROPHY

air-space fighters were set to accompany them to Earth CENTRAL. They were taking no chances with intervention from Bestmarke.

The Star-Commander had informed Rogerton that her presence was requested at CENTRAL and her vacation would have to be postponed again. She wondered if she would ever have another vacation. The Star-Commander didn't volunteer any additional information, and Rogerton didn't ask. She felt something significant was going on that was both fearful and exciting. She hoped her part would be a small one.

Finally loaded and secure, the fleet departed Space Dock for the four hour flight to CENTRAL. The approach to Earth was particularly beautiful, especially for those who had been away a long time. For both women, coming home to Mother was an emotional experience not easily forgotten or dulled by time. It tugged at their primal feelings, helping them appreciate their special bond with this colorful gem floating in space. They began the bumpy, rough flight down through the atmosphere and were relieved when they smoothly settled into sub-sonic speed at cruising altitude.

Both women now glued themselves to the windows, enraptured by the sheer beauty and ever changing views of the terrain below. Their flight pattern brought them in over tree clad mountains with autumn colors blazing at the tops while summer still dominated the lower elevations. The valleys were patched with the gold of ripening grain that surrounded small farming communities which in turn surrounded larger metropolitan and light industrial areas. The connecting high speed transportation lines resembled the spokes of a wheel, all meeting at the hub. Everywhere the land was green with vegetation and dotted with small lakes. Winding streams and rivers appeared as loose threads and ropes from their high vantage point. They flew over areas of heavy industry, usually located on a large river or lake, but still marveled at the greenery and clean organization. Everywhere the air was pure with only the haze of water vapor condensing into white clouds along their flightpath. Their journey slowed as they approached the expansive PCC Space Port sitting on the edge of the plains bordering the great chain of mountains where CENTRAL was located. The space-plane slowly hovered into the hangar and gently touched down. They were finally on Earth.

There was no pomp or ceremony as they exited the space-plane into the cavernous hangar, nor did they expect there to be. It was easy to pick out the PCC personnel assigned to space duty by their distinctive forest green uniforms and even more distinctive purple-tinged eyes. Other disciplines and programs had various colored uniforms to help identify their duties, and the blend made for a colorful pageantry that relieved some of the Spartan starkness of the utilitarian structure.

Three teams of Specialists in totally white uniforms met them at the space-plane. Each team had a low transport vehicle equipped with a shield generator. One team was directed to transport Franelli, hidden inside a personnel capsule. Another was instructed to transport the two pedestals locked inside their cargo crate. The commanding Lieutenant of the third team approached the Star-Commander, came to attention, and saluted with her left fist over her heart. She was tall and muscular, her dark olive skin and shining black hair in stark contrast with her starched white uniform. Near her left shoulder was a single ten-pointed star similar to that worn by the Star-Commander, only the Lieutenant's was pure black onyx, the symbol of the Guardians.

Her dark eyes flashing, the Lieutenant spoke with a husky voice in a proud and confident manner. "Star-Commander, I am Lieutenant Constantine. We welcome you and your crew to Earth CENTRAL. We hope you had a comfortable flight."

"Thank you, Lieutenant, we did," VanDevere answered mildly. "Do you have further instructions for us?"

"Yes, Ma'am, we have been instructed to escort yourself and Lieutenant-Warden Rogerton back to CENTRAL. The other two teams with their cargo will accompany us. Your crew will be escorted to the Base Guest Quarters. I assure you, they will be very comfortably provided for. Does this meet with your approval?" she asked mechanically.

"Yes, Lieutenant, please carry on," stated the Star-Commander.

With minimal and concise orders, the assignments of the three teams were completed. The crew was escorted to another transport vehicle, helped along by Specialists in different colored uniforms. The Star-Commander and Lieutenant-Warden were seated on the transport and watched the completion of the loading. Finally, the last of the teams were seated and the order given to proceed to CENTRAL.

"Shields on!" snapped Constantine as they cleared the fortress-like doors of the hangar. The sparkling edge of the shield-like force field was visible for a split second in the sunlight as they emerged from the shade of the entrance canopy. The wheels of the transport vehicles retracted as the anti-gravity systems took over and the transports floated effortlessly a meter above the ground. The three teams glided quietly along with only a faint hum over the grass way that led the twenty kilometers to CENTRAL.

"How long have they had these vehicles?" whispered Rogerton to the Star-Commander at her side. "These are amazing. I did not realize the development of anti-gravity systems was this advanced.

"Not long, I understand. They are making rapid progress in anti-gravity engineering for space vehicles, too. Fusion engines may be obsolete in a century's time, chemical engines sooner, I would expect."

"I have noticed other air vehicles around us at great distances, difficult to see. Are they escorts also?" whispered Rogerton again, looking up and scanning the sky.

TROPHY

"Most likely, they are probably adding another layer of shielding. They are taking no chances," said VanDevere, also looking up.

The day was beautiful with a clear blue sky, fields of green grass, and leaves in the first stages of autumn. The sunlight filtered through the trees onto the summer's last wildflowers scattered on the forest floor.

Rogerton didn't want to think like a soldier, but as a tourist without a care, on vacation, trusting everyone. She didn't want to think that anyone would harm her on such a day.

The fifteen minute trip was a delight as they quietly hovered along tree clad rolling hills beside a small river. The crystal water swirled and foamed around the colorful stones and mossy boulders. The heady perfume of late summer vegetation filled their senses. In their hearts both officers longed to linger in this tranquility and natural ambiance, appreciating what they hadn't seen, smelled, or felt for months.

Rogerton had never seen CENTRAL before and had no idea what to expect. When they turned the last corner and approached the complex of low-story stone buildings she wondered if they were there yet. Looking around she realized that most of CENTRAL was underground and the approaching buildings were only the receiving areas for personnel and supplies. If the size of the mountains that backed up the buildings were any clue, the underground structures must be enormous. The thought of her being here in the seat of government for the entire earth, not to mention the solar system and nearest star systems, was awe-inspiring and humbling. She could understand why the Star-Commander was here, but why her? Why a young Lieutenant-Warden only in command of a small patrol craft with a crew of six? She suddenly felt very small and inadequate.

Their vehicles glided past the attractive stone and wood buildings with their steep pitched green roofs and under a massive stone-arched opening into a well-lit, expansive tunnel. They continued deeper into the mountain through a series of heavy blast gates into a spacious receiving and entry area. The vehicles lowered their wheels as they came to a stop. The shields and anti-gravity units were turned off.

"Awesome!" was the word in Rogerton's mind as her eyes swept the panorama of the interior. She remembered her feelings upon first sight of the trophy room in Bestmarke's ship. Only here, they were much more intense. The ceiling was like a blue sky with no definition where wall and ceiling joined. The illumination was like the soft golden glow of a late summer afternoon. There were endless varieties of plants and trees growing everywhere, surrounded by water in ponds, creeks, and fountains. Waterfalls could be seen and heard at the distant edges, about a kilometer away. The floor was rich green grass and various ground covers with pathways of polished, richly hued stone. A tree lined boulevard wound through the center. All manner of natural sounds could be heard: a variety of birds and insects, the soft sigh of a gentle breeze, the trickle, drip, gurgle, and flow of ever running water. The air was clean and pure, delicately scented by flowering shrubs and trees. Small animals could occasionally be seen darting or scampering through the low growing bushes. It was as if the luscious outdoor scene they had just traveled through had trespassed inside.

The Lieutenant-Warden and the Star-Commander looked at each other and smiled. Both were at a loss for words and completely overwhelmed by the beauty and serenity of this magnificent foyer into the heart of the Empire.

Rogerton was puzzled by the lack of people. They had seen only a few small groups scattered about and none of them seemed to be in a hurry. Shouldn't it be much busier here at the center of the government? It was just another question to add to her growing list of questions.

Lieutenant Constantine slowly led them along the boulevard to its end, which they reached much sooner than expected. It had appeared to be much farther away. They followed her through a mist into an area that resembled an office lobby environment and then down a number of wide corridors to an area labeled Guest Services. A team of white-uniformed Specialists greeted them, showing them their quarters and accommodations for food and refreshment.

"I will be here tomorrow at 13:00 hours for your appointment with the Guardians," stated Constantine. "Please rest well and enjoy your visit," she said cheerily. She turned and quickly walked away.

The Star-Commander's eyes met Rogerton's. "Well, Lieutenant, tomorrow should prove to be interesting. Would you not agree?"

TROPHY

Chapter XXII

Guardian V was visibly upset as they brought the unconscious Louis Franelli into the Chambers. "Do we have to restrain him like some wild animal?" she asked with concern. "It will just have a negative effect on him when he awakens."

"We have to take some precautions," said Guardian III with a straight face. "He has been so long with Bestmarke we dare not risk having him unrestrained. We quite frankly do not know what he will do."

Guardian V sighed deeply as she watched the Specialists place him in a chair that firmly restrained his arms and ankles, permitting little motion. When the Specialists were finished, they left the room.

"Perhaps we can release the restraints soon," Guardian V said hopefully, walking around the chair, anxiously looking at Louis.

"It will be up to him," Guardian III grunted matter-of-factly. She also walked around the chair inspecting the restraint mechanisms. "If he cooperates and shows no signs of violence, perhaps we can. We will take no chances, though."

"He is a hard one to read and understand," Guardian I remarked, walking up and standing in front of the sedated Louis. "We may have to force him to open up with us," she said, walking to the front of the holographic fire.

"Dare we use a mind probe on him?" asked Guardian II, her face clouded with concern.

"We dare not risk any damage to his incredible mind!" Guardian V quickly responded, horrified at the suggestion. "There must be another way!"

"Your feelings for him run deep," observed Guardian I. "We must remember our priorities ... and our own inherent weaknesses."

Guardian V walked over closely to Guardian I, sighing deeply. "Do my feelings for him show that much? I thought they were dead or at least dormant. But now that he is here, they have awakened with full intensity. These are the same feelings I had for him years ago when we worked together here at CENTRAL as researchers, back before I was a candidate to be a Guardian."

"I remember that you cared for him back then," said Guardian I.

"I did, very deeply. He was always polite and thoughtful, and seemed to return my feelings," said Guardian V. "But he was so focused on his work and frustrated by people constantly questioning the direction of his research. His prison sentence and banishment from CENTRAL were so sudden. I was distraught but buried my feelings and plunged head-on into my own research and studies. I was able to conquer those feelings at the time, but not my memories. I was never able to totally forget him. Perhaps it is not wise that I be here to awaken him. One of the other Guardians should take my place. I am beginning to doubt my own objectivity," she said with resignation as she stood looking into the fire.

"No, you belong here," assured Guardian I, watching her. "You have a unique insight into his thinking the rest of us do not have. Your mild and gentle heart may be what turns him to genuinely helping us and seeing our point of view."

"Then I will stay," said Guardian V. "I do hope we can help him."

"We all do," agreed Guardian II, making final adjustments to her equipment. "Let us revive him now," she said as she administered the reviving agent.

The four Guardians arranged their chairs in a semi-circle facing Louis and patiently waited for the reviving agent to awaken him. After a few minutes he began to stir, trying to move his arms and legs. Feeling the restraints, he sighed deeply. Looking up, he angrily stared at the Guardians, one by one, looking last and longest at Guardian V.

"I thought you were my friend, Sondra," Louis said with disgust. "I can see your loyalties haven't changed."

"I am your friend, Louis," she replied calmly. "And my loyalties have not changed. They are the same as they always have been, to the Empire, and the good of all people."

"The good of all people," he said sarcastically. "Then why am I restrained? Is that part of 'the good of all people'?"

"You are restrained, Mr. Franelli, because you have been aligned with Galen Bestmarke," retorted Guardian II. "Guardian V, Sondra as you know her, objected to the restraints," she said without expression.

"So, Sondra, now you have become a Guardian," he said looking right at her. "But you are not my Guardian. No one is!" he said angrily and turned his gaze to Guardian II. "I am not aligned with Bestmarke! I didn't join him! He abducted me and gave me a choice – I could work for him or go back to an unjust prison sentence. What choice would you make?" he spitefully said. "I simply work on his ship and make things for him. I do not think the way he does nor do I care how he thinks. I do not belong to anyone … not to him, and not to the Empire. I answer only to myself, and that is all."

"Technically we can implicate you in his crimes as someone who has aided and abetted a known criminal," said Guardian III, intently looking at him.

"Yes, technically you can bend the laws to say anything you want. You have done it before!" he said, angrily accusing her. "I dislike playing games. What do you want from me?"

"The truth, Mr. Franelli, the truth," said Guardian II, looking weary.

TROPHY

"Whose truth do you want?" he yelled in frustration. "Do you want what I think is true? That didn't seem to work before. Or do you want me to accept what you think the truth to be?"

"If we cannot have absolute truth, Mr. Franelli, then we at least want your version of it," Guardian II sighed.

"Then put a mind-probe on me," he burst out defiantly. "I have nothing to hide. Ask what you will, Guardians!"

"You would allow that?" Guardian V said with a shocked look. "Are you sure? It could damage your mind if taken too far."

"Well, then, for 'the good of all people', don't take it too far," he retorted, simmering with anger. "I have always told you the truth. What I have said about my relationship with Galen Bestmarke is the truth. If you do not believe me, test me out with a mind-probe."

"Do you trust us?" questioned Guardian II. "Are you not afraid we will hurt you?"

"I ignore fear," Louis said. "What will happen, will happen. Fear is a waste of time," he said pointedly. "And do I trust you?" he asked, his piercing blue eyes fixed on her. The seconds ticked by accompanied only by the crackling fire. With his gaze still fixed on Guardian II he spoke again. "Yes, I trust you to act in harmony with your beliefs. If you believe the laws of the Empire are correct and noble, then I trust you to follow those laws. Trust should be reciprocal, though. Do you trust me?" he demanded, his gaze further intensified. "If you do ... loosen my restraints!"

Guardian I rose and stood directly in front of him, looking him in the face. "What will you do if we free your restraints, Louis?"

"I will do nothing," he said. "I do not lie and I do not attack people."

"If trust is indeed reciprocal, then we ask you ... what do you want from us?" said Guardian I, a gentle expression on her wizened face.

The fire hissed and popped in the background as Louis remained silent, lost in thought, taken aback by this unanticipated line of reasoning. Guardian I leaned over and tapped in the code to release the restraints. Then, still standing in front of Louis, she reached out both her hands. Firmly holding his upper arms, she lifted him up to a standing position. She was tall, as tall as Louis, though with a slighter build. She stood close, her dark eyes bent upon his. "If you could have anything, Louis Franelli, what would you want from us?"

The fire continued to snap and hiss in the silent room. The other three Guardians watched and wondered as Guardian I calmly stood toe to toe with Louis. With his blue eyes intently fixed on the Guardian, he considered his answer for a long moment. Then he said quietly: "I would like my freedom, and to carry on my research … nothing more."

"And that is all?" questioned Guardian I. "You do not want riches or power or vengeance or any other things? Has not Bestmarke offered or given you those things?"

"No. Those things are meaningless to me. I must do my research," he responded, softening his expression. "In fact, I am driven to strive for knowledge. Do you understand me at all?"

"I understand you, Louis Franelli," she smiled. "Will you help us? Will you help us to save our species, the human race, from extinction? We can offer you freedom to do your research and we will care for your other needs, too."

"You would offer this to me, a fugitive for over ten years?" he asked, completely overwhelmed. "Why? Why now?"

Guardian I slowly walked over to the fire and stared at it for a long time, contemplating her next thoughts. "We must bury our differences and past mistakes on both sides, and grasp the unique opportunity we now have before us. What you have discovered, time-travel through the Keyhole, must be used in the proper way to ensure our survival, not hasten our extinction," she said turning to him, her dark eyes shining in the firelight. "We do not have much time left. We can offer you conditional freedom to do your research, right here at CENTRAL."

For a long time Louis continued to stare at her, still overwhelmed. Finally he gave his answer. "I will do research for you. I will not harm anyone nor scheme against the Empire, but I will not give it my undying allegiance either," Louis said. "I will need time to think this through."

"You shall have time, Louis," said Guardian I patiently. "We will place no demands on you. Just concentrate on your research. Guardian V will assist you as needed."

"Don't you mean she will be my jailer?" he accused.

"No, Louis," answered Guardian I. "She will be your helper."

TROPHY

Chapter XXIII

The night's rest was refreshingly long and sweet for Star-Commander VanDevere. Her usually rigid schedule of rising early and reviewing her day's agenda didn't happen as there was no need for it today. Though she knew it wouldn't last, self-indulgence felt very satisfying once in a while. Sleeping late, a long leisurely hot shower, and the anticipation of a delicious gourmet breakfast only further broadened the smile on her face as she walked to the dining hall along the stone floors of the spacious softly lit corridor decorated in tastefully bold colors. Numerous exotic plants and flowers lined the way, their unique fragrances tantalizing the senses. Thought provoking artwork hung on the high walls, and dramatic sculpture highlighted the numerous alcoves lining the way. The high ceilings were like a dark blue sky, glowing with the luster of a late afternoon sun.

At an intersecting corridor she met Lieutenant-Warden Rogerton, also on her way to breakfast.

"Good morning, Ma'am," Rogerton said pleasantly. "I did not realize how late I had slept. It seems an easy thing to do here."

"Good morning, Lieutenant. I do not know when I have slept so soundly. I feel almost slothful," she laughed.

Rogerton smiled. She couldn't remember ever seeing the Star-Commander in such high spirits. Apparently even a short break from her stressful routine was therapeutic for her.

Breakfast was delightful and VanDevere chattered away as if speaking to an equal or a close friend. Rogerton warmed to her even more now that the barrier of rank was set aside, at least for this short while. She felt a sisterly affection for the somewhat older VanDevere, and began to understand the depth of her loneliness which was only too common for those in high command positions. Rogerton was probably only a little older than VanDevere's daughter away at the Academy. Perhaps the Star-Commander was missing that bond and had rediscovered it in the Lieutenant-Warden. Whatever the reason might be, Rogerton was happy to be her friend.

"May I ask you a question please, Ma'am?" she said softly as they sipped their coffee.

"Certainly," nodded VanDevere.

"Why do the Guardians want me here?" she whispered. "Everything I know was recorded."

Instead of showing that down-to-business serious face, VanDevere just kept smiling, allowing nothing to spoil her present mood. "I really do not know. I learned a long time ago not to anticipate the command structure. Trying to second guess the situation will eat you up with worry. Accept it as a challenge, and view it as a positive experience that will help you gain knowledge and grow. You do not know all the answers, nor can you accomplish everything. All you can do is your best, and that is usually more than anyone else expects. We are usually more demanding of ourselves than of others."

Her expressions were like the sun coming out from behind a cloud. "Thank you, Ma'am, that helps a lot," Rogerton said. "Would you like some more coffee?"

"I would love some more, Lieutenant. By the way, do you know the time?"

"Why, it is only 11:09, Ma'am. We have plenty of time before our appointment."

They continued their breakfast enjoying each others company and mundane conversation.

At 13:00 hours, Lieutenant Constantine and a Specialist arrived at the lobby and escorted the Star-Commander and Lieutenant-Warden further inside the complex, past more blast gates, and deeper into the mountain. They finally came to a reception area that widened out with a floor of luminescent white marble and matching walls. The walls ascended high up into what appeared to be clouds or mist with a ceiling like a dark blue sky, the same as the rest of the complex. At the center of the wall were two massive metal doors with a finish like stainless steel or nickel, but having a rainbow sheen, the colors of which seemed to be ever changing, like the reflection from an oil film on still water. Above the doors was a single ten-pointed star of black onyx. Guards, Specialists in white uniforms, were before the doors and came to attention as the four approached.

Lieutenant Constantine approached and stated: "Permission to enter Chambers, please."

The guard checked the identification badges of the Star-Commander and the Lieutenant-Warden, doing retinal scans on both. Satisfied, she allowed them to enter. The Star-Commander thanked the Lieutenant, and the two officers passed inside with the doors silently closing behind them.

Total darkness greeted them except for the pathway of luminescent white marble which glowed in front of them and darkened into blackness behind as they followed it forward. Nothing but the pathway could be seen nor did they hear anything but their own footsteps and nervous breathing. The air was still, but not stifling, and carried a vague odor of electrical circuitry and components. Suddenly, the floor stopped glowing ahead, so they remained on the last portion they could see. A soft voice said: "Please stand still, one meter apart from each other, and close your eyes tightly."

They complied and immediately a very intense light shown on them from all angles. It felt like the burning rays of the sun on a hot day, but from all directions. It lasted only ten seconds and then went dark again, but gave their clothes a newly ironed smell. The soft voice informed them to open their eyes and remain standing until the path was again illuminated in front of them. Their retinal fatigue was strong so they waited, allowing their eyes to adjust again to the darkness. Soon the pathway glowed softly in front of them and they followed it until it stopped at a blank wall. Suddenly, vertical and horizontal slits of light appeared and grew wider as two large doors silently swung open away from them, revealing an interior area like no other they had ever seen. The faint scent of rain washed air rushed to meet them as they entered. A tall, slender, olive-skinned woman with short, wavy blond hair was facing them. She was wearing a simple uniform, white in color, with a ten-pointed star of black onyx near her left shoulder.

"Greetings, Star-Commander VanDevere and Lieutenant-Warden Rogerton, you are right on time, as we expected," she said, extending her hand first to the Star-Commander. "Welcome to CENTRAL. I am Guardian X and we have greatly anticipated this meeting with you."

"Thank you, Guardian, this is a rare privilege for us," replied the awestruck Star-Commander, accepting the Guardian's firm hand shake, and recognizing the minty essence of lavender at the Guardian's approach.

Lieutenant-Warden Rogerton just kept silent, trying to be as small as possible, totally overwhelmed by the whole situation.

"Is this your first visit to CENTRAL, Lieutenant?" the Guardian asked in her soft spoken voice, her blue-gray eyes reflecting the soft illumination. She extended her hand to Rogerton.

"Yes, Ma'am," she replied nervously, extending her hand, accepting the greeting. She was quite unsure whether to say or ask more.

"Please, call me Guardian, my dear," she said reassuringly. "There are ten of us here, ten Guardians. I am number X, the youngest. Our duty, our privilege, is to take care of CENTRAL, the main computer. We are, in fact, inside of it now. That is why you were decontaminated before being allowed entry. Please take no offense, it has nothing to do with personal hygiene."

The two officers walked slowly along with the Guardian as she explained some of the workings and parts of the vast and complicated technology around them. She tried to put it in simple terms and concepts they could understand, but it was still very technical and abstract, even with their high level of education and training.

"Please, Guardian, may I ask you a question?" the Lieutenant-Warden nervously asked.

"Certainly, my dear, how can I help you?" she said, putting her hands together while turning to face the young officer.

"I was wondering about historical data. How far back in the past do the archives reach? Do they precede the New Beginning? Do they have a record of our ancestors?"

The Guardian's eyes briefly met the Star-Commander's, and with a gentle smile said to the Lieutenant-Warden: "The answer to both of your questions is mostly yes. The data bases reach back to the earliest days of computer systems. However, before and after the New Beginning there were some system failures, not total failures, mind you, but enough to leave some gaping holes that so far we have not been able to fill. Most of human history is still there."

"But if you could go back in time, those gaps could be filled, could they not?" asked Rogerton with surprising seriousness.

The Guardian looked at her admiringly. "I am beginning to understand why you recommend our young officer, Star-Commander," she said and then paused. "Yes, Lieutenant, that seems more of a real possibility in view of what you and Star-Commander VanDevere have discovered. I cannot say more now, but soon we will speak in greater depth on these matters."

They continued on for a while until the Guardian stopped and faced Rogerton. "Lieutenant-Warden, in view of your excellent progress and helpful accomplishments, it is my pleasure to promote you to full Lieutenant. Congratulations!" she exclaimed, offering a firm hand to the young woman.

"Yes! Congratulations, Lieutenant!" said the Star-Commander, also giving her a firm handshake. "Thank you very much, Guardian!"

TROPHY

The Guardian and Star-Commander both smiled broadly while Rogerton felt her face flush, growing uncomfortably warm. It was difficult for her to accept praise, even when deserved.

"Thank you ... Guardian," she stammered. "And ... and thank you, Ma'am. I have always tried ... I mean ... It is an honor to serve the New Victorian Empire. I will continue to try ... to try to do my best."

"Yes, that is what we expect of our finest," said the Guardian, continuing her praise. "Let us continue to our chambers where we can refresh ourselves before our meeting." She led them deeper into the vast computer.

TROPHY

Chapter XXIV

The Star-Commander found the shielded chambers in the heart of CENTRAL comfortably austere. The simple furnishings and color schemes were tasteful and relaxing, yet stimulating to thinking and creativity. A river rock fireplace with a realistic holographic fire gave it a homey quaintness that didn't feel out of place, but natural, bringing back memories of the house she had lived in as a young girl. A faint essence of wood smoke completed the ambiance.

Two more Guardians had joined Guardian X and the two officers. All were sitting in comfortable chairs near the fireplace. Behind them at the other end of the room were the two pedestals with their nearly invisible sparkling sheen above each of them.

Guardian II stood up and spoke first. "Star-Commander VanDevere and Lieutenant Rogerton, we thank you for a job well done. Your presence of mind in how you handled this situation has helped us considerably," she said. "We have already had the opportunity to talk with Franelli, quite successfully I might add, and to further examine these pedestals. Because you were instrumental in obtaining them, we want you both to witness the awakening of the ancient man, Martin Charles Bucklann."

"We have already made some progress in our understanding of the nuclear power units in the bases," said Guardian VII. "This is crucial for our restoration of mobility to the man and panther by means of advanced cybernetics."

"Please, Guardian," interrupted Lieutenant Rogerton. "Are you saying you can build robotic bodies for them, so they are no longer trapped in these hideous cages?"

"Yes, Lieutenant, if they will allow that. The choice must be theirs," said Guardian VII. "We truly want to help them, but it is a moral issue ... and they must decide."

148

TROPHY

"But Guardian!" Rogerton cried. "How will the panther decide? The man will no doubt give his opinion. But how can the panther?"

"This is where your help will be needed, Lieutenant," Guardian X said. "You have already spoken to it, have you not? There is already an emotional connection, however small it may be, between you and the panther. It could be the beginning of trust and ultimately communication of some sort. We do not have the answers and success could be a long shot, but are you willing to try? The rewards could be great. Indeed, that is what we hope. I believe you are up for this challenge, are you not, Lieutenant?" she said, her eyes fixed intently on the young officer.

The rank of Lieutenant seemed rather insignificant compared to the four powerful and influential women looking at her now, waiting for an answer. She sighed inwardly, giving the only answer she could, and offered it in good conscience with her heartfelt thoughts. "I will do everything in my power to help this poor creature. I am grateful for this privilege to help."

"Very good, Lieutenant," Guardian II said, smiling broadly. "A program is already in place. You will be working with Guardian VII and her team of Specialists. She will discuss the details with you later."

"Let us now awaken the ancient man," Guardian II determined. "I think we are all very curious of what we will find. Guardian X will take the lead, but the conversation will be open to us all."

The five assembled a comfortable distance in front of the pedestal and Guardian X touched the top plate. The nearly invisible shimmer turned to a sparkling sheen that grew darker. Out of a thick fog a shape began to appear, crystallizing into clarity as the fog dissipated. The head of the ancient man, Martin Charles Bucklann, was directly in front of them, still asleep.

TROPHY

"Did we ever dream we would see such a man as this?" exclaimed Guardian II as the others echoed similar sentiments. "I knew what to expect, but I still find him totally fascinating! Extraordinary!" she gushed, her hands on her cheeks.

"Let us awaken him," Guardian X finally said. "And let us be gentle with him. Remember who put him into this position."

She touched the lower plate and they waited twenty seconds, thirty seconds, and nothing happened. Fifty seconds went by and then sixty. Finally Martin opened his hazel-green eyes and looked straight ahead.

TROPHY

Chapter XXV

A faint hum began to pervade all his senses. His eyes were shut and they wouldn't open. He was trying to wake up, but it seemed as if nothing was happening. He felt more energy flowing to his brain, and finally he was able to open his eyes. He continued to stare as the blur in front of him gradually came into focus. He was confounded by what he saw: five women of different ages and races, three wearing pure white uniforms and two of dark forest green. The eyes of the latter two were tinged purple. They were both white skinned, the younger being taller with large, blue-green eyes and shoulder length auburn hair. She was strikingly beautiful in appearance. The other had a look of authority and was likewise attractive with steel-gray eyes and short blond hair.

The nearest woman in white was tall and looked Italian. Her dark, olive-colored skin complimented her short blond wavy hair and blue-gray eyes. Behind her, also in white, appeared a short, slight, olive-skinned woman with large engaging dark brown eyes and short black hair. She looked to be South American Indian. Beside her was a somewhat heavy-set, kindly faced African woman. She had deep brown mahogany skin, short white curly hair, and was older than the others. Curiously, each woman in white had a ten-pointed black star by her left shoulder. The authoritative woman in green had a matching symbol in silver or platinum. They were all in a living room of sorts with a fireplace burning at the opposite end. Everyone was quiet. The only sound was the muted hiss and pop of the distant fire.

The door at the far wall opened quietly and a tall, slender woman entered and walked gracefully to the others. She wore a pure white uniform, a ten-pointed black star, and intricately beaded leather moccasins. Her gray hair hung in long braids on either side of her finely wrinkled red-skinned face. Her black eyes were alert and full of life. She looked to be American Indian and was, without a doubt, the oldest person there. She stood silently with the others.

Martin closely contemplated the six women standing in front of him. He waited for them to speak, but the silence continued. He had questions that needed answering, so he finally spoke. "Who are you? Where am I? What are you going to do with me?" he said in a determined voice.

The Italian woman in white smiled and spoke distinctly. "You have many questions, Martin Charles Bucklann. In time we will answer them all, but be assured that we mean you no harm, and that we only want to help you. I am called Guardian X and we have rescued you from Galen Bestmarke's ship."

"Did you kill him?" he said with a snarl, his eyes suddenly full of hatred.

"No, Martin," she calmly said. "Unfortunately he escaped this time, but we will ultimately capture him. We did capture his chief engineer who is responsible for your being here and in your present condition. We also captured one more pedestal."

"What's in the other pedestal?" he desperately said. "Have you looked yet?"

"Yes, we did," replied Guardian X. "It is a magnificent black panther, caged as you have been, sadly."

"And that's all? My father's in one, too!" he wailed.

The six women were stunned. They looked at each other and back to Martin with genuine pity. Martin could only groan and cast his eyes downward, feeling thoroughly wretched.

The African woman in white stepped closer assuring him in a kindly, comforting voice. "I am Guardian II, Martin. Please, let us help and comfort you. Your loss is indeed great, but we can help. We have vast resources at our disposal and you have given us a great priority to capture Bestmarke and his ship. We truly want to help you," she said. The soft assurances and soothing tone of her voice was a healing balm on Martin's tortured mind.

TROPHY

"He's so evil. Why'd he do this, first to my father, and now to me?" he moaned. "I want to get my father away from him! He's nothing but a trophy hunter! I hate trophy hunters! They're the ones who should be hung up on the wall instead of all the animals they've killed! Why do they do it? Why? Do they just love to kill things or is it to give themselves glory?" Martin raged, his pent-up anger boiling over. He stopped shouting and was quiet for a moment, trying to calm himself. He looked into the faces of all the women standing by him. "He must be stopped," he said in a subdued voice, his rage turning to dismay, his eyes pleading for sympathy.

The eldest woman in white stepped closer to Martin and studied his eyes, a gentle look on her face. "I am called Guardian I, Martin. My North American ancestors knew much of trophy hunters. Long ago their lives depended on the bison that roamed the plains in great numbers. Do you remember what happened to the bison or buffalo as some called them?"

"Uh, yes, Ma'am, I guess I do," he said, starting to calm himself. "They were hunted nearly to extinction. Sharpshooters killed thousands from the railroad trains and soldiers killed a lot of them, too."

"Why did they kill them, Martin?"

"For sport?" he said, unsure of the answer.

"That is partially true," she said. "Those hunters were glorified for their actions. But the underlying reason for the vast slaughter was to undermine the whole way of life for my ancient ancestors. Without the bison, they could no longer exist in relative peace as they had for many generations. It was more than the bison that were nearly exterminated. So you see, Martin, we understand what trophy hunters are." Then, looking him squarely in the face, she said: "Are you a trophy hunter, Martin?"

"No, not me!" he quickly answered, shocked by the question. "How can you ask that?"

"You are a hunter, are you not?" she said, watching his expression. "What is your purpose in hunting?"

"I hunt for the meat, the food."

"My ancestors also hunted for the food. In fact they used every part of the animal, nothing was wasted," she stated matter-of-factly. "For what other reason do you hunt, Martin?"

"I ... I guess I like the challenge," he said uncomfortably. "I guess I enjoy trying to outsmart the animal."

"Who has the advantage, Martin? You or the animal?"

"I guess I do," he reluctantly admitted. "My rifle has a scope so I can use it from quite a distance. I can decide if I want to pull the trigger, to kill the animal."

"Does your livelihood absolutely depend on your hunting animals as was the case with my ancestors?" she questioned.

"No, I guess it doesn't," he surrendered, his eyes downcast.

"Now do you understand why I asked if you were a trophy hunter?" Guardian I said. "Only you can answer that question. It is a matter of what is really in your heart, in your inmost thoughts and desires. What drives men to be trophy hunters? Is it not really what is in their hearts? Or to put it more accurately, is it not really their lack of heart?" she firmly questioned.

"But men like Bestmarke love to kill. They're not interested in just getting food – they love the hunt, the glory, the bragging rights, and the dominance it brings them. They are violent individuals, killers that don't want to change." Martin looked at her for a long moment. "But I think I see your point," he said, his expression more subdued.

"I am glad you do, Martin," she said. "Guardian X will explain how we can safely get your father back." She nodded at the youngest woman in white.

"Can you really help me?" he anxiously asked. "Can you help me get him back?"

TROPHY

"We will get him back and stop this madness," assured Guardian X. "Our Star-Commander has oversight of the fleet and will concentrate our resources upon Bestmarke."

"We will find Bestmarke's ship," stated Star-Commander VanDevere. "He can only hide for so long."

"How can he hide his ship?" questioned Martin. "What kind of ship is it? He said it was a fast ship. Is it like a submarine? I was just in one room and my father didn't have the chance to tell me anything."

The Star-Commander looked at Guardian X who gently interrupted. "You have many questions, Martin, and we need to start giving you the answers. First, let me briefly explain how you got here. Bestmarke has a star ship – a ship he can use in outer space. Bestmarke's engineer has figured out time travel. He used his ship to travel back in time to the year 1975, captured you, and brought you back to our time, which is the year 475 of the New Victorian Age. The New Victorian Age started in 2065 of your era. That is five hundred and sixty five years ago as you know it."

"Five hundred and sixty five years ago?" said Martin, starting to laugh. "Where are we, really?"

"We are really five hundred and sixty five years in your future, Martin. We can show you our computer records clear back to your time, if you desire," she stated confidently.

The room grew very quiet, only the fire could be heard. "Five hundred and sixty five years?" Martin finally said. "Really? You're not kidding me, are you?"

"Kidding you? That is an interesting expression," said Guardian X, mildly amused. "No, we are not trying to mislead you, if that is what you mean. Bestmarke's engineer, Louis Franelli, whom we now have in custody, used an anomaly, a strange occurring oddity in space, as a portal back and forth through time. He alone has discovered how to harness it. If he will help us also understand its secrets, we hope to reverse the damage he and Bestmarke have done."

"Wow!" Martin exclaimed, desperate to believe. "This is just like that space show we used to watch on television!"

The Guardians and Officers looked at each other again.

Guardian X continued: "Please, Martin, ask as many more questions as you would like. You deserve to know the truth of this situation."

"Okay," said Martin. "You all have a strange accent. Is this the way everyone talks now?"

"Our speech has various dialects depending on what part of the Solar System we are from," said Guardian X. "Our speech sounds normal to us while your speech sounds archaic. It is common for language to gradually change over time."

Martin thought about this for a moment and seemed satisfied. He shifted his gaze to the Star-Commander. "Why do some of you have purple eyes? Bestmarke had purple eyes, too," he said. "Are you really aliens from another planet or is it some new kind of contact lenses?"

"We are definitely not aliens," laughed the Star-Commander. "We are all humans originally from Planet Earth. We have not discovered life anywhere else in the galaxy ... at least not yet. Some of us do come from other planets, though, because we now have cities inhabited by humans on the moon and Mars. We also have space stations throughout the Solar System." She paused, letting this thought sink in. "Our purple eyes are from extended space travel. We create artificial gravity on our ships and the side effect is purple tinged eyes. It is harmless."

"Then it's not contact lenses?" Martin asked again.

"No, Martin," said Guardian II. "We have not needed contact lenses for four hundred years. Most all physical defects can now be corrected on a genetic level."

"Wow," Martin said. "What happened to my body?" he said looking at Guardian X. "How am I still alive? Will I ever be able to get out of this cage?" he sighed.

"I am sorry, Martin, but we do not know what Bestmarke did with your body. He probably left it back on Earth of your time era," Guardian X said. "We do not fully understand how you are kept alive. It appears that some mechanism in the base of your pedestal is responsible and it appears to be nuclear. We hope that Louis Franelli, Bestmarke's engineer, will help us understand more. He is the one that created the pedestals and their processes."

"Is he evil like Bestmarke?" Martin frowned.

"We do not know yet," said Guardian I, stepping forward. "We hope he will help us. His cooperation will enable us to help you at a faster pace."

"How can you possibly help me? Just look at me ...," he said bitterly.

Guardian I looked at Martin for a long moment with pity in her eyes. "Martin, what would you say if we built you a new body? We have the capacity to do so."

"Do you mean you could make me like a robot?" Martin asked.

"That is the basic idea," replied Guardian I. "We could fashion you to look and feel fully human again. Would that be acceptable?"

"Really?" Martin exclaimed. "You can really do that?"

TROPHY

Chapter XXVI

"When you are ready you may awaken it, Lieutenant Rogerton," instructed Guardian VII from the operations center of the cybernetics lab. The Lieutenant was alone in the controlled lab research room where the pedestal with the sleeping panther had been placed. A holographic jungle environment encircled them, complete with realistic sounds. She was sitting four meters away, not directly facing the big cat, but presenting more of a side view to it, her eyes purposely looking away from its eyes. She pressed the remote control activating the bottom plate of the pedestal. She waited sixty seconds for the panther's eyes to snap open. Suddenly a soft growling started. It had spotted her. Continuing to look away, she spoke quietly in a monotone the same words of her first encounter with it.

"We do not want to harm you ... we want to help you ... please let us help you," she repeated slowly many times.

After quite a while the panther finally stopped growling and just stared at her curiously. She slowly turned her head and looked it in the eyes making no sound nor showing her teeth. After a few seconds she looked away again assuming her non-threatening sideways profile while the panther continued to stare.

* * * * * * * * *

On the fourth day Lieutenant Rogerton stood in the control room with her hands on her hips. "Please, Guardian, can you tell me if we are making progress? It stopped growling after two days but nothing else seems to have changed. Perhaps I need to be more patient ..."

"On the contrary, Lieutenant," she replied happily, looking up from her control panel. "We are making excellent progress. We have determined it is a male, and brain scans are showing small

158

but significant growth in crucial areas of his brain. He is growing accustomed to you. It is too early yet to know if fondness and a level of dependency are forming, but we feel they will in time," she said, turning back to her controls, adjusting one of them.

"We have also conducted an extensive analysis on the nuclear power unit and controls found in the pedestal." She continued in her soft, high voice, becoming more animated. "Franelli's genius is extraordinary in the micro-circuitry he developed to allow the head to continue living and thinking with no apparent degradation of brain functions. His connection between the living nervous system and the computer is incredible!"

"Is there any way to speed up the progress?" the Lieutenant asked, sitting down next to her. "Can the controls be fine-tuned or adjusted without introducing negative side effects?"

"We believe they can. We have done so, very minutely, in one area to test our premise. So far, the results have been positive, even beyond our expectations. We need to proceed cautiously, however, as we do not know what the long term implications may be. This is totally new ground we are covering." Guardian VII continued. "By the way, Lieutenant, have you ever been tested for guider training?"

"Yes, back in the Academy we were all tested at least one time. I was tested twice. My rating was 8.5, just below the qualification rating of 9.0, so I was passed over and I concentrated on my other studies." Rogerton looked intently at this small, even delicate woman, a descendant of ancient Inca Indians. She had an inviting, simple demeanor, and a trustworthiness that touched Rogerton's heart, eliminating her fears.

"Lieutenant, a guider/pouncer link may be the only way to effectively communicate with this poor creature. However, it has never been attempted with a wild, adult cat such as this. We believe it is possible, but there are many questions that we frankly have no satisfactory answers for. Would you be willing to try the link? It will be frightening and difficult."

"Is there a danger for me, Guardian? He really cannot attack me, can he?"

"Physically you could not be harmed. But to be mentally linked, having a joined consciousness with such an aggressive, wild animal could be damaging mentally to you ... and to him also," the Guardian said. "We do not know what the results will be. With proper control and safeguards we believe it is possible and ultimately beneficial. But it will not be easy. Obviously it is a decision that only you can make, it cannot be forced. You must be absolutely willing in your own mind for there to be any hope of success. We have no guarantees, it is the unknown we are venturing into," she said uncomfortably.

Lieutenant Rogerton contemplated the Guardian's words, then looked compassionately at the sleeping panther. She finally turned back, quietly looking down. "I know it is possible. Somehow it is possible. The first time I looked him closely in the eyes, I felt his anger, despair, and gratefulness. It lasted only a split second before he fell asleep. The connection is there, though. Somehow I must get through to him. Somehow we must help him. I am willing to try," she determined, looking up again at the small woman sitting next to her.

The Guardian contemplated the young Lieutenant. "We thought, that is, we hoped that would be your answer. We have already begun preparations for the link. We will give you all the protection that we know of. Your willingness and sacrifice for the Empire is commendable, Lieutenant," she said, standing and heartily shaking the Lieutenant's hand.

Lieutenant Rogerton stood and returned the gesture, an unsettled look about her.

TROPHY

Chapter XXVII

Earth Date: 475 N.V.A.
Location: Asteroid Belt

"So, Mr. Bestmarke, let me get this straight," said the Izax. "The heathen Empire has kidnapped your precious chief engineer and you obviously want to get him back. Now you want me to help you. My, what a change from the last time we spoke. You were so sure of the outcome of our little game," he said dryly, looking down his bulbous nose.

"I was hasty, Izax. I was caught up in the moment and emotion swayed my tongue," Galen said, uncommonly apologetic. "Our little game is just that, a little game. Our friendship and loyalty to each other is much more, and goes way back. We have only one real enemy, the Empire," he appealed.

"Yes, Mr. Bestmarke, our common enemy is the wretched Empire, but I have learned to watch my back among so-called friends, too. One can never be too cautious, can one, Mr. Bestmarke?" he mocked. "And what of our little wager, are you going to try and weasel out of that, too? What else did the Empire take besides Franelli?" pressured the Izax. "Oh, come now, pouncer got your tongue?"

"Our little wager is still on," stammered Bestmarke, squirming under the Izax's ridicule. "I just need a little more time to compensate for this unfortunate . . . delay."

"Yes, I am sure," replied the Izax disdainfully. "I am willing to continue our little wager, our little game. It is really not that important to me, although apparently it is to you. Be that as it may, let us get down to more serious business. I have in mind our dear Mr. Franelli. He must be working on some interesting projects for you . . .

161

weapons systems, perhaps? How much will you pay to get him back, safe and sound?"

"You have me at a clear disadvantage at this point," complained Bestmarke. "Just tell me what you can do, and name your price!" he said, his face reddening as he struggled to remain calm.

The Izax looked at Bestmarke with disgust. It was no wonder this buffoon was wanted by the Empire. Bestmarke was known for letting his uncontrolled emotions run his life, bringing him trouble. The Izax was shrewd. He stayed within the law and the PCC left him alone to his business. Bestmarke was a fool.

"You should really have your brother Terran do your negotiations for you, he is so much calmer," rebuked the Izax. "I will tell you what I want. Both of us are rich, so money, credits, precious metals, and things like these aren't worth talking about."

"Then what are we talking about?" asked Bestmarke in a low, steady voice, desperately trying to retain his self control. "What do you want from me?"

"This is where the difficulty comes in, Mr. Bestmarke. What do you give the man that has everything? This truly is a dilemma," he taunted. "You see, I could just help you for no compensation, just out of the goodness of my heart. But how would that affect my reputation? What would everyone else think? Would they say that I am playing favorites? Would they say that I am getting soft and try using a little muscle on me? That would never do!" he said, waving his arms dramatically. "So what I want from you is an option, a choice, as it were. If I can help arrange for the return of Mr. Franelli, then all I desire from you is one thing and I will request it in my own time. Just one thing, Mr. Bestmarke, and I will make my decision when Mr. Franelli is back, safe and sound," he said with a confident smugness. "Of course, I will not choose Mr. Franelli, your brother, or your ship. I am a reasonable man ... I don't want to put you out of business!" he patronized. "What do you say, Mr. Bestmarke, do we have a deal? Is Mr. Franelli worth that much to you?"

TROPHY

"You strike a hard bargain, Izax," surrendered Bestmarke, realizing he had little choice if he wanted help. "Draw up a contract and I will sign it. I need Franelli back, and I don't want him to sit and rot in a prison."

"Very touching, Mr. Bestmarke. "That gets me right here," he said, putting his hand over his heart.

Bestmarke looked at him, struggling to conceal his loathing. The Izax was a pompous ass ... a fat, disgusting mole, living in his hollowed out asteroid. He probably never dirtied his hands once in his mining business and he always played the king. It would be enjoyable to get him out into space and see how tough he was without his muscle men around him.

"I do not use contracts in situations such as this, Mr. Bestmarke. Your word is your bond and I will hold you to it," he said, pointing his finger at Galen. "I keep my word, you keep yours, and we are both happy. I like to be happy, Mr. Bestmarke, don't you? Happiness is good for your health and long life, wouldn't you agree? Do we have a deal?"

"Yes, Izax, we have a deal, you have my word. I will give you your choice or option as you have said. Now, what can we do to get back Franelli?" he said impatiently, nervously shifting his weight.

"Oh, this is the easy part for you, Mr. Bestmarke," he smiled. "Just leave everything to me. I will make all the arrangements. It is much cleaner if I plan it myself. Of course, you will receive all the blame ... that cannot be helped. But you are a wanted man already so it really makes no difference, does it? For me to have any influence I must have a measure of respectability. Surely you can understand that, can't you?"

"Yes, of course," conceded Bestmarke, growing exceedingly tired of the conversation. "I will wait patiently for you to liberate Franelli."

"That's the spirit, my old friend," beamed the Izax, standing and extending his gloved hand to Galen, shaking hands vigorously. "Now you're getting the point! I will start to make all the arrangements at once!"

TROPHY

Chapter XXVIII

Earth Date: 475 N.V.A.
Location: CENTRAL, Earth

"Thank you for this private meeting, Guardian," VanDevere said nervously, sitting in one of the brown, neoleather chairs in Guardian X's office. "I have had many things on my mind, though this was certainly not the least. 'Star-Point' has been much in my thoughts as of late. I was quite stunned when CENTRAL instructed me to talk to you. I have been holding many things in for a long time; it is time to get some answers and direction, please," she said, looking down.

With her blue-gray eyes sympathetically fixed upon her, Guardian X watched and listened quietly to the distraught and anxious Star-Commander, Abigail VanDevere.

"Please, Guardian, I have to know … Is 'Star-Point' my younger sister Michelle? That is the only logical choice my conclusions reach. Am I correct?" she nervously asked, looking into the Guardian's face.

"Yes, Star-Commander, you are correct," she confirmed quietly. After a moment she spoke again in a positive tone. "You probably do not know anything about her now other than her guider training and renegade status, do you?"

"No, I do not. Nor do I know how to feel," she said gazing down again, her voice quivering as she tried to calm her inner turmoil. "I am embarrassed and angry. She is my sister and I love her dearly. How could she leave us? And why? The penalty for a renegade is total and complete banishment, a hopeless situation!" she said, desperately holding back her tears.

TROPHY

The Guardian gently grasped Abigail's hands and looked straight into her eyes. "Your sister is not a true renegade. She is working an undercover assignment. It is so dangerous and risky, we could not tell anyone, not even you, until now. Even her memories were altered to give her a new identity, a clean one."

The Star-Commander could only stare with her mouth open, she was so taken aback. Tears of relief and new found joy filled her eyes. "She still serves the Empire? I do not know what to say!"

"She volunteered. In fact, she insisted," Guardian X continued. "You can be very proud of her."

The Star-Commander was quiet for a long moment, and then stood up and began pacing slowly. "She had so many troubles growing up. I was in the Academy during the worst of it, and I finally talked her into joining. It took persuasion to convince the Board to allow her in. I was doing well, and I really believe they took pity on me and let her in."

"They also could see her potential," added the Guardian. "She was brilliant once she was on the right course."

"She graduated with honors, even higher than I had done," the Star-Commander continued, glancing occasionally at the Guardian. "Then she fell in love. It was a great tragedy when her life-mate died. He had a rare, incurable illness, and it left Michelle devastated when he was gone. She just fell apart and did not seem to care about anything after that. We rarely saw her, and I feared the worst. It was only a few months later that we heard she had become a renegade. Our whole family was devastated."

"We continuously monitor all the graduates," said the Guardian. "When we saw her situation, we immediately helped her with counseling. It was during this program that the opportunity for an undercover assignment came up. She was qualified and insisted she could do it. We explained in detail everything we would have to do to protect her, and she agreed to continue."

"What did you do to her to protect her?"

TROPHY

"We altered her memories so she recognizes herself as Estelle Fairfield, a renegade Victorian officer. We gave her Guider training and a wonderful cat named Tommie with a TMC-7 certification," assured the Guardian. "We inserted into her sub-conscience the driving thought of getting as close as possible to Galen Bestmarke and Louis Franelli. We now know that your sister Michelle and her cat are employed on Bestmarke's ship and have been for a few years. Recent developments led to this suspicion and we have confirmed it with Franelli. Franelli does not know she is your sister. He knows her only as Estelle Fairfield, a renegade Victorian officer."

"Then we cannot destroy Bestmarke's ship until Michelle and Tommie are safe," fretted VanDevere. "Guardian, can her original memories be restored?"

"Yes. It is difficult, but it has been accomplished over twenty times. The success rate has been one hundred percent," Guardian X confirmed. "She still has all of her original memories. We only needed to change a few and those memories can be fully restored. When she received her Guider training, a small implant was attached to her brain stem to facilitate the interface with the guider hardware. Bestmarke will see that on a scan and will expect it to be there. What he will not see is a tiny portion of that implant designed to act as a brain-trigger when we activate it. At the right time and place this will be activated to help finish our task of capturing Bestmarke."

"Why has it not been activated yet?"

"We have not been sure of her location nor been close enough to her," Guardian X said. "Her original orders were to capture or kill the Bestmarke brothers, a difficult assignment, and then capture or kill Franelli. The memory of those orders was blocked or submerged when we gave her a new identity. However, when the brain-trigger reactivates her old memories, she will try to carry out those orders. Obviously, we cannot allow her to harm Franelli. We are relieved that he is safe with us. His knowledge of time travel is of supreme importance. We must rethink how we will capture Bestmarke and his ship. Michelle is not our only concern, though. Do not forget Martin's father and the other trophy pedestals."

"Yes, we cannot forget them," said the Star-Commander. "Do we know when or in what situation this trigger can be activated?"

"No, not precisely, there are too many variables, and can only be best determined by someone in the near vicinity, someone in the field."

"Would that be me, Guardian?" asked the Star-Commander, raising her eyebrows. "Would it be my decision?"

"Yes, Star-Commander. You are the most qualified."

TROPHY

Chapter XXIX

Earth Date: 475 N.V.A.
Location: CENTRAL, Earth

"Why do you want to capture Bestmarke?" asked Martin, gazing into Guardian X's face. "I know why I'd like to catch him, but what about you?"

"He is wanted for smuggling, fraud, and theft," she said matter-of-factly. "He is involved in organized crime and was part of a vicious rebellion twenty years ago that was costly to the Empire. He is directly and indirectly responsible for the destruction of a number of our ships and the loss of their crews. He has taken the lives of our Sisters," she emphasized, her nostrils flaring. "He is an arrogant, selfish, and willfully wicked man. He must be stopped," said Guardian X, barely restraining her anger.

"Why haven't you been able to stop him?" Martin cautiously asked.

"Chiefly because he had Franelli working for him, technologically staying one step ahead of us," Guardian X said, controlling her emotions. "Now that we have Franelli in custody, we hope the balance has shifted. Bestmarke is wealthy and has powerful friends. It is extremely difficult to pin down a man like that," she concluded with disgust.

"So now the Empire can destroy him and his ship or execute him if he's captured."

"It is not that easy," Guardian X said. "Your way of thinking, the ancient way, is one of vengeance. In your day, wars and ethnic strife continued for generations, even centuries, because people and nations had to 'get even'. Under CENTRAL's rule, all life is important, including humans and animals. No animals are unnecessarily killed and no humans are executed."

"But what about justice?" Martin said. "You can't let killers like Bestmarke off the hook. That's not right. Think of all the heartache and misery he has caused. Somehow he has to be held accountable. I want to kill him myself – and you probably feel the same, don't you?"

Guardian X raised one eyebrow and looked at Martin. "You are very observant, Martin. You have sensed my feelings about men like Bestmarke. But to break the cycle of hate and retribution we have to hold to a higher standard and set aside our own personal feelings, no matter how strong they are. The rule of CENTRAL directs us to think of the greater good, the overall needs of the majority, and not our own personal problems or vendettas."

"Well, if men like Bestmarke are not executed, what do you do with them? They can't just go free – what justice does CENTRAL provide?" Martin said, growing exasperated.

"Men like Bestmarke are often killed in battle because they will not surrender. But if they are captured, the Empire has a successful program of rehabilitation which can include neurological micro-enhancement – a program that enhances positive areas of the brain while retarding the negative areas. In most cases that is all that is necessary for the individual to assume a safe and constructive position in society again."

"You said most cases ... what if that doesn't work. What about someone like Bestmarke? You know he'll never give up or cooperate."

"Sometimes we have to do a full neurological reconstruction," Guardian X bluntly said. "Simply put, their brain is wiped clean of all the bad and only good things are put back in."

"But doesn't that make them a different person? Aren't they kind of like a happy vegetable then?"

"That is an interesting analogy, Martin, but essentially correct. Now, however, they are no longer a danger to society and can live out their lives in tranquility. The cycle of vengeance and death is broken, peace is restored, and permanent healing for all involved can begin."

"So, really, hasn't their old personality been executed?"

"Perhaps, in a manner of speaking," Guardian X said. "But they are still alive and no longer pose a danger to the majority. There has to be some expense in order for justice to be satisfied."

Content with the answer, Martin asked another question. "How many countries are there on earth now?"

"Countries?" said Guardian X with a quizzical look. "There are no separate countries. The whole earth is one entity, or as you say, country."

"Well, where on Earth are we now? Where would we physically be right now, back in my time?"

If my ancient geography is correct, we are at the southern end of the Appalachian Mountains – what used to be Carolina, Tennessee, and Georgia in your time. Before that, it had another name," explained Guardian X. "We are inside the mountains, underground."

"Why are we underneath the mountains? Is the air poisonous and polluted outside?

"Not at all, Martin. In fact, the earth is like a paradise … everywhere," said Guardian X. "These mountains are among the oldest and most stable on earth. They are the safest location for our form of governmental operations. Here is where CENTRAL, our government, is located."

"Are you part of a ruling class?" Martin guessed. "You seem to have a lot of authority."

Guardian II stepped forward to continue the explanation. "The manner of rule now is somewhat different than in your time. You had many nations with different types of rule. The rule in your country was by democracy, I believe. Other countries had

TROPHY

monarchies, with royal families passing down the power. Others were dictatorial or authoritarian. Some types had more personal freedom, but less security ... others had the reverse," she continued. "All of them were subject to the thinking, attitudes, and qualities of those ruling. Even good and beneficial rulers eventually died or were replaced by those of less noble character," she said. "Couple that with wars, natural disasters, overuse of natural resources, as well as common human greed, and you have a recipe for disaster on an unprecedented scale."

"But that's the way it's always been," Martin said matter-of-factly. "How can you change such ingrained thinking?"

"By removing most of the human element," Guardian II said pointedly. "We are now governed completely by a giant computer and operating system. As Guardians, we protect and maintain the system called CENTRAL. We, as humans, do not rule. CENTRAL rules." She paused for this thought to sink in. "The study and history of all forms of government was used as a basis to derive the program for CENTRAL. Logic, stability, relative equality, and quickness in problem solving are some of the key principles in CENTRAL's makeup," she proudly said. "It is not a perfect system, but it provides peace, stability, security, and freedom from want for ninety-eight percent of the inhabitants of the Solar System."

"How many other places besides the earth do people live?" Martin asked in fascination. "Have you traveled to the stars yet or around the galaxy?"

"We have recently established new colonies on planets around the nearest stars, the Centaurus system," answered Guardian X, stepping forward again. "Because we have not yet discovered how to warp or fold space, we are limited to less than light-speed travel. Even to the closest stars it takes many years of space travel with the crews in suspended animation. But someday that will change. Once we learn the secret of folding space, the galaxy will be ours to explore," she said hungrily.

TROPHY

"How soon do you think that will happen?" quizzed Martin, completely enthralled.

"Hopefully within a generation," Guardian X excitedly continued. "We have made progress in faster-than-light communications, which is the first important step. Progress may seem slow, but on a cosmic level it is rapid."

"How far is the Centaurus system?" probed Martin. "How long does it take to get there?"

"Those stars are just over four light-years distant," replied Guardian X. "On deep space travel we can achieve speeds approaching ten percent of light speed. The one way journey took about fifty standard years. We recently received our first communications back from the new colony."

"You said ninety eight percent, what about the other two percent?" Martin asked methodically, narrowing his eyes.

"Some have chosen to be renegades, to live free from the regulations and rule of CENTRAL," answered Guardian X. "If that is their choice, it is by their own free will. Some are lawless and have been driven from society, or have escaped from the law and rehabilitation."

"Men like Bestmarke?" Martin sneered. "So far all I've seen are women. Has something happened to the men?"

A silence ensued. Guardian X glanced at Guardian II who continued the history lesson with their ancient pupil.

"To answer this fairly, we need to go back to the beginning; the beginning of the New Victorian Age, four hundred and seventy five years ago. In the Ancient Calendar, your calendar, Martin, that was the year 2065. At that time a great catastrophe happened on Earth. The partial collapse of the ecosystem created a host of diseases including some new or mutated forms of plague. These spread through all the Earth without exception. All the men died!" Guardian II took a deep breath and looked intently at Martin. "Yes, all the men on Earth fell to the disease as did many women, although they seemed more naturally resistant to this particularly virulent strain of plague," she said in a more subdued tone, her hands dropping to her sides.

She paused and looked away for a moment as if recalling a painful memory. Looking back at Martin, she continued, her voice somber, her face less animated. "We called that time the Great Sadness. Words cannot express the grief and sorrow for the entire world of that day. It appeared that chaos and despair would drive the world of that time, all the human race that remained, into extinction ... total extinction," she said, her eyes downcast. Looking up she continued. "But some far-seeing women, notably scientists, computer specialists, doctors, engineers, educators, politicians, and artists, to name a few, collectively worked together earth wide to save humanity. In short, their efforts succeeded after much effort and many tears. They all vowed to never let the Earth return to its divided, corrupt, and greed driven governments that led to this great cataclysm. The idea of an earth wide government by a centralized computer system was born in that same year. Although it took many years to complete and begin perfecting, the start of the New Victorian Age had begun with that brilliant concept and much hard work," she proudly said. She closely watched him as he digested this completely unexpected and profound scenario of prophetic events that now were history.

"But how have humans reproduced if all the men died?" Martin asked, trying to grasp the complete scope of the situation.

"The practice of artificial insemination was a fact of life in your time," Guardian II stated. "And semen banks around the world stored frozen sperm cells at near absolute zero. At such low temperatures the cells were protected from the plague that killed all the men. A smaller number of egg cells had been stored, too. But for some reason, they did not resist the disease and became contaminated. Only the male cells survived," she said matter-of-factly. "By carefully preserving them, the human race has continued to this day. Because all the women were exposed to the disease, all the children born after the Great Sadness have been affected. To this day, all males born have been sterile, unable to reproduce, as well as having no naturally occurring body hair. All females born are fertile, have hair, but pass on the inherited traits of their mothers. Their own male children continue to be sterile and hairless."

"Holy cow!" exclaimed Martin and the Guardians glanced at each other. "This is unbelievable! Do men and women still marry and have families? Artificial insemination was a moral issue and very controversial in my time. Is it now? And what about men? Do they govern, do they work? What do they do?"

"They still marry, Martin. And they help raise families and continue to work," Guardian II said gently. She looked directly at him, her tone serious. "But they do not govern or work in positions of authority. Not any more. In the New Beginning the Founding Mothers, in their great wisdom, determined that now that they had the power to rule, they would never give it up in a return to the old male dominated governments that had been so warlike, corrupt, and ineffective, ultimately leading to the Great Catastrophe and Great Sadness. Some freedoms would never be allowed again," she said resolutely.

"Wow," said Martin. "This is a lot to take in."

Guardian II gazed affectionately at Martin and mildly continued. "To answer your first question, Martin, artificial insemination is still a serious issue and not taken lightly. It is no longer a moral issue when you consider the alternative. Extinction is not a viable choice. The fact that women and men can marry and raise families is still a blessing. They can be happy and lead productive lives within a safe and secure government, CENTRAL."

"But if women rule, won't they have the same problems that men did? Won't some of them be warlike or tyrannical and try to dominate others? Aren't women as imperfect as men?" Martin asked.

"Yes, they are, and if women ruled we would have the same problems as in ancient times," said Guardian II. "But remember,

Martin, women do not rule – CENTRAL rules. Women only serve in positions of authority under the direction and rule of CENTRAL."

"But how can a computer rule? Isn't it just a complicated machine? Does it really think? This is going to take some time to understand," Martin said, his face full of uncertainty. He looked at them all in turn. "Here's my last question for now. What happens when all the semen banks are empty? Is that the end of humanity, as we know it?"

Guardian II paused before she answered. "You are a deep thinker, Martin Charles Bucklann. You see our ultimate dilemma. Our civilization ... our race ... is finite," she said, letting the words sink in. "And yet, you have brought us the most hope. Seeing and talking with you shows us that time travel is possible. And if done with the utmost care and planning, it is possible to once and for all solve our dilemma, and naturally continue the human race forever, as it should."

TROPHY

Chapter XXX

"Guardian, how is the ancient man progressing? Did he agree to a new android body?" Lieutenant Rogerton said, sitting in the spacious control lab of Guardian VII.

"He was enthusiastic about the prospect," answered the Guardian curled in her massive black chair. "We had first started the design soon after we learned of his existence, as the Fleet was returning to Earth. We anticipated his acceptance and continued on at full speed. We could only do so much, of course, until we were physically able to examine Franelli's handiwork in person. Our 'new man' is close to completion now," she said excitedly. "We are very anxious to restore his mobility, as he is. We do not know how much training or therapy will be required before he is back to normal, but so far the results have been beyond our dreams."

"Did you begin a new body for the panther at that time as well?" asked Rogerton directly.

"Yes, we did. In some ways it was simpler because we were forced to make many decisions ourselves instead of waiting to ask questions of the recipient. The human brain overall is more subtle than an animal's. In some areas, however, the panther's brain is exceptionally complex. Those functions that involve hearing, vision, stealth, patience, and sheer ferocity are amazing," she said, looking at the Lieutenant. "For both, the interface between the living tissue and the androidal network has been challenging in the extreme. We are making rapid progress with the panther, as we did with the man. Soon we will be ready to restore the panther, if that is his choice."

"And that is what I need to help him understand." The Lieutenant stood and impatiently wrung her hands. "How soon can we install the link for both of us?" she said, glancing at the Guardian.

"I am sure it will be different than a guider/pouncer program. From what I know, that program is more like a game."

"True, Lieutenant. This will be much more intense as it will be mind-to-mind with no game-program situation. We will place buffers in the link to try and reduce the effect of his ferocity which we expect to be severe," the Guardian said. "It will also be a very frightening and threatening feeling for the panther. He will not understand what is happening. You will understand, however, and it will be up to you to somehow calm him, gain his trust, and ultimately mentally bond with him," she said compassionately. "It will be a very difficult task … it may be impossible. On the other hand, it may happen very quickly. We really do not know."

"I am anxious to try as soon as we can make all the arrangements," said Rogerton. "The waiting is usually more difficult than the actual task."

"You may think so most of the time," cautioned Guardian VII, staring at the young Lieutenant. "This time I fear it will not be so."

*   *   *   *   *   *   *   *   *   *

"The head-gear needs to be somewhat tight, Lieutenant, so any quick movement of your head will not disturb the interface at your brain-stem," reminded the Guardian as she adjusted Rogerton's head-gear. "Emotions and feelings will become visible, as it were, to both of you. If you panic, you will be completely overwhelmed. We will closely monitor you both. If you start to panic, I will end the link. We know the panther will panic. Total calmness on your part is absolutely required," she said, walking back into the control room and sitting down at her instruments.

"I understand, Guardian. I will be as soothing and patient as I can," she assured the Guardian while trying to convince herself and calm her own anxiety.

TROPHY

"It will be necessary, in fact imperative, to search his mind and memories, finding areas he will respond to favorably. We do not know how to guide you in this," Guardian VII said over the intercom. "We have no definite procedure yet … it is still abstract and ill-defined. As you move in certain directions or areas, we will attempt to monitor what part of his brain you are stimulating. We will try to identify where you are and what feelings or memories you are affecting. Perhaps in this way we will be able to offer a measure of guidance."

"The unknown can be fearful, Guardian. Let us proceed with the hope of finally helping this poor creature, no matter how fear inspiring he may be. We as humans owe him that dignity and respect. Let us proceed," she determined, challenging and suppressing her own fears.

The Lieutenant sat in the lab research room two meters from the pedestal with the sleeping panther head. She did not directly face the big cat, but looked away to appear less threatening. A holographic jungle environment encircled them making it as life-like to the panther as possible.

"We are awakening the panther, Lieutenant," she heard in her brain. "We will allow him to stabilize his thought processes before we engage the link. We will count it down for you."

"Thank you, Guardian," she thought back.

The adrenaline was flowing strongly now as she braced her mind for this totally alien and unknown experience before her. She felt as if she was standing on the edge of an abyss.

"He is awake now. Do your best, Lieutenant. We will be with you constantly," she reassured her.

The panther stared at the familiar figure that was now somewhat closer, but showed no alarm. He had accepted her sitting close to him and no longer viewed her as a threat. A mild level of comfort showed on the monitors in the unseen control room.

TROPHY

Guardian VII said gently: "The link will be established in ten seconds, nine, eight ... three, two, one."

Lieutenant Rogerton felt the dream-like confusion of multiple emotions trying to focus as the interface gently pulled her thoughts and those of the panther into the same flowing stream of consciousness. It felt like a river, frighteningly deep, clear, and vaguely greenish, with currents and eddies along the edges. She felt shapes in the depths that were undefined and formless, but one seemed to be growing, like a hidden storm coming up from unseen depths. It was totally black with glowing suns like burning yellow eyes, and a form like a wide, gaping mouth, blood-red and hideous, constantly changing shape. The river all around was churned into brown mire and black whirlpools as the shape rose ever closer, boiling up the darkened waters into huge and frightening waves. Howling winds groaned and growled with merciless intensity, as they swirled screaming in their combined consciousness. The monstrous shape continued to well up from the depths, completely engulfing her, swirling in a vicious frenzy within her mind.

It was all Rogerton could do to remain calm and unmovable, so fearsome was the onslaught of the terrified panther. Never had she felt so small and vulnerable. There was no place to run, no refuge to hide in, or way to conceal herself from the undisciplined rage and terror of her attacker. The depth of her fear was beyond her experience. Only her trained and disciplined mind kept her restrained from total panic. She forced herself to concentrate on her pity for the animal, and why she had wanted to help it in the first place. She mentally shut her eyes and ears to the violent inferno circling around her, and emanated as much love and compassion as she could muster. She began speaking the same words she had repeatedly said previously to the panther: "I do not want to hurt you ... I want to help you." Over and over again she said these words, and tried to fix scenes in her mind of what they meant in relation to the panther.

TROPHY

After what seemed an eternity, she mentally opened her eyes and ears to discover an eerie quietness and stillness so different from the previous horrendous onslaught. The river was clear and calm in its greenish depths. The shapes she felt in it were formless and vague; the menacing black storm could not be sensed.

She reached out and approached one of the shapes that moved closer and surrounded her. She felt trees and plants, a forest with familiar paths and scents, the memories of the panther's ancient home, now long forgotten. A wave of sadness swept over her, and only with great difficulty could she force herself to leave.

She reached out and approached another shape that gently enveloped her, drowning her in memories of panther kittens … brothers and sisters tumbling and playing with each other in the cool grass of a hot summer day. One by one they grew older and disappeared, instilling another wave of sadness and loss; a family born to forget, each departing to go his separate way.

A great sense of loss came over her and she cried with despair in her heart, acutely sensing the loneliness of animals as they struggle through their desperate, often singular and tragic lives. Forcing herself again to leave, she cried at the seeming futility and emptiness that continually stalked them all.

Suddenly, she sensed the black shape approaching again, but more gently, cautiously. Slowly approaching, she lovingly touched it and led it to the shapes of hidden memories she had reluctantly left moments before. It, too, responded in sadness as she had done. Radiating love and compassion, she pictured in her mind a panther running and leaping again, free and strong. She continued to repeat this until finally the black shape glowed with a goldenness, making sounds that could only be construed as purring. The Lieutenant cried out in joy … she now had her answer! The great cat would soon be ready to run again!

She felt again the dream-like confusion as their joined consciousness gently separated; she and the panther were individuals again. She looked at the panther on the pedestal and smiled genuinely, feeling great joy. The panther continued to purr, more content than it had been in a long time.

Guardian VII remotely shut off the pedestal, the panther fell asleep again, and the Lieutenant returned to the control room.

"That was quite an ordeal, Lieutenant. How are you feeling? Your vital signs and brain waves are normal, even somewhat enhanced," the Guardian said, scanning her instruments.

"I am very tired, Guardian, but I feel happy and satisfied. It is hard to explain. It was terrifying, to say the least, but we were successful. He wants to run again! He essentially told me so by his response. Did you hear him purring?" Rogerton asked enthusiastically. "How long did it all take, Guardian?"

"You were linked for almost five hours. We were very concerned about you and the panther," she said seriously. "But you did admirably! Now we will really be able to help this poor creature and give him back his life." She stood and gave the Lieutenant a wide grin. "Please go and get some rest. We have a surprise tomorrow that we do not want you to miss."

"Thank you, Guardian," Rogerton said. "I wonder if it will top this experience?"

TROPHY

Chapter XXXI

Louis Franelli felt angry and troubled as he sat in the soft, black chair by the fireplace. He looked at Guardian V anxiously, remembering the young, tall woman he had worked with years ago. Her once coppery hair was now lightened by age. Her freckles were the same, though, as were her bright, widely spaced green eyes. She had put on a few kilos over the years but still looked trim in her simple uniform. He wondered why she was alone in the room with him, sitting in another chair, facing the holographic fire.

"We are very pleased with the degree of your cooperation, Louis," she said. She looked at him as if contemplating his thoughts. "We frankly thought you would resist completely."

"Then you really do not understand me, do you, Sondra?" he said roughly, staring at the dancing flames.

"Why do you continue to call me Sondra?" she said, turning to him. "Yes, that was my name years ago when we first worked together, but now I am just Guardian V."

"Well, I told you before, you are not my Guardian. No one is. I hate politics! I hate phony loyalties!" he scoffed, his intense light blue eyes brimming with contempt for any and all authority. "The Empire is just another system leading the blind along, stripping their real freedoms and controlling their lives, convincing them to be happy." He turned quickly in his chair and faced her. "Do you know what true happiness is? Do you really?" he asked. He continued his stare.

"To be honest, Louis, I do not know completely. I am content, though, and that is part of it," she said calmly, returning his gaze. "I would suppose that true happiness is too abstract to define absolutely, and that it means something different for each individual."

"Finally you have said something I can agree with," he said, looking at her more kindly.

The Guardian smiled at his answer. She studied him closely, trying to remember him as a younger man. Little had changed over the years. He was still tall and thin with a narrow face, wide shoulders, and large hands and feet. His nose was prominent, but it was his piercing, light blue eyes that drew your attention. His stare could be intimidating, but to her it was wonderfully familiar.

"So you really do not have a strong loyalty to Galen Bestmarke, then?" she probed, still contemplating his features. "Why did you help him so much? Because he rescued you from a prison term?"

"He didn't rescue me, he abducted me. He offered me the choice of 'working' for him or returning to my unjust prison term. I had the choice of comfortable servitude or incarceration. I chose to serve him and he paid me well," he answered plainly, turning back to the fire. "He let me do my work with total freedom. No one was looking over my shoulder and asking questions about moral responsibility. No one was telling me 'No, you cannot do that for this or that reason'. He let me think unhindered. For me, that is true freedom and happiness. Without shackles or blinders, my mind runs free. With controls, my mind shuts down and I am stifled. I want to do pure research, wherever it leads me. I am not concerned with varying opinions on moral values."

"Yes, that is where the problems came in when you were here at CENTRAL years ago," Guardian V empathized, returning her gaze to the fire. "Some did not, could not, accept the direction that portions of your research was leading. They tried to force you in a certain direction and you resisted. You did not follow their rules."

She vividly recalled the compu-court session.

"Mr. Franelli," the Prime Adjudicator had said. "Please tell the court what your position is at CENTRAL."

184

TROPHY

"I am a senior researcher, I am not a killer or a madman as some have stated," he spitefully said.

"Please, Mr. Franelli, just answer the question in an orderly and factual way. Your opinion will not be considered at this time."

"When will it be considered?" Louis said, raising his voice. "Don't my opinions and thoughts matter? This court is a sham, just like other parts of your precious Empire."

"Mr. Franelli, please control your remarks. They will not be held against you but they waste time. We are only interested in the facts ... in the truth."

"Very well," said Louis. "I will answer your questions truthfully."

"Good," said the Prime Adjudicator. "Please tell us the nature of your research."

"I have projects involving cybernetics and artificial intelligence. I have a number of nuclear engineering projects. These involve power supplies of a relatively small scale."

"What would you consider your most important project, Mr. Franelli?"

"The project in which I have invested the most time and resources is the study of the Keyhole Anomaly."

"What do you think the Keyhole is?" asked the Prime Adjudicator. "How dangerous do you think it is?"

"It is my conclusion that it is a conduit through time," Louis said. "It is little understood and extremely dangerous."

"What do you base your conclusions on, Mr. Franelli?"

"Observations and calculations," stated Louis. "The observations are based on factually gathered evidence. The calculations are based, in part, on theory supported by the observations, but not totally so."

"Have your calculations been tested?"

"Not completely," Louis said. "Some parts have ... perhaps thirty percent."

185

TROPHY

"And what did they show, Mr. Franelli?"

"They showed promise in some areas, but were not as conclusive as we had hoped."

"Did you share your results with anyone else?" probed the Prime Adjudicator.

"Yes. Researcher Sondra Anderson helped me gather the observations and develop and test the calculations."

"Is that statement accurate, Researcher Anderson?"

"Yes, Ma'am, we collaborated on gathering the observations and on much of the theoretical calculations," Sondra said.

"Thank you," said the Prime Adjudicator. "Mr. Franelli, did you share your work with anyone else?"

"That's irrelevant – I refuse to answer," Louis stated. "That should not matter."

"But it does matter and that is why I ask you again: Did you share your work with anyone else?"

"I will not answer," said Louis defiantly.

"Did you share your calculations with Carolyn Rogerton, a Pilot on the Research Ship *Rosella*?" continued the Prime Adjudicator. "And did she pilot the *Rosella* into the Keyhole and disappear with a presumed loss of twenty lives and a research vessel?"

"She did do that," admitted Louis. "But she acted presumptuously … against my instructions. I specifically warned her not to attempt to enter the Keyhole."

"Did Carolyn Rogerton understand the calculations, Mr. Franelli?"

"Yes! I was amazed! I could speak to her and she knew what I was saying. She was brilliant and could visualize the calculations and knew how to apply them to the Keyhole. Had I known of her impulsiveness I would have limited my information to her."

"Why did you not tell CENTRAL of her knowledge of the calculations and her impulsiveness to apply them? Surely you were aware of the professional consequences of sharing highly technical and dangerous information with unauthorized personnel?"

"I never dreamed she would try to navigate it until we were sure the calculations were correct," Louis said with a pained expression. "I had warned her many times – I thought she realized the danger."

"Researcher Anderson, were you aware of this situation, that Carolyn Rogerton knew of the calculations and the theory of time-travel through the Keyhole?"

"Rogerton was helpful in our obtaining the astronomical observations as were others on the crew of the *Rosella*, Ma'am. I knew she was interested in our results but I knew nothing of her knowledge of the calculations or applying them."

"Would you say that Mr. Franelli acted with neglect in disclosing the calculations to her?" said the Prime Adjudicator.

"No, not really," Sondra said. "They were theories ... they were unproven. She should never have taken it upon herself to try them."

"Mr. Franelli, you have been accused of wrong doing. Specifically: professional misconduct by sharing highly technical and dangerous information with an unauthorized person or persons. Do you feel the accusation is justified?"

"No, I do not!" he said vehemently. "As scientists we share information and collaborate with each other. Sometimes we gain valuable ideas from people who are not on the 'list'. Many times the results are greater than the sum of the parts. Important breakthroughs have been accomplished by sharing information. To put controls on that freedom is to control our thinking and our progress."

"Mr. Franelli, the Court agrees that you were unaware that Pilot Carolyn Rogerton would take matters into her own hands and attempt to navigate the Keyhole. However, you are held professionally responsible for sharing information with Rogerton that she had no authorization to see or study. Therefore, action must be taken against you for sharing your calculations," said the Prime Adjudicator. "But, the presumed loss of twenty lives as well as the loss of Empirical property requires there must be an accounting. This is a mandatory law of the New Victorian Empire. Violation of the Code of Conduct for Professional Researchers must also be accounted for. Therefore, the Court orders Louis Franelli to be banned from engaging in any and all research at CENTRAL from this time forward. The Court also orders Louis Franelli to serve a term of incarceration, the length to be determined, at the Luna One Rehabilitation Institute. You will be required to leave CENTRAL immediately under full escort. Your term will begin now."

"But Prime Adjudicator, this is not fair!" yelled Sondra. "Louis has done nothing wrong – this is not just!"

"I am sorry, Researcher Anderson. The Court has ruled."

"It is just like I said – this court is a sham!" Louis yelled. "It's a reflection of the rest of your phony Empire. Someday CENTRAL will pay for this injustice!"

"Mr. Franelli, the Court has ruled. Please step down. Guards, take him into custody."

The memories of that day were clear and painful to Guardian V. And yet events had recently turned around with surprising quickness. She studied Louis as he gazed at the fire, lost in thought. "The Guardians desire life and freedom for everyone, Louis. Is that also how you feel?" she asked quietly.

"I am as passionate about life and freedom as they are. I believe in preserving life if I am able. But I speak for myself only. I cannot control those I work for," he said, glancing briefly at her to make his point. "I was bitter with the Empire when Bestmarke took me, so I willingly built weapons for him. Vengeance was all that mattered to me. But I soon tired of his consuming hatred for the Empire. I was dismayed to realize how much like him I was becoming, and I felt a great longing to return to my research and my friends at CENTRAL. But that was now impossible. I was a wanted man, banned from CENTRAL, with no real friends," Louis recalled. "My existence was empty except for my research. Research became my whole life, and that is why I continued to work for Bestmarke. He eventually offered me my freedom but where could I go? He provided all my needs and encouraged my research. Although I often didn't agree with his thinking, he didn't stifle mine in any way," Louis said pointedly. "In fact, it was my idea to develop his trophy preservation systems. He was content to hang their heads on the wall, dead and stuffed. I convinced him to let them live. I realize that their quality of life is not the same, but they are still alive, and perhaps their lives can someday be improved. He gave me freedom to choose, so I did the same with him, nothing more. Like I said, I do not believe in contrived loyalty." He turned back to watch the flames.

These were new thoughts to the Guardian. Never before had Louis Franelli been so candid. Was there a ring of truth in his raspy voice? She hoped so because her feelings of compassion and gentle affection for this brilliant and eccentric man had been growing since his arrival back at CENTRAL. Working together years ago she had felt the same, but his intensity and overwhelming desire for his research projects had left him singularly focused, seemingly without any need for companionship. Perhaps with age and new hope in his life, he was ready for a relationship beyond his work and research.

"I understand you, Louis," she said, turning more toward him. "But how do you feel about real loyalty? What about loyalty among good, close friends, or between two people who care deeply for each other?"

As if lost in thought, Louis stared into the fire and did not answer her immediately. Contemplating her next words and trying to determine their appropriateness she finally blurted out: "I have always cared for you, Louis, but I have never really understood you, until today. I fear that has been a great failing on my part for which I am truly sorry. Can we be close friends, Louis? Will you accept that kind of loyalty?" she pleaded.

Continuing to look away, he seemed torn in his emotions as if struggling to assess his own feelings, contemplating how to answer this bold revealing of deep felt emotions long restrained. Finally he turned and looked her in the eyes. His eyes were more subdued and gentle. "Sondra," he quietly said. "Please, let me call you Sondra for that is what you have always been to me, and we speak now in personal terms. I must speak honestly, I owe you that. Expressing my feelings has always been difficult. You have always been a good friend to me, but I do not know if I am truly capable of that leap of faith, the faith to be loyal to someone other than myself," he said with resignation.

"Think about it, Louis. Ponder over it in your mind and heart … you have to be honest with yourself," she said patiently. "I will accept whatever decision you make."

TROPHY

Chapter XXXII

Earth Date: 475 N.V.A.
Location: Asteroid Belt

"Are you sure that your contact will follow through, Mr. Cedric?" questioned the Izax, contemplating his final decision from his plush, black leather chair in his office. "I do not favor repeating payments when one payment should do."

"Yes, Izax, the Lieutenant in question ..."

"Stop! Choose your words carefully, Mr. Cedric," he cautioned, standing and dramatically raising his gloved hand. "Never tell me names, rank, or any person that could implicate my part in this. Remember, I must not know any names, I am invisible. This must be arranged to appear as Bestmarke's work. They are expecting him to come after Franelli ... we must not disappoint them."

"Sorry, Sir," Cedric groveled, uncomfortably tugging at the collar of his dark gray suit. "Our contact is high ranking and intimately familiar with the layout of CENTRAL. She knows the corridors least monitored, and where the walls are more easily breached. However, there are sensors virtually everywhere, so we are planning to use a device similar to the cloaking mechanism on a star ship."

"But those take enormous power, the kind of power generated by the fusion reactor of a star ship," he said, sitting back down, adjusting his tight, red velvet suit jacket. "How can you possibly get something that big into CENTRAL?"

"That is the beauty of this new device, Sir," Cedric said, trying to appear more confident. "The mechanism is not big at all, only about the size of a large luggage case. The critical part is focusing power to it. We plan to use four star ships in earth orbit at the critical angles of focus. Each will focus a different, very tightly configured energy beam of a specific frequency to the mechanism. The device will then combine the different frequencies to form the proper spectrum to feed the device and generate the power for the cloak. The cloak will be absolute; it will render everyone and everything under it totally invisible to every form of sensor."

"How large will the area of invisibility actually be?" asked the Izax.

"A radius of seven hundred and fifty meters," Cedric said. "It is a huge area and that is why four ships are necessary to generate the enormous amount of power needed."

"Will not your ships be noticed as they generate the energy beams?" said the Izax, squinting at him.

"The energy beams will mimic standard communication transfer beams but with much higher power. Only another ship in very close proximity would notice it. We will just be careful that no other ships are close by."

"Very good!" praised the Izax. "How will you get through the walls into the heart of the great computer?"

"A 'can-opener', a nuclear cutter from an Octopus unit," Cedric proudly said. "We were finally able to obtain one. They are very fast and relatively silent. We can tap the power of the cloaking mechanism to drive it."

"How ironic, for that is how they captured Franelli in the first place," laughed the Izax. "Tell me, how many operatives will you have for this little piece of business?"

"Four should do nicely. With the help of our contact, it will be relatively easy to slip four into the system."

"I see, Mr. Cedric. This all seems very good, very well planned. But just how will you bring in your operatives and take out Franelli with PCC ships everywhere?"

"A small space-plane will be used that also employs a cloaking mechanism, focusing power from the four star ships," Cedric said, brimming with confidence. "Timing will be crucial, but we have been studying the flight patterns and times of regular air traffic. There are a number of opportunities that will work."

"You are quite sure of your plan, Mr. Cedric? What odds do you give for your success?" he asked inquisitively, a gleam in his eyes.

"We are ninety-five percent sure of success," he boasted. "If everything goes as planned and the Empire does not stumble upon us by accident, it should be relatively easy and quick. A little luck is always in the equation."

"I have a small change in the plans that will be to your benefit, and I will still pay you the full price. You see how generous I can be? Here is my little change: Bestmarke's ship will be cloaked and in high earth orbit. You will be given the exact coordinates to rendezvous with him and transfer Franelli. Then our brazen Mr. Bestmarke can make a run for it, and receive all the glorious attention from our beloved Empire. It saves you a long trip back here, and allows you to go about your business immediately, drawing no attention to yourself or, most importantly, to me."

"I like the plan, Izax. However, there is one small question that I have," Cedric said, more seriously. "When and where will I be paid?"

"And that is an excellent question, Mr. Cedric. I must compliment you, you are starting to think like me!" said the Izax. "You make regular freight runs to Luna One, don't you?"

"Yes, Sir, I have a regular schedule, just like clockwork."

"Good. At your next drop on Luna One, after you have delivered Mr. Franelli, your payment in full will be waiting for you at your loading dock. It will be hidden in a scan-proof shipment bound for New London on Mars. It will appear as ordinary food stuffs. At least that is what the blocking device will tell the scanners. Load it as normal and do not open it until you are well on your way and you are sure no one is following you," the Izax said, pointing his finger at

TROPHY

him. "Can you do that, Mr. Cedric? If you are thorough, I am sure we can do business again."

"I am always thorough, Izax. I have to be."

"You will need to be this time, Mr. Cedric," cautioned the Izax, an unusual seriousness about him. "No one in four hundred and seventy five years has broken into CENTRAL."

TROPHY

Chapter XXXIII

Earth Date: 475 N.V.A.

Location: CENTRAL, Earth

"Do you know what the surprise is, Star-Commander?" questioned Lieutenant Rogerton, walking from their rooms to the Chambers where they had first met the Guardians.

"I am not sure, but I think it has something to do with the ancient man. They did not really tell me much, though. I find the situation very intriguing," she said enthusiastically. "We will find out soon enough," she said, smiling as they approached the Chamber doors.

The cozy fire added to the relaxed atmosphere. More chairs were in the room and more Guardians, too, than their first encounter. As before, they wore simple white uniforms, each identified by a ten-pointed black onyx star by the left shoulder. The Lieutenant counted nine in all. Three were familiar as she recognized Guardians I, II, and X. She wondered at the absence of Guardian VII. The other six were new to her, but she felt the warmth and kindness in their gentle demeanor. All were standing except Guardian I who was very old and preferred sitting comfortably by the fire. Had she been standing, she would have been quite tall. Her gray hair was divided into two long braids falling nearly to her slender waist, one on each side of her finely wrinkled, reddish-skinned face. Keen and sharp were her black eyes with a look of great wisdom and tranquility.

She watched the young Lieutenant and caught her eye. Smiling broadly, she motioned for her to come over. "Sit down, please, my dear young Lieutenant," her voice resonated youthfully. "I am Guardian I. We have met briefly before and I have been very anxious to finally speak with you. Guardian VII has kept me informed of your remarkable progress with the panther. You have deep feelings for animals, it seems. That is a gift. You remind me of my ancestors, the Lakota Sioux. Many, many generations ago they lived on the plains of ancient North America. They were a noble race in tune with nature, and they understood the animals and cycles of Earth. That understanding has all but disappeared now," she said sadly. "But sometimes these qualities reappear in surprising intensity," she beamed, looking the Lieutenant directly in the eyes.

Her words touched the Lieutenant's heart and she felt drawn to this wise old woman. "I am deeply honored to meet you, Guardian. I regret that I know little about your ancestors and their obvious great love for Earth. To have that kind of love would indeed be riches beyond compare," she said, gazing into the ageless eyes of the Guardian.

"You are beginning to understand, my dear, and your wisdom and appreciation will only continue to grow," she whispered. "We will talk more of this later. Guardian II now has interesting and exciting news for us."

As if on cue, Guardian II asked them all to sit. With obvious delight and animated facial expressions, she began her presentation. "We are happy to be gathered here for this momentous occasion in the history of the New Victorian Empire. We are seeing historic progress that may help us in solving our greatest dilemma of fully perpetuating the human race forever," she said encouragingly. "As you know, we have been working hard to complete the android body for the ancient man. That has now been accomplished, and Guardian VII has informed us of the successful connection and restoration of the man, Martin Charles Bucklann," she said excitedly. And then with enthusiasm she announced: "I am pleased at this time to present him to you!"

The door at the far end opened widely revealing a happy, smiling, Guardian VII clutching the arm of a tall man walking smoothly beside her. There was, indeed, a collective gasp and then

TROPHY

applause as the couple walked into the room. Guardian VII said with great pride: "May I present to you all, Martin Charles Bucklann!"

The Lieutenant looked at him with admiration. She also realized that the heart of every woman there was instantly stolen by this tall, athletic looking man with looks that harkened back to a time beyond any of their memories but for ancient photographs and legends. Wearing the dark forest-green uniform of the Planetary Control Corps, he stood tall, smiling at them, and spoke in a strong, steady voice.

"I've never had much speaking experience before, but I feel it is important to tell you ladies what's on my mind and in my heart. I am thankful and grateful for being alive. And just look at me – I really can't believe it myself," beamed Martin, holding out his arms to the group. "It's miraculous! It's truly amazing what Guardian VII has done for me. All I can say is thank you from the bottom of my heart. It's hard to find the right words to tell you how grateful I am for what the Empire has done, but you have given me back hope when all my hope was gone. When I was Bestmarke's trophy, trapped in that pedestal, my life looked black with no way out for me or my father. Now it's like the sun has come up and I can see my way again. Now I see how I can help my father, too. For the first time in my life I have a real purpose – you know, something I feel that I must do. I must help capture Bestmarke so we can rescue my father." Martin paused as if reflecting on a distant memory before continuing. Then he stood more at attention and raised his right hand with his palm facing the group. "I promise to serve the Empire in whatever way that I can. I promise to work hard to change the situation that brought me here, and to bring Bestmarke and his cohorts to justice for their crimes against the Empire. I will help in any way I can to prevent the extinction of the human race, and do it in a way that brings dignity, honor, and peace to everyone." He lowered his right arm and with a gentle smile looked at everyone in the room. "Thank you for being my friends, my true friends, when I didn't have any. Thank you for helping me when my life looked black and empty. Thank you, my friends," he said, his voice strong with emotion.

For a few seconds the only sound heard was the hiss and crackle of the fire. Twelve women watched, totally enraptured. Some had tears running down their faces, all had strongly beating hearts. Loud applause and joyful comments followed as they voiced their praise and approval. They could scarcely believe their eyes, so well constructed and life-like was his android body. They all wanted to touch him, to feel his strength and the smoothness of his skin ... to marvel at his perfect physique.

He talked and listened to all the Guardians, especially Guardian I and Guardian II who found it difficult to relinquish their attention to him. Finally, he approached Lieutenant Rogerton and Star-Commander VanDevere and spoke first to VanDevere. "I want to thank you, Star-Commander, because you helped so much in my rescue. Your leadership and guidance made it possible for me to be saved. Thank you so much," he said bowing deeply, completely unsettling the usually stoic Star-Commander. All she could stammer in reply was a quiet, "You're welcome, Martin."

He turned to Lieutenant Rogerton, momentarily gazing at her blue-green eyes, the tiny freckles on her small straight nose, and her thick auburn hair tumbling upon her shoulders, glistening in the firelight. Almost instinctively, he gently took her hand, and bowing low, kissed it tenderly. Letting go, he stood and looked her in the eyes. "I owe the most thanks to you, Lieutenant. You rescued me from Bestmarke's ship and made it possible for me to live and hope again. You saved me from despair. I'm forever thankful to you, Lieutenant Janet Rogerton," he said, bowing low again.

The Lieutenant thought her heart was going to jump from her chest. She sensed the heated rush of blood into her face, totally overwhelmed by the simple beauty and sublime elegance of the moment.

"Thank you, Martin," she softly mustered as if in a daze. She just looked at him, enamored and speechless, taken by the moment and her own hopeful thoughts.

Martin continued to gently study her face until he heard Guardian VII approaching. "Please, Martin," Guardian VII said happily. "Come sit down, we still have some important matters to consider." She took his arm and led him to one of the chairs, all eyes following him as he sat down.

"We want to give our highest praise to Guardian VII, and her staff, for a job well done!" said Guardian II, her expressive face beaming with joy. "Would you all agree that her final results are remarkable?"

Joyous applause ensued, finally dying down, allowing Guardian II to continue. "The completion of the android body for Martin is indeed a milestone and a great accomplishment. However, the general knowledge of this whole situation and how Martin arrived here in the first place must be kept strictly confidential," she said with authority. "If the facts were known that time travel in its truest sense is possible, the repercussions to society within the Empire could be devastating and far reaching. To the lawless factions outside, the temptation of time travel through the Keyhole would be too much for them to resist. We would have to guard it constantly. It would become a continuous battle, and the expense would be great in lives and resources," Guardian II said.

"We cannot hide Martin and ultimately the panther, too, nor should we desire to hide them. Their lives need to be more open and deserving of the dignity we can afford them," Guardian II said. "Therefore, we need to present them as the latest technological breakthrough in cybernetic android research. They will be presented as one hundred percent fully working machines, total androids." She paused for a moment. "Really, this is true for the most part as only their heads are truly alive. We will continue the ruse as a protection

TROPHY

for the Empire, for Martin, and the panther. We will assign them to space duty to limit their interaction with other people."

Guardian II paused again and Martin raised his hand. "Yes, Martin would you like to speak once more?"

"Uh ... yes, Ma'am, I would if it's okay," Martin said. "I really didn't plan to say anything more but I feel it's important for you all to know that I completely agree with this arrangement. It's been seventeen long years since my father disappeared. My mother and I suffered terribly all those years, not knowing what really happened. And now she is suffering even more because I'm gone, too. That really breaks my heart," Martin said, his voice cracking.

The room grew respectfully quiet as he paused for a moment, looking down, struggling to control his emotions. Finally he looked up again, his jaw firmly set. "Like I said, I agree with the plan because it will give me the chance to help capture Bestmarke – to hunt him down, capture his ship, and rescue my father. I hope that time-travel will be figured out so the situation that brought my father and I here can be reversed. I hope that somehow I can reverse the pain that my mother is continuing to go through. Guardian VII has given me great strength and power in my new body. I will continue to look to the Empire for direction in using my new power to accomplish the most good!"

All twelve women immediately rose to their feet with a loud burst of applause. Martin continued to stand, a peaceful look on his face. Guardian II continued to applaud and invited Star-Commander VanDevere to continue.

"As you can see by his uniform, Martin will be assigned a position of responsibility on one of our ships. A rapid and aggressive training program in the rigors of space-duty will be started for him immediately," she said, looking over to him. "Guardian VII hopes to have Martin and the panther working together as a dynamic team. If she is successful we will combine their extraordinary strength, speed, and agility in our quest to capture Bestmarke and his ship."

TROPHY

She sat down and all eyes turned to Guardian I as she rose, lifted up her hands, and concluded. "Four hundred seventy five years of stability and relative peace hang in the balance. History will be the final judge of our decisions and actions, as will the continuation of the New Victorian Empire, as we know it," she said soberly. "We must proceed with careful thought and wisdom, always remembering our ultimate goal of preserving the human race forever."

They all stood and concluded by raising their clenched left fists over their hearts.

TROPHY

Chapter XXXIV

"He looks so real, Guardian. His jet black hair and long tail are perfect! He is so big and muscular ... Look at the size of his paws! His claws appear extremely sharp and deadly looking. He is exceedingly admirable ... but formidable, too," said Lieutenant Rogerton as she watched the screen. "Is he ready to be awakened?"

"In a few more minutes," replied Guardian VII, seated at her controls and instruments, not even looking up. "I want to run a few more tests of his circuitry, particularly the interface between his living tissue and the primary androidal circuits. To this point everything has worked well, just as with our ancient man Martin. He turned out very well, do not you agree, Lieutenant?"

Very well indeed, Rogerton thought to herself, remembering their previous meeting at his presentation to the Guardians. No one before had ever touched her heart like he had done when he gently kissed her hand and spoke those kind words to her. It still resonated within her like a scene from a fairy tale she had read long ago as a young girl. She sighed, absently looking away.

"Lieutenant?" said the Guardian, looking at her curiously.

"Yes, Guardian? ... Oh! ... Yes! He turned out very well. Yes, very well indeed," she quickly said, her face blushing slightly.

The Guardian smiled broadly and looked down again at her instruments. "Martin will be helping us with the panther's training once you and the big cat have fully completed your bonding process. You are both very close now. There is one more critical phase, though. While he was in the pedestal, you were in control. Now he will feel his strength, power, and speed. He may try to dominate you. He is deadly now, and he may figure that out, so we will take every precaution for your safety. If he seems to go out of control, we will shut him off immediately. We fully expect your bonding to hold, but we are prepared if it does not."

"If it doesn't hold, that may break my heart, too," she said absently, her mind drifting off again.

"There, the testing is done. Let us now awaken him," the Guardian finalized, looking up from her controls.

The panther was in a much larger room for this test. Thick tropical foliage and the chirps and cries of insects, birds, and monkeys were faithfully reproduced by the holographic generator. The humid smell of sweet decay completed the authentic jungle landscape.

"Now that he is complete, Lieutenant, he deserves a name. What do you think?" she said, turning to her.

"I have pondered the question with no suitable results. Let us keep it honest, and call him Panther," Rogerton shrugged.

"Panther it will be," she agreed, smiling widely. "Panther! Wake up!" she said, turning on his main power. They continued to watch him on the control room screen, hidden from his view.

After sixty agonizingly long seconds, his large, golden, feline eyes snapped open. He sniffed the air and stretched his great powerful body. His eyes seemed to glow more golden and widen as he excitedly recognized his renewed mobility. He took a few cautious steps before bolting across a grassy meadow the way a young kitten would scamper across a green lawn in the sunlight, its tail cocked at an angle, and its fur raised in the delightful joy of life and movement. He ran, jumped, and pounced to his heart's delight, all seemingly without effort.

"Will he ever get tired?" asked the Lieutenant. "I have never seen so much boundless energy."

"Only if his mind becomes fatigued," stated the Guardian, watching him as if spellbound. "Remember, most of him is nuclear powered. We will let him run for a while. It will be a good test for his circuits and controls."

TROPHY

And run he did. In play, he attacked a fallen tree, ripping
the bark to shreds with his powerful claws. Biting a large branch,
he discovered that his long, sharp teeth still functioned perfectly.
The Guardian and Lieutenant looked at each other wide-eyed at the
forceful, deadly display.

"I hope he still likes and remembers me," said the Lieutenant
sheepishly.

"We will soon find out," cautioned the Guardian. "At first,
I will slow him down so he will not harm you accidentally in his
exuberance." She adjusted her controls. "Is your headgear tight,
Lieutenant? You may enter the room when you are ready. Speak to
him in your mind and reassure him … remind him quickly who you
are. His link controls are permanently wired in, but your headgear is
not. If he plays too rough, he may jar it loose or knock it from your
head. If you feel he should be shut off, tell me immediately. Do your
best, Lieutenant," she said cheerily.

With a lump in her throat and the memory of the roaring lion
on Bestmarke's ship still lingering in her mind, Lieutenant Rogerton
slowly entered the room.

"Panther, it is me," she thought, emanating love, friendship,
and compassion for the great animal that was slowly walking toward
her. The dream-like confusion of shared emotions cleared as the
interface combined their thoughts into the same deep, clear river of
consciousness.

"Panther, it is me. I love you," she repeated over and over in
her mind.

The panther slowly walked toward her. In Rogerton's mind
a black shape from deep in the river of their joined consciousness
approached her cautiously, as if unsure. Slowly and steadily it
began to glow with goldenness as she reassured it of her love and
friendship. At that very moment Panther finally reached her, rubbing
his large head affectionately against her, almost pushing her over. She

laughed and then cried joyfully, stroking his head and neck, hugging him tightly.

"I am turning up his power level to normal," informed the Guardian to Rogerton's side of the link.

Panther started to run while the Lieutenant did her best to keep up. Although she was in excellent physical condition, she was no match for the powerful cat that ran and played with her, instinctively doing so as if with a younger and smaller cat. He tried to be gentle, but his new found mobility sometimes got the better of him, and more than once the Lieutenant went sprawling on the ground. She laughed, making a game of it, and Panther seemed delighted.

He leaped and she dodged a number of times. He leaped again more quickly, but she didn't anticipate his speed. As a result, he hit her directly, knocking off her headgear, and driving her to the ground. Her head forcefully struck the ground and she lay very still.

Guardian VII watched intently, her finger resting on the control that would immediately shut off the great cat, but waited to see his response. Panther just looked at her for a moment, and then slowly walked over. With his large, raspy, pink tongue, he began licking her face and purring loudly. He continued until she woke up, bleary eyed and relieved with his affectionate response. Still purring, he sat next to her and she hugged him again, her head throbbing with pain, but feeling happy. Panther finally curled up and went to sleep as the Guardian slowly shut him off.

Lieutenant Rogerton slowly got up, retrieved her headgear, and stiffly hobbled back through the door into the control room, holding her hand against her aching head.

"That went very well," she said, grimacing from the pain. "He remembered me, even without the link."

"You were extraordinary, Lieutenant, but now you need some medical attention and rest." The Guardian quickly called for the medics. "We have accomplished much today, though. Our next step will be with the ancient man, Martin."

TROPHY

Immediately two Medical Specialists in light pink uniforms arrived and gently helped the bruised and battered Lieutenant to the infirmary.

"You appear to have been through a battle, Ma'am," remarked one of the Specialists.

"It was a battle of sorts," she replied, smiling weakly. "But we won."

TROPHY

Chapter XXXV

"Panther is responding well," remarked Guardian VII as she curled cat-like in her large office chair. "He is progressing just as you have done, Martin. Tell me, do you ever feel tired or fatigued? Yesterday, Lieutenant Rogerton and I observed that our great cat, who is now named Panther, seems to have boundless energy reserves. Are you also experiencing that phenomenon?" she asked.

"Yes, I am, Guardian," he said, his powerful arms crossed on his chest. "My brain seems to get worn out and my eyes need some rest for a few hours each day, otherwise they get sore and red. Physically I never grow tired. I can run and work hard continuously with no pain – and I never need to rest. I'd make the perfect workaholic, I guess."

"Workaholic, Martin?" smirked the Guardian. "I have not heard that expression before, but I get the point," she laughed softly. "Your ancient expressions can be very humorous at times. However, your expressions last week at the presentation were most eloquent. Have you always been so gifted with your speech and manners?"

"No, not at all. In fact, I've always been shy and kept to myself. However, I've had a lot of time to think since my rescue and since you gave me my new body. I don't need much rest so I have plenty of time to meditate on what I learn. I've discovered many new things reading and watching your fancy televisions. Guardian I and Guardian II have answered my questions and have filled me in on a lot of history. But I think I've worn them out since I never get tired," Martin smiled.

Guardian VII laughed again. "I have never seen anyone wear down those tough ladies. I would love to be the proverbial gecko on the ceiling and see how you did it," she teased.

TROPHY

"I guess it's pretty funny now that I look back," Martin grinned. "But they really helped me a lot and made me look at myself in ways that I have never done before. They helped me look deep inside myself and be happy with what I saw. They also exposed things in me I didn't like but showed me what to do about it. I've discovered how to speak my mind and show what's really in my heart. They taught me how to look at people below the surface for what they really are, or what they could be, their infinite potential," he said. "I've grown ... actually, I've been forced to grow. It's been painful at times, but I think the results are positive. Don't you think so, Guardian?"

"I agree, Martin. You have impressed and charmed us all. It has been eye-opening to see your rapid progress, and to be part of it, too," she replied warmly. "I might add that you have made quite an impression on our young Lieutenant Rogerton. She almost seems distracted at times," the Guardian said, watching him closely.

Martin thought deeply before speaking again. "It wasn't my purpose to charm her. If she hadn't taken me from Bestmarke's ship, even unknowingly, I would have been hopeless. She saved me, Guardian," he said with conviction. "She is beautiful and has touched my heart. I would have been intimidated by her before. She is a remarkable woman, and I've tried to truthfully tell her that and how grateful I am for what she did."

"I believe you, Martin." said the Guardian, gazing at him with affection. "And yet your sincere words have done more than thank her. You have touched her heart, too. Accept it as something good and precious. And if the opportunity affords itself, build on it. It could bring both of you great happiness."

"Thank you, Guardian, I appreciate your wisdom." Martin was quiet for a few moments before shifting his thoughts. "All my life I've pretty much kept to myself, kind of like a hermit. Now I'll probably be around more people ... and that's okay. I can see that I need to come out of my shell a little more. I guess what's bothering me is ... well, you know, how will people look at me? What will they think of me and Panther?"

"How do you mean?" asked Guardian VII.

"I know that even though me and Panther are mostly machines we will be presented to the general population as total machines, as androids. I love that word ... 'android'. Maybe it should be ... 'mandroid'," he chuckled. "Anyway, I agree with that decision because time-travel must be kept secret. But how will we be looked at or thought of? Will we be considered freaks? Since Panther is an animal, he will probably be more easily accepted. But how will people look at me?"

"Those of us who really know you accept you as a man, Martin. Unfortunately, we are a small group. Nevertheless, we accept you completely ... one hundred percent. If the general public accepts you differently it will help you learn patience and humility, traits that are essential for true growth and happiness," she continued, tapping her fingers on the desk. "At times your experiences will not be easy, but at other times will be most rewarding. Life forces compromise upon us. How we deal with it reveals our maturity. You will be able to deal with this situation successfully. You have already demonstrated that to us," she encouraged.

"But what if people ask why the androids look like an ancient man and a panther?" Martin said. "Won't that create even more questions?"

"The other Guardians and I had these same questions, Martin. We considered alternatives such as removing all your hair so you would appear as a typical man of this era. What do you think of that plan?"

Martin looked away and lightly touched the top of his head and the side of his beard. With a doubtful expression on his face he turned back to the Guardian. "No ... I don't think I'd like that. I've already lost enough of my body. But I'd do it if you all thought it was the best thing to do," he conceded.

TROPHY

"That option would work well for you," Guardian VII said. "What about Panther, though? Do we remove all his hair, too?" she said, a twinkle in her eye. "Think of the attention that would draw to him ... and also to our credibility, not to mention our sanity!"

"A hairless panther wouldn't inspire much fear," laughed Martin. "Maybe pity. He'd probably be pretty embarrassed, too."

"No doubt he would," laughed the Guardian. "We decided to keep you both as you are and be honest with your looks. We will shield you as much as possible from the general populace. We know you will stand out, but we hope this obvious difference with the rest of society will totally overshadow our ruse."

"Thank you again, Guardian, I have much to think about."

Guardian VII momentarily looked down and the drumming of her fingers stopped. She gazed up at Martin, her smile diminished, replaced with concern. "How are you really feeling inside, Martin? You mentioned that you were saved from complete agony and despair. Do these feelings still haunt and trouble you, even in small measure? Your recovery does seem, indeed, remarkable and swift. But are you putting on a good face for us?"

Martin affectionately smiled at her as a son does his mother and quietly sat down in the chair facing her desk. In silence he folded his hands and gazed absently at the floor, searching his thoughts. "When I first woke up in Bestmarke's ship I was totally confused. I didn't know where I was or if I was waking up from a bad dream. Nothing seemed real. I wasn't even breathing and yet I was alive! The only movement I had was with my eyes and face. Once I started shouting Bestmarke appeared and gloated over me, showing me what he had done to his trophies ... and to me," Martin said. He paused, reflecting on the difficult memory.

"How did you feel at that moment?" Guardian VII gently asked.

Martin looked up into her caring eyes. "I was terrified and outraged ... all at the same time! I have never felt so powerless. There

210

was nothing I could do but scream at him ... and then he laughed at me," Martin said. He looked down again and sat quietly.

"Did Bestmarke then show you your father?" the Guardian asked.

"Yes," Martin said, recalling the nightmare. "When Bestmarke first showed me my father, I was devastated, totally without hope ... not only for myself, but also for my father and my mother. The realization of the anguish and pain that my mother must certainly be going through was unbearable. I have only seen and talked to my father once," he said raising his glance. "After seventeen years I was finally hearing his voice and seeing his face, but everything was all wrong. I couldn't touch him ... or hug him ... or help him at all," Martin said, his voice trembling. "All I could do was look at him! My father was trapped in that wretched chamber just like I was, and Bestmarke laughed at us!" Martin said bitterly. He looked down again and sat quietly, trying to calm himself. "Then Bestmarke shut us off. I haven't seen my father since."

"You know we will do everything in our power to rescue your father, Martin," the Guardian promised.

After a moment he looked up into her sympathetic eyes. "Until my awakening here at CENTRAL, I had been asleep with no thought, no dreams ... completely unconscious. When the Guardians woke me up it was so different than on Bestmarke's ship. You were kind to me. Now I dared to have some hope. I was still bewildered but you answered my questions. I wasn't scared anymore. Once I recovered from the initial shock of when and where I found myself, I was able to put all the pieces of the puzzle together. The Guardians let me stay awake as long as I wanted. Now I could finally think, and I came to the conclusion that my father could be rescued and given a new body just like me. I hoped that with time-travel my mother could be helped and the pain undone. Now I had hope ... true hope!"

"Hope can have a powerful affect on our every thought and action," agreed the Guardian. "But do you not have some despair

TROPHY

and depression at times, Martin? Surely you realize that your efforts to restore things, no matter how noble, will be fraught with difficulty and uncertainty. We will help you, of course, but we do not know what the future will bring or how successful we will ultimately be. It is certainly not our aim to lead you along with false hopes."

"And nobody's done that," he said. "Only possibilities have been shown me, no guarantees. Sometimes I wonder if I'll ever see my father or my mother again. I'm only one person – is there really that much that I can do to help them? If I think too hard about it I start getting depressed. Then I force myself to remember what's already been done with me and Panther and my hope starts coming back. My gut feeling tells me we'll all be successful if we don't give up. That's the hope I'm sticking to ... I have to," Martin said.

Guardian VII could only gaze at him with affection and admiration. "That is how all the Guardians feel, too. We must be successful. Our future, yes, our very existence, depends on hope and the full realization of that hope."

"Thank you, Guardian." Martin gave her an appreciative look and resumed standing. "Please show me what you've done with the great cat."

The Guardian moved to her controls and awakened Panther, lying curled up where he had fallen asleep the day before. On the screen in the control room they watched him run and leap, noticing the coordination and timing of his new body and mind connection. They marveled at his strength and fluidity of movement.

"The Lieutenant will be here shortly," Guardian VII said looking over at Martin. "I talked to her earlier. She informed me she was feeling much better and would like to be here for her appointment. I asked about her head injury and she said that tests for a concussion were negative and the pain was much less. I suspect that even if she were near death she would minimize it and keep her appointments. She is a strong and determined young woman, a fine officer."

"Yes, she is," he said, smiling to himself. "I'll be glad to see her again."

They continued watching the great cat enjoy his new-found mobility. Soon the door opened and in walked Lieutenant Rogerton and Star-Commander VanDevere. Martin briskly stood at attention and bowed deeply to them.

"This is an honor, Star-Commander," said the Guardian pleasantly as she stood and walked over to her, shaking VanDevere's hand. "And it is good to see you again, Lieutenant. Are you in much pain?" she said, extending her hand to Rogerton.

"Very little, Guardian. Thank you, it is quite manageable," Rogerton answered.

"Thank you, Guardian. I have learned that when the Lieutenant says it is manageable, it really means one step above excruciating," teased the Star-Commander.

The Lieutenant just smiled, flushing slightly, as she stiffly moved further into the control lab.

"Good afternoon, Martin," she said, smiling radiantly.

"Good afternoon, Lieutenant. I'm happy to see you again," he said. "Good afternoon, Star-Commander. I'm glad you could join us today for our experiment."

"I am intrigued, Martin," admitted the Star-Commander. "Such a dynamic team is unprecedented."

"Lieutenant, as soon as you are ready we can begin. Panther is already awake and active," stated the Guardian sitting down at her controls. "Remember, the key is to persuade him to accept Martin."

"I have a question before you begin, Guardian," interrupted the Star-Commander. "Will Panther sense that Martin is a hunter and possibly hunted big cats like him? Will that make Panther afraid or even hostile to Martin?"

"The link will probably not go that deep – but we do not know for sure. There is some risk involved," said the Guardian. "Are you willing to take that risk, Martin?"

"Yes, Ma'am," Martin said without hesitation. "For the record, I've never hunted any cats, large or small. I figure the playing-field is even – I'm a hunter and Panther is a hunter. And do we know if Panther has hunted or killed a human before? I'm assuming he hasn't. Look how he has bonded with the Lieutenant."

"You make a good point," said the Star-Commander. "Carry on with the procedure."

"Go ahead, Lieutenant," said the Guardian. "Remember, persuade the great cat."

Rogerton tightly strapped on her headgear. She took a deep breath and slowly walked out the door into the jungle-like room.

The Guardian turned on the link that joined the Lieutenant and the great cat into a single consciousness. Panther recognized her immediately and trotted to her, purring loudly. She hugged him warmly, mentally assuring him.

"She has bonded so well with him," marveled the Star-Commander. "And she did it in such a short time, too."

"Much faster than we had contemplated," said the Guardian.

"Panther," thought the Lieutenant. "Look at this." She imagined an image of two pedestals standing beside each other. The head of the panther was in one and Martin's head was in the other. The river of consciousness became troubled and dark, like a storm brewing. She adjusted the mental picture showing the panther in his newly remade state and then Martin, also whole, in his forest-green uniform. He was smiling and standing peacefully by Panther. She dwelt on this image for a long time finally changing the image to one that included her standing with them, all harmonious, and at peace. Slowly the river calmed and began to clear as the suspicion and fear in Panther's mind subsided.

She signaled to Martin. He slowly opened the door and cautiously entered the room. The Lieutenant focused intently on Martin alone in the pedestal, then made whole, and finally the three of them standing together in peace. Panther didn't move but stared deeply at Martin as if making a decision. Finally he began moving slowly toward him. The river of their joined consciousness remained calm and clear, so Lieutenant Rogerton smiled broadly at Martin, indicating a positive response from the great cat. He walked over to Martin and rubbed against him with his large head and then peacefully sat beside him.

As this was happening, the Guardian adjusted her controls and transferred the Lieutenant's side of the link to Martin's side. He, too, showed the great cat his entrapment in the pedestal and his newly made body and mobility. Panther seemed to understand and rubbed against him, purring loudly. Their bond was beginning. The panther started to run and Martin kept up with him. They crouched and jumped, playing games with each other while still mentally linked. Martin easily kept up with the great cat. Panther had finally found an equal and they played for a long time.

The Lieutenant left the holographic jungle soon after Martin and Panther bonded. She joined the others in the control room and viewed the scene on the large screen.

"Marvelous!" exclaimed the Star-Commander rubbing her hands together. "What a formidable team they will make. I would not want to be the prey!"

"They are bonding deeply," explained the Guardian, looking at the two women. "At this rate, nothing will separate them now, at least in their loyalty to each other."

"I am glad Martin can keep up with him," said the exhausted Lieutenant. "One session was enough for me and I have the bruises and the headache to show for it."

After the others finally left, Guardian VII continued to watch and monitor Martin, the ancient man, and Panther, the great black cat, as they ran, played, and jumped with no letup or tiredness at all. They continued on for hours. The Guardian was beginning to yawn when she turned down the great cat's power and he finally curled up peacefully in sleep.

TROPHY

Chapter XXXVI

Earth Date: 475 N.V.A.
Location: Earth, high orbit

"We are in position and have all the geosynchronous orbit permits and clearances, Cedric," informed the freighter captain sitting at the controls of his ship. "The other three ships have moved into their positions during the last three days. Our permits are good for a week, we have four days left."

"Excellent, we'll move today at 15:00 hours," he said watching the NAV screens. "According to our contact, Franelli is locked down at night, but is with one of the Guardians during the day. Bestmarke implanted a locator chip under Franelli's skin, as he does with all his crew, and we have the code necessary to pinpoint his exact location," Cedric revealed. "The four operatives and the cloaking mechanism are in position. We have a detailed schematic of that area of CENTRAL, and our contact has mapped a course to the lab area where Franelli has consistently been. The cloaking mechanism is an older model originally in a Victorian cruiser. The modified design will hide anything within a fifteen hundred meter circle. That is a large enough area that we can leave the device in one location. When we are safely out, we will focus all the energy into the can-opener and leave the Empire a little surprise."

"Aren't can-openers nuclear? Nuclear-cutters?" questioned the captain. "If that cutter overheats and explodes, it'll make a big mess! Every ship in orbit will be ordered to remain, and we'll be stuck here! They will board and search every one of us down to the last square centimeter!"

"Yes, I know that," said Cedric confidently. "That is why all of us will be clean, free of suspicion. We will just be freighters, doing our usual scheduled business, like we have been doing for months."

"But what if the Empire uses mind-scans on us?" worried the captain. "We can't hide from those!"

"Their own high principles will protect us," Cedric stated. "Empirical law states there must be overriding justification to use mind-scans. They cannot be used casually. Their rigid, unbreakable laws will be used against them, and will be our protection."

"I don't like it," said the captain gruffly. "We already have enough to worry about in order to pull this off successfully. This just complicates it more. Why can't we just quietly do our job and leave?"

"Don't you think they will quarantine us anyway once they realize Franelli is gone?" Cedric reasoned. "As long as we can hurt them, we might as well throw them an extra punch. If we bring down CENTRAL, we can collapse their miserable New Victorian Empire. At least we can give them a crippling blow!" he said, striking his fist in his palm.

"Well, I still don't like it, but you are the boss, Cedric," he shrugged and returned to his seat.

"Don't worry, Captain," Cedric boasted. "With all the credits you make on this job, you can retire early. You'll see."

*　*　*　*　*　*　*　*　*　*

Location: CENTRAL, Earth

"These are the critical circuits, Sondra. They must be adjusted ever so carefully. Hand me that calibrating tool, please," Louis said, bending low over the lab table.

"But how much tolerance should we leave in it, Louis?" she said, handing him the tool. "It will need some flexibility, will it not?"

TROPHY

"You are correct," Franelli agreed. "What is crucial is where we build in the flexibility so it will ..."

"Who are you? How did you get in here?" demanded Guardian V. She walked toward four figures entering the lab. They wore black shielding-suits and darkened helmets.

She was answered with a stun-phaser pointed at her face. Strong hands taped her mouth shut and bound her hands tightly. The same was done to Louis. The four figures pushed and led them back through the door and down a corridor to a round hole in the thick metal wall of the vast computer. The edges were still glowing from the nuclear-cutter as they climbed through into the blackness of the computer's interior. Dull red lights on the abductor's helmets faintly illuminated the narrow maze-like path ahead of them. Guardian V and Louis were quickly marched through the gloom toward a round opening of light in a far wall. Its edges were also glowing faintly and the round plug of the wall was lying in the corridor. Clearing the hole, they started down another corridor towards yet another round hole in the distant wall.

* * * * * * * * *

"What are they working on now, Guardian?" asked the Star-Commander, watching them curiously. "They seem very intent and serious."

"Communication skills," stated Guardian VII, monitoring her controls. "Martin is trying to determine how detailed he can be with our great cat. He is starting with very basic questions and commands."

"Are they using the link again, Guardian?" questioned Lieutenant Rogerton, standing beside her and watching the screen.

"Yes," she said looking up. "They use it most of the time during training exercises. The link circuits are built into both of them. When the link needs to be initiated, either Martin or I can do it."

Suddenly the big cat ran up to the door, pawing at it, and looking back at Martin as if to hurry him along.

"Guardian! Guardian!" Martin yelled excitedly, running to the door. "Panther is sensing trouble! Our collective consciousness is definitely showing something upsetting to him! Is it his body or mine? Is it something outside the room?"

"Both of your bodies are normal, no fluctuations, but he is definitely showing elevated stress patterns," said the Guardian, quickly looking at her controls.

"Is everything alright with the Guardians and with CENTRAL?" Martin hurriedly said.

"Bestmarke!" snapped the Star-Commander, looking keenly at the Guardian. "Where are Franelli and Guardian V?"

"No response!" Guardian VII said. "The computer is not showing them anywhere! How can that be?"

"They have to be somewhere!" cried the Lieutenant. "We saw them only an hour ago in one of the labs!"

"Let me and Panther find them!" yelled Martin, who had been following the conversation.

"Can we risk letting him out yet?" demanded the Star-Commander.

"I can handle him," Martin hastily said. "We need to trust him and do it now!"

The two officers and the Guardian all looked at each other and collectively agreed. The Guardian opened the door and Panther bounded in with Martin right behind. Without even a glance at the three women, the great cat sped for the other door, waiting for Martin.

"Put a map in our link so we'll know where to go!" Martin yelled, racing for the door.

The Guardian instantly inserted the schematic plans for CENTRAL into their link and then sent an emergency signal to the other Guardians.

TROPHY

"Lieutenant Rogerton, strap on your headgear and follow them as best you can. I will hook you into Martin's side of the link. Take this with you," she ordered, handing her a laser-rifle from a cabinet she unlocked.

"Lieutenant-Commander Gornect! Go to full alert: Code-Red-Bestmarke!" Star-Commander VanDevere firmly said to her acting commanding officer aboard the Victorian Cruiser *Daniela* in high earth orbit.

"Yes, Ma'am," she acknowledged. "Code-Red-Bestmarke!"

Martin and Panther ran down the corridor by the Chambers where the two pedestals were still sitting. "Wait!" thought Martin. The panther stopped and looked back at him as Martin ran to his pedestal and opened the back panel. The 8mm rifle and ammunition were still there. Shoving the ammo into his pockets he grabbed the rifle and ran back out the door. "Let's go!" he shouted to the great cat. Following the map in their link, they raced off to the lab where Guardian V and Franelli had been working, only to find it empty and the door half open. Panther sniffed and studied the lab floor carefully for a moment before quickly running back out the door and down the corridor, constantly listening while he watched and sniffed the floor. Turning a corner they discovered a round hole in the metal wall with the plug lying there in the corridor.

"There's a round hole in the metal wall. The edges are glowing hot," whispered Martin over his link to Guardian VII.

"Oh, no!" cried the Star-Commander. "A nuclear-cutter! We should have sensed that immediately, how could they have hidden that?"

"Only a cloak could hide that," reasoned the Guardian, trying to remain calm. "Perhaps that is why we cannot locate Guardian V and Franelli. It would take a fusion reactor to generate that kind of power. Nobody could smuggle that in."

"Could they use an energy feed from outside CENTRAL, somehow?" said VanDevere, thinking quickly.

220

"It is possible, but it would be extremely powerful and noticeable. It would set off numerous sensors."

"Can an energy feed be broken down into different components that are difficult to detect?" continued the Star-Commander, pacing back and forth.

"Yes, that is possible. There are many different beam frequencies that could be used. They could even be standard transfer beam frequencies, but much more powerful," said the Guardian, monitoring her instruments.

"Lieutenant-Commander Gornect, scan for transfer beams from all ships in earth orbit," VanDevere said desperately. "See where they are located and what the beams look like at different wavelengths. Look for especially strong power transfers."

"Yes, Ma'am, beginning searches. I will get back to you."

* * * * * * * * * *

"Guardian, are there lights inside the computer?" asked Martin. "It's pitch-black in there except for small red lights."

"No, Martin. Many of the components are light-sensitive. Only minimal red lighting can be used," Guardian VII said. "Let Panther go first … there may be enough light for him."

"We'll try it," he said. "Okay, let's go in the hole, Panther," encouraged Martin. The great cat went first using his keen night vision and sense of smell with Martin following behind, holding the end of his long tail for direction. Their progress was slower but with his heightened senses the powerful cat led them through the maze of the interior of the great computer to a faint round hole on the far side. It led into another corridor.

* * * * * * * * * *

"I am not sensing them anymore," said the Guardian with concern. "The screens are showing a circular blank area of nearly fifteen hundred meters. That is huge! It must be a modified form of cloak, for they just vanished. We must trust them both now to use good judgment and caution."

"Judgment, yes," said the Star-Commander, nervously. "Caution? They may throw that to the wind. I wish we could see," she complained, pacing the floor. "Did Martin have a weapon with him?"

"Not when he left the room," said the Guardian. "But he and Panther did run down the corridor by the Chambers. His projectile weapon was still in the pedestal there. He could have quickly taken it and the ammunition before they disappeared."

"Oh, great! That is all we need!" said the frustrated Star-Commander. "Now we have a dangerous panther and a zealot with a hunting rifle on the loose!"

* * * * * * * * * *

"Where are you?" thought Lieutenant Rogerton. "I am in front of a cutter hole in the wall. It is pitch-black in there and I have no light."

"We went through," thought Martin in response. "Here's where we are on the map," he mentally indicated. "Can you take a different route? It shows connecting corridors, but they're longer. It may be the only way. We're going through another dark area, through the heart of the computer, and Panther is leading me. If it weren't for him I couldn't do it. Here is where I think we'll come out," he mentally indicated again. "We seem to be traveling overall in a straight line. Try and meet us here at this corridor," he said, mentally showing her the location.

"I will do that," said the Lieutenant, encouraged. "But I will have to run," she replied, carrying the laser-rifle and following the map in her linked consciousness.

TROPHY

"Star-Commander, we have located four ships in parking orbits with unusually strong transfer beam emissions all pointed directly at CENTRAL. We did not see them until we isolated the various wavelengths. They are all different frequencies but combined together give enormous power."

"Is it enough for a cloaking mechanism, Lieutenant-Commander?" said the Star-Commander, still pacing.

"Yes Ma'am, but if we can remove one of the beams the combination will then be incomplete, not capable of powering a cloak."

"Move against the nearest ship. Use the Phase Interrupter Laser and shut them down completely," she ordered quickly. "Call in two Cutters each on the remaining three ships. Order them to stand down, and if they refuse, take whatever action is needed to disable them. If that does not work, destroy them," she ordered.

"Yes, Ma'am, we are moving to intercept the nearest vessel. Estimated time: 10 minutes. The six Cutters are on their way to the three remaining vessels. I will keep you updated, Ma'am."

* * * * * * * * * *

Panther emerged through the round hole into the dimly lit utility corridor with Martin right behind him, finally letting go of his guiding tail.

"Thanks, my friend," he thought. "Now, which way?"

The panther sniffed the ground, examining it carefully. Then he bolted down the corridor with Martin right behind him. They came to an intersection and abruptly stopped. Either direction ended in a short distance with a heavy blast gate. The trail led to the one on the right but it was locked tight. They tried the other one, it was the same.

TROPHY

"Lieutenant, where are you?" Martin thought.

"Here is my location on the map," she mentally pointed. "I have found a device of some sort, about the size of a luggage crate. It is humming softly and has what appears to be a beam generator aimed down the corridor at a nuclear-cutter. It must be the cutter they used to break in. The cutter is by one of the primary walls of the great computer. It is too heavy for me to move. I do not like the looks of this situation."

"Stay there!" he thought, exasperated. "We've hit a dead end ... two locked blast gates. Can you tell from the plan where we are? What's on the other side of these gates?"

"You have to get on the other side of the gate!" she implored. "It is an emergency hangar for space-planes, but rarely used. Usually there is a secret security duct around the gates for emergencies. It is marked differently on the schematic plan, if it is there at all. I am looking ... there it is! See the fine dashed lines ... right here?" she mentally pointed out.

"I see it!" he agreed, running back down the corridor a short distance. Kneeling, he felt carefully with his hands until he found a shallow dimple in the wall just above the floor. He pressed the center and a hatchway opened in front of him, swinging in, revealing another pitch black opening. Feeling around the opening's edge, he clicked a small switch that turned on a faint luminous strip in the floor, stretching out ahead of him in the blackness.

"Come on, Panther," he thought excitedly, as they started single file down the narrow duct. It soon came to an end with a hatchway similar to the first opening. Quietly opening it, they crept out into the spacious, dimly lit hangar.

Keeping in the shadows, Panther heard something as they moved away from the wall. Suddenly they saw lights and people moving toward a small space-plane nearly six hundred meters away. Martin and the great cat began running toward it as fast as they could.

TROPHY

"Panther, go right and come in from the side," he thought, visualizing it for him. Panther responded quickly and disappeared in the darkness to the right. Martin loaded the magazine of the 8mm rifle as he ran straight for the space-plane.

The sound of his quick footsteps finally caught the attention of the dark figures. Two of them began shouting in distinctively feminine voices while firing stun-phasers at Martin. He ran behind a large concrete column and flicked off the rifle's safety. Swinging the rifle around the column, he fixed the cross-hairs of the scope on one of the dark figures and squeezed the trigger. The figure was abruptly thrown backwards to the floor behind where it didn't move. Two more figures started firing continuously at the column. Martin swung the rifle around the other side of the column and squeezed the trigger, dropping another one like the first. Another figure joined them, firing furiously at both sides of the column. Martin peeked around just in time to see Panther bounding from the shadows at the two remaining dark figures. The great cat mastered a tremendous leap, his front legs outstretched with fully opened claws. His yawning mouth revealed huge teeth, gleaming in the dim lighting, and his eyes were a yellow fire. He screamed with a deafening roar. The two figures turned quickly at the sudden noise, their eyes widening at the fearsome animal approaching them.

Without warning, the engine of the space-plane ignited, throwing out dust from the floor and a pillar of flame as it lifted up and hovered above Martin and the great cat. Steadily it moved to the cavernous hangar opening and shot up into the sky.

"Guardian, can you hear me?" thought Martin. There was no response. "Lieutenant, can you hear me?" he thought again.

"Yes, Martin, I am still at the device. I think it is some sort of cloaking mechanism because I cannot get through to anyone but you. I do not know why it is aimed at the nuclear-cutter, but I have a bad feeling about it."

"Stay there and keep me informed. I'll be there soon."

TROPHY

He examined the four figures. Removing their blast helmets, he discovered they were all women, all alive, but unconscious. Their shield-suits prevented the bullets from causing them serious harm. He moved their weapons a distance away and mentally instructed Panther to guard them. Martin grabbed two helmets and his rifle and ran back to the blast gates which were easily unlocked from this side. He started back through the corridors to the Lieutenant's location.

"Martin! The device is emitting a powerful beam toward the nuclear-cutter. If that overheats it will explode, possibly destroying CENTRAL!"

"Is there anything nearby that could deflect or stop the beam?" he thought, trying to run faster.

"I have a laser-rifle but I am reluctant to use it. It could start an energy cascade that would be just as dangerous!"

"Move away from it, back toward my direction. I'll be there soon. Panther is watching our four captives."

He ran as fast as he could, not tiring at all, following the map that was in his head. Finally he came around a corner and found the Lieutenant standing under a dim light. They both ran to the device continuing to emit the intense energy beam toward the nuclear-cutter. The cutter was beginning to glow a dull orange color. An acrid electrical smell was in the air.

"Can I use a bullet on the device?" he quickly asked, staring at it, deciding what to do.

"It is probably safer than a beam weapon, but I cannot say for sure. We do not have much time. It may be our best hope," she said unconvincingly.

"It may be our only chance!" he growled. "Put on this helmet and get behind the corner!" he yelled. They both ran for the corner. Martin quickly put on the other helmet and flicked off the rifle's safety. He leaned around the corner and put the cross-hairs of the scope on the part emitting the beam. "Here goes nothing," he thought to himself and squeezed the trigger. The 8mm rifle roared as the bullet sped to its mark, ripping off part of the device and stopping the energy beam.

With no place for the incoming energy to go, the device began to whine and vibrate faster and faster. Slinging his rifle on his shoulder, Martin picked up the startled Lieutenant, and ran with all his might back down the corridor. The whine turned into a sickening shriek as he ran with desperate speed. The shriek turned into a deafening roar as the device exploded, sending pressure waves and flames racing down the corridors. He huddled in a corner, shielding the Lieutenant with his powerful, android body and waited for the fury to end.

In a few moments it was silent again with an occasional crash and clatter of damaged parts falling to the floor. After a few more minutes nothing could be heard. The blast proof lighting was surprisingly still operating. The smell of burned fabric was about them, but they were unhurt, thanks to the blast helmets protecting their heads. Still huddled in the dusty gloom, they removed their helmets and gazed into each others eyes. The Lieutenant immediately reached her arms around Martin and hugged him tightly. "Now you have saved my life and I will be forever grateful."

Before Martin could speak, the Guardian's voice came through the link. "We can finally see all of you on the sensor grid. Are you hurt? Do you need help?"

Martin sighed, stepped back from the Lieutenant, and answered the Guardian: "We are shaken, but not hurt. Panther's guarding four suspects in the hangar area. Be sure the reinforcements know that he is on our side. A space-plane escaped, probably with Guardian V and Franelli aboard. You should have seen them on the NAV screens unless their ship is somehow cloaked, too."

Martin and the Lieutenant quickly walked back to the explosion site. "We stopped the energy beam aimed at the nuclear-cutter, Guardian. The device was totally destroyed, nothing left but junk," said Martin. "The nuclear-cutter is all blackened but seems okay. The wall it was against is black, too, but seems undamaged. We don't see any obvious structural damage."

"Is CENTRAL safe and operating?" quickly asked the Lieutenant.

"We are running diagnostic tests … so far everything is normal. It was close, Lieutenant," the Guardian admitted.

Specialists in white and light-pink uniforms could now be heard and seen moving quickly toward the two standing by the wreckage.

At the same time Security Specialists were moving carefully into the hangar.

"A panther, Guardian? A black panther? … He is an android? … Yes, I think I understand. We see him now! The four suspects are on the floor, huddled together. Their faces are white! The panther is only meters away from them and roaring loudly. He is frightening, Guardian. I am glad he is on our side. … He is walking toward us! … He stopped! … He is stretching out his front legs and lowering his head to us!"

TROPHY

Chapter XXXVII

Earth Date: 475 N.V.A.
Location: Earth, high orbit

"We are approaching the freighter, Ma'am, and deploying the Phase Interrupter Laser," stated Lieutenant-Commander Gornect. The blue-green beam of the PIL swept out from the *Daniela*. Almost instantly the freighter shut down with only emergency lighting and life support operating. Without their fusion reaction, the powerful transfer beam stopped and the cloak around the space-plane disappeared.

"The space-plane is in our NAV screens now, Star-Commander. It is in the high atmosphere and we are on an intercept course with an ETA of eight minutes. I am calling in two more Cutters to apprehend the disabled freighter. The other three freighters are wisely standing down and will shortly be in custody."

"Very good, Lieutenant-Commander, keep me apprised of the situation. Watch the NAV screens closely. Bestmarke is probably nearby, cloaked and waiting. Are your reinforcements ready?"

"Yes, Ma'am, cloaked and waiting."

"I am going to contact the space-plane on an open channel so Bestmarke can hear us if he is out there, Lieutenant-Commander. Be ready for action."

* * * * * * * * *

"I hope the Izax did not pay these jokers too much," grumbled Galen Bestmarke as he watched the freighters surrendering to the Planetary Control Corps ships. "We will have to change our plan somewhat, Brother. We had better hook up the link. We may need to move quickly very soon."

TROPHY

They both put on the headgear and turned on the Level I interface, mixing their emotions and pulling their separate thoughts into the same flowing stream of consciousness.

"The space-plane has uncloaked. Fools!" Bestmarke continued complaining. "The Izax should know that if you want to do something right, you have to do it yourself. It is amazing he has achieved what he has, depending on others."

"We may have to skim the atmosphere," thought Terran, changing the subject. "A Victorian Cruiser is on an intercept course with the space-plane. We can beat the Cruiser if we go underneath it, closer to the planet."

"Have you done that before? ," Galen asked, looking over at him.

"Yes. If we get a good run at it we can coast through without the engines," Terran said.

"I do not care if the engines are toxic to the atmosphere, Brother."

"Nor do I, but if we are coasting, we can be cloaked. We can then come right up to the space-plane and pull them in the port. We will snatch them from right under their nose."

"I like that," said Galen, grinning slyly.

"Wait!" Terran interrupted. "Something is coming over the open channel."

"Space-plane L3971 leaving Earth, this is Star-Commander VanDevere of the New Victorian Empire ordering you to stand down."

"Not a chance, Commander. We have two very important people we need to safely deliver. If you want them to remain safe you will leave us alone. It is very simple. I repeat, leave us alone and they will be safe. This ends our conversation."

"Space-plane L3971 … space-plane L3971 … "

"Short and sweet," laughed Galen, slapping his arm-rest. "Johnny, take us to maximum starting thrust as soon as you can.

230

Stelle, get plugged in with the Pouncer. Everybody strap in tight. We will be skimming the atmosphere and it will be a rough ride."

"Maximum initial thrust in thirty seconds, boss. Prepare to drop cloak and go to full shielding," Johnny said.

"They used an open channel to try and pull us in," Terran reasoned.

"That is obvious," thought Galen. "They want us to show our hand and we will, right under their noses. Perhaps we will give them a bit of a bloody nose, too," he promised bitterly as he charged all his weapons.

At thirty seconds the twin Zenkati fusion engines roared to life at maximum starting thrust. Pushed back hard in their seats by the oppressive g-forces, the inertia dampers struggled to maintain a safe level of gravity. Terran plotted his course along the top of the atmosphere. "Space-plane L3971," Terran said, contacting them on a secure channel. "We will be skimming the atmosphere, cloaked. Be ready to move in close when you see us uncloak. We will grab you with the extension arm. Shut off your engine then and we will pull you in. Do you have any questions?"

"No, we understand. We are almost out of the upper atmosphere and we will maintain our present course. A Victorian Cruiser is behind us, so watch your back."

"We see them. Watch for us, you will need to move quickly when we arrive."

"Full thrust coming up," Johnny acknowledged as the ship vibrated under the increasing strain of the powerful engines. "Full shut-off in five seconds with full cloak."

* * * * * * * * *

"They are skimming the atmosphere below us, Ma'am," informed Lieutenant-Commander Gornect. "They have cloaked again at high speed. We can calculate their trajectory and timing as well as see their target."

"Bestmarke is playing too obvious or he is desperate," said the Star-Commander. "He will try something. Remember, the safety of Guardian V and Franelli is paramount."

"Acknowledged, Ma'am."

* * * * * * * * * *

"It is blazing hot in here," griped Galen, holding onto the seat as they bumped and bounced along the upper atmosphere.

"Remember, Brother, space is always cold. All we have ever needed was heat. Don't worry. We are rising up into sub-space now. It will start to cool off soon. Two minutes to intercept."

"Braking thrust and cloak drop in two minutes," monitored Johnny. "Space-plane port is ready to open and extension arm is at stand-by."

Two minutes counted down and the braking thrust matched their speed to the space-plane. "Space-plane in position and port is open," said Terran. "I am taking us in just a little closer. Put the arm out, Johnny."

"Space-plane hooked and pulling it in," Johnny said. "Port is closed and tight. Space-plane will be secure in twenty seconds."

"Setting new headings," thought Terran. "Go to maximum thrust when you are ready, Johnny," he said out loud. "Let's see what these engines can do."

* * * * * * * * * *

"He has dropped cloak again and is using braking thrust, matching speed with the space-plane," reported the Lieutenant-Commander. "They have pulled the plane in and have increased speed tremendously on a different heading. Should we go to full pursuit, Ma'am, with our reinforcements?"

"No, not this time."

"Ma'am?" she questioned in disbelief.

"That is correct, Lieutenant-Commander. Do this, however, before they cloak again. Send this coded message I am relaying to you in a one-second burst on the COM laser. It will penetrate their shields and is brief enough they may not notice it or pay attention to it. Send it quickly. This may be our last opportunity before Bestmarke disappears completely."

"Complying now, Ma'am ... it is done. Is that all, Ma'am?"

"Yes, Lieutenant-Commander. Bring the ship back to its parking orbit," sighed the Star-Commander.

TROPHY

Chapter XXXVIII

Earth Date: 475 N.V.A.
Location: Leaving high Earth orbit

"Why didn't they follow us?" asked Galen, quite perplexed. "I was ready for a fight."

"It is because our new guests are too precious to them, and they don't want to risk a battle," laughed Terran. "But we did get a burst on the COM laser frequency. It was so short I thought at first it was static."

"What was it?" questioned Galen suspiciously.

"Just these words: 'Good-bye Galen Bestmarke'."

"That is all?" he said, growing worried. "Why send that? Is it coded?"

"No, not at all, I checked it out. They are just trying to get inside your head, trying to make you worry over nothing. They are playing psychological games with you," Terran said, laughing at him.

"That won't work with me! Why do they think that will work with me? Do I look like a sucker? Are you sure it wasn't coded?" Galen said, growing more agitated.

"You see, it is working," Terran said, laughing harder.

"That's not funny! Nobody plays games with me!" he scowled and stomped away.

* * * * * * * * *

Estelle Fairfield was ready to fight. She was strapped into her battle-seat in the defense cube linked to Tommie, her TMC-7 cat.

"They backed off? They didn't pursue us? Why? They always have before. That's alright, though, isn't it, Tommie?" she said to her only close friend on the ship, her orange striped tabby.

234

TROPHY

"Stelle, you and the Pouncer can relax," Bestmarke said over the COM. "Our good friends have decided not to visit tonight."

"Thank you, boss," she acknowledged. She removed Tommie's headgear and straps, and then her own. She started to get out of her seat when a sudden sensation in her mind made her dizzy, causing her to lose her balance, and fall dazed to the floor. It wasn't a pain … it was more of a blinding flash. She struggled back into her seat and fell into a deep sleep, so deep she appeared to be dead. Tommie started meowing, licking her hand, and rubbing against it. He climbed into her lap and curled up, purring and meowing softly, concerned for his best friend.

*　*　*　*　*　*　*　*　*

With a drawn stun-phaser, Galen Bestmarke walked to the space-plane port accompanied by two crew members, each armed with a laser-rifle. The port atmosphere had just been restored with the green light and chime signaling 'safe to enter'. The three strode quickly in with the crew members moving to each side, their weapons raised.

The space-plane hatch swung open. The pilot and his assistant emerged slowly, walking out with their hands raised up.

"You can put your hands down, I will not shoot as long as you do not anger me," Bestmarke sneered. "You are doing better than your friends, at least. All four freighters surrendered to the PCC. I would imagine they will all now have a permanent retirement program just for them. I admit, your little scheme almost worked. At least you brought me Franelli," he said, holstering his weapon. "As a reward, I will let you live. Our heading takes us near Luna One. We will remain cloaked and you will be allowed to leave near there. If you are careful, you should not have any problems," he said, standing with his hands on his hips. "Is Mr. Franelli alright? Did you bring a guest along with him?"

"Yes, Sir," said the frightened pilot. "Mr. Franelli is in perfect condition and so is the woman with him. Thank you, Sir, for allowing us to go," he groveled. "Do you want me to get them? They are locked in the back compartment."

"By all means!" Galen said. "We certainly do not want to leave our guests locked up!"

"Sondra," Louis whispered quietly in her ear. "You said you would accept whatever decision I make?"

"Yes, Louis, I did," she whispered back, sitting closely to him and holding his arm.

"Then I must play this out, Sondra. I must play it out. Wait . . . I hear someone coming . . . they are unlocking the door . . ."

"Follow me," said the pilot. "Mr. Bestmarke wants you to come out."

Louis walked out first, followed by Guardian V.

"Louis!" exclaimed Galen Bestmarke. "I am so glad to have you back! It has not been the same without you!" he said sincerely as he walked up to him.

"Hello, Boss," Louis said in his raspy monotone. "I was wondering when you would get me out of that stifling hole they call CENTRAL."

"Is this a friend of yours, Louis, this pretty woman all in white?" he taunted. "Who is she?" he said looking straight at her.

"I am Guardian V, Mr. Bestmarke," she calmly said, looking him in the face. "You may speak directly to me. I am not cowed by you or your reputation."

"Ah, yes, always the principled one, aren't we?" he said, mocking her. "Did you say Guardian? Guardian V? How charming. We will speak more later," he said. Then he turned abruptly to Louis. "Is she a friend of yours?" he sternly asked again.

"I worked with her many years ago when I was doing research at CENTRAL, boss. That's all. They are all the same there. They didn't like what I was doing then and still don't like what I am doing now. She was allowing me to do my research, keeping me occupied, and out of trouble," he said without any expression on his narrow face.

"I was worried, Louis," Galen said pointedly. "I feared you might want to stay there."

"Boss, you give me freedom to do my work without always looking over my shoulder. Why would I want to leave that?" he said, staring at Galen without emotion.

Bestmarke accepted his answer, unwilling to press him further. Then he pointed at the pilot. "You and your assistant ... remain here in your ship. You can leave in a few hours."

"Louis, your old quarters are ready for you," he stated. "Show our new guest to her quarters and keep a guard outside the door," Bestmarke bluntly said to his two crew members. "We will have dinner for our guests and to celebrate Louis's return tonight at 20:00 hours."

* * * * * * * * * *

Estelle slowly woke up from her deep sleep to find her cat, Tommie, lying on her lap and purring, intently looking at her.

"Tommie," she said softly, reaching for him. "Why are you here? Were you worried about me? My mind is so fuzzy ... I need to wake up more."

He jumped from her lap as she sat up slowly, rubbing her short blond hair. Her head didn't hurt, but she felt confused, unable to focus her thoughts. All she could remember was the blinding flash in her mind. Her thoughts felt like a great puzzle all in pieces, and she was attempting to reassemble it. Tommie was her corner piece. At least she had him as a beginning focal point.

The longer she thought, the more pieces started to fit together. The memories of the last three years fell into place and felt like genuine memories, no longer like an unconnected dream. There were other memories, though, that she couldn't grasp or make sense of. How did they fit? Ideas would float through her mind, but were just out of reach. She tried to grasp them, but they were elusive, disappearing as she touched them. Maybe she just needed to wake up more. She tried to relax with only mundane thoughts. Tommie meowed and nudged her hand. He was hungry. "Alright," she said and slowly stood up. "I'll get you something to eat."

Her quarters were separate from the rest of the crew as she needed to remain close to the defense cube in the bow of the ship. A place for Tommie was also provided as he needed to stay near her, not wandering about as a common cat would do. Behind her quarters was the bridge. A small passageway let her bypass it directly to the mess hall and general crew quarters.

"Hi, Cookie," she said, entering the mess hall. "I need something for Tommie, please."

"The usual, Miss?" he asked, giving her a wink and a smile.

"That will be fine," she said, returning the smile. "You look extra busy today. What are you cooking? It smells really good. Is something special happening?"

"The boss wants a special dinner tonight. Franelli is back and the boss wants to celebrate. He has another guest, too, but I don't know anything about that. He was in a good mood and that's reason enough to celebrate," he said quietly.

Estelle smiled, thanking him, and took the provisions back to Tommie, waiting patiently. "Here you go, little guy," she said, giving him his food. He purred as he started eating. The rank smell of the cat food was a sharp contrast to the luscious kitchen air.

"Louis Franelli," she said to herself, her mind stuck on his name. "I feel like I need to do something, but ... what is it?"

Her train of thought was interrupted by the COM system: "Stelle," boomed Galen's voice, "Please join us for dinner tonight at 20:00 hours in the Captain's dining room. We have a special guest. I think you will find the evening most interesting."

TROPHY

"Thank you, Sir. I will be there at 20:00 hours," she said politely, pondering his words. In all her time with him, he had never asked her to dine at the Captain's table. "I don't trust Galen Bestmarke," she said out loud.

Saying the name, Galen Bestmarke, made it stick in her mind the same as Louis's name had done. "What is going on?" Her thoughts flew to the date on the subprogram. "Perhaps I was not meant to see that. It was only on the subprogram once before it was changed back to the present date. Was that a mistake?" she said and shrugged the thoughts away. She turned and walked to her wardrobe cabinet to find suitable clothes for the special dinner.

* * * * * * * * *

"Do you really think it wise, Brother, inviting Estelle to the dinner?" said Terran, demanding his attention. "She is our last line of defense if we are attacked. Do you want to risk alienating her? That could jeopardize her performance as a guider if she has it in her heart to pay us back for some embarrassment."

"I am not going to embarrass her! I just want to have a little fun with the Guardian," Galen said, looking annoyed. "Stelle hates the Empire just like we do. She was banished, remember? She is a renegade. She could care less about that woman, that so called Guardian. Stelle will spit in her face if we give her the chance! You worry too much, Brother."

"That is part of my job to worry and reason things out. One of us needs to be practical," he said, looking at him and shaking his head. "If we always did things your way, we would probably both be dead now."

"And if we always did things your way," countered Galen, "we would most likely be dead from boredom. But come now, Brother, let us not argue. You know I am always right," he said, teasing him. "I will not embarrass Stelle. I just want a little sport with Her Majesty."

239

TROPHY

"I hope it doesn't come back to haunt you one of these times," conceded Terran.

TROPHY

Chapter XXXIX

Estelle took a last look in the mirror before making the short walk to the Captain's dining room. It had been a long time since she had rubbed a little Europa-Spice perfume on her neck or had worn her powder-blue outfit. It was dressy enough and well tailored. It still fit her perfectly and it matched her eyes. She checked her short blond hair that she had teased up, admitting to herself that even it looked good. "I wish my life-mate could see me now," she sighed. "Blue was his favorite color." She forced another smile upon herself, trying to sweep away her sudden melancholy thoughts. "Funny, I haven't thought of him for a long time. Why should I do so now? It's all very odd . . ." She dismissed the thought and headed for the dinner.

Estelle Fairfield walked down the short corridor to the dining room and in through the wide door. Being the first to arrive, she took her time and looked about the room. It was her first time to see it. The paneling and ceiling were dark wood. Hand woven carpets and tapestries gave it a luxurious feeling. The heavy furniture was finely-grained dark wood, smelling faintly of polish. The tableware was pure platinum, complimenting the handmade china, crystal and fine linens. It was truly opulent. She was quite taken back. Her thoughts were interrupted as Galen and Terran entered the room.

"Ah, Estelle," Galen said pleasantly, using her full name for once. "I am glad you are here. You look stunning tonight. I almost didn't recognize you," he said patronizingly.

"Thank you, Sir," she said politely.

"Please," he urged. "Just call me boss."

"Yes, boss," she returned. "That is what we are used to." She smiled halfheartedly noting his black suit with pure gold edging and buttons.

TROPHY

"You look very nice tonight," Terran said wholeheartedly as he walked up to her. "Do you approve of our Captain's dining room? We tried to incorporate early Victorian decor. I find it very comfortable. I hope you do, too."

"Thank you, Terran," she said. "Yes, I find it very comfortable, quite impressive, in fact," she said, complementing him and noting how well dressed he was, too. His light gray suit was not as formidable as his brother's and she liked the black edging and buttons and the breezy hint of Mercurian Musk. Now, at least, she could tell him and Galen apart.

"Where do you put all this furniture when we have a battle situation?" she asked him.

"Oh, yes, Louis helped us with that," he answered. "We store the small items in special drawers and the large pieces are magnetically locked down. We have had no shifting or movement. Louis is a genius."

"Yes, he is," agreed Estelle.

At that moment Louis and Johnny walked in the door. Estelle walked up to the tall, thin man. "Welcome back, Louis," she said in greeting. "I hope you weren't ill treated at CENTRAL."

"Hello, Estelle," he said nervously. Social situations were difficult for him. "I was well treated. But I am relieved to be back in my own lab again."

"Did you see anyone you had worked with before?"

His eyes darted and he appeared troubled, as if not knowing how to answer. He looked at Estelle. "Only one and she is with us tonight. She will be here soon, and then you will see," he said quietly.

She didn't know quite what to make of his cryptic answer and gave him a puzzled look. She was about to ask him another question when the door opened a final time and Guardian V walked in, leaving her escort in the corridor.

"No, not this!" Estelle thought. "They have captured a Guardian! No wonder Louis was nervous. This is the real reason

242

Bestmarke asked me here. He assumes I will react to her with scorn and hatred. " She concentrated her gaze on the Guardian. "She seems familiar, but I can't get my thoughts to focus. I feel I should know her name, but how?"

"Welcome to our special dinner, Guardian," spoke Galen, breaking the silence. "Let me make introductions, please. This, of course, is Louis, my Chief Engineer. And this is my First Officer, Johnny. He fills in when Louis is not here," he said sarcastically.

Louis and Johnny bowed slightly. The Guardian did the same and smiled at them both.

"This is my brother, Terran," he said proudly. "He is my full partner and our Pilot."

"The pleasure is all mine, my lady," Terran gushed, bowing deeply. "We hope you enjoy our hospitality tonight."

"Thank you, Mr. Bestmarke," she said, returning the compliment. "I hope your heart is as pleasant as your words," she said, smiling sweetly.

Galen's eyes narrowed as he observed his brother. Clenching his jaws, he fought to control himself. Quickly recovering, he said: "And here is our defensive weapons expert, our guider, Estelle Fairfield," he gloated. He paused for a moment and then spoke with a threatening smoothness. "Perhaps you already know her?"

"I am pleased to meet you, Ma'am," Estelle said quietly, her eyes downcast as she bowed slightly.

"And I am pleased to meet you, Estelle Fairfield," noted the Guardian, smiling gently. "I hope at some time you will enlighten me on how you came to be in Mr. Bestmarke's employ. And perhaps why he thinks that we should have previously known each other," she concluded, smiling first at Estelle, and then at Galen.

"Yes, yes," Galen said impatiently, growing slightly red in the face, and becoming frustrated with the direction of the conversation.

Composing himself again, he invited them all to sit at the impressively set table with himself at the head. "Louis, please sit at my right, and Johnny next to him. Guardian, sit at my left with Estelle next to you. And Terran, please take the foot, if you will," he pointedly said. Terran rolled his eyes.

A far door opened as Cookie appeared with two more crew mates bringing rich, dark red Burgundy wine, and sharp cheese with stone-ground bread as appetizers, filling the room with tantalizing aromas. In time, this was followed by a classic Waldorf salad and more wine, most of which was consumed by Galen, Terran, and Johnny.

"Estelle and Louis are not drinking much," thought the Guardian. "Good. We must be careful with our words."

Cookie entered again and announced: "Our main course tonight is the Boss's favorite, and one of Louis's, too," he said, beaming with pride. "Beef pot roast with pot roasted potatoes, carrots, and onions. We also have whole-wheat soft rolls with fresh butter and a pickle relish. Save room for dessert, which is Black Forest cake and freshly ground Martian-Mocha blend coffee!" he said, most triumphantly.

With strains of Stravinsky in the background, all the party ate and drank with minimal conversation.

Finishing the cake and sipping her coffee, the Guardian spoke. "Well, Mr. Bestmarke, that was certainly delicious ... my most hearty compliments to the chef. I have not eaten this richly in a long while."

"Do you mean the queen bees of the Empire are not fed that well at CENTRAL?" he said slurring his words, the wine loosening his obnoxious tongue. "I would think you would eat like royalty there, sitting on your thrones," he sneered.

"We eat very simply, Mr. Bestmarke. We choose to eat that way. It brings us good health and long life," she said, staring at him fearlessly. "Speaking of life, what do you intend to do with me, Mr. Bestmarke?"

"I have not yet fully decided what to do with you. I want to know more about you, starting with your name. What is your name? I grow tired of these 'Guardian' titles," he said arrogantly.

"Our names are unimportant. Guardian is not a title … it is a task, a responsibility. We are servants, really, of the great computer, CENTRAL. The Guardians take care of it," she calmly said.

"I know all that!" he angrily retorted. "Our mother tried to force your insipid ideals down our throats years ago. We do not care about or accept your Empire! Just tell me your name!"

"My name, years ago, was Michelle," she stated calmly.

"You knew her back then, did you not, Louis?" Bestmarke said accusingly. "What was her name then?"

"I always knew her as Sondra," he said flatly, pausing for a moment as he smiled at Galen. "But Sondra is her middle name. Her first name is Michelle, but she always wanted to be called Sondra," he stated without emotion, looking at the Guardian.

"Michelle, you say?" Galen said, deflated as he glanced sourly at Louis. "And your last name?" he asked, looking darkly at the Guardian.

"Anderson, Mr. Bestmarke. My last name was Anderson."

Estelle was sitting quietly drinking her coffee and thinking. "I know her name is Sondra. I can't remember how I know it, though. And Michelle . . . that name is important, too, but how? How does this all fit together?" she wondered absently, not paying attention to the ongoing conversation.

"Is that not right, Estelle?" demanded Galen, staring at her.

"What, boss? I'm sorry I . . ."

"I told her highness, Michelle Anderson, that you are a renegade from her precious Empire!" he barked, visibly upset. "Is that not right, Estelle?"

"That is correct," she confirmed, looking down. And then, her temper rising, she looked him in the eyes. "I left the Empire on my own, boss. I wasn't thrown out!" she sternly said.

TROPHY

"Well, yes, that is true," he confessed, backing down a little.

"We do not make a practice of chasing down our citizens, Mr. Bestmarke, unless it is a judicial matter," calmly interjected the Guardian. "If Estelle chose to leave, that is indeed our loss. She has free will. We are not tyrants, Mr. Bestmarke, whatever you may think."

His sport with the Guardian was not going the way that Galen intended it and he was becoming even more upset.

"You still have not answered my question, Mr. Bestmarke," pressed the Guardian. "What are you going to do with me?" she demanded.

His thinking clouded by wine, Galen yelled and jumped to his feet. "I will show you what I am going to do with you! Everybody, come with me!" he bellowed, grabbing the Guardian roughly by the arm and leading them all down the central corridor of the ship to his prized trophy room. He unlocked the hatchway and they all followed him in.

Galen shoved the Guardian as he released his grip on her and ran to one of the pedestals, touching the switches on the side. He did the same with another. The faint sparkling sheen above them darkened, and shapes began to form above each, as if through a thick fog.

"Here is what I am going to do with you!" he screamed like a mad man. "I will preserve you alive, and torture you for the rest of your miserable life!" he shouted with hatred. "This is what you will become!"

The first pedestal came horribly to life with an angry lion's head, viciously snarling and roaring, escalating the hatred manifest in the room. The second pedestal brought forth a marked contrast as a bleating deer's head cowered in obvious fear, unable to find any escape from its frightening environment.

Galen stood between the pedestals, his eyes wild with rage, screaming at the Guardian. "This is what you will become! Louis will

246

put you in one of these, won't you Louis?" he yelled, looking at him directly.

"Whatever you want, boss," he said with no expression. So matter-of-fact was his response that all the others suddenly looked at him.

All the others, that is, except the Guardian. "You still cannot frighten me, Galen Bestmarke," she calmly said. "Even as we speak, you are being hunted down by our fleet. Star-Commander VanDevere will finally catch you whether you imprison me in this monstrous, inhuman device or not. You will never defeat us. Your own hatred will defeat you, and everyone that thinks like you and follows you. Star-Commander VanDevere will see to that!" she emphasized.

Estelle could hardly believe the hideous scene unfolding in front of her. She wondered why the Guardian was pushing him so hard. Where was she going with this and what does she hope to accomplish? Didn't she realize that this will force him to take deadly action against her?

Estelle looked at Galen with loathing. Then she fixed her gaze on the Guardian and felt deep admiration, even affection, for this seemingly defenseless woman. A strong protective feeling swept over her and she wondered where those sudden feelings came from. How did she know this Guardian so that she wanted to protect her – even with her own life? Was it something in Estelle's past she was trying to recall? Estelle held her head with both hands moaning to herself. "Why can't I focus? Why are my thoughts so confused?"

Amidst the dreadful uproar surrounding them the Guardian calmly maintained her watch on Estelle, following her closely, until Estelle finally lowered her hands and looked up, straight into the Guardian's eyes. They stared long at each other. The Guardian quietly said a name but said it only once.

"Why did she do that? What did she say?" thought Estelle as she tried to mouth the word. "Van ... Van ... De ...Vere ... VanDevere ... Star-Commander VanDevere. That's what the Guardian said.

And she said it twice to Bestmarke! That name must be important ... but why?" Estelle continued to say the name over and over in her mind. "VanDevere! VanDevere! I know that name. I am starting to remember. Somehow I know my name is VanDevere. That feels right ... Fairfield does not," she continued. "But what is my first name? Estelle feels wrong. What names did the Guardian say? Sondra ... Michelle ... is it one of those? Sondra doesn't feel right – that's the Guardian's name. What about Michelle? Yes, that might be it. It's starting to feel right. Yes. Michelle is right. Yes! My name is Michelle! My REAL name is Michelle! ... Michelle VanDevere! ... I can remember! I can finally remember!"

She repeated her name, many times, and each mention further opened the floodgates of her memories. She trembled and nearly collapsed from the overwhelming rush of hidden thoughts surging back into focus. She took a deep breath and slowly stood up, continuing to gain back her strength. "Everything is clear now! I remember all of my training and its purpose! I am not a renegade! Now I remember why I am here!" she said to herself, her blue eyes fully alive as she looked intently at the Guardian.

The Guardian returned her look and smiled. "She knows now. Now she remembers."

TROPHY

Chapter XXXX

"I cannot let him continue," thought Terran. "The drunken fool is out of control. I have to stop this madness!" he reasoned as he quickly walked to both pedestals and turned them off. "Come, Brother, we have had enough excitement for one night," he said, trying to calm him.

"No!" screamed Galen, his face red with anger. He lunged at Terran who quickly sidestepped causing Galen to sprawl face first on the floor by one of the pedestals. Pulling himself up, he rushed at Terran, yelling: "Traitor!"

Terran sidestepped again and gave him a hard left jab to the solar plexus followed by a vicious right hook to the jaw. Galen crumpled to the floor, completely unconscious. A deathly quiet followed.

"Please, I beg everyone's pardon for my brother's irrational behavior," Terran said, still trembling from the rush of adrenaline. "I was afraid this would happen if he drank too much. I am sorry the evening has ended this way. It would be best if we each returned to our own quarters," he apologized. He called for the Guardian's escorts. "Please see the Guardian back to her quarters, and then come and put Galen in his," he plainly ordered.

During the confusion Estelle had quietly moved into a protective position in front of the Guardian, preparing to spring at Terran as he finished off Galen. Guardian V reached forward and gently squeezed her hand. The message was plain. Estelle relaxed and stepped back taking the Guardian's hand in hers, squeezing it affectionately, and quickly letting go. She slowly moved away unnoticed. Then two crew members came to the hatchway for the Guardian who walked with them back to her quarters.

TROPHY

Terran approached Estelle and spoke mildly. "I apologize for any embarrassment you may have suffered, Estelle. My brother, as you know, can be unpredictable at times. He should not drink, it only makes the situation worse."

"Thank you," she replied. "I appreciate your concern. It would be best if I went back to my quarters now." She turned and walked up the corridor to the front of the ship.

As Estelle walked along the long central corridor she marveled at the Guardian's brilliance in forcing Galen to reveal his plans and motives. Estelle could fully remember everything now, including her original assignment to capture or kill Bestmarke and Franelli. But the Guardian had stopped her. Why? Has the plan changed?

*   *   *   *   *   *   *   *   *   *

Wearing her dark colored fatigues, she crept silently out of her room and down the small passageway past the bridge to the mess hall and general quarters. It was 02:00 hours and all were asleep as she stealthily moved by in the dim light on her way to Louis's private quarters. The door was unlocked. She quickly went in and then realized it was vacant. She then set out for his lab, moving cat-like through the shadows and dimly lit corridors.

The only sound was the slight hum of the ship's climate control as it pushed the stale, slightly bitter smelling reprocessed air throughout the system. The big ship was coasting now, its mighty engines silent, having reached cruising speed hours ago. Their destination was somewhere in the Asteroid Belt, a few weeks distant.

Estelle found the lab door unlocked. Louis was at the far end, totally absorbed in his work with his back to the door. She drew her battle knife and moved slowly toward him, the fifteen centimeter black titanium alloy blade gleaming dully. She swiftly pulled him backwards to the floor and jumped on him, pinning his arms with her legs. She set the knife firmly against his throat. His eyes were wide with anger. He could utter no words, only gasp.

"I will not allow any harm to come to the Guardian, Louis," Estelle quietly said. "I will not let you or Bestmarke harm her in any way. I am sworn to guard her with my life, and I will kill you and Bestmarke quickly if I have to, starting with you now, then Galen Bestmarke. I am not bluffing. You have thirty seconds to tell me why you should not die."

"I have never killed anyone!" he hoarsely said.

"Yet you approve of what Bestmarke accomplishes, don't you? You do his bidding; you make his hideous trophies, am I correct? I heard you say you would do whatever he wants to the Guardian, to Sondra. You said that, didn't you?"

"Yes, yes, I said that!" he grimaced as he felt more pressure on the blade at his throat. "But I only said it to stall him. I could never hurt Sondra. Never!" he trembled.

"Why should I believe you, Louis?" she calmly asked. "Fifteen seconds left."

"Because ... because I ... I care for her," he stammered. "Because I love her!" he admitted, trembling harder with fear. "I cannot hurt her. She is the only person that has ever cared for me and helped me, really helped me. I may have to take unusual means to save her."

"I am listening," she said without backing off.

"Bestmarke wants to take off her head and keep it alive as a trophy. I do not have the materials for the nuclear power unit. She will die if the chamber is not immediately ready and operational. He is an irrational, impatient man. He may order me to remove one of the animal trophies and use that chamber. I cannot do that. I have a plan to stall him."

"How will you do that?" questioned Estelle, still not moving.

TROPHY

"I will convince him that the connection between the living tissue and the power unit is different for humans. I may have to put Sondra into a cryogenic state to protect her."

"You may have to freeze her?" questioned Estelle. "Will that harm her?"

"No, what it will do is buy us time, time for Star-Commander VanDevere to find us. I know how to send a locator signal without Bestmarke's knowledge. You could help me," he said, imploring her.

"I will risk giving you a chance, Louis," she said, unpinning his arms as she quickly jumped up. She removed the deadly blade from his throat, but did not sheath it.

"And there is one more reason, Estelle," he continued seriously. "I know how to use the Keyhole to travel through time."

"You can really do that?" she said ... flabbergasted.

"Yes, I finally worked out and perfected the formulas. I realize now that if used properly, time travel could solve our great dilemma of the continuity of the human race. It is wrong to use it as Bestmarke has done. Sondra helped me to appreciate and understand that. I have to save her," he said, stifling his tears. "My last words to her in the space-plane were: 'I have to play this out'. She understands that. She trusts me."

"I hope that is true," she said, her knife still in her hands. "If it is, I will help you. If you are lying, I will take you out quickly. Then I will take out Bestmarke, too."

"I am not lying. But be careful with Bestmarke. He is dangerous and ruthless ... do not underestimate him."

"Don't worry about me," she quietly said as she started back to her quarters.

* * * * * * * * *

"Well, Brother, how are you feeling this morning?" said Terran scornfully.

252

TROPHY

"My head and stomach hurt, but I cannot remember why," Galen complained. "I must have had a good time, right, Brother?"

"You cannot remember, can you?" accused Terran. "You cannot remember because you are a stupid, drunken idiot! Fool! All you can think of is yourself!"

"You cannot talk to me like ..."

"Shut-up! I will talk to you any way I feel, you deserve it!" Terran said, hissing his words through clenched teeth. "And if you give me any trouble now, I will take you down like I did last night! Just remember that I am tougher than you, and a lot more patient. Otherwise you would probably be dead by now!"

"I was that obnoxious?" he said sheepishly.

"Your complete memory loss when you drink is your perfect alibi," Terran said bitterly. "Someday I will make a recording so you can personally see how revolting you can actually be. It is no wonder we are either shunned or wanted by the law everywhere in the Solar System."

"Oh, my head," Galen groaned, holding his head with both hands. "What did I say?" he asked after a pause.

"If you cannot remember, then I am not saying," Terran replied bluntly. "You had better be on your best behavior and make some apologies, though. I am sure you can figure out to whom."

"Oh, my head," Galen moaned again, slowly getting up and returning to his quarters.

* * * * * * * * *

"Hello, boss," Louis said in his deep voice. "I did not expect to see you today. Are you feeling better?"

"Yes, Louis, I am," Galen replied with rare graciousness. "Ah ... Louis ... ah ... I wanted to ... to apologize for last night. My brother informed me I was out of control."

253

"Apology accepted, boss," he said, with no change of expression. "Is there anything else, boss?"

"Yes, there is, Louis," he said cautiously. "This Guardian … what do you know about her?"

"I have already told you, boss. We worked together years ago, nothing more," he stated, hiding his true feelings. "Why, boss? Do you want me to prepare a trophy chamber for her like you mentioned last night?"

"Did I say that last night? I admit, I cannot remember."

Louis noted his uncommon embarrassment. "I told you I would help you. But now I have discovered a complication. I do not have the materials I need for the proper kind of chamber and interface connection," he said, blankly looking at him.

"What do you mean, Louis?" Galen asked, puzzled.

"The chamber controls are somewhat different for a human than an animal. I do not have what I need for a human's chamber. Didn't I ever tell you there was a difference?" Louis asked, staring at Galen.

"No, you did not," Galen admitted, bending under Louis's gaze. "What can we do? I am concerned she will cause problems or send a message locating us to their fleet. The more time she has, the more trouble she could cause."

"I could put her in cold storage, boss."

"Really, would that work?"

"Yes. We have a cryogenic system on board. It would take a few modifications, but I could have it operating in a day."

"Are you sure it will work?" Galen asked again.

Louis stared at him, expressionless.

"Right!" Galen said, lowering his gaze. "Let me know when it is ready." He turned and walked out of the room.

"I will, boss," Louis said, smiling faintly.

* * * * * * * * *

TROPHY

"Mr. Bestmarke, did you bring me here to this lab to apologize for the threats you made three days ago or is it to carry them out?" questioned Guardian V, showing no fear.

"I can only offer vague apologies because I cannot remember what I said or did, Guardian," he said insincerely. "But I will soon be giving you a place of honor. You will be unique, the guardian of my trophies, the envy of the Solar System. Think of it! I am almost giving you immortality. Almost, because you will soon wish you were dead," he said, mocking her.

She looked to Louis, then to Galen: "I have always used my life for good, Mr. Bestmarke. I would never wish to die, but I am prepared to do so for what I truly believe in," she firmly said. "Can you say the same about yourself?"

"Does it really matter to you what I think?" he asked callously. "Your precious Empire cares little for those of us who do not agree with you."

"That is not true, Mr. Bestmarke," she answered. "We do care. Freedom of thought and expression is encouraged. But breaking the laws and living outside them is not. A peaceful and just society must be based on laws and principles. The greater good of all people depends on that."

"The only good I am concerned about is what is good for me, Guardian. Deep down we are all animals, completely selfish, and sooner or later that trait manifests itself in all of us. Your 'greater good' is just false sentiment that will eventually be exposed," he said. "Entropy, Guardian, entropy. Everything eventually runs down, wears out, or is lost. Even your precious Empire will go back to the dust someday. It will be gone forever, including all your laws, principles, and greater good," he sneered. "You know I am right. That is why I believe only in myself. Everything else is hopeless ... everything else is futile."

"I have never met anyone as negative as you, Mr. Bestmarke. Your lack of joy and the shallowness of your existence sadden me.

Real happiness comes from truly giving of yourself and your talents to help and enrich others. I am afraid you will never be truly happy unless you change your way of thinking."

"You remind me of my mother with all of her high principles. My brother and I both left when we were old enough to make it on our own. We have been happy. And we have never looked back, not for her, and not for you, or any other part of your wretched Empire," he arrogantly said. "Do what you need to do, Louis," he said with finality. "The next time I want to speak with our Guardian, I will just touch the power switch. I am going back to the bridge now. Let me know how it all works out," he said as he left the lab.

Louis listened to his departing footsteps, closed the door, and quietly locked it.

"I told you that I had to play it out, Sondra," he softly said to the Guardian. "Do you still trust me?"

"Yes, Louis, more than ever," she replied, gazing into his eyes. "My life will be in your hands."

"I am going to put you into a cryogenic state. Do you fully understand what that entails?"

"You will freeze me, instantaneously. Is there a great risk, Louis?" she questioned. "I am not afraid of death. What I do fear is not ever seeing you again."

"The risk is minimal, Sondra, and there is no pain involved. You will have no thoughts … it will be like a deep, dreamless sleep. I will take care of you and guard you with my life. Estelle said the same."

"So, you have talked to Estelle?" Sondra said curiously. "What convinced her to spare you, Louis?" Sondra continued. "She would have to be convinced before she turned back her weapon. She is one of the Protectors … the highest level."

"I told her that I care for you, Sondra," he said tenderly. "I truly care for you. In fact, I love you very much," he assured her, holding her tightly in his arms.

TROPHY

Chapter XXXXI

Earth Date: 475 N.V.A.
Location: Earth, CENTRAL

"How are you feeling, Martin?" said Guardian VII, standing next to him and Panther in the cybernetics lab. "You seem to have suffered no ill effects from the explosion."

"I guess our android bodies saved us, Guardian, and CENTRAL, too. Me and Panther were able to run without tiring," Martin said as he absently scratched behind the big cat's ears. "Since our brains are connected with the link, it speeds us up and we make faster decisions. The more we use it, the easier it gets. I never thought in a million years I could talk with an animal like him. I'm really blown away," he said, meeting her gaze.

"You are not the only one who is 'blown away', Martin. All of the Guardians are fascinated with the progress of you both. How often do you use the link?"

"Most of the time I forget that it's on and we stay linked for hours. Neither of us is afraid. We seem to have accepted each other completely. It's kind of weird to have that close of a relationship with someone, especially an animal. I guess we have a special bond, with our minds being connected. Does that bother you, Guardian? Is it unnatural?"

"It does not trouble me," she calmly replied, folding her hands together. "Is it unnatural? Technically, yes. It has never been done before at your level. For years we have had guider/pouncer teams with no negative affects, but their links have not reached nearly the level yours has. I am thinking of making his side of the link more accessible to him."

"What do you mean?" he said with a puzzled look.

257

"Presently, only you control whether the link is activated. I would like to try giving him an equal choice," she said. "However, both you and I will still have control as to whether he is awake or asleep. That will not change."

"Why give him more freedom of choice?"

"Call it research, my dear, pure research," she said, smiling at him, a twinkle in her dark eyes.

*   *   *   *   *   *   *   *   *   *

"The Guardians tell me no structural damage has occurred and that CENTRAL is in perfect condition," stated Star-Commander VanDevere, standing before the fireplace in the Chambers. "You, though, have suffered hurt again, Lieutenant. Are your burns healing without too much pain? We owe you a proper vacation leave, but I am afraid it will again have to wait."

"I am in little pain, Star-Commander. The burn medication is wondrous except for the smell. It really stinks!" said Lieutenant Rogerton, making a sour face. "With all of their advances in medicine, could they also not make it smell nice?"

"You make a good argument," she agreed, risking a smile. "Seriously though, you, Martin, and Panther have averted a great catastrophe. The Empire is indebted to the three of you. I personally want to thank you for your courage and presence of mind."

"Thank you, Ma'am," Rogerton replied, slightly flustered.

"Our assignment now is obvious," VanDevere confirmed, beginning to pace in front of the fireplace. "We must concentrate on the safe return of Guardian V as well as Franelli and Martin's father, still trapped on Bestmarke's ship. We know Bestmarke's final heading before he cloaked his ship. There is no doubt he will change that. We do not know his destination, but someone on his ship may contact us. We are not sure how, so all sensor stations and ships in the Solar System have been placed on heightened alert. Even the smallest, faintest clue will be taken seriously," she said, looking at the Lieutenant.

"Is there any hope at all, Star-Commander?"

"Very much so, we feel. I cannot say more at this time, but we can be optimistic." She stopped pacing and with a confident gleam said to the Lieutenant: "You are going to need a new ship. Would you like to see it?"

"Yes, I would, Ma'am, very much," she said surprised. "But how, it is not here at CENTRAL, is it? I thought they were assembled at the PCC Space Assembly Plant in high orbit?"

"That is correct. However, all the assembly work is monitored here at CENTRAL. We can watch them working on it right now, it is almost finished." They walked to a small side office with a monitor screen on the wall. VanDevere spoke again. "Computer, show us PCC-SAP, dock C-17… There it is," she said, proudly pointing to it. "What do you think of it?"

The Lieutenant stared, mesmerized by the ship on the large screen.

"Well, Lieutenant?" she gently prodded, watching her face.

"Oh, Ma'am, it is unbelievable!" she exclaimed, radiating excitement. "What is it? I have never seen anything like it before. The design is so sleek, so radical, so different. It almost looks alive."

"It almost is, Lieutenant. The pilot and commanding officer are both linked with the ship's computer, although still remaining separate from each other. They do not have a joined consciousness. I do not fully understand and I am only repeating what the Guardian told me. The Guardians have made tremendous strides from their success with Martin and the great cat. You will, no doubt, understand what they mean more than I," VanDevere admitted.

"What is it called, what model is it?" She stared at the screen, thoroughly fascinated.

TROPHY

"It is an entirely new design called a Clipper. Of all the ancient wind driven ships, the clippers were the fastest. This one is the same. It is even faster than a cruiser."

"Is it as fast as Bestmarke's ship?"

"Faster! Look at this close-up of the engine and you will start to see why." She commanded the computer to zoom-in.

"Zenkati, D-Class," read Rogerton with delight.

"The very latest and best," the Star-Commander said proudly. "It has cloaking ability, is guider/pouncer capable, and has a host of weaponry, almost as much as a cruiser. But it is small, only fifty meters in length, and carries a crew of ten. Do you think Pilot Kolanna will approve?"

"She will be so happy her face will split apart from grinning," said the Lieutenant with a laugh. "Will I retain the rest of my current crew, Star-Commander?"

"Yes, Lieutenant, if that is your desire. We will add what we need, but three will be special members."

"Special members, Ma'am?"

"Yes, in fact the Guardians recommended it, even insisted. Can you not guess, Lieutenant?"

"Are two of them Martin and the great cat, Panther?" she said, silently hoping.

"That is correct! The third is a Medical Specialist hand-picked by Guardian VII to care for the unique needs of Martin and Panther." VanDevere paused for a moment and then confessed: "Actually, Lieutenant, I envy you. You are young, in the prime of life, and in command of the fastest, most advanced ship in existence. And you are teamed up with a handsome, dashing young man, and a dynamic and unforgettable black panther," she sighed. "It does not get any better than that! Oh, that I were your age again," she wistfully said, looking at the screen again.

"But Star-Commander, you deserve to command that ship. Why should I be given such an honor?"

TROPHY

"You tempt me greatly, Lieutenant," she replied, narrowing her eyes and looking sideways at her young officer. Then she broke into a wide grin. "It is your time and place for this assignment. You are the best fit. You have already proved that. Think of the dynamic team you will all make. You will be unbeatable!" she said with pride, and sighed again.

"Thank you, Star-Commander. Thank you!" Rogerton said. She paused, staring at the sleek new vessel. "When will the ship be finished, and how soon can we depart?"

"We have been working hard on this ship for months. And now, it is non-stop at a feverish pace since the abduction of Guardian V and Franelli. In two or three days it will be finished. Tomorrow, Pilot Kolanna will be here to receive her brain-stem implant and undergo some critical training. She will also meet Martin and Panther. That should be interesting, do you not agree?" she said, raising her eyebrows.

* * * * * * * * *

"It is like a dream, Lieutenant, and I don't want to be awakened!" exclaimed Pilot Kolanna Montoombo, completely overwhelmed by the new ship, new assignment, and new additions to the crew.

"It is just like a dream, Kolanna," Lieutenant Rogerton said. "The Shipyard Superintendent told us they need six more hours to finish loading supplies and running the final tests on the circuits. I wish we could depart now. Bestmarke is getting farther away by the hour." She grew more impatient as they watched the final loading of supplies into their new Clipper Class ship. As they looked through the thick windows of Dock C-17 a familiar crew member approached them.

"Lieutenant-Warden Archer reporting for duty, Ma'am," she announced, walking up and standing at attention.

TROPHY

"Congratulations on your promotion, Lieutenant-Warden," Rogerton heartily said. "As a Lieutenant-Warden you could have your own ship. Thank you for staying with us."

"Even having my own Cruiser would not match this assignment, Lieutenant," she exclaimed, marveling at the sleek new ship. "This is a rare privilege, a once in a lifetime opportunity."

"I agree," smiled the Lieutenant. More crew members arrived, reporting for duty, all expressing similar sentiments. When all but two had reported for duty, Lieutenant Rogerton addressed them.

"You have all been briefed on our two special crew members, our two androids," she stated seriously. "Remember, please, that they have been extensively programmed. The man android will look and act just as a real man, an ancient man. You will think of him and treat him as a real man. That is my requirement. The same applies to the panther. He is programmed to be as a real panther, with some behavior modifications. He is very docile and genuine to those on his side. He will not eat you!" she said grinning, drawing a round of laughter.

Hurried and excited voices in the distant corridor prompted the Lieutenant to say: "They are approaching now; we will greet them with professionalism and dignity. Please stand at attention," she ordered calmly.

As Martin and the great cat approached, the Lieutenant watched the eyes of her crew grow larger and larger, their mouths opening in unbridled awe. Remembering their orders, they closed them quickly.

Specialists Martin and Panther reporting for duty, Ma'am," he said, standing at attention and bowing deeply to the Lieutenant. Panther also bowed following Martin's lead.

"Welcome aboard to you both," she said, giving Martin a knowing look. Bending down, she hugged the great cat causing him to purr so deeply the air rattled around them.

TROPHY

"Please, let me make introductions," she said to the thoroughly overwhelmed crew. Moments later, they entered the ship through the connecting tubes, beginning the process of familiarizing themselves with their unique and powerful ship.

* * * * * * * * *

"The *Clipper* is ready, Star-Commander," Rogerton reported to VanDevere at her post on the bridge of the Victorian Cruiser *Daniela*. "All systems are functioning perfectly and ready for operation. The Superintendent has just signed off on the last of her inspections. We are ready to leave immediately, with all due haste."

"The squadron will move out in two hours," VanDevere stated. "Our course will be toward the Keyhole. Beta and Gamma Squadrons have departed and are en route to the general area. We can only assume that Bestmarke will try to use the Keyhole again now that he has Franelli back. And we can only hope that he does not immediately go there. We do have some ships in the area, though, but not enough to stop him."

"Could the *Clipper* alone stop him, Ma'am?" she asked directly.

"It is very possible, Lieutenant."

"May we have permission to leave now at our greatest speed, Ma'am? It would be a good test for the ship."

"I do not favor the idea of your lone ship advancing against him, but we may have no other choice," said the Star-Commander reluctantly. "I will not order you to do that, Lieutenant. It must be your decision."

"Then we are leaving, Star-Commander. We will keep you apprised of any and all situations. Thank you, Ma'am."

"Please, Lieutenant, take great care."

"We will, Ma'am," she said to herself as she strapped into her gravity seat. "Pilot Kolanna, use the steering thrusters and depart the station. Once outside, give us full chemical thrust. When we are at the safe-point, go to maximum starting thrust on the Zenkati fusion engine. Let us see what this ship can do!" she said excitedly, turning and grinning widely to an exuberant Kolanna sitting beside her.

TROPHY

Chapter XXXXII

Earth Date: 476 N.V.A.

Location: Asteroid Belt

"Is the Guardian safe, Louis?" Estelle whispered. It was after midnight, and she was slowly pacing the floor in the dim lights of his lab.

"Yes, she is safe now, asleep in the cryogenics chamber," he said, sitting at his desk. "She is out of Bestmarke's reach."

"Good. Thank you." She sat down next to him. "Have you worked out a way to send a message to the Fleet?"

"I have an idea that will work if they are listening," he said, looking in her eyes. "I designed many of the systems on this ship including the COM systems. I know how difficult it will be to compromise any of them. Even a very subtle try will be detected, so we will have to use a different approach.

"Every fusion engine has a different signature. Like snowflakes, none are exactly the same. Certain frequencies are generated by the engine ... this is normal. Observed on an instrument, these frequencies each have their own specific wave pattern," he said, gesturing with his hands.

"And they are all different?"

"Yes. Ships can be traced and located by their signature frequencies. People that do not want to be traced, like Bestmarke, add an electronic device to the engine that masks or hides the generated frequency, essentially making them neutral ... unreadable.

"Electronic parts are very stable, but sometimes they do fail. If one of the parts in the masking device were to fail intermittently, it would unmask the signature of the ship," he continued. "If there was a pattern to the unmasking, not just randomly done, it would be detected quite soon."

"That is, if somebody was looking for it," Estelle said, standing back up.

"CENTRAL knows we will have to be very subtle, so they will be looking for anything unusual, no matter how faint. I check the reactor, engines, and circuits daily. It will be simple to insert a modified part into the masking device. It will appear as a normal part that has become defective, if it is discovered." He looked at her with a satisfied look. "I will take care of it first thing tomorrow."

"For this all to work, the engines need to be operating. Is that correct?" Estelle said, pacing again.

"Unfortunately, that is true. Braking thrust will work, but generally the engines only then run for a short while. It may be enough, however."

"Do you know where we are going now, Louis? Will we engage our braking thrust soon?"

"We appear to be headed to the Asteroid Belt. Terran mentioned the name Izax when talking to his brother. Are you familiar with that name?"

"We went to a specific asteroid after you were first taken from the ship. The fact that another party broke into CENTRAL indicates that Galen asked for favors or hired someone to do it. That must be where this Izax comes in. Bestmarke probably now needs to pay him." She paused with a disgusted look on her face. "Knowing Galen Bestmarke as we do, the situation could get ugly. I don't trust any of these characters ... these businessmen."

"I have heard a little about this Izax," Louis said. "You and Tommie should keep a sharp eye on the whole affair."

"Thanks, Louis," Estelle quietly said as she left the lab, silently returning to her quarters.

* * * * * * * * *

"Braking thrust and cloak drop in ten minutes," monitored Louis in his deep voice.

"Stelle!" Galen yelled, his voice booming: "You and the Pouncer get plugged in. Keep your eyes sharp on the NAV screens."

"Yes, boss," she confirmed.

"Do you expect a welcoming party, Brother?" said Terran, turning and looking at him.

"I do not know what to expect," Galen said seriously, returning his gaze. "I do not trust him and I know he does not trust me. I made a mistake at our last meeting. I showed weakness, groveling in front of him, and submitting to his demands. This time it will be different ... I will be in control."

"I do not think he will look at it that way, Brother," Terran said with a worried look. "I suggest we go to full shielding with all weapons at ready when we drop our cloak. If he tries anything, it will be done quickly at first, or when we are leaving, especially if he is not happy with the results."

"I agree," Galen said, looking down at his controls. "I am charging up my weapons now."

Finally Louis said: "Thirty seconds to braking thrust and cloak drop. Everybody strap in."

"Full shields when we drop cloak!" Galen ordered.

The engines roared to life with their braking thrust as the cloak dropped and full shielding took effect. No other ships could be seen.

"I do not like this, Brother," said Galen as he looked at the NAV screens. "The Izax should be here."

"He is here, but he is cloaked. I caught a shimmer on the NAV screens. Perhaps he was hoping to catch us unprepared with our shields down."

"He should know us better than that. We will just wait him out. He cannot fire on us as long as he is cloaked.

"Look, Brother, we do not have to wait. He is not that close, though. Probably two hundred kilometers away, and is fully shielded with his weapons locked on us. Where is our friendly welcome?" he said.

"He wanted room to maneuver and thought he could catch us napping. We will have to teach him a lesson on hospitality before we leave," Galen said grimly.

"What an ugly ship he has! He would be laughed out of a space port with that old bucket."

"What do you expect for an asteroid rat. He lives like a mole. He needs to get out more instead of burying himself in his big hollow rock," Galen said with disgust. He waited a few more seconds and touched the switch for the COM system. "Izax, good to see you, old friend!" he bellowed on a secure COM channel. "Bring your space-plane over. You kept your end of the deal, and now I will keep mine."

"Humph! We shall see, Mr. Bestmarke, we shall see," the Izax said haughtily.

"His rust-bucket ship is moving closer, still fully shielded. You are right, Brother. He does not trust you." They watched the screens as his ship drew closer. "He is stopping ten kilometers distant and a space-plane is departing his ship. I will focus an opening in our shields for his ship to enter, and then close the opening immediately."

"Johnny, take four crew members with laser-rifles to the port. Open the doors and extend the arm. Bring his space-plane in, I will join you there," Galen said, strapping a stun-phaser to the waist of his black flight suit. He walked quickly to the space-plane port.

Instructing his men to spread out along the back wall with their laser-rifles pointed up, Galen walked out alone to greet the Izax.

"Welcome to my humble ship, old friend," he said, his arms outstretched in greeting. "Perhaps you would like to stay and have dinner with us and enjoy our hospitality."

TROPHY

"I will enjoy making my choice and then leaving quickly, Mr. Bestmarke," he said, dryly. "I do not have time for frivolous social functions."

"Very well, Izax. Come with me, please, to my Trophy Room and you shall have your choice."

He was accompanied by two large, muscular men with stun-phasers at their waists. They were all dressed in light gray protective suits.

"Your men will have to leave their weapons here," Galen bluntly said. "If not, they must stay here."

"Just stay here," Izax ordered, after noticing the four men with laser-rifles. "Let us continue, Mr. Bestmarke," he said icily. "Show me what you have."

There was no small talk as Galen led the way to his Trophy Room. Galen walked with large measured strides while the shorter, portly Izax struggled to keep up in his quick short steps.

"I do not know how you can live in these cramped quarters, floating out in space. I would go mad," said the Izax, out of breath and sweating.

Galen looked at him with disgust and walked faster. Finally reaching the room, Galen unlocked it and the two went inside.

"Please, Mr. Bestmarke, do not turn these trophies of yours all the way on, just leave them sleeping. It is so much quieter that way, don't you think so?" he said with a wheeze between deep breaths. Taking a red handkerchief from his pocket, he wiped the sweat from his head and face.

"Make your choice, Izax," Galen said passively, after touching the top switch on all the pedestals.

Izax walked around them all, studying them carefully. "Exquisite!" he remarked at one trophy. "Marvelous!" he said of another. He continued on for a while before looking at Galen. "Mr. Bestmarke, I believe you are holding out on me. I was expecting to find a beautiful woman among these. That is what my heart is set on."

"These are all my trophies, Izax. I keep them all here. I have no others. Make your choice," he said plainly, sweeping his arm all around.

"Mr. Bestmarke, really!" Izax exclaimed in mock surprise, shaking his right hand, index finger extended. "I was informed that you had a Guardian delivered to you. That is who I want. Whether or not she is in this room is immaterial to me. She is my choice!"

"That is not how the deal works, Izax," Galen said, becoming impatient, his hands on his hips. "We made the deal with what I possessed when I came to you. Not for what I might have in the indefinite future. Besides, your hired lackeys made a bungling mess and they all got caught. I had to step in and finish the job myself. You should pay me for that," he sternly reminded him. "Your choice is any one thing in this room, nothing more."

"Very well, Mr. Bestmarke, I can see there is no point in my insisting. I have a reputation for keeping my word; it is obvious that you do not. Be that as it may, and to keep the peace between us, I will take this one … this one right here, Mr. Bestmarke. The one you call 'The Hunter'," he said, patting the heavy wooden pedestal.

"That is what I expected, Izax," he said with a sarcastic sneer. He turned off the pedestal and called for two crew members to bring a dolly, wrap up the trophy carefully in packing blankets, and wheel it to the space-plane waiting at the port. Neither said a word as they walked back, more slowly this time, through the long corridor.

Without a word they supervised the loading. As the crew finished, they turned and faced each other. "Your word, Mr. Bestmarke … your word," the Izax said haughtily, holding his head up and looking down his short, bulbous nose.

"Get off my ship!" Galen said with a growl, and then turning, walked quickly back to the bridge.

"Fire up the engines and go to maximum thrust as soon as the space-plane clears the shields. Everybody strap in. Keep a sharp eye on the NAV screens, Stelle," ordered Galen, quickly strapping himself in.

"Did it go as you expected, Brother?" asked Terran, looking up at him.

"Exactly as I expected," he said, giving him a quick glance. "He will most likely take a parting shot or two."

"Space-plane is away and the port is tightly sealed," reported Johnny.

"Everyone strap in. Maximum starting thrust in ten seconds," said Louis over the COM. The two powerful engines roared to life, shaking and propelling the large ship forward with incredible acceleration.

Estelle flipped the separator switch off to engage the link with Tommie. Her thoughts began racing across what felt like a closely trimmed, bright green lawn, infinite in size. There was Tommie, an orange striped tabby cat, sitting on a small bump of a hill, waiting for her with anticipation. His ears were straight ahead and his golden eyes glowed in the warm sunlight.

"Play?" thought Tommie.

"Yes, play!" lovingly thought Estelle. "Let's start now." She engaged one of the training programs she daily practiced with him. If the Izax fired at them, she and Tommie could switch programs instantly and handle the real situation. She continued the practice session with Tommie.

"The space-plane has reached his ship," monitored Terran. "Do you think he will follow us in that old bucket? I don't think he can."

"He does not need to. Look!" Galen said, excitedly pointing to the NAV screen at the object steadily following them, slowly gaining. "What is it?"

TROPHY

"I see it, boss," said Estelle. "It's a fusion interceptor. It flies up the wake of a fusion engine, and when it gets close enough to the ship, it launches two projectiles perpendicular to it. They make a tight arc forward, penetrate the hull of the ship and explode. It is old technology, but deadly."

"How do you defend against it?" he quickly asked, his apprehension growing. "Should I shut the engines down?"

"No, it has already locked on to us. I've only read about them, but I know that the missile is hardened and nearly impossible to knock out. Keep us going as fast as possible."

Galen fired the hyper-lasers and the ion phase pulse-cannon, but with no success. "Nothing seems to work!" he said with frustration as it slowly continued to gain on them.

"Tommie and I can get the projectiles, but it will take exact timing. I need control of the ship."

"You have control," he said resignedly, tapping in the transfer code.

To Tommie and Estelle, the missile appeared in the program as a slow moving tortoise, crawling over the hills of the fine green lawn, inching its way closer and closer. Tommie attacked the tortoise with all his claws and teeth, but just slid off, not affecting it at all.

"Be patient, Tommie. Wait!" thought Estelle. The missile continued to grow steadily closer. "Get ready!" thought Estelle. "Get ready!"

It was very close now, continuing to gain. Suddenly, two projectiles exploded from it, shooting straight out each side, perpendicular to its line of flight. They started to form tight arcs to bring them back to the sides of the ship.

Estelle and Tommie saw these as two white rabbits running in opposite directions from the tortoise. "Quick, Tommie," urged Estelle.

Tommie bolted after the closest one as fast as he could. At the same time Estelle mentally rammed the engine controls to one hundred fifty percent, and violently turned the great ship toward the rabbit Tommie was chasing. With two more leaps Tommie was on the rabbit, teeth and claws holding tight. She mentally hit the hyper-laser trigger and the projectile was destroyed. Tommie saw the rabbit disappear and raced off toward the other.

Estelle rammed the engine controls to one hundred seventy-five percent. Fusion overload warnings screamed as they were pushed deep into their seats by the even more oppressive g-forces. The heightened speed and directional change increased the size of the last projectile's arc, giving them additional microseconds. Tommie's strength was impressive, even with the heavy g-forces, as he bounded toward the rabbit, finally leaping onto it, and gripping firmly with his teeth and claws. Estelle hit the trigger and the second projectile was destroyed. To Tommie, the rabbit just disappeared. The tortoise was gone and the playing field was empty, only green grass and sunlight remained.

Estelle backed down the howling, overheated engines and returned the controls fully to Galen. "Good boy, Tommie," she praised. "Good boy," she continued, projecting warmth and love.

Flipping the separator switch back on, she ended the program with her thoughts racing backwards, the golden sun reddening as it set over the infinite green lawn now glowing silvery in the moonlight that darkened and glimmered out, a few last stars twinkling and fading.

"Good job, Stelle!" Galen yelled.

"Shut down the engines and go to full cloak, Louis!" he ordered.

"Turn us with the thrusters after we are cloaked, Brother, and bring us up behind the Izax's ship," he growled. "We will just coast in and give him a taste of his own medicine."

"His shields are at fifty percent, Louis. Can we burn through them?"

TROPHY

"Focus all four hyper-lasers on one spot. In two seconds it should open a hole large enough to fire the pulse-cannon through."

"Get a little closer, Brother," Galen muttered, closely watching his NAV screen. "Take us in at an angle. We can decloak, fire on him, and cloak again. We will leave our engines off so he cannot use another missile."

The great ship coasted closer, silent under its protective cloak, finally coming into range. Galen locked on the four hyper-lasers and readied the pulse-cannon. "Drop cloak!" he yelled. "Fire!" he screamed as the hyper-lasers focused their beams. "Fire!" he yelled again, and the hot blue pulse of the cannon sped through the shield breach straight to the reactor, damaging it extensively, shutting it down. The old ship lost its shields, weapons, and main power.

"Cloak on!" said Galen. "Change course with the thrusters. We will just coast on by," he said with a grin, watching the emergency power turn on in the stricken ship.

"How do you like that, Mr. Mole?" he said, jeering at the screens. "Go back to your stinking asteroid, fat man, and leave space for us," he gloated.

"We could finish him off," Terran said, pursing his lips as he looked at Galen. "He is completely at our mercy now."

"Yes, he is," agreed Galen, returning his brother's gaze. "That is the point I want him to remember. Besides, I want my trophy back. Someone like him doesn't deserve it."

"Where to now, Brother?" asked Terran, turning to his screens again.

"Io Station. We need more supplies, and Louis needs special parts for his next project," he said as he turned to his controls. A cruel smile began to form on his thick upturned lips.

TROPHY

Chapter XXXXIII

Earth Date: 476 N.V.A.
Location: En route to the Asteroid Belt

"Lieutenant Rogerton, this is Star-Commander VanDevere. What is your status?" she said, speaking on a secure channel. "How is the *Clipper* functioning?"

"Brilliantly, Star-Commander! Her speed is unbelievable. Pilot Kolanna has total mental control of the ship's movement. The ship's response is extremely quick … we cannot wait to show you in person."

"I cannot wait either, Lieutenant. We have new coordinates to readjust your heading."

"Have you located Bestmarke's ship?" Rogerton guessed, her eyes brightening in anticipation.

"Yes. Ships near Mars detected a faint fusion engine signature pulsing on and off, following a regular pattern. We traced the signature back to the manufacturer, Zenkati. Two engines were originally sold to Louis Franelli and one of them matches this signature. He must have purchased them for Bestmarke when he refitted his ship years ago. Proceed to the new coordinates with all speed and due caution. If Bestmarke is in the area, he could be cloaked. We are four hours behind you on the same heading."

"Thank you, Star-Commander, we are complying now."

"New headings, Kolanna," instructed Rogerton, looking over at her.

"I have them, Ma'am," she said cheerfully, watching her controls. "This is so easy! All I have to do is think about it, and then direct it with my mind."

"Maximum thrust in two minutes," said the computer. "Please strap into your gravity seats."

"I don't even have to talk," said Kolanna. "The computer does it for me. I may get very lazy!"

"What is our ETA?"

"Our heading is based on two identified locations," Kolanna said, studying the readouts on the screen. "If Bestmarke's heading and speed remain unchanged, we will intercept in seventy five hours at the far edge of the Asteroid Belt."

"Wow, as Martin would say!" exclaimed the Lieutenant. "That is fast … faster than any ship I have ever seen!"

The ten second warning was followed by the powerful thrust of the engine and the increasing g-forces, tempered successfully by the redesigned inertia dampers.

Sitting beside the Lieutenant in the bridge of the new ship, Kolanna turned and looked her in the eyes. "Ma'am, may I ask you a personal question?"

"Do I have a choice, Kolanna?" she teased. "Please, ask me anything."

"You really like Martin, don't you? I see it in your eyes and your expressions," she said, watching her closely. "And what's not to like? If only he were completely real … I mean, Ma'am, if only there were more like him … that were real … sorry, Ma'am, … do you know what I mean?" she struggled, growing embarrassed.

The Lieutenant started to laugh. "Oh, Kolanna! He affects you the same way he affects me. And the same with any other female that has seen him. You should have seen how the Guardians fussed over him, especially the older ones," she said, making a funny face. "Perhaps we can clone him."

"He and Panther were Bestmarke's trophies, weren't they?" she asked quietly, abruptly changing the mood, her expression serious.

Stunned, Rogerton just stared at her. "What makes you say that, Kolanna? How do you know that?"

"They told me," she admitted, looking down. Worried, she looked up again at the Lieutenant. "Not directly, I sensed it. They are not total androids, are they?"

With a blank face, the Lieutenant just looked at her, quite taken aback. "No, Kolanna, they are not. Their heads are completely alive, but they have android bodies. You must not tell anyone about this, it is strictly confidential."

"But why would CENTRAL portray them as machines?" she said puzzled. "It's not fair to Martin and Panther."

"Perhaps not, but it is for their protection ... and ours. Where do you think they came from?"

Kolanna sat thinking, her eyes away from the Lieutenant. Suddenly they opened wide and she put her hands over her mouth. "They are from the past! Bestmarke brought them through the Keyhole!"

"Yes, you see it clearly. Can you understand the great danger if this becomes generally known, that we can travel back and forth through time?"

"It could undermine the Empire! People could just disappear ... vanish! We would have continuous war with criminals or rebels. Everything would be out of control," she said, sensing the consequences.

"There could be even greater consequences. We just do not know. The Guardians are very concerned, but hopeful, too. This knowledge of time travel could save the human race from extinction. We must safely keep the secret of Martin and Panther. Only one other person on this ship knows their secret and that is the Medical Specialist. She was hand-picked by the Guardians. Obviously she needs to know. Do you understand why confidentiality is so important?" she said, intently looking at her.

"Yes, I do," said Kolanna. "Wow!"

"Wow, indeed," said Rogerton. "Now, tell me again how you sensed all this."

"When I am linked to the computer, and Martin and Panther come close to me, I pick up mental images. I don't mean to, it just happens. I am not purposely snooping, it just happens."

"Kolanna, there are four of us on this ship with links that connect us in different ways."

"I am beginning to see what that means. I guess I really didn't know what to expect. Sometimes the feelings are very strange, even frightening. I feel at times like I am not in control of my mind anymore," Kolanna said, her smile changing again to a worried look.

"This is new for all of us, even the Guardians are learning new things. We should allow nothing to surprise us, really," Rogerton calmly reasoned. "I have had those feelings myself, Kolanna. The strangeness, even the fright, should end when you realize what your boundaries are. The interface only goes so far, so deep. Realizing that principle is what finally helped me understand and cope with my feelings.

"I think I understand, Lieutenant," she remarked, looking down, momentarily lost in thought. "You still haven't answered my question, though," she brightened, looking up with a grin. "You really like him, don't you?"

"Yes, I do, Kolanna," Rogerton answered quietly, lowering her gaze. "He saved my life, and I fear he has also touched my heart."

"He thinks of you often, at least when he is close to us. You saved his life and have touched his heart, too! ... Oh, I'm sorry, Ma'am," she said with a distressed look. "Again I am relating things I shouldn't see, matters that are private. This is why it is so frightening. With these links, will we lose our private thoughts? I don't know where my boundaries are yet. I don't want to invade anyone's privacy, nor do I want mine invaded," she confessed, tears forming in her large, dark eyes.

TROPHY

"Kolanna," Rogerton kindly said, touching her arm. "We are all in a growing process ... we will have some growing pains. Relax and ride it through. Learn from it, and above all else, do not lose your sense of humor. Okay?"

"Okay? What does that mean?" Kolanna said, sniffing back the tears.

"That is another ancient expression I picked up from Martin," Rogerton said, rolling her eyes. "It means 'do you understand?'"

"They had some interesting expressions back then, didn't they?" asked Kolanna, her smile returning. "Are Martin and Panther training today? We haven't seen them."

"Probably. Without as much room to run, Martin has been concentrating on mental exercises with the great cat. His progress so far has been astounding."

"Perhaps he will have Panther talking soon," Kolanna said. They both laughed at the thought of it.

* * * * * * * * * *

"Lieutenant, long range sensors are picking up something faint in the proper location for Bestmarke's ship," Kolanna stated as she sat in her control seat, concentrating on the NAV screens. "Should we maintain course and go to full cloak?"

"Do it," Rogerton calmly ordered. "We will sneak in behind him and have a look. I will inform the Star-Commander before we cloak."

"Will he detect us, even cloaked?" Kolanna asked.

"Hopefully not, but Franelli did work on his systems, so anything is possible," Rogerton said. "We will need to be cautious as we draw nearer."

* * * * * * * * * *

279

"Nothing on the sensors, Brother," Terran said, rubbing his chin as he stared at the NAV screens. "When do you want to cloak the ship?"

"Not until we start picking up traffic near Io Station. Keep an eye open, I am going to take a nap," Galen said, loosening his collar buttons as he walked to his quarters.

* * * * * * * * * *

"That's him, Lieutenant," confirmed Kolanna. "I'll keep us just out of weapons range."

"So far there is no indication he detects us," said Rogerton, strapped into her control seat. "Let us hope it stays that way. Go to full alert."

* * * * * * * * * *

"Good, you are back," said Terran, rubbing his hands together and stretching as he looked up at Galen. "I was about to awaken you."

"Is there a problem?" asked Galen. "Have you seen something?"

"Not really, at least nothing specific," he said, turning back to his screens. "It is more of a feeling when I watch the NAV screen, like a very faint shadow that appears and just as suddenly is gone."

"Could it be a cloaked ship?"

"If it is, it is small and is staying out of weapons range. Does the Empire have any small ships with cloaking ability?"

"Not that I know of," said Galen. "It would take impressive technology to accomplish that, although I am certain one day it will happen. If they now have that capability, we will need to make adjustments quickly. I will talk to Louis about this."

"I am going to start the engines and bring them up to half-thrust for thirty seconds. If there is a ship following us, they will have to drop their cloak and use their engines if they want to keep following us."

"Go ahead and try it. Let's see what happens," Galen agreed, nervously drumming his fingers on the console.

Terran went to half-thrust and the shadow revealed itself to be a small ship.

"You were right, Brother!" Galen yelled, pointing at the screen. "Why would they come after us with only one small ship?" he said, lowering his eyebrows. "Outrun them!"

"Maximum thrust," Terran said as the inertia dampers struggled to keep up with the rising g-forces. "It's amazing, Brother! They are keeping up, even gaining on us!" he said, his dark eyes wide with astonishment.

"Listen!" Galen said with surprise. "They are contacting us!"

"Galen Bestmarke, this is Lieutenant Janet Rogerton of the New Victorian Ship, *Clipper*. You are ordered to stand down and surrender. If you do not comply, we will be forced to fire upon you."

"Are they serious?" questioned Galen in disbelief. "What can that little dinghy do to us?" he yelled with annoyance. "Here is your answer, Janet Rogerton!" He fired the ion phase pulse-cannon.

With satisfaction he watched the hot, blue pulse speed straight at the small ship. At the last second, however, the small ship dodged and the pulse harmlessly flashed by, missing completely.

"What?" he cried in shock, his eyes wide open. He fired again and again, continuing to miss.

"How can they dodge my fire?" he demanded, his face reddening. "Even the hyper-lasers are missing! I cannot get a lock on them, they are jumping all around! Speed up, Brother!" he ordered, clenching his jaw. "Speed up!"

* * * * * * * * *

TROPHY

Mentally linked to the ship's computer, Pilot Kolanna saw the barrage coming. "It is like a slow-motion dream. I see the pulses and the laser-beams coming and I still have time to move the ship. It's as if this ship is alive!"

"Kolanna, they are speeding up," thought the Lieutenant, also mentally linked to the ship's computer. "Take us in fast and close. I will lay a row of pulses down the side of their shielding."

"Yes, Ma'am, here we go." The *Clipper* quickly gained on Bestmarke's lengthy ship. "They are increasing hyper-laser fire. It is harder to dodge this close. Our shielding may take some hits. It could be more damaging this close."

"Agreed. Take the ship in fast, the recharge time on our new pulse-cannon is almost immediate."

Kolanna guided the nimble ship close to the edge of Bestmarke's shields and quickly sped the length of his ship. Rogerton laid a string of twenty pulses at the side of his shielding before Kolanna swooped out in a tight arc from the big ship, continuing to dodge his incessant fire. The string of brilliant, blue pulses exploded nearly simultaneously in a spectacular display, violently shaking the great ship, but not slowing it down.

"Their shields are down to fifty percent, Ma'am. Do you want to go in again?" She looped the *Clipper* around for another strafing run from behind.

"Hold off, I will contact them once more," said Rogerton, reaching for the COM switch.

* * * * * * * * *

"They are coming in close and fast, Brother! How can they do that?" Galen shouted, as his ship shuddered violently from the exploding pulses, shaking them in their seats.

282

TROPHY

The COM announced again: "You are ordered to stand down, Galen Bestmarke. Comply immediately or your engines will be targeted."

"Fire the modified-projectiles, Brother! All of them!" Terran fervently yelled. "It is all we have left!"

"Right!" Galen agreed, quickly lunging for his controls. "Get us out of here! Get us cloaked and turned!" he said in desperation as he hit the trigger.

* * * * * * * * *

"Modifieds incoming," thought Kolanna. "There are too many to dodge, I'll have to make a run for it!"

"Give it everything you can!" said Rogerton. "I am firing the interceptors, but we need more distance for them to catch the modified-projectiles."

"What the interceptors don't get, I can almost outrun. Can you pick off the stragglers with the hyper-lasers, Lieutenant?"

"I can finish them all, but now Bestmarke is getting away. He will be cloaked before we are safe," she thought, her frustration evident. "We almost had him, Kolanna, but now we at least have a way to trace him." She mentally aimed the hyper-lasers at the last incoming projectiles.

* * * * * * * * *

"Aim us at the Keyhole!" blurted Galen, still shaken, sweat beading on his bald head. "After we are cloaked, turn us and proceed to Io Station. Those ruthless females will expect us to try the Keyhole now that we have Franelli, but we need supplies and repairs. Have you ever seen a ship like that before, Brother?"

"Never," he admitted, his eyes fixed on the NAV screens. "What a radical design. They must be using links, it seemed to be alive. We need something like that if we want to stay in business and keep living! One more hit and we would have been finished."

"We have fallen behind the Empire. New technology will be our priority," Galen emphasized, returning his brother's worried look.

"Talk to Louis as soon as possible," Terran said. "We cannot take any more close calls like this."

* * * * * * * * *

"We destroyed all the projectiles, Kolanna! Which direction did they go before they cloaked?"

"Toward the Keyhole," she answered, monitoring her screens. "Do we follow them?"

"No. They will need repairs and supplies. Where are the closest colonies or stations?"

"There are two stations near Jupiter's moons."

"Bestmarke will be watching us to see which way we go, so point us at the Keyhole," ordered Rogerton. "Once we are cloaked, change our heading to Jupiter. Keep a sharp eye on the screens for their engine signature."

TROPHY

Chapter XXXXIV

Earth Date: 476 N.V.A.
Location: Io Station

"Io Station still looks the same," Galen sneered, watching his screens. "It is a mystery why anyone would want to live here."

"We do have some fond memories, though, don't we, Brother?" said Terran, glancing over and smiling faintly. "We found our first jobs here after we left home."

"If you call them jobs," he scoffed. "As I remember, it was long shifts on a recycle barge, plowing around the outer Solar System."

"There was definitely no glamor to it," continued Terran. "But we did meet a lot of people ... the right people. They helped get us started."

"You make a good point," Galen said, recalling old memories. "Perhaps some of them can help us now with the parts we need. Louis needs some nuclear items, things hard to come by. They will probably be expensive," he sighed, rolling his eyes. "But they will be worth it for my final trophy."

"Is Louis going to the Station with us on the space-plane?" Terran asked.

"No, he gave me a list and insisted that he stay. He wants to work on his latest research, whatever that is," he said indifferently, not looking up. "Johnny will be in charge while we are gone. It should only take us a few hours. We will need to watch our backs, however. Some of our old clients may not appreciate seeing us again." He looked up with a grin, his gold rimmed teeth glinting in the dim instrument lights.

TROPHY

"You are probably right," Terran said. "We will leave the ship cloaked, close to the Station. We can open a hole in the cloak when we leave and return. The fewer eyes that see us, the better. I will go start preparing the space-plane." He stood and walked towards the door. "Meet me there when you are done here, Brother."

* * * * * * * * * *

"We are picking up Bestmarke's engine signature again, Star-Commander. Now it is at Io Station."

"Interesting, Lieutenant-Commander, a typical ruse," VanDevere said with no emotion. "He started for the Keyhole and shifted after he had cloaked. Instruct the Fleet to continue to the Keyhole vicinity and wait. We will take the *Daniela* to Io Station. Bring us in slow and cloaked, Lieutenant-Commander."

"Should we risk a message to the *Clipper*, Ma'am?"

"No. Knowing Lieutenant Rogerton, they are probably almost there. We will meet them at Io Station."

* * * * * * * * * *

"Go to braking thrust on the far side of Jupiter, Kolanna, so we will not be seen," ordered the Lieutenant, running her fingers through her thick hair. "Cloak the ship and slowly bring us around the planet to Io Station. We know Bestmarke is there, we saw his engine signature when he braked."

"He will no doubt be cloaked, Ma'am."

"No doubt. Watch for any clues, especially transfer ships … where they come from, and where they go."

"Yes, Ma'am," she confirmed, looking back at her instruments. "The computer is monitoring all activity."

"Martin, are you and Panther ready for action?" Lieutenant Rogerton asked over the COM. "We are approaching Io Station with an ETA of ten minutes."

"Yes, Ma'am," answered Martin. "Panther is itching for revenge – he's ready for an all-out fight."

"Itching?" said the Lieutenant looking at Kolanna, both smiling widely. "How do you know he is 'itching' for revenge?" she said, trying to keep from laughing.

"He told me so, Ma'am."

"What? Have you even taught him to speak?" she exclaimed, her and Kolanna both laughing.

"He still has trouble with some words," he said seriously. "His furry lips give him difficulty with the letters 's' and 'f'."

"Where does he come up with this?" laughed Kolanna, tears running down her cheeks.

"Have you taught him phonics, yet?" squealed the Lieutenant, laughing uncontrollably.

"I tried, Lieutenant," Martin replied straight-faced. "But he told me his kitten-hood memories of that subject weren't very good, so I gave up." He waited for the laughter to subside. "Seriously, we are prepared and will position ourselves by the Octopus boarding unit when you order it."

"What weapons do you have?" Rogerton said, still shaking, trying to stifle her laughter.

"Stun grenades, a stun-phaser, and my 8mm rifle."

"Do you think it wise to use a solid projectile weapon inside a spaceship? Could it not cause a big problem?"

"Only if I miss, Ma'am," he answered in all earnestness. He then heard laughter again through the COM. "Ma'am, that wasn't meant to be funny." The laughter only increased.

* * * * * * * * *

"Two hours so far and no activity to speak of, Ma'am," whined Kolanna, her eyes heavy from boredom. "Three transfer vessels and their main ships, all uncloaked ... just ordinary freighters," she said, stretching her long arms and legs.

"Space-plane departing Io Station," stated the computer in its soft feminine voice.

"Maybe we have something now," said the Lieutenant, sitting up in her seat, her eyes glued to the screens. "Watch it carefully!"

"Look!" said Kolanna, excitedly pointing at the screen. "An opening is forming, barely visible. The ship is going through, and now it is closing. Nothing can be seen now. It has to be Bestmarke."

"Use the thrusters and coast over, Kolanna," she ordered, her full concentration on the screens. "Get up close. Be ready to drop the cloak and set shields at full. Martin, you and Panther station your team at the Octopus."

"Moving into position now, Ma'am," verified Kolanna, awake with exhilaration.

"Drop cloak! Full shielding! Activating Phase Interrupter Laser! Attempting to shut down their reactor!" yelled Lieutenant Rogerton, her adrenaline flowing strongly.

Suddenly the cloak dropped on the big ship, and the fusion engines began their start-up sequence. Intense hyper-laser fire from Bestmarke's ship crackled along the edge of the *Clipper's* shielding.

"The shields are taking a beating, Ma'am, but they are holding," said Kolanna with wide eyes, staring at her screens and instruments. "We cannot take much more at this range. They are already down to ninety percent."

"I am countering with our hyper-lasers and still trying the Phase Interrupter. I am unable to get past their shielding!" complained the frustrated Lieutenant. "The frequency is shifting too rapidly!"

"Our shielding is at eighty percent, Ma'am," monitored Kolanna, her exhilaration turning to concern. "Try going deeper with your link, it will slow everything down."

"I am trying to, Kolanna," Rogerton said. She forced herself to relax, letting her mind stretch out with the dream-like program she was mentally linked to.

"I can see it better now. Their changing frequencies are like numbers flashing quickly by. Now they are slowing down and I can read them. There are blank spaces now and then ... it is a pattern. What if I insert my numbers into the blanks?"

"Shielding at sixty percent, Ma'am, and dropping rapidly," reminded Kolanna, her concern growing.

"More spaces opening ... I can barely keep up. Slow it down even more ... There! Almost all the spaces are blank ... putting numbers in them all ... Now all of the spaces are showing our numbers!" she yelled in triumph.

"Enemy fire has stopped!" exclaimed Kolanna, cheering loudly. "His reactor and engines are dead! You did it, Lieutenant!"

"Wow, the link is amazing! This ship is almost alive!" She locked down the controls on the Phase Interrupter Laser.

"Thanks, Kolanna, you gave me the key," she said, trying to slow her mind down to its normal speed. "Move into position and activate the Octopus. Boarding crew ... take your stations!"

Kolanna positioned the nimble ship over the central cargo area and lightly touched down, the extended arms of the Octopus immediately grasped the big ship's hull.

"Activate the nuclear-cutter," Rogerton ordered. "Okay, Martin, now it is in your hands. Be careful, remember your space-training. And do not forget who you are up against."

* * * * * * * * *

"Port door is closed and atmosphere restored," stated Johnny. "You can safely leave the space-plane now. I'll send for some crew members to help unload, boss."

TROPHY

"Thanks, Johnny," Galen said. "We will wait here to direct them. Then we will come to the bridge."

"Louis will be happy," Terran mentioned, walking toward the cargo hatch door. "We found all his parts at a good price."

"Surprisingly, everything went smoothly," Galen said, walking by Terran. "Maybe we should come back ..."

Suddenly the defense alarm began braying loudly. "Now what?" muttered Galen as they both started running to the bridge. "What is going on, Johnny?" he shouted, quickly glancing at the NAV screens.

"The same small ship that was following us just appeared out of nowhere, boss," he quickly explained. "They are sitting beside us firing hyper-lasers, and some sort of beam weapon with a blue-green color. I fired our hyper-lasers and activated the engine start-up sequence."

"They are trying to shut our engines down!" Galen yelled, pounding his fist on the console. "Keep firing the hyper-lasers! We will burn through their shields and destroy them!"

Suddenly the engines, the weapons, and the main power system of the ship stopped. It was deathly quiet for long agonizing seconds. Galen could not believe it. "No! No!" he shouted, running back and forth to his lifeless controls. "How can this be? They cannot do this to me!"

In the dim glow of the emergency lighting, they all looked up as they heard the Octopus unit tightly gripping the ship's exterior hull. The hollow sound and reverberation echoed ominously in the strangely quiet ship.

"Sensors are off," growled Galen. "It sounds like they are over the cargo area. Everyone put on shielding suits and blast helmets. Activate the night-vision screen on your helmets. Take stun-phasers and laser rifles. Stay back from the boarding hole, they will probably throw in stun grenades. Let them come in and then we will hunt them down," he hissed.

TROPHY

Galen ran to the defense cube hatch, locking it with Estelle and Tommie inside.

"We could use another hand, Brother! Why did you lock her in?"

"She is only a defensive fighter," he said pointedly. "And I do not trust her, you know that! Where is Louis?"

"I don't know! The COM is down. He is probably in his lab," said Terran, running to grab his weapons.

"Let him stay there! He is not a fighter. . . . Let's go!" ordered Galen, pointing out directions. "Split up and take different corridors!"

*   *   *   *   *   *   *   *   *

"The lid is secure and the equalizer tube is in place," said the Specialist. "Aren't you going to throw stun grenades in first?"

"Not this time," Martin said, calmly looking at her. "That's what they're expecting. Me and Panther will go in first. Wait until you hear action. Don't come down any sooner. Okay? ... I mean, do you understand?"

"Yes, we understand."

"It's eight meters to the floor. That's an easy jump for us, but you'd better use your ropes."

With his rifle on its sling over his shoulder, he lowered himself into the hole and dropped quietly to the floor, moving quickly to the side so Panther could join him. Moving into the darkest shadows behind some tall containers, they allowed their eyes to adapt to the low light.

"How many? ... Where?" thought Martin.

The great cat looked intently in all directions, sniffing the stale, unmoving air. He listened carefully for the slightest sounds.

"Two ... far end," Panther thought, mentally indicating the direction.

291

TROPHY

"Good, I'm going to throw something loud." Martin quickly threw two stun grenades into the far end and waited for the explosions that shook the room.

"Let's go!" he thought. They bolted toward the end of the room as the two Specialists dropped down on ropes.

Martin mentally signaled the panther right as he went left. Standing behind a metal column he saw one man lying on the floor and an open door a few meters behind him. He cautiously stepped out and started toward the man. Suddenly, another figure jumped into the doorway and fired a laser-rifle at him. With his heightened reflexes, Martin instantly jumped to the side and the laser bursts missed. The figure quickly ducked back behind the wall. Martin again positioned himself behind the column.

Panther saw what happened and crept along the wall to the doorway and crouched, ready to spring. Martin stepped out and the figure jumped into the doorway again. Before he could fire his weapon, Panther sunk his left front claws in the man's leg, pulling him down, while his right front claws ripped away the laser-rifle. Screaming in pain the man fell to the floor, knocking loose his helmet. Panther pinned him, growling ominously in his face. Turning white with fear, the man passed out. The two Specialists sedated both men to keep them out.

The door led into another dark cargo area. "How many? ... Where?" Martin thought again to the great cat.

"Two ... each corner," Panther mentally indicated.

There were numerous crates in this room, making it more difficult to maneuver. Martin crouched and moved to the right while directing Panther to the left. A small red laser dot suddenly appeared on the wall beside him followed by a blinding light. Martin hit the floor as laser beams crossed over him. The light went out. He had seen this trick before, but this time it would turn out differently. Quietly he slid to the center of the room and readied the 8mm rifle. He felt the floor around him for something to throw and found a loose bolt. He threw it against the wall where he had been standing. The loud clattering brought the bright light and intense laser fire in the direction of the noise.

He quickly aimed his rifle and squeezed off a shot sending the bullet through the wrist holding the light. The light fell to the floor as the man screamed in agony. The light continued to shine along the floor, creating distorted shadows as Panther rushed into the left corner at the two figures looking the other way.

They looked back too late as he roared a deadly greeting, springing on the first man and driving him to the floor. Panther ripped off his helmet and snarled in his face. The second man ran toward the other two and all three bolted through a doorway, locking it behind them.

"Good work, Panther," praised Martin. The Specialists arrived and sedated the man.

"How strong can this lock be?" he said, grasping it firmly and twisting with his android strength. He felt the metal give, finally breaking, and the door swinging open. He just looked at the Specialists and smiled.

"Let's go, Panther," he thought, moving through the open door. They had an easy trail now with blood drops along the floor, guided by Panther's keen sense of smell. Cautiously they crept along the dark main corridor of the long ship, slowly working their way forward.

"Wait ...," Panther mentally indicated to Martin. "Hear something ..." He crept ahead slinking very low to the floor, his tail twitching. He stopped before a connecting side corridor, listening and sniffing the air, then quickly springing around the corner with a great scream. Laser beams shot wildly in the air as Panther brought down another man, pinning him and growling fiercely. The Specialists came, rendering him unconscious along with the others.

"Two left that we know of," thought Martin, rubbing the big cat on the back of his head. "Let's follow the trail"

TROPHY

Panther stealthily led the way down the dark, side corridor to another locked door.

"Can you hear anything?" Martin asked.

"No ...," Panther mentally indicated. "Something ... wrong." Panther stood sniffing the air, continuing to listen carefully.

"I feel it, too," Martin said with increasing concern. "Quick!" he yelled, grabbing Panther and pulling him back from the door. "Back to the main corridor!"

Moving as fast as he could, Martin picked up a startled Specialist under each of his arms, and ran back down the main corridor following Panther. Reaching the cargo hold, they jumped through the doorway to the floor as a huge explosion thundered through the corridors they had just been in.

"Stay here!" he told the Specialists, after confirming they were not hurt. He and Panther ran back through the smoke and dust to the room they had almost entered. Charred walls with pieces falling to the floor were all that remained. The trail was lost.

Suddenly, Panther mentally said: "Quick ... hear sound ... this way." They forced their way through a blackened doorway on the other side of the room into a corridor. Panther led the way to a room with thick windows looking out on a space-port. There was blood on the floor. Looking through the windows, Martin saw two men, identical twins, trying to ready a space-plane. He quickly stepped through the space-port hatchway and yelled: "Galen Bestmarke!"

The man with the bloody wrist looked up as Martin raised his rifle and squeezed off a shot, hitting him in the shoulder where the shielding suit had a narrow gap. Galen was thrown to the floor. "Well met, indeed!" Martin screamed with vengeance as Panther came bounding past him. The twin grabbed Galen, dragging him into the space-plane. As he struggled to shut the space-plane door, Panther viciously raked his arm and leg, leaving blood on the floor and dripping from his lethal claws.

TROPHY

With rage engulfing their collective consciousness, Martin suddenly realized their great peril. "Panther! Quick!" he screamed. "Come back to the hatchway! Now! Come back, now!" Panther looked up at Martin, hesitating for a moment. Then he started to run back to him.

All at once the explosive bolts of the space-port hangar door detonated, blowing the door out into space, evacuating the air and heat and anything else that was unsecured. Martin grabbed a metal railing and screamed with dread as Panther was swept along the floor toward the gaping opening. Panther hit the landing strut of the space-plane where he somehow managed to twist himself around and hang on with his front claws. Martin knew they only had a few seconds before the vacuum of space would completely expand and freeze them. "Shut your eyes and mouth! Hold on tight!" he mentally ordered Panther. "I'll help you!"

Martin jammed his rifle in the hatchway door behind him, keeping it partially open. He wouldn't have the strength to push it open if it slammed shut. The air rushing out the partially open hatchway was like a hurricane as the vacuum of space progressively pulled the air out of the huge ship. He desperately looked around and then seized the power transfer cable still attached to the space plane. Yanking it from the wall coupling, he quickly tied the end to the railing. Squinting and tightly holding the cable, Martin worked his way back to the space plane and grabbed Panther. Wrapping his arm around the great cat, Martin pulled them back to the rushing hatchway. With all his strength he shoved the door open and they both squeezed through. It slammed shut, leaving them weakened and lying on the floor. With a rumbling vibration, the space-plane fired up its engine, lifted up, and turned toward the opening, spewing a jet of flame across the interior of the space-port. It slowly flew out the opening.

TROPHY

"Destroy it, Janet! Destroy it!" begged Martin, hoping for an end to the nightmare. He lay on the floor beside Panther, totally exhausted, his head throbbing with pain.

* * * * * * * * *

"Space-plane leaving the ship, Ma'am," reported Kolanna, angry and frustrated. "He is on the other side of the ship and we are still attached. We can't move to shoot him down and we don't have interceptor missiles!"

"He is heading straight for Io Station," said Rogerton, equally frustrated. "If we fire at him and miss, we could hit the Station. We cannot take that risk. Notify the Station. Tell them to intercept with deadly force if necessary."

TROPHY

Chapter XXXXV

Earth Date: 476 N.V.A.
Location: Io Station

"Archer, come with me!" ordered Lieutenant Rogerton as she jumped up from her control seat and strapped on a stun-phaser. "Kolanna, you have the bridge. Call the medic to accompany us. Take a stun-phaser with you, Lieutenant-Warden."

"Sensors show the two Specialists and their prisoners in the forward cargo hold. Martin and Panther are at the space-plane port, Ma'am," stated Kolanna, quickly reviewing her instruments. "All are alive," she announced with relief, looking up at the Lieutenant.

"Thanks, Kolanna," Rogerton said, returning her glance, relieved that no one was killed. Hurrying to the Octopus, they descended into the silent ship.

"If this ship follows the usual layout, engineering should be up this corridor. Yes, here it is. Louis must have a lab close by. This might be it, but the door is locked," she said, perplexed. "Louis!" she yelled, banging on the door with her fist. "Louis, it is Lieutenant Rogerton!" she shouted again, but received no answer.

"Kolanna, can you tap into their circuitry and open this door? It is labeled EL-1," she mentally said, still linked with her ship.

"I am looking, Lieutenant. Here it is and it appears to be on the emergency circuits. I am trying it now." In a few seconds the lock softly clicked open.

"Thanks," she replied, carefully opening the door. As she started to step in, a stun-phaser burst harmlessly hit the wall, two meters away. Quickly withdrawing, she yelled: "Louis! Louis Franelli! I am Lieutenant Rogerton from CENTRAL! We were sent to rescue you and Guardian V! Do not shoot! We are your friends! I am coming in slowly with my hands up!"

She slowly walked in looking carefully around the dimly lit lab. Finally she saw him sitting in a back corner, his head in his hands, and a stun-phaser on the floor in front of him. Rogerton slowly walked toward him and spoke calmly. "Louis, are you all right? Are you hurt? Has something happened to the Guardian?"

"I have never fired at anyone before. I had to protect her, I swore my life on it," he said somberly, still looking down.

"Is the Guardian all right?" she patiently asked again, looking down at him.

"Yes," he croaked, finally collecting himself and looking up at her. "She is in the cryogenic chamber, she is frozen. It was the only way I could keep her safe from Bestmarke."

"Is she safe now, with the fusion reactor shut down?"

"Oh, yes. She is safe. We will need more power to awaken her, but she is safe now," he said with relief.

"Do you need medical assistance, Louis?" Rogerton asked again.

"No, I am fine. I will stay here with Sondra."

"Stay here, please. Keep the door locked and protect the Guardian. We must find Martin and the great cat." She left quickly with her two companions. "The space-plane port should be nearby," she yelled, running down the corridor ahead of the others, fear in her eyes. "In here!" she said. The other two quickly joined her.

The Medical Specialist immediately went to Martin. "Look in my eyes," she gently ordered, gravely concerned. Using a small instrument from her bag, she meticulously examined his eyes for a few moments. "No permanent damage," she concluded, looking up relieved. "A little bruising, but it will heal completely. Let me look at Panther," she said, equally concerned. After another long moment, she smiled. "He is the same, no permanent damage. It will heal quickly, too"

TROPHY

"How do you feel, Martin?" asked the medic. "Do you have any pain or confusion?"

"My head hurts and feels tired, but my body feels fine. Let me try standing up," he said, attempting to get up, his legs shaking. The Lieutenant grabbed him from behind firmly around his chest, helping him stand.

"I feel my strength returning," he gratefully acknowledged. "Let me stand for a moment, then I'll help Panther."

Even Panther was wobbly for a few minutes, but slowly his strength returned.

"Kolanna," thought Rogerton. "Do the sensors show anyone else aboard that is not accounted for?"

"One person and a small life-form in the very bow of the ship, Ma'am."

"Thanks," she thought. "Could this be our guider/pouncer team?"

"Martin, can you and Panther walk?" Rogerton asked.

"Yes, our strength's coming back more quickly now."

"Good," she replied, turning to leave. "We are going to the bow of the ship. Please follow us at your own pace. We have one more person to meet. This should prove interesting for Panther, too," she said, affectionately rubbing his head as she walked by.

Arriving at the very front of the ship, Rogerton and Archer drew their stun-phasers, positioned themselves, and unlocked the door, swinging it open. Facing them stood a woman with short, blond hair, blue eyes, and a slight build. Somehow she looked familiar, and she held an orange striped tabby cat in her arms. Immediately she stated: "Please identify yourselves and explain what you intend to do with us."

"I am Lieutenant Janet Rogerton of the New Victorian Empire. We have captured this ship belonging to Galen Bestmarke. Unfortunately, he and his brother have escaped. Everyone else has been taken prisoner."

"Everyone?" she questioned, looking her straight in the eyes, shifting her weight and tensing slightly.

"Everyone, except Louis, that is. He is still in his lab caring for something," Rogerton answered cautiously, setting her guard. "Who are you? What is your name?"

"My name is Estelle Fairfield," she replied, relaxing her posture. "And this is Tommie," she said, looking down at him, petting him gently.

"You are a guider/pouncer team, then?" said the Lieutenant, holstering her weapon. "Are you New Victorian trained?"

"Yes, Lieutenant, we are extensively trained. Tommie has a TMC-7 rating," she said proudly.

"Do you submit to us, Estelle Fairfield?" she asked seriously, following conventional protocol.

"Yes, in the name of the New Victorian Empire," she answered, extending her hand, watching the Lieutenant's expression.

Rogerton gripped her hand firmly and looked deeply in her eyes. "I am feeling something," she thought. "Images, I feel strong mental images about her."

"Who are you, really?" asked the Lieutenant, releasing her hand. "You are not really Estelle Fairfield, are you? I sense you have a position of great authority. Am I correct?"

"You are very perceptive, Lieutenant. You must also have a link. I am one of the Protectors, a Level Ten."

"You could have taken us all quickly," admitted Rogerton. "We are grateful to you, and humbled, Protector. Please pardon our insolence," she said, bowing slightly with her eyes down. The other two officers followed suit.

"Nonsense, Lieutenant," she exclaimed, reassuring her. "You are a good officer, loyally doing your duty. When you said Louis was in his lab caring for something, I knew the Guardian was safe."

"But Protector, Estelle is not really your name, is it?" Rogerton continued with a questioning look.

TROPHY

"It was for three years while I had this assignment, an undercover assignment, to get close to Bestmarke and Louis. It now appears to be over, at least this phase of it. My real name, Lieutenant, is Michelle… Michelle VanDevere."

"Michelle VanDevere?" said Rogerton, stunned, her eyes open wide. "You are the Star-Commander's sister? You are not a renegade?"

"Yes, I am Abigail's younger sister. And my renegade status was a ruse, necessary for my assignment. Even my sister didn't know."

"Now I start to understand her pain," Rogerton said, thinking back. "How relieved she will be!"

"Do you know my sister well, Lieutenant?"

"As well as a junior officer can," she admitted. "Please, let me introduce you to two very special members of our crew. Specialists Martin and Panther," she said, smiling proudly.

Tommie and Michelle's eyes grew wide as Martin and the great cat walked around the corner. Martin and Panther stood at attention and bowed low.

Michelle smiled and looked deeply into their eyes for a long time. "I understand who you both are, and where you came from. I am happy that you are now free."

"Thank you, Ma'am," said Martin, lowering his eyes and bowing slightly. Panther began purring loudly, looking straight at her and Tommie.

"Please, Lieutenant," Martin said, distress in his voice. "Can we go to the Trophy Room? I must see my father!"

"Of course, Martin, let us go at once. I will have Kolanna unlock the door for us," she said, acutely sensing the pain he had hidden for so long. They all set off, moving quickly towards the center of the long ship.

Finally reaching the hatchway door, they all went inside. "There are two switches on the side of each pedestal," explained Rogerton, pointing them out to everyone. "Just push the top one."

TROPHY

They turned them all on, waiting. One by one the form in each appeared as if out of a thick fog. Finally all were clearly seen ... all of them asleep.

"He is not here," Martin said quietly, sighing deeply. Anguish and pain defined his questioning face. "Where could he be? After all this time and effort, I still don't have him back."

The atmosphere of the room darkened as they all realized and shared in Martin's disappointment. The Lieutenant moved closer, her arm around his back, tears forming in her eyes. "I am so sorry, Martin," she cried. "We have all tried so hard."

"But where could he have been taken?" Martin asked, perplexed and devastated.

"I have an idea," said a deep voice, just entering the room. "I feel somewhat responsible, too," said Louis. He walked up close to Martin and looked him in the face. "Galen had a deal with a man called Izax who lives in the Asteroid Belt. I believe he is responsible for capturing Guardian Sondra and myself. The trophy of your father was given as payment to Izax. The captured men may know more details. I am very sorry, Martin," he said, with great remorse, putting his large hand on Martin's shoulder.

"We will find him, Martin," assured Michelle, moving closer to him. "My sister and I will see to it. It will be done!"

Martin stood silently for a long moment. His head was bowed as if deep in thought or lost in a memory. Finally he looked up into the eyes of those standing near him. "Thanks for all your concern and sympathy," he said, resigning himself. "The pain is real and intense. But I know now what we can do as a team, and I'm thankful to have good, loyal friends. I've had bitter disappointments before and I'm sure I'll have some more. One thing is for certain, though, we now have a trail to follow. And if we have a trail, we still have hope," he said stoically.

TROPHY

Panther rubbed against him purring loudly, sensing his innermost pain, trying to console him. Suddenly the great cat looked up and excitedly ran to one of the pedestals.

"What is it? What does he want?" asked Michelle.

"He has found his mate!" exclaimed Rogerton, joyfully sensing the great cat's innermost thoughts and feelings.

"Bestmarke must have taken them both together. Panther is happy now. At least one family can be reunited," Martin replied. "Guardian VII will be busy when we get back."

TROPHY

Chapter XXXXVI

Earth Date: 476 N.V.A.
Location: CENTRAL, Earth

The flames of the holographic fire crackled in the river-rock fireplace with convincing reality. The Chambers of CENTRAL were comforting – more so now with the confirmed capture of Bestmarke's ship and the rescue of Guardian V and Louis Franelli.

"CENTRAL has granted a conditional pardon for Franelli," said Guardian III as her eyes followed the dancing flames. "I have to admit ... I am somewhat surprised. But it is a logical conclusion seeing that he saved the life of Guardian V."

"And the pardon is conditional," Guardian II emphasized. "It only makes sense that we continue to monitor him for a while." She paused in thought for a moment. "Franelli is a strange man ... he marches to no drum beat but his own. Nothing has turned his head except Guardian V, and he insists on calling her Sondra," she sighed. She shifted position in her comfortable, black chair, her eyes also fixed on the mesmerizing flames.

"Did I not mention that Guardian V's mild and gentle heart would prevail?" smiled Guardian I, her black eyes glistening as she turned to the two older women beside her.

"Indeed, you did," Guardian II acquiesced. "Franelli may now be more malleable to our concerns," she said, a gentle expression on her motherly face. "If CENTRAL can accept Franelli, then it is our duty to fully support the decision."

"Once the squadron returns to Earth we can focus our full attention on time-travel through the Keyhole," said Guardian III. "With Franelli's help we can implement the regeneration program."

TROPHY

"Do we have more details yet on that program?" asked Guardian II. "Is more data needed from Franelli?"

"So far we have only a brief outline," admitted Guardian I. "We hoped that Franelli's engineering files would vastly speed up and enhance our understanding of how time-travel works. But all his files are gone ... wiped clean from the ship's computer," she lamented.

"Could Bestmarke have taken them when he escaped to Io Station?" asked Guardian II. "A full investigation for him and his brother is already underway."

"Franelli thinks so," Guardian I said. "Franelli assures us he has all the information in his head – and that it will not take long to input into the computer again. He is also confident that Bestmarke cannot understand or implement the data himself."

"Is there someone else with a mind like Franelli's that could understand and use the data?" asked Guardian III.

"I asked him that very question," replied Guardian I, her smile slowly fading. "He stated it would be difficult ... but not impossible. He knew of no one, but he is a recluse, and has been out-of-touch with main stream research for nearly ten years."

"If Bestmarke remains hidden, eventually he could use or sell his data to someone as clever as Franelli," said Guardian II. "They could begin using the Keyhole again for time-travel."

"That is a possibility," agreed Guardian I. "It is remote, but we cannot discount it. We know Bestmarke's resourcefulness. Franelli also mentioned a 'human relocation program' that Bestmarke was planning. Louis did not know the details, but it may be as Guardian IX feared – a slavery system that snatches biologically sound people from another time era to sell to the highest bidders in our time."

"The idea is monstrous!" said Guardian III. "It undermines the Empire's most basic principles! We must capture Bestmarke soon!"

"Indeed, we must!" said Guardian I. "Oh, here is another tidbit drawn from the captured freighter captain and verified by

305

Franelli. Bestmarke implants a locator chip in each of his crew members."

"So that is how the abductors found him and Guardian V so quickly when they broke into CENTRAL," said Guardian II. "We will need to remove that from Franelli and presumably from Michelle VanDevere and Tommie."

"I agree, we must remove it from Franelli," said Guardian I. "But Bestmarke locked Michelle and Tommie in their quarters. For all he knows, they were captured or escaped. Bestmarke still knows her only as Estelle Fairfield," Guardian I said slyly. "She may be able to get close to Bestmarke again."

"It will be a difficult assignment. He will trust her even less than he did before," said Guardian III. "She will need help. Perhaps we can use our team of Lieutenant Rogerton, Martin and Panther."

"We will keep all our options open," Guardian I said quietly. "CENTRAL will give us our directions at the proper time."

* * * * * * * * * *

Location: En route to Earth from Jupiter

"Wake up, Sondra," Louis gently coaxed, as she finally opened her bright, green eyes. "How do you feel?"

"I feel awake and alive. That is a wonderful feeling, isn't it, my dear," she quietly said, looking up into his face. "Where are we?"

"We are on Bestmarke's ship, but do not worry, he is not here. Estelle, I mean, Michelle VanDevere is our Commander and Pilot. We are in Star-Commander VanDevere's squadron, heading home to Earth. Michelle is the Star-Commander's sister. Our other friends are with us in a new ship called the *Clipper*."

Sondra started to sit up, but could not support herself. Immediately Louis reached over and gently propped her into a sitting position on the side of the padded platform of the cryogenics unit.

"Thank you, Louis. I am not in pain, but I feel very weak. How long will this last?"

"A few hours ... a day at the most," he said. "You need to have some food – especially water."

"I will, Louis," she said. "But please, answer my questions first. What happened to Galen and Terran Bestmarke? Were they captured or killed?"

"Neither," he said. "Lieutenant Rogerton followed them to Io Station and attacked them there. Bestmarke's ship was boarded. Martin and Panther wounded them both but they escaped in the space-plane heading toward the Station. They just seemed to vanish. . The Station authorities could not find them or their space-plane."

"I see," Sondra said. "That is unfortunate. It means somebody is protecting them. Io Station is a desperate place, known for its lawlessness. Bestmarke will be able to buy friends and help."

"That is not all," admitted Louis. "They took all my work on the Keyhole ... all my files are gone. I can remember everything, but it will take time to replace it."

"Does CENTRAL know this?"

"Yes. I have discussed it thoroughly with Guardian I."

"Will this slow down our work on time-travel through the Keyhole?" Sondra asked. "Time-travel is the only way we can solve our dilemma of continuing the human race."

"It will only slow me down a few weeks, perhaps a month. I am confident we can repeat time-travel and do it for the right reasons," Louis said. He paused and gave Sondra a worried look. "I am concerned that someone else will use my calculations for the wrong reasons. Bestmarke was planning a human relocation program – a slave trade."

"We are concerned about that possibility, too," she said. "Could Galen or Terran figure out your calculations?"

"No. Of that I am certain," Louis said. "But years ago I heard there were others doing research on the Keyhole. They were passionate about their work, too. I did not know who they were, but they were not working for CENTRAL."

"If Bestmarke teamed up with them, they could navigate back and forth through the Keyhole ... back and forth through time."

"Yes, they could," Louis continued. "But my greatest fear is that they could damage or shut down the Keyhole."

"Is that possible?" gasped Sondra.

"My calculations indicate the possibility," Louis said bluntly. "The Keyhole appears to be very powerful, which is true. It is also, in fact, quite fragile. Any disruption to it could be disastrous. Something like a powerful weapons discharge or a fusion reactor overload could affect it."

"What would happen to it?"

"That is uncertain ... maybe nothing," Louis said. "But it could be damaged extensively, even permanently collapsed ... I just do not know."

"Then we must guard it and be the first to use it, Louis," Sondra said with determination. "We cannot afford to lose our only hope of saving the human race."

* * * * * * * * *

"Michelle!" cried an exuberant Abigail VanDevere as she climbed down through the equalizer tube into the captured ship, coasting along with the squadron. "I am so happy! I am so relieved! When Guardian X told me the truth, the whole story, I could not wait to see you again. The remaining time you spent on this ship only increased my anxiety," the Star-Commander admitted.

Michelle VanDevere smiled widely as she hugged her older sister, reluctant to let go. "Oh, Abby! It's so good to be with you! When I finally remembered everything, all the pieces of the puzzle came together. Now I remember who I am and what I want to do. I want to be closer to you, Abby, and serve the Empire together. We have difficult challenges ahead and we'll need each others strength," Michelle said.

"What do you think of our dynamic team – the ancient man, Martin, and the great cat, Panther?" Abigail said with a grin.

"Tommie and I were quite surprised," Michelle said, laughing. "But then I realized who they were ... Bestmarke's trophies. I had been on the same ship with them and didn't realize it," she said more seriously. "I am incensed at his cruelty! I cannot wait to capture him and his brother!"

"That assignment may come soon," Abigail said. "We also need to find Martin's father."

"He was given in payment to the Izax, a felonious character with his own mining asteroid," Michelle said. "His location could be in this ship's log or possibly extracted from the men taken captive."

"Those men know nothing about your condition or location," said Abigail. "All they know is Bestmarke locked you in your quarters. None of them, including Bestmarke, know whose side you are on," she said. "All they know is that you are a renegade. We may have to continue our ruse."

"If we can capture the Bestmarke brothers, it will be worth it," said Michelle. "Right now I am the happiest I have been in years!"

"I am, too," Abigail said, hugging her again.

* * * * * * * * *

Alpha Squadron was coasting through space, full speed to Earth. Two additional vessels accompanied the Star-Commander's ships: a huge battle damaged freighter and a much smaller, sleek, futuristic looking ship called the *Clipper*.

Aboard the *Clipper* the reports were all filed and the questions finally answered. The ship was on auto-pilot – synched to the Victorian Heavy Cruiser *Daniela*, the flagship of the Empirical fleet. There was nothing left to do but enjoy the long trip home. Although the ship was small, the crew all managed to find a private place to relax.

"Do you still dream, Martin?" asked Lieutenant Rogerton, sitting on a sofa in the small lounge.

"What do you mean, Lieutenant?" he said, turning his chair to face her.

"We are not on duty now, Martin. Please, call me Janet. I call you Martin, I have a first name, too," she gently teased. "As I said … do you still dream?"

"Well, I daydream a lot … mostly it's about my mom and dad," Martin said. "I think about the good times we had together back when I was young. It seemed like we didn't have any cares at all. I'm sure they had plenty of worries. Trying to make a living and pay all the bills was hard back then. But I was just a kid and with both of them taking care of me, I had no worries. Those were the best years of my life."

Janet contemplated his words for a moment. "I feel almost envious," she said looking down. "I did not have a real father and my mother's ship was lost when I was eight years old. My foster mother treated me wonderfully and my foster father was a good man, but I never drew close to him. I can only imagine how content you were, Martin."

"I am sorry about your mother, Janet. I know how difficult it is to lose someone and never find them. There are so many unanswered questions. It's like all your hopes and feelings are frozen."

"I know. I guess we both have been in that situation," she said. "Tell me more about your youth."

Martin looked at her and admitted: "I was satisfied then. Life was so simple and good. I wish it was like that again. I want to change things back to what they were … but that's impossible."

"It may not be totally impossible," Janet said, her face brightening. "If we can perfect time-travel we may be able to reverse the difficult situations. We are only beginning to realize the good things we can do. We must keep believing – never give up hope!"

Martin gazed with admiration at the young woman sitting across from him. "You're really amazing," he affectionately said. "I've never known anyone as positive as you."

Janet smiled wider. "What else do you think about, Martin? With such dramatic changes in your life and your environment, surely you must be curious about ... about everything, I would guess."

"Everything? That's for sure!" he chuckled and then paused, turning his face aside. "I have so many questions I don't know where to start. I guess one of my biggest is about the earth: the mountains, the forests, the oceans, the changing seasons, all the living things. The earth has always been my first love. I really want to see what's happened to it – to see and feel the forests where I grew up – if they're still there. Are the birds and animals the same ... or are they gone, extinct? I have to know – these questions tug at my heart."

"I know you will be pleasantly surprised. The care and conservation of Earth is at the greatest level in recorded history. When we return perhaps we will have some leave time. I would be glad to show you how Earth has been so beautifully restored."

"Can I add that to my dream list?" Martin said.

"Of course. That will come true," she said. "What other dreams do you have, Martin?"

His smile faded and his face took on a melancholy look. "Probably my biggest dream is somehow getting my father back alive. I don't know how we'll do it or if we can ever find this Izax character. The Asteroid Belt is a pretty big place to search. Do you think we have any chance at all of finding him?"

"Yes, I think our chances are extremely good," Janet said. "Michelle and Louis have both been near his mining asteroid and the computer-log on Bestmarke's ship may give us the coordinates. If mining is the Izax' legitimate business, it should be relatively simple to track him down. The hard part will come once we locate him."

TROPHY

"What do you mean? Can't we just go in there and rescue him? We certainly have the fire-power to do so."

"There is no doubt we have the military strength – that is not the issue," she said. "We may not have the legal means to search the Izax' property and seize your father's pedestal. If we can prove the Izax is any part of organized criminal activity, then we can use military force. Without convincing evidence on our side, he has the full legal protection of the Empire."

"If that is true, my father is nothing more than the Izax' personal property," Martin said with dismay. "Couldn't the Guardians insist that his return is necessary for their studies on time-travel to help save the human race?"

"They probably could, but then their knowledge of time-travel would become generally known, and with potentially disastrous results. Every criminal and rebel organization would be desperate to use or control the Keyhole. War would be constant," Janet said. "Time-travel under those circumstances might be impossible. It must be kept a secret as long as possible."

"And without time-travel the human race can't be saved from extinction," Martin said. "And my father and I won't be able to return to our own time. Isn't there any other way?"

"There is always another way," she slyly said, her eyes narrowing. "It may be more clandestine, however. A fast, cloaked ship and a dynamic team make the possibilities endless."

Martin returned a narrow smile. "I see what you mean, Janet Rogerton."

THE END

312

TROPHY

APPENDIX

NEW VICTORIAN EMPIRE
PLANETARY CONTROL CORPS

Order of Rank:

1. Star-Commander
2. Commander
3. Lieutenant-Commander
4. Lieutenant
5. Second-Lieutenant
6. Lieutenant-Warden
7. Warden
8. First-Officer
9. Second-Officer
10. Specialist

PCC Patrol Class Ship:

Length: 25 meters (82 feet)
Crew: 6 standard, plus 4 Specialists on short missions
Drive: 1 P-Class Fusion Engine - Deep Space Capable
Weapons: 2 P-Class Hyper-lasers, 1 projectile cannon, 5 SPM-3 mines, probe bombs

PCC Flagship: Victorian Heavy Cruiser- *Daniela*

Length: 600 meters (1,968 feet)
Crew: 550
Drives: 2 HC-Class Fusion Engines – Deep Space Capable
Features:Cloaking ability, guider/pouncer capable, dispensary, repair bays, canteens, Multiple docking ports
Weapons:4 C-Class Hyper-lasers, 4 Modified Projectile Cannons, 2 Ion-Phase Pulse-Cannons, 1 Phase Interrupter Laser (PIL), SPM-3 Mines, 4 Octopus Units

PCC Clipper Class Ship, Series A - *Clipper*

Length: 50 meters (164 feet)
Crew: 10

TROPHY

Drive: 1 Zenkati 'D' Class Fusion Engine – Deep Space Capable

Features: Cloaking ability, guider/pouncer capable, direct pilot-to-ship interface, direct commander-to-ship interface.

Weapons: 1 Ion-Phase Pulse-Cannon, 2 C-Class Hyper-lasers, 2 Projectile Interceptors, 2 Projectile Cannons, 1 Phase Interrupter Laser (PIL), 10 SPM-3 Mines, Probe Bombs, 1 Octopus Boarding Unit

PCC Cutter Class Ship

Length: 60 meters (197 feet)

Crew: 10 standard, plus 6 Specialists on short missions

Drive: 1 CT-Class Fusion Engine – Deep Space Capable

Features: Optional: Patrol Class or Research Class

Weapons: Patrol Class: 2 C-Class Hyper-lasers, 2 Projectile Cannons, 10 SPM-3 mines, probe bombs

Research Class: 2 P-Class Hyper -lasers

BESTMARKE'S SHIP:
MODIFIED HIGH-VOLUME CARGO VESSEL

Length: 500 meters (1,640 feet)

Crew: 10

Drives: 2 Zenkati 'B' Class Fusion Engines – Deep Space Capable

Features: Cloaking ability, guider/pouncer capable, direct pilot-to-gunner interface, Space-plane and port

Weapons: 4 C-Class Hyper-lasers, 1 Ion-Phase Pulse-Cannon, 2 Projectile Launchers

TROPHY

GLOSSARY

Asteroid Belt – The region of space between Mars and Jupiter that contains thousands of small, rocky, sun-orbiting objects ranging in size from grains of sand to 12+ kilometers in length.

A.U. – Astronomical Unit, approximately 150,000,000 kilometers (93,000,000 miles), or the distance from the earth to the sun.

CENTRAL – The massive computer-government that rules the Solar System and nearest star system in the Centaurus region.

Guardians – The caretakers of the great computer, CENTRAL.

Io Station – One of the early exo-Martian colonies constructed in 386 N.V.A. It originally served as a research and industrial area before falling into decay. It is located in orbit around Jupiter near the moon Io.

Kuiper Belt – A division of space beyond Neptune that extends from 30 – 1,000 A.U. This region contains trans-Neptunian objects, the two largest being Eris and Pluto. Over 1000 objects have been discovered as of March 2009, and most are larger than 100 kilometers (60 miles) in diameter.

Protectors – An elite devision of the Planetary Control Corps whose purpose is to protect the Guardians at all costs, even with their own lives if necessary. They are all women, highly trained in the martial arts and all manner of military technology.

TROPHY